Storing Up Trouble

Books by Jen Turano

Storing Up Trouble

JEN TURANO

BETHANYHOUSE

a division of Baker Publishing Group
Minneapolis, Minnesota

© 2020 by Jennifer L. Turano

Published by Bethany House Publishers
11400 Hampshire Avenue South
Bloomington, Minnesota 55438
www.bethanyhouse.com

Bethany House Publishers is a division of
Baker Publishing Group, Grand Rapids, Michigan

Printed in the United States of America

Library of Congress Cataloging-in-Publication Data
Names: Turano, Jen, author.
Title: Storing up trouble / Jen Turano.
Description: Minneapolis, Minnesota : Bethany House Publishers, 2020. | Series:
  American heiresses ; 3
Identifiers: LCCN 2019051155 | ISBN 9780764231698 (trade paperback) | ISBN
  9780764236266 (cloth) | ISBN 9781493425082 (ebook)
Subjects: GSAFD: Romantic suspense fiction. | Christian fiction.
Classification: LCC PS3620.U7455 S76 2020 | DDC 813/.6—dc23
LC record available at https://lccn.loc.gov/2019051155

This is a work of fiction. Names, characters, incidents, and dialogues are products of the author's imagination and are not to be construed as real. Any resemblance to actual events or persons, living or dead, is entirely coincidental.

Scripture quotations are from the King James Version of the Bible.

Cover design by Dan Thornberg, Design Source Creative Services

Store shelves and part of counter courtesy of Josephson's Clothing Store, Red Wing, Minnesota

Cash register courtesy of Goodhue County Historical Society, Red Wing, Minnesota

Base, column, and finial of glove holder courtesy of Pottery Place Antiques, Red Wing, Minnesota

Author is represented by Natasha Kern Literary Agency.

20 21 22 23 24 25 26   7 6 5 4 3 2 1

For Al

Because surviving thirty years of marriage to me certainly deserves a bit of recognition.

Love you!

Jen

CHAPTER 1

The truth of the matter was this—she, Miss Beatrix Waterbury, had been banished from New York, and all because she'd had the great misfortune of landing herself in jail . . . twice.

Granted, misleading her mother about Mr. Thomas Hamersley and the romantic relationship they didn't share, what with how Thomas was now engaged to another woman, hadn't helped the situation. Nevertheless, she truly hadn't thought her mother would make good on her threats to ship her off to stay with Aunt Gladys, but apparently she'd been wrong about that.

Smoothing red curls that had escaped their pins back into place, Beatrix lurched against the small sink of the retiring room as the train came to yet another screeching stop. Realizing the train had probably stopped at Crown Point Station, which meant Chicago was only an hour or so away, she hurried out the door and toward the Pullman car she'd been enjoying on her long journey from New York City to Chicago.

Even though she was hardly looking forward to a stay with her aunt Gladys, a lady she barely knew but distinctly remembered as being a somewhat querulous sort, Chicago was considered an up-and-coming city, which meant . . .

"Watch where you're going."

Beatrix stumbled to a stop, her forward progress brought to a rapid end due to the large man who'd stepped in front of her and whom she'd just barreled into, a man who was certainly solid and most assuredly surly, given the tone of his voice. When she lifted her head, the apology she'd been about to voice got stuck in her throat as her gaze settled on the man now blocking her way.

That he was not what she'd been expecting to see in a Pullman car was an understatement.

Dirty dark hair straggled over the man's face, but it wasn't the hair that held her attention; it was the vivid white scar running from the man's hairline down to his chin. It was a scar that suggested the man was used to rough living, a notion further encouraged when Beatrix shifted her attention to his small, beady eyes that were filled with something that caused the hair on the nape of her neck to stand to attention. Uncomfortable with the manner in which the man was looking at her, Beatrix dropped her gaze, sucking in a sharp breath when she realized the man was grasping a deadly looking pistol in his beefy hand—a pistol that was aimed her way.

Her head snapped up. "Have you taken leave of your senses?" she demanded, which had the man blinking his beady eyes. "This is hardly an appropriate setting to have a pistol out, so I'll thank you to tuck that right away."

"I ain't the one that's taken leave of my senses. This is a holdup, it is, and I'll thank *you* to stop yapping and hand over that bag you got swinging from your wrist."

Hoping she'd misheard what sounded like ominous words indeed, Beatrix glanced around the compartment, finding many of the passengers sitting still as statues, the gentlemen looking furious, while some of the ladies were dabbing at their eyes with handkerchiefs.

Any hope she'd been mistaken died in a single heartbeat.

Switching her attention back to the man who was evidently intent on robbing her, Beatrix frowned. "Shall I assume the train hasn't stopped at Crown Point?"

"'Course not. We'd hardly be successful robbin' a train at a station, would we, but enough with the questions. I'll have that bag, and quickly if you know what's good for you."

Beatrix clutched the bag closer to her. "This bag has no monetary value and was made for me by a dear child who'd be devastated to learn I no longer have possession of it."

The man took a step closer to Beatrix, so close in fact that the pistol he was holding pushed into her side. "You're tryin' my patience."

"I'd give him the bag if I were you," a gentleman called out from behind the man sticking a pistol in her side.

Although Beatrix knew that was sound advice indeed, the idea of handing over her belongings to a thief left a sour taste in her mouth.

She was not a lady tolerant of those who sought to rob innocents of their possessions. However, the man *was* threatening her with a pistol, which meant her only course of action as far as she could see would be to cooperate—to a certain extent.

Forcing herself to meet the man's gaze, she refused a wince when she detected a hefty dose of temper in his eyes. "You're more than welcome to the contents of my bag if you'll allow me to keep the bag because, as I mentioned, it has no monetary value."

"If it'll stop you arguing with me, fine, keep the bag, but get on with it. Hand over all the contents, and fast-like. I ain't got all day."

"I'd be a lot faster if I could empty my bag without that pistol distracting me."

Thankfully, the man took a step away from her, even as he began muttering something about "peculiar women" under his breath. Ignoring the mutters, Beatrix fumbled with the contents of her bag, throwing them into the leather satchel the robber was thrusting her way.

In went a lovely handkerchief that had taken her hours to embroider, an oatmeal cookie that the Waterbury cook had slipped into Beatrix's bag in case she got hungry, two pencils, one half-eaten apple she'd forgotten to throw out, one lone earring, three pennies, two nickels, one folded-up slip of paper, and . . .

"Don't think you can fool me by handing over such rubbish," the man snapped, causing Beatrix to jump. "I'm only interested in your money, and not the measly coins you've found so far."

"You said you wanted the contents of my purse, so that's what I've been giving you."

"Get to the good stuff."

Rooting around her bag, Beatrix stilled when she discovered an object lingering at the bottom of her reticule, something she'd completely forgotten about, but an object that could very well put a rapid end to the unfortunate situation currently taking place. Struggling to control nerves that were now jangling, Beatrix pulled out a deceptively innocent-looking rectangular coin purse.

Flipping open the side that held her pin money, she riffled through the accordion compartments, dumping all the change directly into the satchel. After every last cent was gone, she drew out the few bills nestled against the side of the purse, the bulk of her money safely stowed away in a special pocket in the waistband of her traveling gown.

"There you go. That's all my money."

"What ya got stashed on the other side of that purse?"

Turning the coin purse over, Beatrix flipped out a trigger that had been expertly concealed against the bottom of the purse, leveling the purse on the man with a hand that was surprisingly steady, even though she was well aware that she'd just put herself in certain peril.

"This is what's called the Frankenau Pistol Purse, and what's stashed on this other side is a clever five-shot pinfire revolver, one that, as you can see, is trained on you."

The man's brow furrowed. "You say you got a pistol in there? I don't believe you."

"Shall I pull the trigger to prove it?"

"You ain't got the nerve, even if there is a pistol in that purse. You're a woman, and everyone knows that women ain't got the stomach for shooting a—"

Whatever else the man had been about to say got lost when

there was suddenly a loud thud, and then the man crumpled to the ground, his pistol and the leather satchel falling from his hands. Glancing up, Beatrix discovered a gentleman standing a few feet away from her, holding a colored glass bottle that still had some water swishing around in it.

For the briefest moment, she merely gawked at the man.

He was unusually tall and his shoulders seemed to be broad, although it was difficult to say with any certainty because his jacket was baggy and ill-fitting. Long brown hair was sticking up in a most unusual fashion all over his head and looked as if it hadn't seen a comb in weeks. His eyes were an icy shade of blue, and his nose, though rather normal, was slightly red on the end, as if he were recovering from a cold.

That this gentleman had been the one to take down the man depriving her of her possessions took Beatrix completely aback. She'd certainly noticed him over the hours and hours they'd traveled together, since he'd been sitting only a seat away from her, but not once had she seen him speak to any of the other travelers on the train, instead preferring to spend his time buried in paperwork.

Frankly, she was surprised he'd even realized the train was being robbed, and . . .

"That was one of the most foolish actions I've ever witnessed in my life, especially from a woman" were the first words out of the gentleman's mouth. "If you'd only taken my advice from the start, I imagine the man would already be on his way instead of lying here unconscious, which is certain to cause us all sorts of trouble."

Beatrix drew herself up. "I don't recall you extending me any advice."

"I told you to give up your bag—advice you clearly didn't heed—instead deciding to take down the man with your purse." The man gave a shake of the bottle he was still holding. "You're fortunate I had the presence of mind to render this man senseless with this because I'm convinced that if I'd not acted, he would have called your bluff—right before he decided to shoot you because you were definitely testing his patience, something that's not advisable when dealing with a train robber in possession of a seemingly well-used pistol."

Any thought of thanking the man for his timely assistance disappeared in a flash. "Why would you think I was bluffing?"

"You're a woman, and everyone knows that women aren't possessed of the qualities needed to shoot a person—qualities like steady nerves and the actual ability to fire a pistol with accuracy."

"Given how close I was to the man, I hardly believe that I would have been anything other than accurate."

"And I believe that there was a very good chance you'd take out your own eye, or worse yet, shoot a fellow passenger. Pistols tend to recoil when they're shot, something very few women, if any, are prepared for when they fire a weapon for the first time."

"It would not have been my first time firing a pistol."

"And while I'm skeptical about that, allow us to put this absurd conversation aside because we have more pressing matters to attend to."

Beatrix had certainly encountered her fair share of gentlemen who believed ladies were, in essence, useless and expected to leave troubling situations to the discretion of men. But because she *was* Beatrix Waterbury, one of the great American heiresses, she was quite unaccustomed to anyone speaking in such a condescending manner to her.

The gentlemen of her acquaintance were always unerringly considerate of her and her "delicate feminine sensibilities," as they liked to call them, and none of them would have ever contemplated speaking so rudely to her.

Realizing, though, that now was hardly the time to deliver a blistering lecture, Beatrix swallowed the words that were on the very tip of her tongue. She then gave a jerk of her head toward the man lying in the aisle. "Shall I assume that pressing matter revolves around getting this man secured?"

"You should assume nothing of the sort. The pressing matter I mentioned revolves around us—as in you and me—getting off this train."

"I have no intention of departing this train with you, Mr. . . . ?"

"Nesbit. Norman Nesbit, and you are?"

"Beatrix Waterbury, but I can't get off the train with you because it would hardly be proper. And, besides, you could very well be a madman out to murder me, quite like the madmen I read about in the gothic novels I enjoy. And I have to believe any danger has vanished because you knocked out the man who was threatening us."

For the briefest of seconds, Mr. Norman Nesbit considered Beatrix, a flash of curiosity flickering through his eyes, but then he stepped over the man lying on the floor and took hold of her arm.

"I'm not a madman."

"I imagine that's a proclamation most madmen make before they do in their victims."

A vein began throbbing on Norman's forehead as his lips thinned. "An interesting theory, but one I have no time to debate with you because we have to get off this train."

"No."

"Did you not hear what the man disclosed to you before I rendered him senseless?"

"He disclosed he was a thief, intent on relieving me of my possessions."

"Not that, the part where he said, and I quote, 'We'd hardly be successful robbin' a train at a station.'"

Beatrix frowned. "Are you of the belief he's not acting alone?"

"Of course he's not acting alone, and because the man charged directly for me when he entered this car, something you missed when you made a trip to the retiring room, I'm convinced I was the main target of this train heist. Robbing the other passengers was only a ploy to distract from the real reason behind this particular train being held up."

"How did you know I'd gone off to the retiring room?"

"I'm very observant. I'm also very rational, which is why I feel it's prudent for me to get off this train in order to avoid bodily harm done to my person."

"And you feel it's prudent for me to go with you?"

He nodded. "Indeed." He gestured to the unconscious man. "There's little hope that when this man comes to he'll be feeling charitable toward you, what with you threatening to shoot him." Norman gestured to Beatrix's hair. "And because red hair is uncommonly rare, what with how scientists believe it's only seen in a small percentage of the world's population, some believing it's as small as one percent, it's highly likely this man will recognize you again and likely he'll be able to give a credible description to his fellow train robbers when they . . ."

"When they what?" Beatrix prodded when Norman stopped talking, narrowed his eyes on something behind her, then snatched up the leather satchel the train robber had dropped.

"We're running out of time" was all Norman said as he hustled her toward the door, shoved it open, and all but dragged Beatrix through it.

Chapter 2

Tripping over the hem of her traveling gown as she followed Norman off the train, Beatrix regained her balance and looked up, frowning when she saw the clear dose of annoyance in his eyes.

"Why are you regarding me in such an unpleasant fashion?" she asked.

"I was planning on assisting you."

"I'm perfectly capable of getting off a train by myself," she said shortly as Norman began tugging her toward a grove of trees located a few yards away from the tracks.

"Are you always so argumentative?" he asked.

"I'm rarely argumentative." She squinted as she caught sight of three horses tied to a tree and immediately tried to angle toward them, which had Norman slowing his pace.

"Is there some part of 'we're soon to be set upon by other robbers' that you're not comprehending?" he asked.

She nodded toward the horses. "I imagine those are the robbers' horses. We need to take them."

"I'm not a horse thief."

"I hardly think taking horses that don't belong to us from robbers who most assuredly want to deprive us of our possessions—if not our very lives—makes us horse thieves. Besides, taking their horses will make it all but impossible for them to catch us."

Shrugging out of Norman's hold, Beatrix raced toward the horses, untying two of them swiftly and leaping into the saddle of a large chestnut with ease. Taking a second to adjust her skirt to make riding astride more efficient, she shoved her pistol purse into her bag, gathered the reins into a practiced hand, then leaned forward to snag the reins of the horse closest to her, kneeing her horse forward and bringing it to a stop in front of Norman. That man, annoyingly enough, was still standing exactly where she'd left him, shaking his head as his gaze traveled over the horse she'd brought him.

"Need I remind you that we're in imminent danger?" she asked.

"I'd rather take my chances with the thieves over that dreadful beast."

"There's nothing dreadful about this horse, so I'll thank you to stop dithering and get in the saddle." She tossed him the reins, which he didn't bother to catch.

"Ah, thank you, but no."

"Why not?"

"I don't find riding horses to be a pleasant pastime."

"I'm not asking you to accompany me on a leisurely ride through a park. You said yourself that we need to get away from here as quickly as possible. I highly doubt you'll be able to escape from those men on foot, especially if—"

A gunshot split the air.

Lifting her head, Beatrix discovered a man running toward them, who was, concerningly enough, aiming a pistol at Norman. Snatching her pistol purse from her bag, she fired off a shot that was less than accurate but had the fortunate effect of having the man dive behind one of the train cars.

"Come on," she yelled to Norman, who, thankfully, jolted into motion. Instead of pulling himself into the saddle, though, he merely flung himself over the horse, his arms dangling over one side and his legs dangling over the other.

"How do you expect to ride like that?"

"I don't ride horses," he mumbled. "Haven't been on one since I was seven and suffered a horrendous accident."

Another shot from the train robber sent the horse she was on skittering to the left. After reining it in, and after realizing this was not the moment to argue with an unreasonable man, Beatrix urged the horse forward, snatching up the reins of the horse Norman was lying across before she headed for the trees, additional shots ringing out behind her.

For how long she rode, she couldn't say, although it was at least thirty minutes—thirty minutes in which Norman went from yelping to then grunting before he finally settled into reciting what sounded like an obscure list of numbers.

"You do know," Beatrix said finally, "what with how you're all but bellowing out numbers, that you're making it remarkably easy for one of those thieves to follow us, don't you? You do recall that we left one horse behind."

The recitation of numbers ceased. "Simple logic suggests we're not being followed because I haven't heard any sound of pursuit. That means the thieves found the satchel I left behind, which was what they were after in the first place, so they have no reason to chase after us."

Beatrix reined to a stop and turned in the saddle, finding Norman still lying across his horse, his eyes squeezed shut.

"You should have said something about dropping your satchel. I could have swung around and scooped it up before we headed into the trees."

One of Norman's eyes opened. "I left it on purpose."

"Because you wanted to make life easier for those criminals by giving them what they wanted?"

His other eye opened. "Hardly. I gave the thieves what they *think* they wanted. The research papers in my satchel are altered. I changed some conclusions and mathematical equations, which, in essence, makes the papers worthless."

"Research papers?"

"I'm a scientist and have been having some breakthroughs with electricity lately. I'm just on my way home from a meeting with some of the greatest minds of the day, and while I spoke with many noble gentlemen at that meeting, there were also many men there who were clearly possessed of unscrupulous natures. That's why I decided to provide myself with a decoy if someone tried to abscond with the research papers I took with me to discuss in New York." He gave a wave of his hand. "You may continue forward. I have no desire to be on this horse longer than necessary and can only hope we'll soon find our way out of this forest and into some manner of civilization."

"I've no idea how to go about finding civilization."

"Just keep heading north. We'll run into a road eventually or, if not, Lake Michigan. But now, if you'll excuse me, I need to return to distracting myself with division by three."

"Most people find descending into prayer or singing a cheery song works like a charm when in need of a distraction. I've never heard of anyone using mathematics to accomplish that."

"I'm not most people" was all he said before he closed his eyes and began reciting random numbers again, with a "divided by" and "to the third power" occasionally interrupting his recitation.

"You're definitely not most people," Beatrix muttered as she turned in the saddle and kneed her horse forward, pulling Norman's horse behind her.

She continued riding for a good twenty minutes but was forced to stop when a rushing stream spread out in front of her. Turning in the saddle, she found Norman with his eyes firmly closed, his mouth moving rapidly as numbers spilled through his lips. Clearing her throat, which did nothing to attract Norman's attention, she cleared it again, louder than the first time.

"I could use your opinion right about now," she was finally forced to call in a voice so loud that it echoed through the trees surrounding them.

Norman opened his eyes. "You don't strike me as the type of woman who puts much stock in the opinions of others."

She stiffened in the saddle. "You don't know me well enough

18

to understand what type of woman I am. And while many people find me to be possessed of a pleasant nature, I have to admit that I'm not currently feeling pleasant thoughts toward you because, forgive me, but you have to be the rudest man I've ever had the misfortune to meet."

"I'm not rude, just direct."

"Whoever told you that bit of ridiculousness was not doing you any favors. And while I normally don't bother asking rude men their opinions at all, I have no choice at the moment." She gestured to the stream. "We'll need to cross this at some point, but I'm not sure which direction I should lead us to find a shallow spot."

"I'm afraid I have no ready opinion for you because I don't have a good vantage point from my current position."

"Perhaps you should consider getting off the horse so you'll have a better vantage point."

"But then I'd have to climb back on. I really don't think I'm up for that type of trauma again today."

"Get off the horse."

Norman's blue eyes narrowed. "Does your husband allow you to get away with speaking to him in such a demanding fashion?"

"I'm not married."

"Which explains much," he returned right before he began shifting around on the horse, all but tumbling to the ground a second later. Rising to his feet, he wobbled as if his legs were having a time of it holding him upright.

"What did you mean by that?" Beatrix asked, turning her horse around to face him.

Norman stopped his wobbling. "Mean by what?"

"I believe you said 'Which explains much' after I told you I wasn't married."

"At the risk of being accused of additional rudeness, I don't think it would be in my best interest to answer that."

Beatrix's lips thinned. "If you've forgotten, I still have possession of my pistol purse, and it's a five shot, which means I still have a few left."

To her annoyance, Norman smiled. "Because you're a woman, I doubt you have the stomach to shoot an unarmed man."

"My stomach has never given me difficulties."

Norman's smile faded. "How disconcerting."

"I imagine it is, and with that settled, what did you mean?"

"You're very tenacious—which is not a compliment, if you're wondering—and that also lends credence to the conclusions I'd made about you and your unwedded state."

Regret over encouraging Norman to explain his statement was immediate, but before she could figure out how to get him to stop, he opened his mouth again.

"Even with your evident problem with a tenacious nature, the main reasons I wasn't surprised to learn you're unmarried are this—you're well past the first blush of youth, and you're also traveling on your own. Those two circumstances already suggested you're a confirmed spinster. I've now concluded that your spinster state was undoubtedly brought about because you're an opinionated and impulsive woman, traits that gentlemen find less than appealing in a woman they might be considering marrying."

"It *would* have been in your best interest to refuse to answer my question because you've just proven without a doubt that you *are* the rudest man I've ever met."

"Exactly why you shouldn't have pressed me for a response," he said calmly before he turned and began moving to the stream, stumbling over a tree branch a second later.

Unfortunately, he then knocked into his horse, which then jolted forward into Beatrix's horse right as she was beginning to dismount from it.

Losing her balance, she landed on the leaf-strewn ground in a heap of billowing fabric, the pistol purse she'd stowed on her lap for easy access landing with a clunk on the ground a foot away from her. To her utmost horror, a gunshot split the air, and then Norman was flying off his feet, dropping like a stone to the forest floor in the blink of an eye.

CHAPTER 3

Of anything Mr. Norman Nesbit had been expecting on his journey back to Chicago, being shot—and by a woman no less—hadn't crossed his mind, one that many people said was one of the most remarkable minds of the day.

He was a man known for presenting the world with a detached and, some might say, emotionless demeanor. However, as he lay on the ground, most likely bleeding to death, he couldn't deny he was feeling less along the lines of detached and more along the lines of aggravated.

It was beyond curious how it had come about that he'd been thrust into the company of Miss Beatrix Waterbury, a progressive woman if there ever was one, and the type of woman he normally avoided like the plague. He never willingly stayed in the company of women who were incapable of taking sound advice, such as putting away her pistol to protect the innocent, advice Beatrix evidently didn't believe was sound, even though she'd actually shot him, which proved his advice had been very sound indeed.

Sucking in a breath of much-needed air, which had his chest burning in protest, he released it right as Beatrix materialized above him, her lovely green eyes, something he only just noticed, filled with what seemed to be genuine concern.

Before he could dwell further on that thought, another thought chased it straight away, one that questioned why he was wasting precious time noticing that Beatrix's eyes were lovely. It was hardly the moment to ponder such nonsensical matters and certainly suggested he might have suffered a blow to the head because it was very unlikely him to become distracted by lovely eyes in the first place.

"Lie perfectly still while I see if I can locate where the bullet struck you," Beatrix said, interrupting his disconcerting thoughts as she began patting him down, her hands starting at his face, which clearly didn't have a hole in it, and moving downward.

"Stop that," he muttered around a hand that was now covering his mouth.

"Don't argue with me. I'm trying to do a thorough assessment, and you're disturbing my concentration."

Before he could muster up an argument, Beatrix ripped open his jacket, popping off buttons in the process. Why she'd chosen such a dramatic manner to open his jacket was curious since it wouldn't have taken that much longer to simply unbutton it. However, since she was now thumping her hand against his chest, the thumping setting his teeth on edge, he found himself lacking any incentive to question her methods.

Her thumping abruptly stopped. "Why does your chest seem unusually firm, and why is it giving off an odd pealing sound?"

Norman peered through untidy hair that was almost obscuring his view. "I'm wearing plates of steel under my vest that one of my fellow scientists gave me. He's a metallurgist and is working with different metals, hoping to create a stronger product. He gave me a sample after I met with him in New York."

"But why are you *wearing* plates of steel?"

"Thought they would come in handy to protect my research papers, the ones the train robbers really wanted, from any weather elements as I traveled back to Chicago."

A second later, Beatrix was unbuttoning his vest, something he was grateful about since he was fond of this particular vest and didn't want its buttons to go the way of the buttons of his jacket. Shoving open the vest after she'd gotten it completely unbuttoned, she let her gaze travel over the steel plate he'd secured around himself with a belt.

"Do you often encounter unexpected weather elements when you travel?" she finally asked.

"No, but that's not to say I *couldn't* have encountered unexpected weather, such as a torrential rainstorm, which could have ruined my papers."

"But you were traveling on a train, not in an open carriage."

"I'm not on a train now."

"True, but it's not raining."

"True, but my papers could even now be getting a drenching from the blood I'm most certainly spilling because, if you've forgotten, you shot me."

Her green eyes widened. "I did forget about that. Where do you think the bullet entered?"

Norman frowned. "Not sure."

"Where's the greatest pain?"

"My chest."

That answer had her returning her attention to his chest, or rather to the belt that was keeping the steel plates in place. Divesting him of the belt and the top plate, she peeled away his research papers, then paused when she got to the second steel plate that was lying directly against his shirt. Leaning closer, she plucked the plate off him, turning that plate over and over again as she considered it.

"There's no hole, and I don't see any blood on your shirt" was all she said, tossing the plate aside before she picked up the first plate again, which she then brandished in front of him.

"Look, there's a dent here that suggests the bullet might have ricocheted off this plate." She tossed the plate to the ground and began patting his jacket down again, causing him to jump when her finger poked him in the side.

"What *are* you doing?" he asked.

"Looking for the bullet." She bent over him, her hair tickling his nose as well as allowing him to get a whiff of her hair, which smelled like lemon mixed with a bit of lime.

"Got it," she said cheerfully, taking the scent of her hair with her as she straightened, holding a small bullet in her hand. She turned a bright smile on him, drawing his attention to a freckle that rested directly next to her bottom lip. That lip, he realized, was once again moving, which meant she was speaking, although what she'd just said, he had no idea.

"I *must* be suffering from a blow to the head," he muttered.

"Why didn't you say something sooner?" she demanded, tossing the bullet aside and probing his head with her fingers. She lifted his head as she continued feeling around the back of his neck until his head was nestled directly against her bosom, not that she seemed to realize she'd placed him in a spot she probably didn't want him lingering.

A different scent immediately captured his senses, one that smelled of lilies, sunshine, and . . .

He shook his head as he realized the scent was beginning to muddle thoughts that were unused to being muddled.

"You're pulling my hair," he murmured through the fabric his face was pressed up against, a less-than-truthful statement since she was being remarkably gentle with him, but it was the only thing he could think of to get her to release him, which would hopefully have his thoughts returning to fine working order.

She released him abruptly, causing his head to land with a thud against the hard ground and earning a grunt from him in return.

Beatrix winced. "Sorry about that, but you'll be pleased to learn that your head seems to be fine, as does your chest." She picked up one of the abandoned steel plates and nodded. "You must make sure to tell that scientist friend of yours that he's on to something with this steel because it appears that his plate prevented the bullet from hitting your skin."

"I suppose I should be relieved I've not actually been shot."

"You *have* been shot, but you aren't going to die from it." She caught his eye. "Do know that I didn't intentionally shoot you, although I didn't actually shoot you, the ground did. With that said, though, I feel dreadful about the accident and am much relieved to know you're going to live."

"I'd feel much relieved if you'd agree to give me that pistol purse of yours so you won't unintentionally shoot anyone else."

"I'm not giving you my pistol purse. These are dangerous times for a lady traveling alone, and that pistol purse lends me a sense of security."

"Your pistol purse lends me an ache in my chest where that bullet would have torn my skin if I'd not had the presence of mind to gird my chest with plates of steel to begin with."

"If you'd not been so clumsy as to stumble into your horse, which then bumped into mine, I wouldn't have tumbled to the ground, nor would I have dropped the pistol purse, which then caused it to fire—a rare occurrence I'm sure since I've not read any reports in the newspaper about this particular weapon firing at random."

"You read?"

"I don't believe I need to dignify that with an answer." She rose to her feet and dusted off her hands.

"I'm not questioning whether you *can* read," Norman clarified. "I was questioning the idea that you read newspapers."

"Of course I read newspapers."

"There's no need to sound so indignant. You must know that electing to read newspapers is a peculiar choice for a woman. I can't claim to know but three women who read the daily newsprints."

"You must not be acquainted with many women."

"I'm acquainted with lots of women, but again, they've never brought it to my attention that they read newspapers."

She let out a bit of a snort. "That's only because women are brought up to believe that gentlemen do not want to spend time with bluestockings, so most women keep their true reading habits to themselves to spare them disdainful conversations like the one I'm currently *not* enjoying with you." She tilted her head. "Out of curiosity, though, have you ever asked a woman what she prefers to read?"

"And be bored silly as that woman would, of course, expound on the delights of Jane Austen or the like?"

"I'll take that as a no." She dusted off her hands again. "And with that settled, shall we get moving?" She gave him a tight smile. "I'm afraid if we spend too much time together, I may very well be tempted to drop my pistol purse to the ground again, preferably aimed in your direction."

He was relatively certain she wasn't jesting. "By all means, let us get on our way, although I don't believe I'm feeling settled enough just yet, after having been shot, to climb back into that saddle."

"You were never *in* the saddle, merely sprawled over it."

"I told you, I suffered a riding accident in my youth. As I recovered from that accident, I decided that I'd never ride a horse again."

Beatrix held out her hand to him, and even though he was surprised by the gesture, he took it, surprised again when she hauled him to his feet.

"Didn't your parents believe that it's always best to get right back on a horse after you've fallen off?" she asked, releasing his hand.

"I couldn't very well have gotten right back on that dastardly horse because I suffered two broken arms, a broken leg, fractured ribs, and a concussed head."

"You did take quite the spill, didn't you?"

"Indeed. I was confined to my bed for months. Today is the first time in over two decades that I've been up close and personal with a horse."

Her nose wrinkled. "But if you'd gotten back in the saddle after you'd recovered, you wouldn't now be hampered by a fear of horses."

"I have no issue with my fear of horses."

"It takes a confident man to admit that."

He shrugged. "I've never been overly concerned with what others think of me. I'm well aware that many people find me eccentric, a notion that doesn't bother me in the least."

"Why do people find you eccentric?"

"I have an unusual mind."

"Undoubtedly."

He tilted his head. "Aren't you curious why I believe I have an unusual mind?"

"I don't believe you need to give any further explanation." She smiled. "I am curious, though, how your parents allowed you to avoid riding again, what with how horses are a necessary means of transportation."

"Do you not have a mother?"

"Of course I have a mother."

"Then you really shouldn't need more of an explanation than that. My mother suffered tremendously after I was thrown from my horse, so because of that, and because she also decided I was a fragile sort, she didn't bat an eye when I declared I was never mounting a horse again."

"You don't look fragile."

"I made a concerted effort to improve my physical form after I was permitted to leave my sickbed. To this day, I maintain a strict schedule devoted to physical activity."

Her gaze traveled over him. "That strict schedule is clearly effective. But returning to your refusal to ride horses . . . while I understand your mother's decision, what of your father? Did he not have a say in the matter?"

"My father enjoys keeping a harmonious relationship with my mother." Norman brushed a leaf from the sleeve of his jacket before he lifted his head and frowned. "I find myself curious, though, about your understanding of my mother's decision. I've often wondered about spinsters and their outlook on life, but now feel as if my theories may be off the mark."

Beatrix narrowed her eyes at him. "What theories?"

"Well, one of them has always been that because spinsters are not mothers, they don't develop the expected maternal feelings their counterparts do, which would then make it more difficult for them to understand emotional reactions such as my mother had."

A flash of temper flickered through her eyes. "While it's bewildering to me why you would even contemplate such nonsense, what with how you claim to have a brilliant mind, I don't believe spinsterhood is responsible for depriving a woman of maternal instincts. Frankly, I find such theories insulting and have to wonder what your wife thinks about all that."

"I'm not married."

"That explains much." She crossed her arms over her chest. "What theory would you come up with about me if I told you that not only am I a spinster, and one who has no interest in marrying at the moment, I'm also an avid supporter of the suffrage movement?"

"I'd say it's fortunate you have no interest in marrying because men do not care to become involved with suffragists, whom everyone knows are simply women disgruntled with their lot in life."

For a long moment, she stared at him, until she spun on her heel, stomped over to her pistol purse, scooped it up from the ground, then turned back to him.

"You're not intending on shooting me with that, are you?" he finally forced himself to ask when she continued regarding him without speaking a word.

"Tempting, but no." With that, she tucked the pistol purse away, walked over to her horse, took the reins, then sent him a nod. "This is where I bid you *adieu* and wish you luck in finding your way back to civilization."

"You're going to leave a man you only recently shot, and one whom you know is incapable of riding a horse, out here in the middle of nowhere?"

"Yes."

Before Norman could compose a suitable argument, Beatrix jumped on her horse and galloped away, leaving him behind.

CHAPTER 4

Knowing there was nothing to do but go after Beatrix because he couldn't very well leave a spinster woman unaccompanied in the middle of a remote forest, Norman strode to the horse Beatrix had left behind. Taking hold of the reins, he resisted the urge to drop them when the horse let out a nicker.

"This is not the time for such nasty business," he said, earning a nibble from the horse, which had perspiration beading his forehead and his stomach roiling.

"You lost, mister?"

Turning, Norman discovered a young boy standing a few feet away from him, holding an empty bucket in one hand and a stick with a line attached to it in the other.

He wasn't a man comfortable around children, never knew what to say to them even though he had numerous nieces and nephews. However, since he *was* lost at the moment, Norman nodded.

"I'm afraid I am lost. I've also misplaced the woman I was traveling with and was about to go on a quest to try and locate her. Any chance you'd be willing to help me out? I have a feeling she's off to find the nearest road or train station."

The lad smiled, revealing a large gap in his front teeth. "Is a quest the same as an adventure?"

"I suppose it is."

The boy nodded. "That sounds almost as fun as fishing, so sure, I'll help you." His smile faded. "Don't know how we can go about finding your lost woman, though, but the road that'll take you to the Merrillville train station is that way." He pointed the stick to the right. "Want me to lead the way?"

"That would be most appreciated."

After retrieving the steel plates and research papers, and after taking a moment to re-gird his chest because there was a possibility Beatrix might reappear at some point and because she *was* still armed, Norman took hold of the horse's reins and fell into step beside the boy.

He soon learned that the boy's name was John Nelson, and he also learned that John was eight years old and had annoying sisters who didn't care for fishing. The look he sent him after that disclosure left Norman with the distinct impression John found that more than a tad confusing. The little boy then launched into all the reasons why fishing was his favorite activity, and since he didn't expect Norman to do more than nod every few minutes, Norman found their walk through the forest to be surprisingly pleasant.

Stepping from the trees almost an hour later, Norman came to an abrupt stop when he heard something behind him. Turning, he frowned when Beatrix cantered into sight, leaving him to wonder if she'd been following them the entire time—a concerning notion since he'd not had the smallest inkling she was trailing after him.

"Couldn't find your way back on your own?" he called.

Beatrix reined her horse to a stop as her nose shot straight into the air. "I turned around to come back for you because I was worried about your mother, which should have you reconsidering your conclusions about spinsters and our supposed lack of maternal feelings."

"What does my mother have to do with anything?"

"I figured she'd be beside herself if you didn't return to Chicago within the next few days. I wouldn't have been able to live with myself knowing that if you came to an unpleasant end, I could have spared your mother such anguish. So, here I am, but how fortunate this boy came across you and was so helpful with leading you out of the forest and to a road." With that, Beatrix slid gracefully from the saddle and strode over to John.

"I'm Miss Beatrix Waterbury," she said, smiling at John, who was watching her with wide eyes. "What's your name?"

"I'm John Nelson, Miss Waterbury, and I ain't never seen a lady wearing such a fancy dress get off a horse so smoothly."

"I've been riding since before I could walk," Beatrix said right as the sound of barking rang out, which sent John bolting forward.

"That's Charlie," he called over his shoulder. "He's lookin' for me. Don't want him to worry, so I'll be right back."

As John dashed away, Beatrix's smile widened. "What a delightful boy."

"I suppose he is, although he's very chatty for one so young."

"Am I correct in assuming you don't converse in idle chitchat with children?"

"I don't have an aptitude for participating in idle chitchat with anyone."

"How unfortunate for you. I've always found it to be a wonderful way to engage in pleasant interludes with strangers who then often evolve into friends." Beatrix turned from him as John came racing into sight, a large dog of indeterminate breed keeping pace beside him, its tail wagging furiously.

A second later, as Beatrix knelt to greet the boy and his dog, she was knocked to the ground by Charlie, peals of laughter escaping her as the dog immediately proceeded to lick her face.

Norman suddenly felt the most unusual urge to laugh with her, an idea that took him so aback that any amusement he'd been feeling disappeared in a flash.

He was not a man who laughed often, preferring to embrace a somber attitude, one that befitted a serious man of science.

The very idea that he'd felt compelled to join in Beatrix's

amusement left him with the concerning notion that his well-structured world was slowly becoming anything other than structured.

Taking a firm grip of the horse's reins, he tugged the horse forward, not bothering to even flinch when it let out a nicker. Frankly, there was no time for flinching, not when it was becoming clear to him that his well-structured life was in certain jeopardy.

For the sake of his sanity, he realized that he needed to part ways as quickly as possible with Miss Beatrix Waterbury because even though he barely knew the woman, he was now convinced she had the ability to disrupt his world, which would then disrupt his work, and that was something he couldn't—or rather wouldn't—allow anyone to do.

After thanking John for getting Norman out of the forest, Beatrix couldn't resist a roll of the eyes when Norman threw himself across the saddle again. He then asked her to keep their pace at a sedate level, stating his chest was still sore from where she'd shot him and he didn't care to be jostled about.

Because she *had* shot him, though, she didn't set her horse to galloping, letting it meander down the road at a pace that left much to be desired.

It quickly became apparent that Norman had not been exaggerating when he'd claimed to have no aptitude for chitchat. The few times she attempted to engage him in conversation during their ride were met with grunts or silence, which was why she eventually abandoned any effort in that regard, spending the time it took to get to the small train station listening to Norman spout out random numbers every few seconds.

Steering the horse to a hitching post once they reached the station, Beatrix dismounted and tied the reins around the post, doing the same to the reins of Norman's horse. She then watched in disbelief as Norman slid clumsily off his horse, landing on his backside, but before she could offer him a hand up, he was on his feet, stamping one foot and then the other against the ground and wincing with every stamp.

"I'm trying to get rid of the tingles," he said when he noticed her watching him. "Must have lost the circulation at some point."

"That wouldn't have happened if you'd ridden in the saddle."

"No, but if I'd done that then there's a good chance I'd have fainted from terror at some point, and then where would we be?"

"You'd still be lying on the road, where I would have left you because I don't believe I would have been sympathetic to your plight a second time."

"And yet another reason why you're not married."

Her lips twitched, but not wanting Norman to know he'd actually amused her instead of annoyed her, Beatrix spun on her heel and strode to the ticket window, purchasing them two tickets to Chicago. Delighted to be told the train to Chicago would be leaving in fifteen minutes, she took a moment to explain their situation to the man in the ticket booth, who hurried to assure her that he'd see after the horses, and then returned her money, saying she deserved a free trip after the trouble she'd experienced.

"Did that man give you back your money?" Norman asked, falling into step beside her after she handed him his ticket and strode for the train.

"He did."

"That was hardly a prudent business decision on his part. You were obviously capable of paying since you'd already done exactly that, although I was intending to pay you back for my ticket."

"He was trying to be kind."

"But he lost the sale of two tickets."

Beatrix stopped walking a few feet from the train. "Do feel free to choose a seat far, far away from me."

He frowned. "I was already intending on doing that."

"Good." As she marched her way onto the train, her disappointment was swift when she realized all the seats were occupied save two—and those seats, unfortunately, were together.

"And here I was hoping to get some uninterrupted time on

the ride to Chicago," Norman said behind her. "Highly doubtful that'll happen now, not when you talked almost nonstop on the ride here."

"No, I didn't," Beatrix said. "You're the one who was never silent."

"I was working on an elusive mathematical equation, which demanded I talk out loud because that helps me puzzle equations out."

"You do know that talking out loud to oneself can be construed by others as rather rude behavior, don't you?" Beatrix asked as she headed for the two empty seats, sitting down in the one directly by the window, Norman taking the seat next to her.

"No one has ever mentioned that they find my talking out loud rude, not even the decorum instructors my mother hired for me in my youth."

"You had decorum instructors?"

He nodded. "My mother has always been determined to take her place as one of *the* society leaders in Chicago society. But the lessons stopped when I turned twelve, though, after Miss Addleson, my last decorum instructor, decided I was a hopeless case."

"Your family is society?"

He nodded again.

Beatrix's brows drew together. "Don't you find society events difficult because you don't enjoy idle chitchat?"

"I'm only required to attend a few events every Season." Norman smiled. "My mother is well aware that I'm somewhat lacking in social graces, which is why she's content to simply tell everyone I'm occupied with my work. She only insists I attend events that are deemed significant, which, thankfully, are few and far between."

The train chugged into motion, picking up speed as Beatrix took a moment to appreciate the scenery now flashing past her window. "How did your family become involved in Chicago society?" she asked, turning back to Norman, who was in the process of retrieving an apple from his pocket, which he promptly gave to her before retrieving another one for himself.

Beatrix smiled. "Thank you." She took a bite, swallowed,

then nodded. "Returning to your family, have they always been society?"

He took a bite of his apple, chewed it for a few seconds, then shook his head. "No, at least not on my father's side. My grandfather began mining iron ore back in the forties. He found a large deposit on some land he'd purchased, which then led him to build an iron foundry in Chicago a few years later. That foundry became quite profitable, which allowed my grandfather, and then my father, to expand into steel mills. With their success came invitations to society events and introductions to the reigning belles of the day, of which my mother was one." With that, Norman took another bite of his apple and descended into silence, seeming to be perfectly content to end the conversation there.

Beatrix frowned. "You really *are* inept at the whole chitchat business, aren't you?"

"I never said I was inept. I said I don't have an aptitude for it."

"You admitted you've had decorum instructors, so I have to imagine those instructors broached the subject of how to go about participating in proper conversations. With that said, you've just neglected a basic rule of conversation—that being when someone has inquired about your life, you reciprocate by inquiring about theirs."

"You're upset that I didn't inquire about your societal standing?"

"*Upset* wouldn't be the word I'd choose. *Curious* would suit the occasion better."

Norman polished off his apple and shrugged. "I was trying to spare you the embarrassment of admitting that you don't have any societal standing."

Of anything Beatrix had been expecting him to say, that hadn't crossed her mind. "Why would you assume I don't travel in society?"

"Because you're a confirmed spinster. You're also traveling alone, which suggests you're not a lady of means. Ladies without means are rarely of the society set."

That he kept bringing up her spinster status set her teeth on edge and had her abandoning any thought of disclosing the fact that she *was* a lady of means, and great means at that, or that she was a member of the illustrious New York Four Hundred.

"I'm beginning to feel you might be right about idle chitchat, that it is, indeed, overrated," she muttered, which earned a nod from him in return.

"Of course I'm right."

She narrowed her eyes. "Or perhaps I should amend that and say any attempt at idle chitchat with *you* is doomed to failure because you're completely inept with it."

"I'm *not* inept. I simply don't enjoy it."

"Then by all means, feel free to return to your mathematical equations. I'm perfectly capable of entertaining myself."

"An excellent suggestion." He closed his eyes and immediately began mouthing numbers instead of speaking them out loud, something that suggested he'd never realized how annoying his unusual habit was until she'd mentioned it, and was actually making an attempt *not* to annoy her.

However, because the numbers were coming out of a mouth that appeared to be clenched, it was clear he wasn't finding elusive mathematical equations to be the distraction he'd evidently been hoping for, something that left Beatrix smiling.

CHAPTER 5

"If you've neglected to notice, the train has stopped. I believe there's now the expectation that we're meant to get off the train, unless you'd like to continue on with whatever you seem to be in the midst of contemplating."

Norman's eyes flashed open, disgruntlement running through him when he realized that the train *had* come to a stop, something he *had* neglected to notice.

This curious lapse on his part was concerning, especially when he'd always prided himself on his observational skills—skills that seemed to be failing him rather spectacularly at the moment.

It was also concerning that his attempt at distracting himself with his tried-and-true habit of dividing sums by three had not worked at all because while he had been trying to concentrate on numbers, thoughts of Beatrix had wormed their way through the numbers, or rather, the notion that she apparently found him lacking, or worse, inept.

Pushing his disturbing thoughts aside as Beatrix got out of her seat and began moving down the aisle, Norman followed her, stepping off the train and on to a wooden sidewalk.

"Do you think our original train finally made it here after being robbed, and if so, do you think we'll find our luggage stowed somewhere?" she asked.

"Only one way to find out." He gestured her forward and began making his way through the crowd toward the main depot. When he realized Beatrix had broken into a trot to keep up with him and was rubbing her side, as if she'd developed a stitch, he slowed his pace.

"Was I moving too quickly?"

"Not if you believe we're being chased by a pack of rabid wolves," she returned, dashing a hand over a forehead that was now beaded with perspiration.

His lips twitched. "Fortunately there are no wolves chasing us. I'm merely accustomed to moving quickly to save time." He frowned. "Have you ever considered taking a daily run to improve your physical stamina? I run a few miles every day and find that activity to be greatly beneficial with keeping me in fine form."

"I'm not really keen to embrace an activity I feel is comparable to torture," she said before she headed into the main depot and charged toward a man sitting behind a counter, moving remarkably fast for a woman who'd only recently suffered from a stitch in her side.

By the time Norman reached her, she'd already informed the man about their run-in with train robbers, which had the man rising to his feet and escorting them into a nearby office.

As the man hurried from the room, telling them he'd be back directly, Beatrix took a seat in front of a battered desk while Norman elected to remain standing.

Men soon streamed in to join them, one of whom introduced himself as Agent Mahoney, a member of the Pinkerton Agency. Agent Mahoney immediately directed his attention to Beatrix, questioning her about the robbery.

Beatrix didn't hesitate to launch into an explanation about what had occurred, giving Agent Mahoney an excellent recollection of what the man who'd tried to take her reticule looked like, as well as giving a surprisingly detailed account of the second train robber who'd shot at them after they'd gotten off the train.

Ten minutes later, she nodded to Norman. "Have I left anything out?"

"I believe you were more than thorough with your recollection of the events that occurred. You did, however, neglect to disclose that your decision to turn your pistol purse on the robber escalated the danger we were in since I was of the belief, before you brought out your pistol, that the matter was soon to be resolved since the robber had possession of my satchel, which was what I'm convinced they were after in the first place."

Temper immediately flashed through Beatrix's eyes. "Are you suggesting that everything that happened after I pulled out my pistol purse was my fault?"

"It wasn't a suggestion."

Her lips thinned. "Then allow me to counter with this—if you'd not snatched up your satchel after telling me we needed to get off the train, we would have never been chased by the other robbers, nor would we have had to duck a barrage of bullets as we tried to get away."

"We wouldn't have experienced any of that if you'd only had the good sense to cooperate with the robber when he asked for your bag."

"I wasn't giving him my bag. It's sentimental to me, and—"

Agent Mahoney held up his hand. "While I'm sure both of you have valid points, let's return to the satchel for a moment. What did you have that these criminals wanted?"

Norman settled his attention on Agent Mahoney. "Research papers."

"And these papers were pertaining to what?"

"Electrical currents, or more specifically, my theory on how to rotate an electric field within a motor using an alternating current instead of a single current. I've recently exchanged a brass ring for a steel one because brass is not magnetized, but I'm—"

Norman stopped talking when Beatrix took to clearing her

throat loudly. He frowned. "I say, Miss Waterbury, should we ask one of these men to fetch you a cup of tea? You seem to be having difficulties with your throat, no doubt brought about by how much smog is in the air today in Chicago."

Beatrix returned the frown. "I haven't noticed an unusual amount of pollution in the air."

"Which is why it probably snuck up on you." He nodded. "Unfortunately, pollution is often found in and around Chicago, what with how many ironworks and the like are operating at all hours."

"It wasn't the smog that had me clearing my throat."

"Perhaps you're coming down with a cold?"

"I'm not coming down with a cold." She turned to Agent Mahoney. "Was there any other information you needed?"

Agent Mahoney looked up from the notes he'd been taking and smiled at Beatrix, a smile that, oddly enough, seemed to hold a trace of relief in it. "You've been more than helpful with your accounting of the troubling events you experienced." He shot a glance to Norman. "As have you, of course, Mr. Nesbit."

Norman frowned. "But I didn't finish explaining about my research papers."

Agent Mahoney looked at his notes, then lifted his head. "From what I could gather, they have something to do with electrical currents."

"That hardly does my research justice." He drew in a breath and then launched into a detailed explanation regarding his theory but was forced to stop his explanation in midsentence when Beatrix began coughing in earnest, although it almost seemed as if her coughing had a rather theatrical ring to it.

"Maybe we really should get someone to bring you a cup of tea," he said.

Beatrix waved that aside. "I'm fine, but before you return to explaining more about your research, which sounds downright titillating, I'm sure I speak for everyone when I say that none of us have the least little idea what you're going on about."

"I've made my explanations as simple as possible."

"Which would be lovely if any of us gathered here were fluent in electrical talk, which I'm confident with saying we're not."

Norman nodded to Agent Mahoney. "But he asked me about the research papers."

"True," Beatrix said. "However, I'm going to assume he only wanted a basic description of the contents of the research, something along the lines of—'it's electrical in nature.'"

"That's an insult to my research."

She released a breath. "Agent Mahoney doesn't need all the details. He just needs to know the gist of your research so that if he happens to retrieve a leather satchel filled with papers on electrical currents, he'll know it's your satchel."

Norman blinked. "Oh."

"Exactly," Beatrix said, returning her attention to Agent Mahoney. "And with that now settled, was there anything else you needed from us before we conclude this meeting?"

Agent Mahoney looked through his notes again, then nodded to Norman. "I would like to know if you have any idea who might be behind the train heist. Any enemies or business associates who might want access to your research?"

Norman nodded. "Quite a few names spring to mind."

Agent Mahoney flipped to a fresh piece of paper. "Ready when you are."

It took exactly nine and a half minutes to rattle off the list of men Norman thought could be considered suspects, although it would have only taken seven minutes and fifty-two seconds if Beatrix hadn't distracted him when she'd accepted a cup of tea from one of the men who'd evidently decided her throat needed soothing, no matter her protest about that. She'd smiled so easily at the man that Norman had faltered in his recitation of names, until he'd realized that Agent Mahoney was about to tuck away his list of suspects, which had immediately brought Norman back to the situation at hand and had him continuing on.

"Mr. Stephen Millersburg, who is currently working with Mr. Westinghouse, is the last gentleman I can think of who should be listed as a suspect. He was very interested in trying to secure my agreement to allow him to work with me on my research, going so far as to imply he and Mr. Westinghouse wouldn't be opposed to paying me for what I've accomplished so far," Norman finished, which had Agent Mahoney lifting his head after he'd scribbled that name on to his second-to-last sheet of blank paper.

"You've given me almost a hundred names," Agent Mahoney said.

Norman shrugged. "It's important research."

"Then here's hoping we'll be able to retrieve it for you," Agent Mahoney said.

"There's no urgency with that," Norman said. "I'm afraid I neglected to mention this earlier, but the research that was stolen was not my true research, merely a decoy in case someone tried to rob me. The only benefit from you being able to recover the satchel would be that it may very well lead to the culprits behind the robbery, which will then allow you to close your case."

"But this decoy research still had something to do with electricity?" Agent Mahoney asked.

"Have a care with your questions, Agent Mahoney," Beatrix said before Norman could respond. "Unless you're willing to sit through another detailed explanation of how he purposefully flawed his research in case it was stolen, I think we should all agree that this would be the perfect time to end this meeting."

Norman was not amused when Agent Mahoney muttered, "Too right you are" under his breath, then closed his notepad with a snap and stood. He presented Beatrix with a bow. "It's been a pleasure, Miss Waterbury, although I'm sorry we had to meet under such unusual circumstances."

Beatrix smiled, which drew attention to a dimple that was right next to the freckle Norman had noticed earlier, although he'd not noticed the dimple until just then, and found it to be—

"Perhaps we'll meet again under normal circumstances," Beatrix said, rising to her feet. "Do feel free to call on me if you need any other questions answered. I'll be staying at my aunt Gladys's house for the next few months."

"That's very kind of you," Agent Mahoney said, opening up his notebook to the one and only page that still had some room on it. "I'll just need your aunt Gladys's address, as well as her full name."

Beatrix's smile faded. "In all honesty, I don't know my aunt's address off the top of my head, and I'm afraid the scrap of paper on which I jotted that address down is long gone since I tossed it into the satchel Mr. Nesbit left behind for the train robbers." She tucked an errant strand of hair behind her ear. "Aunt Gladys was supposed to meet me here at the depot, but I don't know if she's still waiting for me, or if she came to the conclusion I'd missed my train and would arrive later."

"There's no need for you to worry, Miss Waterbury," Agent Mahoney said. "I am a Pinkerton detective after all, so if you'll give me your aunt's full name, I'll find her address for you, as well as send someone to see if she might still be waiting for you here."

"That would be much appreciated, Agent Mahoney," Beatrix returned. "My aunt's name is Miss Gladys Huttleston, and I believe she lives at the north section of Hyde Park."

It took a great deal of effort for Norman to keep his mouth from dropping open. "Your aunt is Miss Huttleston?"

Beatrix nodded. "She is. Are you acquainted with her?"

"I believe most people in Chicago are acquainted with Miss Huttleston," Norman said. "She enjoys a reputation of being somewhat . . . odd."

"Odd how?"

Before Norman could respond, Agent Mahoney instructed one of the men in the room, a Mr. Engle, to find out what he could about Norman and Beatrix's trunks, as well as ascertain whether or not Miss Huttleston was still waiting for her niece. After the man quit the room, Agent Mahoney turned back to Beatrix.

"I'm certain we'll soon have you on your way, but perhaps you'd be more comfortable retaking your seat and finishing your tea while we wait."

Beatrix sent the Pinkerton a most charming smile, one she'd never sent to Norman, as she retook her seat, where she and Agent Mahoney, who'd claimed the seat next to her, immediately began chatting as if they'd been friends forever, with Agent Mahoney going on and on about what sights Beatrix should make sure to take in during her stay in Chicago.

"I'll make certain to visit that Washington Park Club you mentioned," Beatrix said five minutes later. "Although I am disappointed to learn that the American Derby occurs every June, since clearly I've missed it."

Before Norman could point out that the Washington Park Club was a racetrack that catered to the very well-heeled, of which she was apparently not, Mr. Engle hurried into the room. "Good news, Miss Waterbury. Your aunt *was* here. However, when she was informed by some of the other passengers that you'd departed from the train, she evidently decided to return home and took your trunks with her." He sent Beatrix a weak smile. "And while I'm sure you must find that somewhat concerning, what with having your aunt mosey back home after discovering her niece was missing, Miss Huttleston did arrange to have a hansom cab made available for you if you eventually showed up here."

Beatrix's brows drew together. "That is considerate of her, although I'm beginning to wonder if I'm going to be staying with her long, what with how she seemed less than concerned I was missing."

Mr. Engle nodded. "I'd be wondering the same." He nodded to Norman. "We found your trunks as well, sir. They're right outside."

"Then I suppose this is where all of us part ways," Beatrix said briskly, setting aside her teacup and rising to her feet. She sent Norman a nod. "It's been interesting, meeting you."

"And I can say the same of you, while also adding that our time together has seemed much longer than the single day it actually was."

"Has it really only been a *day*?"

"Shocking, I know, but yes. However," Norman continued, "before we part ways for good, if you'd be so kind as to allow me just another moment of your time, I feel compelled to revisit the subject of your aunt." He arched a brow at Agent Mahoney, who immediately bobbed his head before he took hold of Beatrix's hand, an action that left Norman feeling somewhat annoyed, although why that was, he couldn't say.

"Thank you again for your assistance, Miss Waterbury," Agent Mahoney began. "I'll have that hansom cab waiting for you right outside." With that, Agent Mahoney strode from the room, the remaining men in the room following after him.

"Why do I get the distinct impression I'm not going to like what you have to say about my aunt?" Beatrix asked, resuming her seat.

Norman settled into the chair Agent Mahoney had recently occupied. "Because no one enjoys hearing less-than-pleasant tidbits about their relatives, but before I disclose anything, how well do you know your aunt?"

"I've only met her a few times, so not well."

"And do you not have any other family you might be able to call on in what I've only recently determined must be your time of need?"

Beatrix wrinkled her nose. "Why would you think I'm in a time of need?"

"That's the only reasonable explanation I could draw, given that Miss Gladys Huttleston is not a lady I believe anyone, not even a niece, would willingly travel to visit unless that was the only option available."

"I assure you, nothing could be further from the truth. My mother wanted me to spend time with her older sister, so that's why I'm in Chicago."

Norman tilted his head. "So you've not recently lost your parents?"

"Both of my parents are alive and well."

"Does your mother not care for you, then?"

"I'm sure my mother loves me very much."

Norman frowned. "An idea you might want to revisit because I wouldn't think a mother who loves her daughter would send her off to stay with a woman as terrifying as Miss Huttleston, something I assure you everyone in and around Chicago believes, whether they are society or not."

"Aunt Gladys is a bit querulous from what I recall, but not terrifying."

Norman leaned toward her. "When I was younger, my sister told me all about your aunt. She lurks about the city in the company of a hulking brute of a man, searching for orphans she then takes home with her—and those orphans are never seen again."

A snort escaped Beatrix's lips right before she began to laugh.

"Abducting the orphans of the city is no laughing matter," Norman said.

She released a hiccup of amusement. "May I assume this sister of yours is older than you?"

"What does that have to do with anything?"

"Everything, because older siblings are known to torment their younger siblings, and clearly that's what your sister was doing with you." She released another hiccup. "I have two older brothers who enjoyed tormenting me endlessly in my youth with farfetched stories that I certainly *did* believe at the time. However, when I reached the age of eight, I realized my brothers were jesting with me, which put a rapid end to their stories." She shook her head. "You're evidently a literal sort—so literal, in fact, that you apparently never realized your sister was telling you some very tall tales."

"My sister is not one to tell fibs."

"While I hate to disillusion you about your sister, I fear she was amusing herself at your expense. However, because you're hardly going to listen to my argument, allow me to appeal to what I've concluded is a very logical mind. Don't you think that if orphans had truly begun disappearing, and my aunt's house was the last place they were seen, that the authorities would have stepped in by now and carted my aunt off to jail?"

Norman opened his mouth, then closed it again as the logic of what she'd said registered. Rising to his feet, he helped Beatrix to hers, then took her arm.

"You've just presented me with a most valid point," he said, steering her for the door. "And one that I'll be broaching with my sister the next time I'm in her company."

"I'd love to be a fly on the wall during that conversation."

"I'm sure you would enjoy it immensely, but enough about that. If you're agreeable, I'd like to escort you to your aunt's house."

She raised a hand to her chest. "Be still my heart. Here I thought you'd had just about enough of me today, and yet you're now suggesting you desire to spend additional time in my company, even though there's really no need."

"Of course there is," he countered. "I need to see for myself that you won't be in danger. And once I'm satisfied that I won't be leaving you to the machinations of a madwoman, then and only then will I bid you good-bye."

CHAPTER 6

To Beatrix's surprise, Norman, instead of retreating back to his mathematical equations as they rode through the crowded streets of Chicago in a hansom cab, took to telling her all sorts of tidbits about the city, making the ride downright pleasant instead of uncomfortable.

He started with explaining about the great fire of 1871, which saw a good portion of the city go up in flames, then moved on to telling her about Potter Palmer. That gentleman had evidently been influential with the recovery of State Street, making improvements to that area that would not have been possible if many of the derelict buildings both on and surrounding that street had not been consumed by the fire. He then pointed out stores he thought she'd find interesting on State Street, including Marshall Field & Company, before launching into a list of the churches available throughout the city, as well as parks.

"Why are you telling me all this?" Beatrix finally asked as Norman settled back on the seat next to her.

"Because you accused me of being inept at chitchat, and I'm now determined to prove you wrong."

"And here I thought you were trying your hand at being charming."

"I can be charming."

"Tell me about this Hyde Park where my aunt resides. Is it a fashionable part of town?" Beatrix asked, seeing no point in getting into an argument with Norman yet again, even though she had much to say about his charm, or lack thereof.

"Hyde Park is a perfectly respectable area, and it's located not far from where I live on Prairie Avenue, which is north of Hyde Park."

"If Prairie Avenue is closer, perhaps we should have the driver drop you off first and then I'll continue on to my aunt's house."

"I can't determine if you'll be safe at your aunt's house without personally assessing the situation."

Beatrix waved that aside. "For goodness' sake, Norman, my mother is hardly likely to send me off to stay with a mad relative, even if she is rather put out with me at the moment."

Norman arched a brow. "You lent me the impression you enjoy a lovely relationship with your mother. Why is she put out with you?"

"It's not unusual for mothers to occasionally become put out with their daughters."

"My mother is never put out with my two sisters. They always seem to be in complete accord with one another, but again, why is your mother put out with you?"

"Aren't we almost there yet?"

He consulted his pocket watch. "We have approximately twenty-four minutes before we arrive at your aunt's house." He tucked his watch away. "That means you have plenty of time for an explanation."

She blew out a breath. "I suppose there's no harm in telling you the story behind me being banished from New York."

"You've been banished?"

"For lack of a better word, yes. My mother, you see, became exasperated with me after I managed to get myself arrested while marching with hundreds of fellow suffragists through the streets of New York . . . and arrested twice, at that."

Norman blinked, just once. "You were arrested twice?"

"I'm afraid so."

He frowned. "You do realize that it's a futile movement, don't you? The majority of women enjoy having men take care of them, and men enjoy taking care of their women. Because of that, the movement is doomed to failure, which means you would be better off to find a different, less volatile cause."

"And to that I would say this—men have all the say in our lives especially after a woman gets married. They have complete control over our finances, unless a woman is fortunate enough to have a father who has some wealth and foresight in setting up a separate account for his daughter, but most women don't have that luxury. Men also have the final say in where we live, how we deal with children, and . . . well, I could go on and on. Many women want the right to vote because laws affect us, and yet we have no say in what laws are passed."

"And you were willing to get arrested for pushing the right to vote?"

"It wasn't as if I planned on getting arrested either time. The first rally was supposed to be a tame affair, but then the police showed up, someone threw something, and the next thing I knew, I was locked behind bars." She shook her head. "The second time I'd gone to listen to a lecture. After the lecture, some of the women decided to take to the streets, wearing their *Votes for Women* sashes. I just happened to be trailing after them when yet another ruckus broke out, and before I knew it, I was behind bars *again*." She sighed. "After my father posted my bail for the second time, my mother decided I needed a change of scenery."

"Your mother must be exceedingly put out with you if she's making you spend time with Miss Huttleston. I also have to imagine you're put out with her because of the banishing business."

"I don't blame my mother. And because I'd *almost* gotten arrested during a frenzied protest about labor conditions in Five Points a few months before I *actually* got arrested those two times, my mother had good reason to be concerned." Beatrix winced.

"And then if you add in what happened with Mr. Thomas Hamersley, I really can't claim to be surprised that my mother bought me a train ticket and sent me west."

"Who is Mr. Hamersley?"

She rubbed a hand over her face. "I wasn't intending on telling you about him, but he's a friend of mine, and not of the romantic sort."

"Is that because Mr. Hamersley no longer views *you* in a romantic way after you got arrested? Not that I would blame him for that," Norman continued before Beatrix could respond. "No gentleman wants to court a woman with progressive ideas *and* an arrest record."

Beatrix's lips thinned before she gave a sharp rap on the ceiling of the cab, which brought the cab to a smart stop a moment later.

"Why did you stop the cab?" Norman asked.

"Because the only way I'm going to be able to resist pulling out my pistol purse again is to remove myself from your company." She reached for the door. "I imagine now is the perfect time for me to try that running business you mentioned earlier."

"You can't run all the way to your aunt's house," Norman argued. "You don't even know where she lives."

"Given that my aunt seems to have quite the reputation, I'm sure someone will be able to point me in the right direction. And with that, allow me to say good-bye." Ignoring the protest Norman called after her, Beatrix hopped from the cab, told the driver to take Norman to Prairie Avenue, then set off down the road at a good clip.

"You're not wearing shoes that are conducive to a brisk excursion. You're certain to develop numerous blisters," Norman said, loping up beside her.

She picked up her pace, something that had Norman picking up his pace, as the hansom cab followed them from a few yards behind.

"Normally when a person bids another person good-bye, it's a cue that their time together has come to an end," she said, increasing her pace again, which he met with ease.

"I'm not letting you go to your aunt's house unaccompanied."

"I've traveled all the way from New York unaccompanied. I'm perfectly capable of making the last mile or so of my journey on my own."

Norman stopped in his tracks, a wonderful opportunity, as far as Beatrix was concerned, to put some distance between herself and the annoying man. Unfortunately, she'd barely made it half a block before he was at her side again.

"You never explained why you were traveling alone. Was I correct in assuming your family did not have the funds to hire a traveling companion to travel with you?"

"Has anyone ever told you that it's not acceptable to question a person about their finances?"

"I believe every one of my decorum instructors mentioned that at some point in time."

"And yet you've apparently decided to ignore that particular rule even though, clearly, I don't care to discuss my financial situation with you." She slowed her pace and ignored that she was already developing a blister on her heel. "But to answer your original question before you take to pestering me, I was traveling alone because the lady who was supposed to accompany me to Chicago came down with a nasty stomach ailment."

"Was she one of your friends?"

Beatrix decided it would take far too much effort to explain to Norman that Miss Munn was more of a casual acquaintance of Beatrix's who'd been hired by her mother for the sole purpose of accompanying Beatrix to Chicago. Or that Miss Munn had only agreed to the position because she'd recently experienced a disappointment of the heart. Or that her sudden "stomach ailment" might have been a direct result of a certain gentleman by the name of Mr. James Elliott showing up at the train station with flowers in hand after Beatrix's parents had made their departure. She settled for a nod instead.

"Do you still consider her a friend?"

"I wouldn't abandon any friendship simply because of unforeseen circumstances."

"But she left you to travel alone. I imagine if she hadn't done so, she also would have cautioned you against pulling out your pistol purse, which would have then spared both of us our dramatic experience today."

"Miss Munn wouldn't have been able to dissuade me from threatening that man with my pistol purse, not when I was all but ambushed by that thief and acted instinctively."

"I would say you acted impulsively, which is a great deal different from acting instinctively."

She stopped walking. "Impulsively, instinctively, they're not that different."

"They are, and before you argue with that, consider that you reacted impulsively when you all but leapt from the hansom cab to dash off to your aunt's house, when, if you'd acted instinctively, you would have known that it wasn't a prudent plan because you're ill equipped to travel such a distance in shoes that have an inappropriate heel on them for strenuous activity."

Surging into motion again, she forced herself to keep an even gait, even though the blister on her foot was really beginning to make itself known. "Surely I must be closer to Aunt Gladys's house," she muttered.

"It's just another two blocks."

"Thank goodness for that." As she strode down the remaining two blocks, she noticed that the lots were getting larger and larger, and she stopped when she caught sight of a tall, wrought-iron fence that seemed to go on for an entire block.

"That fence surrounds the entirety of Miss Huttleston's house," Norman said, stopping beside her. "It's like a fortress."

"A comforting thought since I won't have to worry about anyone breaking into the house."

"Or a worrisome thought because the fence could be there to keep people from escaping."

Beatrix glanced to the fence again. "There is that." She bent down and began unlacing her shoe, tugging it off a second later. Straightening, she handed it to Norman before unlacing her other shoe.

"Why are you taking your shoes off?"

"Because I'm getting a blister, and I've decided I'll only get more blisters if I keep my shoes on."

"But we're almost to your aunt's house."

"Which means I won't have to walk far without my shoes, nor will I aggravate the blister I already have on my foot."

Norman took her other shoe from her. "Why didn't you take your shoes off when your foot first started hurting?"

"I didn't want to give you the satisfaction of knowing you were right."

She wasn't certain, but it almost seemed as if Norman's lips twitched. "I see."

"I'm sure you do." With that, she strode forward, enjoying the feel of the cool cobblestones under her feet, which helped to diminish the pain in her heel.

As she traveled alongside the wrought-iron fence, she got a glimpse of an imposing house sitting back from the road, one that was almost completely obscured by the many trees scattered about the front lawn. Coming to a stop when she reached an iron gate that wouldn't have been out of place guarding a fortress, she gave the gate a rattle. "How do you suppose we get in?"

Norman nodded to a plaque Beatrix hadn't notice. "It says *Pull the bell string.*"

"So it does." Beatrix moved to a black rope that was attached to an iron post, gave it a yank, then smiled when a resounding gong sounded from the vicinity of the house. "How clever."

"It *is* clever," Norman said, eyeing the bell string. "It must run across the yard, and look, the gate is opening."

Directing her attention to the gate, she shuddered a bit when the wind took that moment to whip up, sending branches on a nearby tree scratching against the iron fence. It was an eerie sound and sent a sense of foreboding swirling through her.

Blowing out a breath, she nodded to Norman. "You really don't need to come with me. I'm sure I'll be . . . fine."

"I'm not leaving you now," Norman said, taking her arm and

then walking with her through the gate and down a gravel path, the gravel causing her to wince with every step.

"You should put these back on," he said, handing over her shoes.

"I'm not putting them on. They were killing my feet," Beatrix said, coming to a stop before she reached the covered porch to look the house over.

It was an imposing structure almost completely covered in ivy. Three stories high, it sported two turrets on either side of the house, as well as intricately paned windows, light pouring from many of them. Shifting her attention to the covered porch, she watched as the front door slowly opened, revealing the large form of a man.

"That's Lurch," Norman said, tightening his hold on her arm. "He's the butler."

"His name is Lurch?"

"According to my sister Alice, yes."

"The same sister who fed you the story about disappearing orphans?"

"Are you suggesting my sister made up a name for your aunt's butler?"

"I am, unless that man now gesturing for us to enter the house tells us his name is Lurch, which I highly doubt he's going to do."

"Ah, Miss Beatrix, you're exactly as your aunt described," the man said in a booming voice that caused Beatrix to jump.

"We've been expecting you, but allow me to say that I find myself relieved to discover that your aunt was quite right about your possessing an independent nature. You've found your way to us after all. We *were* expecting you to be in the company of a female traveling companion, though, but I'm sure there must be a story about where she is and what you're doing with a gentleman, who, if I'm not mistaken, is Mr. Norman Nesbit."

"He knows who I am?" Norman asked in a hushed tone even as his hand further tightened on her arm.

Sending him what she hoped was an encouraging smile, Beatrix stepped forward, even though Norman was trying to hold her back. Tugging Norman beside her, she walked through the door of her aunt's large and somewhat unnerving house, turning her smile on the man holding the door for her.

"I lost my traveling companion, Miss Munn, before I even got out of New York, and then acquired the company of Mr. Nesbit when we ran afoul of some train robbers."

"An interesting development to your day, I'm sure." The man inclined his head and smiled. "I'm Edgar, Miss Beatrix. Edgar Bosworth, butler to Miss Huttleston."

Beatrix turned to Norman and lowered her voice to the merest whisper. "You really might want to consider having a bit of a chat with that sister of yours. Lurch indeed."

"Edgar's not much better, nor is Bosworth," Norman whispered back.

Ignoring that, she smiled at Mr. Bosworth. "I'm delighted to make your acquaintance, Mr. Bosworth."

Mr. Bosworth's smile widened. "I can also see your aunt was right about you being a charming sort, but there's no need to call me Mr. Bosworth. Edgar is fine, and it's what everyone calls me, except for some of the mischievous children who live in these parts." He sent her a wink. "They enjoy calling me Lurch, and I must say I find that amusing and have been known to take a turn around the street, hunching my shoulders as I go, which does keep those children in a state of high anticipation."

Beatrix grinned as some of the anxiety she hadn't realized she'd been holding about coming to stay with an aunt she barely knew disappeared. "I imagine it does indeed."

Edgar inclined his head, his rheumy blue eyes twinkling. "And with that settled, allow me to welcome you to Hyde Hall." He gestured around the hallway. "It's a lovely house, filled with the treasures your aunt has collected on her many journeys, and I hope you'll enjoy your stay with us. Your aunt has been looking forward to your visit and hasn't stopped talking about the plans she has for you since it was decided you were coming to Chicago."

"She has plans for me?"

"She does, but I'll leave it to her to explain."

Realizing that Norman was being far too silent, Beatrix glanced his way, finding his eyes narrowed on something behind Edgar. Craning her neck, she peered around the butler and found at least twenty cats sitting in a perfectly straight line against the wall, their heads turned her way, staring at her with unblinking eyes.

"Your mother must be *incredibly* put out with you," Norman said, nodding toward the cats. A second later, he sneezed, sneezed again, and again, then began digging into his pocket, pulling out a handkerchief, which he promptly sneezed into.

"God bless you," Beatrix told him when he finally stopped sneezing and turned watery eyes her way.

"It would be a greater blessing if God would take away my sensitivity to cats, as well as pollen, smog, and numerous other things, but thank you for that."

"You're sensitive to cats?"

"Why do you think I'm sneezing?"

"I thought you were recovering from a cold. I noticed on the train that your nose was red."

"You noticed that?"

"You're not the only one capable of being observant."

Norman dabbed at his nose again. "Apparently not, but my symptoms on the train were a direct result of the cloying perfume the woman wearing the purple hat had on, which is why I abandoned that seat and moved closer to you, even though I was hesitant to do so because you'd proven yourself to be a chatty sort. You, however, weren't wearing a cloying perfume but a more pleasant scent, one I got a better whiff of later when you . . ."

"When I what?" Beatrix prodded when Norman stopped talking right as a cat came streaking past them with what looked to be a dead mouse in its mouth. The cat stopped, turned, then trotted back toward them, depositing the mouse at Norman's feet and releasing a purr before slinking off down a dim hallway and disappearing from sight.

"How unusual," Edgar said. "Phantom never shares his mice, but it seems he's taken to you, Mr. Nesbit, something I've never seen that cat do before."

Norman dabbed at his nose and nodded. "Cats seem to sense that I'm sensitive to them, and being rather interesting creatures, they also seem to enjoy tormenting me by leaving dead birds and mice at my feet. Once I even had one climb a tree to slip through my open window." He shook his head. "Couldn't breathe for a good few days after that surprise."

"Is that a dead mouse lying on the floor?"

Recognizing the voice as belonging to her aunt Gladys, Beatrix turned, but her greeting got stuck in her throat the moment her gaze settled on her aunt.

Dressed in trousers that had been cut off at the knee, and wearing striped stockings and a large, billowing shirt that looked as if it might belong to a pirate, Aunt Gladys was an unexpected sight, especially since her face was covered in something that looked, unfortunately, like blood.

Before Beatrix could process that sight, or determine why her aunt might be covered in blood in the first place, Norman appeared directly in front of her. To her utter astonishment, he then picked her up as if she weighed nothing at all and strode for the door.

CHAPTER 7

"I insist you set my niece down at once, sir, and also insist you explain to me why you're trying to hustle dear Beatrix out of my home when she's only just arrived."

A tingle began creeping up Beatrix's spine when Norman, instead of setting her down, tightened his hold on her and continued for the door.

It was unexpected, the tingle, as well as confusing, because he'd proven himself time and again to be one of the most irritating men she'd ever encountered. Still, irritating or not, he was currently being downright chivalrous as he tried to protect her from her aunt. And while she was perfectly capable of looking out for herself, his chivalry was making her feel all sorts of curious things.

"What do you want me to do?" Norman asked, his breath tickling her ear.

"She wants you to put her down so she can properly greet her favorite aunt," Aunt Gladys called out before Beatrix could respond.

Norman caught Beatrix's eye. "Miss Huttleston is your favorite aunt?"

"She's my only aunt."

"Ah well, that explains much." He frowned. "Frankly, though,

I got the distinct impression that you don't think of her as being one of your favorite—"

Beatrix placed her hand firmly over Norman's mouth, muffling the rest of his words, right as the sound of footsteps drew her attention. Those footsteps apparently drew Norman's attention as well because he slowly turned around, drawing her closer when Aunt Gladys came into view.

Unfortunately, Aunt Gladys's appearance was less than reassuring the closer she got to them.

A red substance that did look like blood was dripping from her face and onto her billowing shirt, but Aunt Gladys ignored that as she smiled at Beatrix, which was rather frightening because the red smeared all over her face was in sharp contrast to the whiteness of her teeth.

"Ah, there's that face I haven't seen in far too many years," Aunt Gladys began. "Why, you've turned into a most beautiful young lady, something I always worried about because you were rather homely as a child. How delightful to see that you've grown out of that stage."

"Good thing you're accomplished with chitchat because I wouldn't know how to respond to a statement like that," Norman muttered.

"I'm afraid I'm at a loss as well," Beatrix muttered back. "But you may set me down now, Mr. Nesbit. It's beginning to feel rather peculiar being held in your arms this long."

"I believe, given the adventure we've shared today, that it's perfectly fine to address me as Norman," he said, right as Aunt Gladys took another step toward them.

"On my word, you're Norman Nesbit," Aunt Gladys exclaimed.

Instead of setting her down, Norman drew Beatrix closer to him. "I am Norman Nesbit, but I must admit I'm taken aback that you're familiar with who I am."

Aunt Gladys gave a wave of her hand. "Your mother, Mary, and I share a delightful disdain for each other—which is why I've taken it upon myself to learn everything I can about the Nesbit family." She winked. "I always find it best to gather pertinent information about one's nemesis because you never know when such information might be useful."

Norman bent his head closer to Beatrix. "I'm confident I can outrun your aunt as well as Lurch—er, I mean Edgar. Just say the word."

Aunt Gladys let out a huff. "There's no need for that, Mr. Nesbit. I assure you there's nothing to flee from."

"I beg to differ, unless you have a reasonable explanation for whatever madness was responsible for . . ." He waved a hand in her general direction.

Aunt Gladys exchanged a look with Edgar, who was still standing in the hallway. "Whatever is he talking about?"

Edgar winced. "I believe he's referring to your face, one that currently looks as if you've recently participated in something concerning."

A booming laugh was Aunt Gladys's response to that. "Oh my, I completely forgot. I must look a fright right now. Why, it's little wonder poor Mr. Nesbit is trying to whisk Beatrix away from me." She laughed again, hardly an encouraging sound since her laughter echoed around the hallway, eliciting a rousing round of howls from the cats still sitting in a perfectly straight line.

With a last chuckle, Aunt Gladys nodded to Norman. "No need to fret you're about to deliver my niece into the hands of a madwoman, Mr. Nesbit. There's a perfectly reasonable explanation. The condition of my face is a direct result of a new beauty regime I'm testing out."

"Begging your pardon, Miss Huttleston," Norman began, "but I've got two sisters, neither of whom would ever embrace a beauty regime that leaves them looking as if they've been in a brawl."

"A most excellent point, and one I'll be certain to pass on to Miss Blanche Bell, the inventor of this beauty product, which is, if you're curious, made out of clay." Aunt Gladys patted her face, albeit gingerly. "We, as in myself and the women who are currently waiting for me in the parlor, decided the original color of the clay was less than appealing, which is why we added a smidgen of red paint to the mix, hoping that the brighter color would appeal to women with whimsical natures."

Norman's brows drew together. "Begging your pardon yet again, Miss Huttleston, but I have to believe that what you're currently wearing on your face would repulse whimsical women, although it might appeal to women possessed of bloodthirsty natures."

"Duly noted," Aunt Gladys said cheerfully. "Perhaps we'll try a nice shade of yellow next."

"Which is a color that tends to make one appear sallow," Norman pointed out. "In my humble opinion, lavender would be the wisest choice because scientific studies suggest that people find lavender a most relaxing color, which should, at least in theory, encourage consumers to purchase such a beauty product, if it does, in fact, result in any beneficial beauty results."

Aunt Gladys tapped a finger against her chin. "A worthy consideration to be sure. However, because Blanche is convinced that this particular beauty remedy must remain on a woman's face for at least thirty minutes to ascertain whether or not it will draw out impurities, there's no point in mixing up a new color until we know if it works."

Norman nodded. "A logical decision."

"I'm nothing if not logical," Aunt Gladys returned before frowning. "But speaking of logic, is there any logic in continuing to hold on to my niece? Surely both of you have determined that I don't present a threat to Beatrix, unless . . ." She smiled. "Could it be that the two of you have formed an attraction to each other, and you're using this most unusual situation as a way to enjoy unexpected closeness?"

Beatrix found herself back on her feet a split second later, the rapidity of her return to the ground causing her to lose her balance and stumble into Norman, who steadied her and winced.

"Sorry about that."

"As you should be. Was there a reason you just dropped me like a hot potato?"

"Of course there was. I've often been the victim of many an aunt, sister, mother, grandmother, or random stranger who've set their sights on me as a potential suitor for one young lady or another. A bachelor gentleman is evidently difficult to ignore for women with matchmaking on their minds, even though I've been able to steer relatively clear of that because of my work. I don't have time for romantic nonsense." He shot a glance to Aunt Gladys. "Thought it best to nip any thoughts of matchmaking your aunt may be harboring in the bud before they got out of hand."

Aunt Gladys laughed. "My dear boy, while I'm sure you would make Beatrix an admirable suitor, even with your reputation of being an eccentric, I've got plans for her that don't include gentlemen . . . yet. But do know that I've now taken your reluctance about matters of courtship into account, and with that settled, what say we repair to the parlor for some refreshments? We were just about to enjoy some lemonade before we partake in some dancing."

"See if he'll agree to a few turns around the parlor with us," a voice called out from behind Aunt Gladys. "It would be awfully nice to have a strapping young man to dance with for a change— not that we mind dancing with Edgar or Hubert, but Edgar tends to get winded after a while and Hubert *is* missing a leg."

Beatrix directed her attention past Aunt Gladys and found they'd been joined by at least ten women, all of whom had faces smeared with red and all of whom were wearing unusual ensembles of clothing, quite as if they'd rummaged through old trunks and thrown on anything that wouldn't be missed if it was ruined.

The woman who'd just invited Norman to join them in a dance waggled her fingers Norman's way.

Aunt Gladys blew out a breath. "Honestly, Mamie, how many times must we go over this? It's not appropriate for you to blurt out observations about strapping young men." She turned to Beatrix. "Mamie's only recently come to us from a dance hall off of Twenty-second Street. She spent almost three years there playing the piano, but now she's given up that life and is determined to improve her circumstances."

"How's she determined to do that?" Norman asked. His obvious determination to avoid addressing the flirtatious batting of the lashes from Mamie made Beatrix's lips curve.

"By improving her knowledge of proper etiquette and behavior, which will hopefully then see her achieving some success with obtaining employment with a reputable orchestra. Truly, her skill with the piano is something that cannot be denied."

Norman glanced to Mamie and then quickly back to Aunt Gladys after Mamie blew him a kiss. "Have you been meeting with much success?"

"She's still a work in progress." Aunt Gladys sent Mamie a fond smile before she nodded to Norman. "Do say you'll join us for some refreshments."

"And dancing," Mamie called over her shoulder before she followed the rest of the women out of the room.

Norman shuddered before he shook his head. "Regrettably, I must decline, Miss Huttleston. I've been away from home for a few weeks and have matters that I need to attend to this evening." He tilted his head. "I am curious, though, about what was said regarding a man named Hubert. Does he really dance with only one leg, and how does a person go about that?"

Aunt Gladys leaned to the right and gestured someone forward. The sound of uneven clomping rang out, and then a man appeared through the dimness of the hall, walking over to Norman with a distinct limp. Bending over, he rolled up his pants, revealing a peg leg that had been painted a bright yellow.

"Hubert Barrett, sir," Hubert said while Norman bent over to get a closer look at the man's leg. "As you can see, I do have a leg of sorts, one that allows me to enjoy a few turns around a room. Mind you, I'm not capable of doing a full polka because that vigorous dance leaves the stub right below my knee throbbing something fierce."

Norman dropped to a knee and peered at the wooden apparatus

attached to Hubert's knee. "Did the physician who fit you with this wooden leg take his time measuring you? It seems to me as if the cup that goes over your knee and keeps the leg attached is not fitting properly."

"They don't make them individual-like. I was simply shown a room where they had a few legs, picked one out, and the good doctor showed me how to pull it on and keep it on with suspenders attached to my belt."

"Seems a bit antiquated," Norman said as he straightened. A loud clock began clanging as it marked the time, which set the cats to scattering, one of which slunk across the floor to snatch the dead mouse Phantom had left behind, disappearing with it down a hallway.

"And here's where it's time for me to take my leave," Norman said firmly, turning from where he'd been watching the cats to nod at Beatrix. "You're sure you'll be all right if I leave you here?"

"I'll be fine."

"Then this is where we part ways." Norman took Beatrix's hand, surprising her when he brought it to his lips and kissed it. "You're an unusual woman, Beatrix Waterbury, and even though you've annoyed me more than any woman I've ever known—and that's with us only spending a day together—it's been a very interesting day and one that, oddly enough, was somewhat enjoyable at times." He caught Beatrix's eye. "Do try to not unintentionally shoot anyone else while you're in Chicago."

"Can't make any promises," she said, to which he might have actually smiled before he turned to Aunt Gladys, inclined his head, then turned on his heel and strode down the hallway, disappearing through the front door without another word.

Aunt Gladys moved to stand beside Beatrix. "I must admit that the last person I expected to show up at Hyde Hall with you was Mr. Norman Nesbit, but he's not nearly as odd in person as I always assumed he'd be. Do you imagine he'll visit you often while you're in Chicago?"

"As he mentioned, I frequently annoy him, and he definitely

annoys me, which does suggest he'll not be paying us a call anytime soon, if ever."

"How disappointing, but enough about Mr. Nesbit for now. We need to discuss the plans I have for you, ones I came up with after your mother asked if I'd be willing to have you come for an extended stay."

"She said I'm here for an *extended* stay?"

"Did Annie not tell you that?"

"I'm afraid she didn't."

Aunt Gladys took hold of Beatrix's arm. "I'm afraid you've finally pushed poor Annie too far, my dear, what with your propensity for havoc and becoming embroiled in the most unlikely of situations. She must be at her wits' end to resort to sending you here, which will see you missing the New York Season."

"I've been wondering if Mother might have done me a favor by banishing me for the Season, since word has certainly gotten around about Mr. Thomas Hamersley getting engaged to someone who isn't me. He's been shielding me for years from being pursued by other gentlemen, but with him out of the picture . . ." She smiled. "Perhaps it's good I'm here for an extended stay after all."

Aunt Gladys returned the smile, looking more terrifying than ever. "It is indeed, and frankly I don't know how you managed to get through six Seasons when I couldn't make it through one." She pulled Beatrix into motion. "My father—your grandfather— moved to New York after my mother died. I was eighteen and decided I wanted nothing to do with living in a big city like New York after having only been there a month. I returned to Chicago even though Father stayed in New York, where he met and married your grandmother, Erma, and they had your mother a year later."

Aunt Gladys drew Beatrix toward a room where she could hear the tinkling of piano music. "Your grandmother was a lovely woman, but she was firmly of the social set. She invited me back to New York, which I agreed to, but only because I knew my father expected that of me. However, after I made my debut, I knew that that life was not for me. Father then set up an account for me that allowed me to build Hyde Hall, and I've not had a reason to regret my decision to stay in Chicago."

Beatrix stepped with Aunt Gladys into a room where the women covered in red clay were waiting for them.

"Ladies, you'll be amused to learn that Mr. Norman Nesbit has all but fled from our presence."

"There's nothin' amusing about having a fine-looking gentleman like that get away from us," a woman wearing a bright purple turban on her head declared. "We don't get many gentleman callers as it is, and that we've apparently caused one of them to flee, well, it's cause for concern."

Aunt Gladys leaned closer to Beatrix. "Della used to work for one of the big houses over on Prairie Avenue. She got dismissed because she set a friendly eye on her employer's twenty-two-year-old son."

"Ain't nothin' wrong with a little flirting, and me and George were the same age, and . . ." Della released a huff. "It's not like we would have gotten married or anything, but his mother found out about the flirting and sent me packin'."

"Della's now trying to learn how to operate a typewriter, but I'm not certain that's the best option for her since she does seem to have an eye for the men, and men are usually the ones hiring women proficient in using a typewriter," Aunt Gladys said before she launched into introductions.

Fifteen minutes later, Beatrix had not only been introduced to Blanche Bell, Mamie Stewart, Della Hayes, Nancy Collins, Arwen Daugherty, Colette Balley, Roberta Shaw, Clara Davis, Susan Morris, and Dorothy Brown, but she'd also been divested of her clothing, given a pair of short trousers and a billowing shirt, and had red clay pressed to her face.

"And now that you've met everyone and heard a bit about what they do," Aunt Gladys said, "tell us something about yourself."

Not knowing what to say about herself after hearing how all of the women gathered in the room had overcome great odds and horrible circumstances—those being abusive relationships, repugnant bosses, horrible working conditions, and the list went on and on—Beatrix caught her aunt's eye.

"I'd rather hear how it came to be that you became involved with all these women."

"Your aunt's a well-known supporter of the suffragist movement," Blanche Bell said before Aunt Gladys could speak. "Many of us became acquainted with her while participating in marches and listening to speeches. Then, after she heard our stories, she took it upon herself to assist us when no one else would, even offering us rooms in this house until we got on our feet."

Beatrix's brows drew together, a tricky feat since the clay on her face was already beginning to dry. She looked at her aunt. "You're a suffragist?"

"Been one since 1872—the election year when Susan B. Anthony took a stand and insisted on being allowed the right to register to vote in her hometown of Rochester, New York. She was forced to read aloud the Fourteenth Amendment to the inspector overseeing the registration, which then had him, albeit reluctantly, allowing Susan and her sisters to register. Word soon got out about that and women began showing up in other wards in that part of the state to register, but after Susan actually cast a vote a few days later in the election, she was arrested. She was then charged with voting without having the lawful right to do such a thing." Aunt Gladys nodded as the women around her began *tsk*ing. "I thought that was a most grave miscarriage of justice, and from that moment on, it's been my goal to further the advancement of women and the right to vote."

"Does my mother know you're a suffragist?"

"Hard to say. With me being so much older than Annie, we don't actually have that much contact with each other."

"But I thought Mother sent me here to keep me well away from anything related to the suffragist movement."

"And that very well could be, but by sending you here, she's clearly expecting me to use my own judgment as to how your time should be spent."

"And how *do* you want me to spend my time?" Beatrix asked slowly.

"I'd like for you to find your true purpose in life because, what with all the shenanigans Annie told me you've been involved with over the years, I've concluded that you're floundering."

"Floundering?"

"Indeed. You lack true commitment to any cause."

"I most certainly do not lack commitment," Beatrix argued. "I assist at numerous missions, support the suffragist movement, help out my friends, and I even volunteer at Grace Church, teaching lessons of faith to the children."

"All very commendable acts, my dear, and I don't want you to believe that I find any of that objectionable. However . . ."

"Why do I get the distinct impression I'm not going to enjoy hearing what you're about to say next?"

"Because it's occasionally painful to have truths pointed out to us. And your truth is this—while you've thrown yourself into philanthropic endeavors, your privileged life has left you at a distinct disadvantage. So in regard to the suffrage movement, I don't believe you truly grasp the reason why women are so desperate to obtain the vote, no matter that you want to support the movement by attending rallies and marches."

"I understand why women want the right to vote."

Aunt Gladys inclined her head. "In theory perhaps, but you don't know what it's like to be at the mercy of an employer who can level abuse on you at his whim, and you have no alternative but to take it because you have mouths to feed or rent to pay. That right there is why I've decided that the best way for you to spend your time in Chicago is to take up a position."

"A position, as in . . . a position of employment?"

"Quite right." Aunt Gladys gave Beatrix's arm a pat. "I'm sure you'll be delighted to learn that I've arranged for you to have an interview with Mr. Bailer at Marshall Field & Company. He's expecting you tomorrow morning at nine o'clock sharp."

Chapter 8

Norman had the uncanny feeling someone was watching him.

Lowering the newspaper he'd been reading in the breakfast nook of his mother's grand house, he discovered a young boy gazing back at him from across the table.

Norman set the paper aside, took a sip of coffee, and frowned. "Do I know you?"

The boy nodded, a less-than-helpful response if there ever was one.

"We're not related to each other, are we?"

"Of course you're not related to him, Norman. That's Oscar Weinhart."

Looking past Oscar, Norman found one of his sisters, Constance Nesbit Michelson, bustling into the room, dressed in a gown of green, paired with an enormous hat that had four birds with different colored feathers attached to it.

"Am I going to suffer a lecture if I admit I still don't know who he is?" Norman asked, which earned him an eye roll from Constance as she helped herself to a cup of coffee from the silver pot resting on the buffet table.

"He's Marian's son."

"Still don't know who he is."

"Do not tell me you've forgotten that Marian is my best friend, have you?"

"I've not forgotten that you're friends with a Marian, but that Marian's last name is Shaw and you stated this boy's name is Oscar Weinhart."

"Because Weinhart is Marian's married name. Surely you must remember her getting married twelve years ago because you were present at her wedding."

Norman raked a hand through hair that was longer than ever, him having neglected to make time to visit his barber since he'd returned from New York, unsurprised that his sister was watching him as if she were afraid he was suffering from some dastardly illness.

He couldn't say he blamed her because he wasn't one to forget events he attended, but he'd obviously forgotten all about Marian's wedding. The only explanation for that curious lapse was that he was apparently still suffering from the effects of his encounter with Beatrix Waterbury, even though it had been seven days since he'd parted ways with her, a sufficient time to recover, but . . .

"What's wrong with you today?"

Shaking himself from his musings, Norman found that Constance had abandoned her coffee and was advancing his way, determination in her every step. Norman summoned up a smile. "There's nothing wrong with me, and of course I remember attending Marian's wedding." He turned and nodded to Oscar. "I'm sure I just didn't recognize you because it's been ages since I've seen you, but you must be friends with my nephew Christopher."

Oscar immediately looked disgruntled. "Christopher's only four, Mr. Nesbit. I'm eight and friends with Gemma—your niece, if you've forgotten."

"I haven't forgotten who Gemma is, but she's a girl."

Constance released a snort. "Of course Gemma's a girl, Norman, but I don't understand why you find it surprising that Oscar and Gemma are friends. You're friends with Theodosia Robinson, and she's a girl, or rather, a woman."

"I wouldn't say Theo and I are friends. We're colleagues who share an interest in science."

"And because I have no desire to spend the morning arguing with you about whether or not you're friends with a woman you spend an inordinate amount of time with, let us move on to why I'm visiting Mother today." Constance nodded to Oscar. "Gemma and Oscar have been pestering me for over two weeks to bring them here, which is why I've stopped in for the past seven days once I heard you'd returned from New York, but you've not been here until today." She caught Norman's eye. "Where have you been?"

Because he wasn't comfortable telling his incredibly nosy sister that he'd been taking the train the short distance to Hyde Park every day, and then had spent hours running through the streets, doubling back time and time again to run past Hyde Hall, Norman ignored the question. Instead, he returned to his eggs and bacon in the hopes that his sister would grow tired of waiting for an answer and move on to a different subject.

It was disruptive, this preoccupation he had with Beatrix. Every time he tried to settle into a relaxing bout of mathematical equations or attempt to draw a diagram of an improved electrical motor, thoughts of Beatrix interrupted his work.

He'd never had thoughts of a lady disrupt his work before, which was why he'd decided that to cure those disruptive thoughts once and for all he needed to travel to Hyde Park to make sure she was not suffering mistreatment at the hands of an aunt who was certainly odd and who could also be slightly mad.

The problem with that decision, though, had been that after he'd run past Hyde Hall three times on the first day, approaching the house from different vantage points and then peering through the slats of the iron fence that encompassed it, he'd not gotten a single glimpse of Beatrix. That had left him more concerned than ever, which was why he'd traveled to Hyde Park for the next five consecutive days, choosing different times each day to improve his chances, but even with being so diligent, he'd never caught sight of her.

Unfortunately, while he'd been running past her aunt's house yesterday, he'd almost run over Edgar, who'd stepped directly into Norman's path right as Norman had been craning his neck as he ran, hoping to see Beatrix roaming around her aunt's extensive grounds.

It soon became clear that Edgar had taken note of how often Norman had been running past the house. And even though Norman had tried to convince Edgar that he'd been running the streets of Hyde Park for a change of scenery, the amusement in Edgar's eyes had suggested he didn't believe Norman's story.

Edgar had then proclaimed in a voice that held a trace of laughter that Miss Beatrix was currently not at home, having taken up a position at Marshall Field & Company.

Instead of alleviating Norman's concerns, learning Beatrix had evidently been forced to seek out employment had left him reeling.

Everyone in Chicago knew that Miss Gladys Huttleston was a woman of means. The notion that she'd insisted her niece, who was obviously a woman of limited means, take up a position suggested that Miss Huttleston was a stingy woman, unwilling to extend even a small bit of her fortune to the niece who'd come to stay with her.

It was disturbing, Beatrix's unfortunate situation, but what he could actually do about rectifying her situation was a puzzle he'd yet to figure out.

"I hope you realize that the longer you take to answer what I originally thought was a fairly easy question is only going to increase my curiosity about the matter."

Norman polished off the last of his eggs, took a swig of coffee, and elected to continue ignoring his sister. He turned to Oscar instead. "Do forgive me, Oscar," he began, earning a blink from Oscar in return, "I've neglected you most dreadfully. To rectify that, tell me why you're spending your time sitting across from me when you could be doing something vastly more amusing. Where's Gemma?"

Oscar shifted in his chair. "She's off seeing a new doll her grandmother purchased for her."

Norman smiled. "Ah well, I can see why you chose to sit at the table with me instead of accompanying Gemma to retrieve a new doll. I was never one to care for dolls even though Alice, my oldest sister, used to try to get me to play with hers."

"Gemma doesn't like dolls," Oscar muttered.

"Gemma doesn't like dolls?" Norman repeated, glancing to Constance, who was taking a seat beside Oscar.

"Not really. She prefers her chemistry set," Constance said.

"Gemma has a chemistry set?"

"I bought it for her on her last birthday."

"You bought your daughter a chemistry set?"

Constance shrugged. "I always enjoyed playing with chemistry sets when I was her age, so when she asked for one, I saw no harm in getting it for her."

"You never had a chemistry set when you were young."

"Well, I didn't have my *own* set, but I freely admit that I took liberties with yours whenever you were away from the house."

"No wonder my supplies were always dwindling more rapidly than they should have." Norman frowned. "I distinctly remember you telling Mother that I was careless with my supplies when I complained to her about the situation."

"I couldn't admit that I was the culprit, not with how adamant Mother always was about how unacceptable it was for girls to be interested in science." Constance shook her head. "She became suspicious of me after I invented this soap that I tried out in the washing machine. I obviously used too much sulfate because, before I knew it, the washroom was filled with bubbles. Mother found me standing in the midst of those bubbles, and while she never outright accused me of anything, she did begin buying me doll after doll, evidently hoping I'd abandon my interest in science and adopt a love of doll collecting."

"You do have an impressive doll collection," Norman pointed out.

"One that is currently collecting dust in my attic." Constance smiled. "However, when I realized that Gemma was fascinated with science, I decided that instead of hindering her interest, I'd encourage it."

Norman set aside his napkin. "Aren't you afraid you're allowing her false hope because there are limited opportunities for girls in science?"

"I'm hopeful that by the time Gemma is old enough to seek a higher education, there'll be more colleges and universities admitting women."

Norman frowned. "Don't let Mother hear you speaking that way because you know she'll conclude you're sympathetic to the suffrage movement, and I can't even imagine the drama we'll be forced to endure if she comes to that conclusion."

"I *am* a supporter of the suffrage movement, something Mother is well aware of but chooses to ignore."

"You support the suffrage movement?" Norman asked weakly, feeling as if his world truly was turning topsy-turvy and not only because of Miss Beatrix Waterbury.

Constance merely smiled before she quirked a brow and got a far-too-familiar look on her face. "Returning to why you've been absent from the house this week . . ."

"Your brother is clearly in the middle of trying to puzzle out some new invention or mathematical equation, which is why he's been going off to Hyde Park to run, evidently needing a change of scenery to do his thinking."

Relief was swift as Norman watched his mother, Mary Elizabeth Dupee Nesbit, breeze into the room, dressed to perfection in a walking gown of blue. His relief disappeared in a flash, though, as a troubling thought sprang to mind.

"How do you know I've been running in Hyde Park?"

Mary sent him an indulgent smile. "The Pinkerton men I hired to keep you safe until the miscreants from the train are caught have been keeping me apprised of your movements."

Norman pushed back his chair and rose to his feet. "You hired Pinkerton men to follow me?"

Mary raised a hand to her throat. "Do not tell me you have yet to notice them. They've been at it for almost a week, taking shifts."

The next thing Norman knew, he was pushed back into his chair. His mother wasted no time in placing her hand on his forehead while his sister smacked both of her hands against his cheeks, ignoring the wince her smacking caused.

It didn't take a genius, which he most certainly was, to conclude that both ladies were now convinced that he was certainly suffering from some type of dreadful illness. What they didn't know, however, was that what he was suffering from was actually far worse, and it had a name.

Miss Beatrix Waterbury, to be exact.

CHAPTER 9

"He doesn't feel hot to me, Mother," Constance said.

"But he must be ill. What other explanation could there possibly be for him being unaware of the Pinkerton men?" Mary returned.

"Have either of you considered that I may have been distracted with matters of science?"

Constance and Mary exchanged telling looks right before they launched into speculation about what dreadful ailments he could be experiencing that could cause him to be so unobservant.

Norman settled back in his chair, knowing there was little point in interrupting their discussion because he had nothing of worth to add to explain his symptoms, which had been caused by Miss Beatrix Waterbury. Nor was he willing to broach the subject of Beatrix because that would open up an entirely different can of worms. Wincing when Constance tugged his hair in her attempt to ferret out some place on his head where he might show signs of a fever, Norman felt a sliver of relief slide over him when Gemma, his niece, strolled into the room, carrying a porcelain doll under her arm. She promptly thrust that doll into Oscar's hands as her gaze traveled from Constance to Mary and then settled on Norman.

A blink of an eye later, she was rushing his way, inserting herself between him and his mother.

"Uncle Norman," she exclaimed. "I've been longing to see you for days and days and now you're finally here."

He couldn't help himself, he grinned. "Should I ask why you've been longing to see me?"

"We want to see your wagon," Oscar said, sitting forward. "Gemma told me it runs on an electric motor."

Gemma leaned closer to Norman. "Oscar doesn't believe you have an electric wagon that works, and he's been very vocal about his disbelief regarding the matter."

Norman shook his head. "It's not a wagon. It's a conveyance vehicle, complete with an electrical engine."

Gemma's nose wrinkled. "It looks like a wagon."

"It's far too complex to be considered such a lowly vehicle."

"Then maybe you should build a better frame for it that complements the complexity of the engine."

Norman caught Constance's eye. "She really is unusually intelligent, isn't she?"

"She reminds me of you at her age," Constance said as Gemma grabbed hold of Norman's hand and tugged him from the chair. "Can we show Oscar the wagon now?"

Having no reason to balk, Norman allowed Gemma to hustle him from the breakfast room, Oscar hurrying to join them as they stepped into the backyard. They then began making their way to one of the three carriage houses located a good ways from the main house.

"I'm curious how you know about my latest invention in the first place," Norman said as they passed the first carriage house, a building where numerous horses were kept and one that he avoided entering whenever possible.

"I saw it while you were in New York when I was . . ." Gemma's voice trailed off. She shot him a guilty look, then dropped his hand and hurried ahead.

It took him all of five seconds to catch up with her. "When you were what?"

"When she was looking for scraps to finish off one of her own inventions," Oscar supplied when Gemma didn't respond.

Oscar didn't even flinch when Gemma stopped in her tracks and scowled at him. "Uncle Norman might not let us test his electrical wagon if you keep telling him tales."

"He's more likely to let us if you don't hide why you were sneaking around his workshop."

Gemma's nose shot straight into the air. "It wasn't sneaking, because I knew Uncle Norman wouldn't care if I helped myself to the discarded items he tosses into that bin in his workshop." She jolted into motion again, passing the second carriage house a moment later, leaving Norman and Oscar behind.

"She's got a good stride for a girl," Norman said.

Oscar shuddered. "Don't say that around Gemma. She doesn't like when people use that 'for a girl' comment. Tends to make her grumpy."

"Duly noted," Norman said, falling into step beside Oscar. "So what was Gemma trying to invent that she needed my old scraps for?"

"A boat that could be operated like one operates a bicycle."

"Did she succeed in building that?"

"She did build it, or rather, she used me as the muscle to build it while barking out instructions." Oscar grinned. "Gemma's real bossy at times, but I thought she was on to something. Problem was that after we mounted an old rowboat over the bicycle Gemma got for Christmas last year, and then put fins on the tires like paddle-wheels, we left a few tiny openings in the boat and . . . it sank within minutes of launching."

"Were you and Gemma in it at the time?"

"We were, but we both know how to swim. Your sister, Mrs. Michelson, was furious when she found out what happened."

Norman stopped walking. "You told my sister what happened?"

"'Course not. Your brother, the other Mr. Nesbit, told her, even though Gemma suggested he keep that information to himself."

Norman frowned. "How did Stanley find out about your adventure with the rowboat?"

"Uncle Stanley followed us to the lake," Gemma said, stomping up to join them. "He'd been keeping an eye on me, thinking Oscar and I were acting suspicious, so when we loaded our invention into my pony cart and headed for the lake, he trailed behind us." Gemma blew out a breath. "I couldn't stay mad at him for telling on us, though, because he did manage to retrieve my bicycle."

"I didn't realize Stanley was so involved in your life," Norman said slowly.

"He's my uncle, so of course he's involved in my life, although you're my uncle as well, but I suppose you're not as involved because you're always so consumed with your experiments." Gemma flashed him an unexpected grin. "But I'm not complaining. We scientists are known to become consumed with our work, so it's fine that you don't spend much time with me."

A sliver of what felt like guilt slid through Norman.

Gemma was right. He'd not made much of an effort to be involved in her life, or involved in any of his nieces' or nephews' lives, which didn't speak highly of him in the least. He was certainly going to have to make amends for his clear neglect, although how he was going to go about that while still being able to devote enough time to his work was something he was going to have to plan out in detail, perhaps make a few charts and even a graph or two, laying out a detailed schedule that would allow him to dedicate more time to being a proper uncle.

"Are you feeling well, Uncle Norman?" Gemma asked, breaking into Norman's less-than-pleasant thoughts. "You look like you're about to toss up your accounts."

He summoned up a smile. "I'm fit as a fiddle, Gemma."

Gemma grinned. "Thank goodness. That means there's no reason to delay showing Oscar and me how your electric wagon works. We're hoping you'll let us test it out, but we need to hurry. Mother and Grandmother will certainly be joining us soon, and while Mother won't balk if you agree to let us try out your wagon, Grandmother might be another story."

"I never said you could try out my *electrical conveyance vehicle*."

Gemma immediately took to looking stubborn. "I don't know

why you'd object to that. I overheard you and Theo speaking about the difficulty you were having marking the distance the wagon could travel because the weighted bags you were using kept falling off when the wagon traveled over bumps."

"Me and Gemma are real good at staying on things that move," Oscar added. "And we know that you need something that weighs over a hundred pounds, but not more than one hundred fifteen pounds, which is why you couldn't put Theo on the wagon because she weighs one hundred twenty-two pounds. So right now we're your most convenient option."

Norman tilted his head. "How do you know for certain the two of you weigh a combined weight of less than one hundred fifteen pounds?"

Oscar shrugged. "Gemma insisted on weighing us this morning, knowing you'd ask this question, which is when we confirmed that I weigh fifty-four pounds and Gemma weighs forty-nine pounds."

"And how did you obtain those numbers?"

"Gemma used my seesaw."

Norman turned to Gemma. "You used a seesaw to weigh yourself?"

Gemma gave an airy wave of a small hand. "It wasn't difficult. Oscar and I used bags of flour we knew weighed five pounds, setting those bags on one side and then adjusting them until we achieved a perfect levelness as we sat on the other side."

"And you went through all that bother so that you'd be able to tell me your combined weights are approximately one hundred four pounds?"

Gemma nodded.

"Then I suppose with that level of determination that I can't very well deny the two of you a chance to try out what isn't a wagon, but an—"

"Electrical conveyance vehicle," Gemma finished with a grin, falling into step beside him as he headed toward the third carriage house, which housed his workshop on the first floor and his bachelor apartments on the second.

"Oscar and I decided that ladies will probably be more keen to drive electrical vehicles over men," Gemma declared.

"But I'm trying to invent an electrical vehicle for my own personal use, and clearly I'm a man," Norman countered.

Gemma nodded. "True, but you're a man who loathes horses." She shrugged. "Most men adore their horses, so they won't want to give them up, not when they seem to enjoy looking very, well, manly on the back of a horse."

Before he could consider what was an excellent observation on Gemma's part, she snatched Oscar's hand and they ran right up to the door of his workshop, disappearing into it a second later.

"Don't touch anything," Constance called out from behind Norman, materializing by his side a moment later.

"Where did you come from?" he asked.

"I've been behind you the entire time. Don't tell me you were unaware of that, were you?"

Unwilling to chance having her pat his face for a fever again, Norman smiled. "I imagine your footsteps were drowned out by Gemma's voice. She's far more talkative than I remember her being."

"She was talking up a storm by the time she was two."

Another dose of guilt swept over him.

"Hurry up, Uncle Norman," Gemma called, poking her head through the door of his workshop. "We've already uncovered your electrical conveyance vehicle, but I know better than to touch it without you here." She shot a grin to Constance. "We wouldn't want to get electrocuted by mistake because you'd never forgive Uncle Norman if that happened."

"Too right I wouldn't," Constance returned with a grin of her own.

The next ten minutes were spent pushing his invention out of the workshop, and then getting Gemma and Oscar settled into it. After making certain they were securely seated, Norman attached a few cables to the battery and switched the motor on.

To his relief, it sputtered to life, earning squeals of delight from

Gemma and Oscar. Taking a second to show Gemma how to steer the wagon with a lever that was attached to the middle of the floor, he stood back and watched as she set the wagon into motion, traveling at what was probably no more than three miles an hour.

"It works," Constance exclaimed.

"Of course it does. It just doesn't work for long." Norman nodded to a large oak tree that was exactly an acre and a half from them. "It'll die right past that tree, which, unfortunately, suggests the work I've been doing on double electrical currents still leaves much to be desired."

"Unfortunate indeed," Constance said somewhat absent-mindedly before she lifted her chin and turned to him. "Who is she?"

Of anything he'd been expecting her to ask, that had not been it. "Beg pardon?"

Constance crossed her arms over her chest. "Don't turn all scatterbrained scientist on me, Norman. You know very well what I'm asking you, so out with it. Who is the woman responsible for your unusual lapses of observation? May I assume she resides in Hyde Park, which would explain why you've chosen to run there this week, even though you normally prefer to run along the lakeshore?"

"Parts of Hyde Park are directly beside the lake."

"You're being deliberately difficult. Who is she?"

Norman turned his attention back to Gemma and Oscar, who were slowly approaching the tree he'd pointed out to Constance, their speed at a mere crawl, proving that his battery was incapable of holding a charge for long. His invention drifted to a stop, and then Gemma jumped out of it right before she, for some unfathomable reason, began speaking to the tree.

"Why's Gemma chatting with the tree?" he asked, but instead of answering him, Constance looked him up and down with concern in her eyes.

"Gemma's not talking to the tree," his mother said, sneaking up behind him and causing him to jump. "She's talking to the Pinkerton man who was watching you from behind the tree. Of course I'm sure you must have noticed him and were attempting to distract your sister from questioning you about a mysterious woman." His mother caught his eye. "So who is she?"

Norman rubbed a hand over a forehead that was beginning to perspire. That he'd not noticed his mother stealing up behind him was troubling, but that he also hadn't noticed a Pinkerton man lurking behind the tree . . . well, clearly he must be coming down with an illness, because surely a wisp of a woman by the name of Beatrix Waterbury couldn't be disrupting his normal keen observational skills so much . . . could she?

"You must have misheard the conversation Norman and I were having, Mother," Constance surprised him by saying. "We were simply discussing Hyde Park and why he's taken to running over there."

Mary frowned. "I distinctly heard you ask him about a woman."

Constance waved that aside before she nodded to what looked to be an invitation in Mary's hand. "Anything of interest delivered today?"

For a moment, Norman thought his mother was going to press the issue, but then she turned her attention to the heavy vellum piece of paper she was holding. "We've been invited to Mrs. Potter Palmer's first charity ball of the year. It's to be held at the Palmer House come late October, and"—she handed the paper to Norman—"you've received a personal invitation as well. You're to bring a guest."

Relieved to have the conversation turn to a more innocent topic, Norman glanced over the invitation and smiled. "Mrs. Palmer always serves an impressive meal, so this event is one I may actually look forward to attending."

Mary's gaze sharpened on his face. "Are you certain you're feeling quite well? You never look forward to any society event, no matter the circumstance."

"Again, I'm fine."

Mary took a step toward him. "You're acting peculiar, but if you're sure you're not unwell, allow me to return to Mrs. Palmer's ball. I've come up with three young ladies I believe are appropriate guests for you to choose from—Miss Paulina Dinneen, Miss Caroline Ashburn, or the oh-so-delightful Miss Francis Elks."

"I didn't find Miss Elks oh so delightful when she sat next to me last year. She almost nodded off into her soup as I was explaining the difference between a cirrus cloud and a stratus cloud and the impact Mr. Luke Howard had on the science of meteorology."

"Why would you choose to lecture a young lady about meteorology at a formal dinner engagement?" Mary asked.

"Miss Elks is the one who broached the topic of how charming she thought the clouds had been in the sky that particular day." Norman shrugged. "I thought she'd be keen to learn more about clouds in general."

Mary blew out a breath. "I doubt Miss Elks will be willing to risk receiving another lecture from you, so that leaves Miss Dinneen and Miss Ashburn."

"I'm perfectly capable of asking a lady of my choosing to attend the Palmer affair with me."

"The last few times you've chosen a lady on your own, you've chosen Miss Theodosia Robinson."

"I enjoy her company."

"She's not a suitable escort for you."

Norman frowned. "What's wrong with Theo?"

Mary returned the frown. "Well, for one, the fact that she seems perfectly content to allow everyone to address her as Theo. Second, she's currently sporting the shortest hair I've ever seen on a woman. And third, she has no sense of fashion and attends society events wearing the drabbest of gowns."

"Her hair is only short because one of our experiments caught fire, setting fire to her hair as well."

Mary's lips thinned. "She's not an appropriate guest. You'll need to ask Miss Dinneen or Miss Ashburn, unless you have some other lady in mind. Perhaps that mystery lady I know you were discussing with Constance?"

An image of Beatrix immediately flashed in front of his eyes, and, curiously enough, the thought of asking her to attend the ball with him was oddly appealing. That appeal, however, only lasted a few seconds after he realized his mother was watching him far too closely, which would then, as was her habit, lead to a barrage of questions he didn't care to answer.

"I'm taking Theo and that's the end of it," he said.

Mary released a huff. "Fine, but you'll need to visit your tailor and get some new formal attire before the Chicago Season begins. You'll also need to order some everyday clothing as well because that jacket you wore home from New York was ill-fitting and missing most of its buttons."

"I bought that jacket in a slightly seedy shop in New York after someone tripped into me on the street, depositing the jelly-filled pastry he'd been carrying all over my perfectly fitted jacket."

Another huff was Mary's response to that. "If you don't care to visit your tailor, just say so and I'll take your measurements and order your clothing for you."

"I never said I didn't care to visit my tailor. I was merely explaining why my jacket didn't fit me well. But since you've now broached what you seem to believe is the sad state of my wardrobe, I'll amend that situation straightaway." He tilted his head. "Would Marshall Field & Company have everything I need to purchase?"

Mary's gaze sharpened on him again. "You want to personally go to Marshall Field & Company and shop on your own? Have you ever even been there?"

"Can't say that I have, but I've heard it's a splendid store. It also has two working elevators I wouldn't mind seeing, so perhaps I'll rearrange my schedule and take the afternoon off to do some shopping."

"Good heavens, there *is* something wrong with you," Mary proclaimed, Constance nodding in agreement.

Not caring to be interrogated about what was really an unexpected decision on his part, as well as not caring to dwell on the true reason he'd decided to visit Marshall Field & Company, Norman forced a smile. "For the hundredth time, there's nothing wrong with me. And now, if you'll excuse me, I believe it's past time I introduced myself to that Pinkerton man. After he and I get a few matters cleared up between us, I'll be off to Marshall Field & Company, and no, I don't need either of you to accompany me there."

CHAPTER 10

"These gloves are not the ivory I need. Show me another pair, and quickly, if you please. I'm meeting ladies for lunch and time is rapidly getting away from me."

During the week Beatrix had been employed at Marshall Field & Company, she'd dealt with ladies like Mrs. Hermann Davis on an hourly basis—ladies confident of their superiority over a salesgirl they believed was far beneath them, a notion that left Beatrix holding her tongue time and time again.

Granted, she'd seen more than her fair share of ladies who were members of the New York Four Hundred treat members of the serving class rather deplorably. However, she'd never been reluctant to share her opinion regarding their unacceptable behavior with them, earning her a few disgruntled remarks from the ladies in question. But because she *was* one of the great American heiresses, what with her father being one of the wealthiest men in the country, those ladies always seemed to be on better behavior the next time she ran across them, which was why it was now so difficult to swallow the reprimands she longed to voice.

"This is no time for dawdling. Do you have other ivory gloves or not?"

Beatrix shook herself back to the situation at hand. "Of course

I have more, Mrs. Davis," she said, not bothering to add that she'd already shown her over twenty pairs of gloves, all of which the lady had found fault with for some reason or another.

In Beatrix's humble opinion, having to fetch a single pair of gloves from the drawers that were built into a cabinet behind the glove counter was a waste of time. It would have been far more efficient if she could display numerous pairs at once for her customers to peruse. However, Marshall Field & Company had specific rules about such matters. And because she didn't want to be dismissed from a position she found fascinating, even with all the aggravation she dealt with as a mere salesgirl, having not had the experience needed to be given the more coveted title of saleswoman, she returned the gloves the lady had dismissed with a sniff to their proper box. Pulling out another pair of ivory gloves, she spread them carefully onto the glass counter.

"Perhaps you'll find this pair more to your liking," Beatrix said as Mrs. Davis leaned over the counter, inspecting the gloves with an eagle eye. "If I may direct your attention to the label sewn into the glove, you'll notice it's the famed Alexandre Kid Gloves, produced only in France." She ran a finger over the fine leather. "Marshall Field's is the sole agent of these gloves in America, having been given that honor after A. T. Stewart's store fell on questionable times after his death."

Mrs. Davis's head snapped up. "You say that only Marshall Field's sells this glove?"

"Indeed, and while it does come with a dearer cost than the other gloves you've seen today, there's no finer glove to be had."

"And does it come in other shades of ivory?"

Knowing there was nothing to do but pull out every shade of ivory the Alexandre Kid Glove came in, Beatrix set about doing just that, keeping a smile on her face as Mrs. Davis inspected every glove as if it were a life-and-death situation.

"I'll take twenty in every color of ivory you have," Mrs. Davis finally said with a nod. "See that they're delivered to my residence this afternoon and charge them to my account."

"Very well, Mrs. Davis," Beatrix returned, flipping open the notepad where she kept track of her sales and poising her pencil over the page. "I'll simply need your address."

"You don't know my address?"

"I'm afraid I don't because I've only recently come to Chicago and—"

"I don't need to know any of that," Mrs. Davis snapped before she rattled off her address, forcing Beatrix to write down that information so quickly that her handwriting was almost illegible.

"Will there be anything else I may do for you today, Mrs. Davis?" Beatrix asked, lifting her head and blinking when she realized that while she'd been scribbling away, Mrs. Davis had taken her leave without a single word of appreciation for all the time Beatrix had spent assisting her.

"Aunt Gladys was right," she muttered, closing her notepad. "I truly had no idea what the world was like for working women."

"Miss Waterbury, have you not had an opportunity to completely read the handbook I know you were given on your first day of employment with us?"

Summoning up yet another smile, because Marshall Field & Company expected their employees to sport a smile at all times, Beatrix turned and found Mrs. Goodman, supervisor of the first floor neckwear, trimmings, notions, coat check, and glove department, standing a few feet away. Her pursed lips and sour expression were less than encouraging.

Beatrix nodded. "I have read the handbook."

"Cover to cover?" Mrs. Goodman shot back.

"Yes, although I found some parts of it more riveting than others."

"Shall I assume, then, that you were bored by the part regarding how much information our employees are expected to disclose to our customers about the products available here, unless directly asked?"

Before Beatrix could formulate a suitable reply to that, because she had read the part Mrs. Goodman had just broached but hadn't agreed with it in the least, a sharply dressed gentleman stepped up to join them.

Standing before her was none other than the esteemed Mr. Harry Selfridge. Mr. Selfridge was known to be a most ambitious gentleman, and during the time he'd been at the store, he'd risen from stock boy to the assistant to Mr. J. M. Fleming, the superintendent of retail, within a remarkably short period of time. Rumor had it that Mr. Selfridge now had his eye on Mr. Fleming's position, and given what little Beatrix had already observed about the man, she was relatively certain he would win that position within the next few years.

"Is something amiss, Mrs. Goodman?" Mr. Selfridge asked, his gaze never dropping from Beatrix as Mrs. Goodman gave a wave of her hand.

"Nothing that need concern you, Mr. Selfridge," Mrs. Goodman returned. "This is Miss Beatrix Waterbury, newly employed here, and I was reminding her of a few of our rules."

Mr. Selfridge's eyes narrowed. "Which rules would those be?"

Beatrix cleared her throat. "I wasn't familiar with where Mrs. Davis resides and asked her to provide me with that information."

Mr. Selfridge crossed his arms over his chest. "I see. And how did Mrs. Davis react to that?"

"She took me to task and then interrupted me after I tried to explain why I didn't know her address."

Mrs. Goodman released a sniff. "You're supposed to get that information from the credit department if you're in doubt."

"But what if there is more than one Mrs. Davis, ma'am?" Beatrix countered. "By asking her what was really only a simple question, I was given the proper address, even if I'm still going to have to double-check with the credit department because she rattled off the information so quickly that I'm now unable to read part of my handwriting."

"It's never ma'am, always Mrs. Goodman."

Beatrix nodded. "Quite right. I do recall reading that in the handbook."

Mrs. Goodman's lips pursed. "Then I would expect you to remember from this point forward that we address everyone, whether they be employees or customers, by Mr., Mrs., or Miss, unless you're speaking to one of the young cash boys or errand girls, of course. And do not, under any circumstances, address anyone as *dearie*."

"I don't believe I've ever called anyone *dearie* in my life."

Mrs. Goodman leveled a stern eye on Beatrix as Mr. Selfridge cleared his throat. "Were there any other rules you needed to address with Miss Waterbury?"

Mrs. Goodman turned to Mr. Selfridge. "Only the one pertaining to disclosing too much information about a product to a customer."

Mr. Selfridge quirked a brow in Beatrix's direction.

Beatrix forced another smile. "I thought Mrs. Davis would be impressed by the Alexandre Kid Gloves if I explained they can only be purchased in America at Marshall Field's. And because she ended up purchasing twenty pairs of every shade of ivory we carry, which is seven shades, I was able to secure an impressive sale. Twenty multiplied by seven is, after all, one hundred and forty, which you must admit is a rather significant amount."

For the longest moment, Mr. Selfridge stared at Beatrix, until he finally turned to Mrs. Goodman. "I don't believe Miss Waterbury needs to be reprimanded further about the matter, Mrs. Goodman. As she said, the sale of one hundred forty gloves to a single customer is most impressive." He turned back to Beatrix and nodded to her notepad. "Allow me to give you Mrs. Davis's address again, sparing you a trip to the third floor."

After Mr. Selfridge gave her the address, speaking slowly as she wrote the information down, Beatrix thanked him for his assistance, thanked Mrs. Goodman for hers, then excused herself, telling them she needed to package Mrs. Davis's order to make certain it was delivered by late afternoon.

Thankful that Mrs. Goodman didn't linger after Mr. Selfridge took his leave, Beatrix counted out the proper number and shades of gloves, wrapping them in brown paper. She then pushed one of the two buttons attached to the back of the glove counter, the one that would alert Mr. Ford, who was head of the delivery boys on the floor, that she had a package that needed to be taken to the delivery docks. The other button was only pushed when she had a cash sale and needed a cash boy to run the money up to the third-floor cash room and then return with any change the customer needed.

Less than a minute later, a young boy by the name of Bertie scampered up beside her, smiling shyly as he took the package of gloves.

Marshall Field's employed many children in its store on State Street, as well as in their wholesale building located at Madison and Market Streets. Beatrix had been appalled to discover that these delivery boys, cash boys, and errand girls earned a scant two dollars a week. But when she'd broached the subject with Miss Louisa Brennon, a young woman who worked the handkerchief counter, Louisa had told her to have a care in case anyone was listening. Louisa had then, in a very hushed tone, explained that working at any other retail establishment was considered low class, but working at Marshall Field's was considered respectable, which was why the positions were always in such demand, and why most everyone who worked there accepted their low pay with few complaints.

Beatrix had been less than satisfied with that explanation, although that was the beginning of her realization that she truly had been woefully ignorant about the plight of the working class.

Clearly, the working class was suffering, and women most especially. Salesgirl positions such as the one she currently held started off with a salary of seven dollars a week—a week that encompassed six days of work. Women who worked in the workrooms, sewing garments for the sales floor and for custom orders, made a little more, but their salary was only ten to twelve dollars a week. Many of the salesmen, on the other hand, made up to twenty-five dollars a week, although Beatrix had been told that they would have to secure a promotion to increase their salary from that point forward.

It was a humbling thought that Beatrix often spent more on a single gown from Worth than the employees who worked the floors of Marshall Field's made in several years.

"Got anything else for me to take to the docks, Miss Waterbury?" Bertie asked, drawing her from her musings.

"Not just yet, Bertie, but give me another hour. I'm sure I'll have another customer soon."

Sending her a grin, Bertie hurried away as Beatrix began tidying up her counter, a responsibility she took quite seriously since it had been mentioned more than once that she could be dismissed out of hand if a supervisor found an area in disarray.

Turning around after she'd returned the last glove to its proper drawer, Beatrix discovered a gentleman standing a few counters away from her, holding on to the arm of a lady dressed in a drab gray blouse and matching skirt—a gentleman who was staring Beatrix's way, and who just happened to be none other than Mr. Norman Nesbit.

CHAPTER 11

The most unexpected feeling of relief swept over Norman the second he clapped eyes on Beatrix.

She was standing behind a glass counter, wearing a plain white blouse, her brilliant red hair pulled back in some manner of knot at the nape of her neck, little wisps of curls escaping that knot.

Pulling Miss Theo Robinson, an associate of his, into motion, he strode toward Beatrix, unusually pleased when she sent him a smile that held not a trace of annoyance in it.

"Why are you dragging me across the room?" Theo demanded, trying to shrug her arm from his.

"I'm not dragging you," he replied, refusing to let go of her arm as he continued forward. "I'm merely getting you to the, ah . . ." His gaze shot to the items displayed in the glass case Beatrix was minding. "Glove department in an efficient manner."

"I don't need any gloves."

"Of course you do." He stopped directly in front of Beatrix and smiled. "Good afternoon, Beatrix."

"Good afternoon, Mr. Nesbit," she returned, her smile never wavering. "What a surprise to see you shopping at Marshall Field & Company."

He frowned. "Why are you addressing me as Mr. Nesbit?"

Beatrix glanced around and lowered her voice. "I've already been taken to task for addressing one of my supervisors as *ma'am* earlier. Best not to chance any additional repercussions if I'm heard calling you by your given name."

"But you know me."

"True, but even if my aunt were to pay me a visit, I'd have to call her Miss Huttleston instead of Aunt Gladys."

"Are there many rules an employee has to adhere to at Marshall Field & Company?"

"Indeed, but they're not difficult. I simply haven't gotten all of them down quite yet." She nodded to Theo. "However, with that said, one of the rules is to discover the names of all of our customers, but you've yet to provide me with the name of your companion."

Norman glanced to Theo, who was fidgeting with her hat, trying to pull a stray string from the brim of it, which only succeeded in having the stitching unravel, leaving a gaping hole behind.

He suddenly realized that Theo, a woman he spent an extraordinary amount of time with, what with how she could always be counted on to lend a helping hand with any of his many experiments, often fidgeted when she was in the vicinity of other women.

It was curious, that, and almost suggested Theo was uncomfortable in the company of women, although why that was, he had no idea.

Beatrix shot him a look of exasperation before she turned to Theo. "Since Mr. Nesbit is apparently thinking far too strenuously about how to provide me with your name, I'm Miss Beatrix Waterbury, and you are . . . ?"

"She's Theo, Theo Robinson," Norman supplied when Theo just blinked back at Beatrix, seemingly at a loss for words.

Beatrix's smile faltered for the span of a second, but then she hitched it back into place. "Forgive me, Miss Robinson, but I noticed that you winced when Mr. Nesbit introduced you as Theo. May I dare presume he's being his usual insensitive self and doesn't realize you might not care to be addressed as Theo, which I'm also going to presume isn't your full name?"

"Everyone calls her Theo," Norman said when Theo still didn't say a single thing and stared back at Beatrix as if she'd never met anyone quite like her in her life, which she probably hadn't.

Beatrix didn't spare him a single glance, keeping her gaze on Theo. "Be that as it may," she began through teeth that seemed to be clenched, "I get the distinct impression Miss Robinson may prefer everyone use her full name that might be . . . Theophila?"

"Theodosia," Theo mumbled.

"How lovely," Beatrix exclaimed. "If I had a name as delightful as Theodosia, I would definitely prefer that instead of having people shorten it to Theo."

"Her own father calls her Theo," Norman felt compelled to point out when Theo retreated into silence again.

"And my father occasionally reverts to calling me *pumpkin* at times, but that doesn't mean I enjoy anyone else calling me that," Beatrix shot back.

Theo considered Beatrix for a moment, then nodded. "Before I was born, Father was convinced I was a boy and decided I was going to be a Theodore. But because my mother died in childbirth, leaving him to raise me on his own, he apparently found it too much of a bother to come up with another name, so he decided a version of Theodore would do just fine. Someone suggested Theodosia and that's what he named me, evidently relieved that he could still shorten the name to Theo because he'd gotten used to thinking of me as a Theo before I was born."

Norman blinked. "You've never told me that before."

"You never asked."

"Why does that not surprise me?" Beatrix muttered with a shake of her head. "You have my sympathies, Miss Robinson, for the death of your mother. I imagine that has caused you all sorts of difficulties over the years, unless, of course, your father remarried and you have a stepmother."

"Father's much too busy with his work to take time to find another wife."

"How unfortunate," Beatrix returned. "But tell me this, Miss

Robinson, why, if you don't care for the nickname, have you not bothered to correct Mr. Nesbit? I assume the two of you are friends, which means it's perfectly acceptable for you to disclose your preference when it comes to your name."

"We're not friends," Theo declared firmly. "We're acquaintances who share an interest in science."

Beatrix blinked before her lips began to curve. "Ah, well, that explains it. You're just like him."

Theo turned to Norman. "Am I mistaken in taking that as something less than a compliment?"

"Hard to tell," Norman admitted. "During the time I spent with Beatrix, she was very vague at times with her words, but if I were to hazard a guess, given the frequency in which she insulted me, she might very well have just done the same to you."

Theo frowned. "When did you spend time with her? You've not mentioned anything about her before, although is that why you insisted we come to Marshall Field's today?"

"I wouldn't think Mr. Nesbit knew I worked here," Beatrix said, catching his eye. "You didn't know, did you?"

Unwilling to admit that Edgar had disclosed Beatrix's employment situation to him, Norman turned back to Theo. "I'm sure I must have mentioned my encounter with Beatrix to you. She's the woman who got off the train with me after the train heist."

Theo shook her head. "No, you never mentioned her, and frankly, you've not said much about your experience with the train robbers except to tell me how you foiled their efforts to rob you of your research papers. The only other thing you told me was that the robbery was the reason you're currently being trailed by Pinkerton men."

"You're being trailed by Pinkerton men?" Beatrix repeated.

Relieved that the conversation was taking a more acceptable turn, Norman nodded. "I'm afraid so. My mother is convinced I'm in dire jeopardy, even though I've explained to her numerous times that it's highly unlikely anyone will try to accost me again, what with how the thieves believe they absconded with my real research. And since the research I included in those false documents was very complicated, it'll take someone months to wade through it and realize they've been duped."

Theo shoved back her hat. "What if whoever is responsible for stealing your research is just as brilliant as you?"

"It's highly unlikely that will be the case because there are only a handful of men in the country who are currently at my level with electricity and currents. Why, besides Nikola Tesla, I'm confident in saying there aren't any other men experimenting with double currents."

"What if Nikola Tesla is the man behind the theft?" Theo pressed.

"Mr. Tesla is far too arrogant to stoop to theft to further his theories on electricity."

Theo bit her lip. "I'll have to take your word on that because I've never personally met the man, what with me being a mere woman and all." Her cheeks began turning pink, as if she just revealed something she'd not meant to, something that suggested she held a bit of resentment over the fact she was blatantly excluded from the scientific set because she was a woman.

Not knowing what he could possibly say to Theo's disclosure, he glanced to the gloves displayed in the counter before he nodded to Beatrix. "We're here to purchase new gloves for Theo."

"I don't need new gloves."

"Then I'll not show you any, Miss Robinson," Beatrix said firmly, sending him a look that dared him to contradict her, which had him stepping closer to the counter and pointing to a pair of ivory gloves that had buttons marching up the side of them.

"I'd like to see that pair for Theo," he said.

Mutiny flashed through Beatrix's eyes. "I think not. Miss Robinson has been perfectly—"

A loud clearing of a throat from behind him drew Norman's attention. Turning, he discovered an older woman standing a few feet away from the glove counter, her lips pursed and her eyes narrowed on Beatrix.

"Is there a problem here?" the woman asked.

Beatrix beamed a bright smile at the woman. "Not at all, Mrs. Goodman. Miss Robinson and Mr. Nesbit are simply deciding if Miss Robinson needs a new pair of gloves." She inclined her head to Mrs. Goodman. "May I presume you're acquainted with Mr. Nesbit and Miss Robinson, or if not, would you care for me to perform a proper introduction?"

When Mrs. Goodman drew herself up and began looking rather scandalized, Beatrix's smile dimmed ever so slightly before she hitched it back into place, muttered "pesky rules" under her breath, then squared her shoulders. "Forgive me, Mrs. Goodman. Clearly you're already acquainted with these two customers, and—"

"I've never met Mrs. Goodman in my life," Norman interjected, which had Mrs. Goodman turning her gaze on him. "Frankly, I've never stepped foot in Marshall Field & Company, so if you ask me, Miss Waterbury's inquiry was warranted." He presented Mrs. Goodman with a bow. "Mr. Norman Nesbit at your disposal, Mrs. Goodman." He nodded to Theo. "And this is my acquaintance, Miss Theo . . ." He stopped talking when Beatrix sent him a pointed look. "Ah, or rather, Miss Theodosia Robinson."

Mrs. Goodman inclined her head. "I'm well aware of who the two of you are, Mr. Nesbit, but thank you for reaffirming your identities to me."

Uncertain where he was supposed to go with the conversation from there, while not wanting Beatrix to intervene on his behalf because she'd certainly suffer some manner of discipline from the unpleasant Mrs. Goodman if she did, Norman settled for doing what he always did when he felt indecisive.

He stared at Mrs. Goodman.

For some reason, that particular action always made people uncomfortable, probably because he was capable of staring without blinking. Mrs. Goodman rapidly proved his theory correct, because less than thirty seconds later, she excused herself, telling him she had other customers to see after.

"Impressive," Beatrix breathed as Mrs. Goodman stalked away.

"Works like a charm," Norman said. "But before she decides

to return to check on your progress with selling us some gloves, why don't you show Theo a few selections?"

"Again, I don't need new gloves."

"And again, I'm going to respond to that by saying of course you do. According to my sister Constance, ladies always purchase new gloves, as well as new gowns, for the opening ball of the season. You'll need new gloves for Mrs. Palmer's charity ball."

Theo's nose wrinkled. "How did you know I'm attending Mrs. Palmer's ball?"

"You're going with me."

"I don't recall you asking me to attend the Palmer ball with you."

"I haven't gotten around to it yet, but you often accompany me, so I'm not certain I understand why you're suddenly turning difficult about the matter."

"I'm not being difficult, although I will admit to feeling the most unusual sense of annoyance toward you."

"Why would you be annoyed with me?"

Theo descended into silence again, although her cheeks took on a decidedly pink tinge.

He'd never seen Theo blush, and that she'd now taken to doing so more than once in the span of a few minutes meant he was going to have to devote time to ponder the matter more thoroughly, but now was hardly the moment for that. Instead, he turned to Beatrix. "Would you have an idea why Theo's annoyed with me?"

"I have several," Beatrix began, "but since I really cannot be seen chatting with the two of you for too long, I'll disclose the main reason I think she's annoyed. You assumed, which is something *I'm* going to assume you do often, that Theodosia would be attending the ball with you. However, *you* didn't bother to extend her the courtesy of asking her if she wanted to be your guest."

"But she must have known I was going to ask her because I've taken her with me before when I've received invitations I can't decline."

"How could she have possibly known that?" Beatrix asked

before she stiffened, then spun on a heel, pulled out a drawer, and retrieved a pair of gloves, which she immediately spread out on the counter. "Mrs. Goodman is circling closer," she whispered before she was smiling brightly again, her smile turned on Theo. "Am I mistaken in concluding you're attending this ball with a gentleman who isn't Mr. Nesbit?"

Theo, to Norman's disbelief, gave a bob of her head, the action causing her short hair to bob as well under her unraveling hat.

"What do you mean you're going with someone else?" he all but sputtered. "Or better yet, who would that someone be?"

Theo's face turned from pink to red. "Mr. Harvey Cabot."

"Surely not."

Theo's eyes flashed in a very un-Theo-like manner. "Do you not believe I'm capable of drawing a gentleman's interest?"

"Don't be ridiculous. Of course you're capable of drawing interest. Why, I've always been very interested in almost everything you have to say, and I'm a gentleman."

"You're interested in *almost* everything I say? What, pray tell, have I ever said, or done for that matter, that didn't interest you?"

His collar suddenly felt unusually snug. "If you must know," he began as Theo glowered at him, "I don't find it all that interesting when you show me those fashion advertisements from different newspapers."

"I showed you an advertisement one time because I was trying to seek your opinion on whether or not your mother would find me more acceptable as your escort to that charity ball we attended last February if I wore one of the gowns displayed in the advertisement instead of the gown I always wear."

"Why didn't you tell me that instead of leaving me to try to decipher on my own why you were taking an interest in fashion?"

Theo's nose shot straight into the air. "One would think, what with that stellar mind of yours, that you wouldn't have needed me to explain why I was asking you about fashions. You must know that I'm challenged in that regard, but you do have two sisters, so I assumed you'd be able to lend me at least a smidgen of advice, but sadly, that didn't happen." She blew out a breath. "And because your mother looked me over at that specific ball as if I was something unpleasant one finds on the bottom of her shoe, I've concluded I was quite right to consider purchasing a new gown, although I truly have no idea which style, or . . ." Her voice trailed off as she shot a look to Beatrix, then immediately descended into silence again.

Beatrix leaned closer to Theo. "If you're in need of a new gown, Miss Robinson, the second floor is where you should visit next. The saleswomen will have models parade in front of you with styles they believe will suit you. All you'll need to do is allow them to measure you after you settle on a gown and they'll have it made up for you."

Absolute horror flickered through Theo's eyes. "I don't really need a new gown. The one I have is fine."

Beatrix winced. "Forgive me, Miss Robinson. I'm not supposed to offer advice to our customers unless asked. I was being far too forward."

Norman shook his head. "You weren't. She does need a new gown because I noticed the last time she accompanied me that the gown she always wears is becoming frayed around the, ah . . ." He gestured to his chest. "Bosom area."

Beatrix gave a very uncalled for rolling of her eyes. "I hope you realize it's really not quite the thing to embarrass Miss Robinson like that in public." She lowered her voice. "Besides, did you ever consider that Miss Robinson may not care to spend the funds required on a new gown right now?"

"Theo has an entire fortune to her name, and doesn't even need to seek out her father's permission to access that fortune." He nodded to Theo, who was once again looking annoyed with him, so he quickly returned his attention to Beatrix. "Her father, Gus Robinson, is a brilliant engineer in his own right, but his father, Theo's grandfather, very kindly left him the fortune he'd made in shipping, which Gus wisely invested in George Pullman's railroad company." He glanced to Theo. "That means there's no reason for you to not indulge in a new gown, which may allow you to get a small bit of enjoyment out of the Palmer ball since I doubt you're going to enjoy the company of Mr. Harvey Cabot."

If he didn't know Theo so well, he would have sworn she was fighting an urge to strangle him, given the increased temper in her eyes.

"I'm sure I'll enjoy Mr. Cabot's company."

"You won't. Harvey doesn't come close to being as intelligent as you, and don't even get me started on all the inventions he brags about to one and all, even though I've never seen him complete an invention or receive a patent for one." He narrowed his eyes on her. "I imagine you're only going with him because you know it'll please your father since the Cabot family has recently invested in the Pullman company, which has allowed George Pullman to expand his operation, thus increasing your father's profits."

Instead of replying to that, Theo stepped up to the counter, looked over the pair of gloves Beatrix had spread out over the glass, then lifted her head. "I've decided I *will* need to purchase some new gloves for the Palmer ball, Miss Waterbury. In fact, I may decide to purchase numerous pairs." She glanced to Norman. "It shouldn't take me more than an hour or so, but because this glove business was your idea, I expect you to wait patiently. And do not even think about trying to give me your opinion as I look through the selections Miss Waterbury shows me. At this moment, your opinion is the very last opinion I'd put any stock in."

CHAPTER 12

It took Beatrix a mere two minutes to discover that Miss Theodosia Robinson had not been exaggerating when she'd claimed to be challenged when it came to fashions.

Theodosia had not known there were different styles of gloves, her eyes widening when Beatrix pulled out a glove Theodosia had pointed to, and then explained that the glove wasn't appropriate to wear to a ball because it was meant to be worn while riding a horse.

"Is that why it only goes up a short distance from the wrist?" Theodosia asked, admiring the driving glove she was now wearing.

"It is. Makes it easier to handle the reins if your arm isn't encased in fine leather."

"Fascinating," Theodosia breathed, stripping the glove from her hand and laying it aside. "I'll take it."

"Are you sure you want it in this particular color?" Beatrix asked. "Red is a bold color, unless, of course, you have a riding habit that has a bit of red in it."

Theodosia's shoulders drooped. "I only have one riding habit and it's brown."

Beatrix's heart gave a lurch at the dejection she saw in Theodosia's eyes. Pulling a piece of brown paper from beneath the counter, she set the red gloves on top of the paper. "Red gloves would certainly add a nice splash of color to a brown riding habit."

"Or Theo could purchase a new riding habit that would match the gloves," Norman said, looking up from the notepad he'd pulled out of his pocket a second after Theodosia had proclaimed she was going to purchase some gloves. "Perhaps, Theo, after you finish selecting a pair or two of gloves, you should take Beatrix's suggestion and go visit the salon on the second floor."

Horror flickered through Theodosia's eyes. "I'm not going to the second floor." Her hand reached up and touched what Beatrix hadn't neglected to notice was very unevenly short hair before she gestured to the customers mingling around the different counters. "All these ladies are finely dressed and have their hair styled to perfection. I hate to imagine what the saleswomen would think of me if I, dressed as I am right now and with my hair all but burnt off, showed up on the second floor."

Even though Beatrix longed to tell Theodosia that the saleswomen would find it a privilege to assist her, she knew that because Theodosia was currently wearing a dress of the dullest shade of gray she'd ever seen, along with sporting numerous stains as well, it would be less than the truth.

The reality of shopping at Marshall Field & Company was this—ladies shopped not only to purchase new items but to be seen in their finery. Enormous and well-decorated hats were a must, as were proper gloves, brooches, fine reticules, and even parasols, if it was overly sunny outside.

Unfortunately, the leather gloves Theodosia had taken off before she'd tried on the riding gloves were worn and cracked, and her hat, an outdated style that suggested Theodosia had purchased it at least five years prior, was missing a good deal of stitching and didn't sport so much as a single flower or feather on it.

Beatrix had no doubt that if she were to encourage Theodosia to mosey up to the second floor, that woman would soon find herself being scrutinized by the most snobby of saleswomen, even if they would greet her with a smile.

"How are you going to get a new riding habit if you don't purchase one here?" Norman asked, which earned him a scowl from Theodosia in return.

"I'll order one from a catalog, just like I order all of my clothing." Theodosia nodded to Beatrix. "I find the Montgomery Ward catalog to be very convenient, and they send the orders right to my house, which saves me the bother of shopping in a store."

"But how can you know that clothing will fit you properly?" Beatrix couldn't resist asking, having never ordered anything in her life from a catalog.

Theodosia shrugged. "I've never been one to bother much with that. I just hack off the hem with a knife if a garment arrives too long, or use pins if something's too large."

Norman's brow furrowed. "Why don't you use a needle and thread to hem your garments instead of hacking at them with a knife? Seems to me your method would cause the fabric to unravel."

"Have you ever hemmed any of your garments?" Theodosia tossed back at him.

"Of course not, but I'm a gentleman, and no one expects a gentleman to be proficient with a needle and thread."

"Unless you're a tailor," Beatrix said, which earned her an unexpected smile from Norman before he nodded to Theodosia.

"You about finished?"

Theodosia's nose shot into the air again. "I've barely begun."

It took a great deal of effort to swallow the laugh that was bubbling up her throat. Clearly Theodosia was still put out with Norman and was, if Beatrix wasn't much mistaken, prolonging her time at the glove counter as a way to punish him for all the annoyance the man had caused her that day.

"If you'd agree to tell Mr. Cabot you're unable to attend the ball with him, you could then abandon the glove counter, since you must know it doesn't matter to me if you wear old gloves while in my company," Norman said.

Theodosia's eyes flashed. "I'm not going to the ball with you, nor will I disappoint my father by changing my mind about attending the ball with Harvey Cabot."

"You don't even like Harvey."

"I don't dislike him, and he's an attractive gentleman, what with his dark hair, somewhat broad shoulders, and a gaze that seems to linger on me quite often." Theodosia smiled. "He told my father he finds me to be an intriguing lady, giving him hope that Harvey is soon to approach him about courting me."

"You don't want a man like Harvey courting you," Norman said firmly.

Realizing she was rapidly losing control of the situation, and because Mrs. Goodman was making yet another circle around the glove counter, Beatrix decided an intervention was desperately needed. "Perhaps, Mr. Nesbit, if you'd allowed Miss Robinson to know of your interest in her, she wouldn't have agreed to attend the ball with Mr. Cabot."

The squabble Norman and Theodosia had been in the midst of came to an abrupt end as the two of them burst into laughter, Theodosia laughing so hard that she came down with a case of the hiccups.

"What an amusing conclusion you've come to, Miss Waterbury," Theodosia said before she hiccupped again, exchanged grins with Norman, then hiccupped once more.

"Indeed," Norman agreed before he turned his grin on Beatrix, the unexpectedness of his grin causing her to lose her train of thought, until Norman continued speaking.

"As Theo stated before, we're acquaintances, and neither of us has any interest in changing our acquaintance status. But before you decide to launch into a full-blown argument about that, I believe I'll remove myself from your presence and go off to do a bit of shopping for myself." He consulted his notepad. "I need new collars, a few belts, some shirts, and if time permits, I might see about ordering a few jackets." He lifted his head. "Where might I find those in this monstrosity of a store?"

"You'll find the collars and belts in Men's Furnishings on the other side of this floor, while jackets may be found in Men's Clothing on the second floor."

"Wouldn't it make more sense if those two departments were located side by side on the same floor?"

"A valid point," Beatrix said. "But I suspect the reasoning behind the layout rests with having customers travel from one floor to another so that they may purchase items they'd not been intending to."

"An impressive marketing plan," Norman said before telling Theodosia to meet him in Men's Furnishings when she was done selecting gloves and then wandering away.

"I find I'm in no hurry to join him," Theodosia said after Norman disappeared from sight.

"Can't say I blame you for that. He can be trying at times."

Theodosia nodded before she frowned. "If I do wear the gown I always wear, what gloves would you recommend?"

"Depends on the cut and the color."

"It's got a high neck, long sleeves, and the color is, well, it was once a shade of ivory but it's somewhat yellow now."

"Are you certain you don't want to pay a visit to the second floor?"

"And be mocked by everyone up there? Thank you, but no."

Since Mrs. Goodman was making another circle, Beatrix held her tongue, fetched a pair of ivory gloves that had a hint of yellow in them, then proceeded to fetch ten additional pairs of gloves for her to try on after it became clear Theodosia really wasn't in a hurry to rejoin Norman.

While Theodosia tried on pair after pair of gloves, exclaiming over every pair she tried on, Beatrix had to excuse herself time and again to assist other customers. Thankfully, those customers knew exactly what they wanted, which meant Beatrix didn't need to spend an inordinate amount of time with any of them.

"I think all these should do it," Theodosia exclaimed as Beatrix sent young Bertie on his way to the delivery room with a package that needed to be delivered to a Mrs. Sterling's residence later that afternoon.

"You've made some nice choices," Beatrix said, looking over Theodosia's selections. "Now all that's left to do is for you to tell me how you'd like to pay for these, give me your address, and then I'll make certain your purchases are delivered to your house by late afternoon."

"I'm perfectly capable of carrying my gloves home with me."

"Then I'll wrap them up for you and you may take them with you."

"Why would ladies bother having their gloves delivered to their homes?"

"Most ladies stop by the glove department first, then venture into other areas of the store to continue on with their shopping. By the time they're done, they've usually acquired quite a few items."

"A logical explanation, but because I have no intention of any further shopping today, I'll take my gloves with me." Theodosia opened up a battered bag that was swinging from her wrist and pulled out a wad of bills.

"Good heavens, Miss Robinson, have a care. That's a great deal of money you're showing right now, and one can never know when unscrupulous types are lurking about."

"I'm not really the type to secure the interest of anyone, let alone unscrupulous types. People tend to give me a wide berth."

Having no good response to that, Beatrix tallied up Theodosia's purchases, took some of the cash Theodosia was still holding in her hand from her, then pushed the button for the cash boy. Thirty seconds later, a young boy by the name of Robert appeared at her counter, and after giving him the money and telling him how much change he needed to return to her, she nodded to the money Theodosia was still clutching in her hand.

"You should put that away now, even if you don't believe anyone would try to deprive you of it."

Theodosia stuffed the money back in her bag. "No one would deprive me of it because, again, no one ever notices me."

"Harvey Cabot has apparently noticed you," Norman said, striding up to join them. He raked a hand through his hair and nodded to Beatrix. "I need your help."

110

"More than you probably realize, but how exactly do you need my help now?"

"There are too many options for collars, and the salesman was less than helpful." Norman raked his hand through his hair again. "He was all but fawning over Mrs. John Hamline, who is married to Mr. Hamline, a broker and president of the Chicago Stock Exchange, information I obtained through listening to the salesman who was doing all that fawning."

"Since I've just finished with the gloves," Theo began, "I can help you select a few collars."

Norman frowned. "When was the last time you selected men's collars?"

"Well, never, but I'm sure it can't be that difficult."

Norman turned back to Beatrix. "While I have to admit I'm surprised by Theo's offer, I don't believe she's got the experience needed to assist me in picking out proper collars. I'd like you to come with me and pick out collars for me."

"I can't abandon my counter. I'll be dismissed for certain."

"I'll watch over the gloves for you," a woman said from behind her.

Turning, Beatrix discovered Miss Darlene Wheeler, who was responsible for the umbrella counter that was next to Beatrix's. "Won't Mrs. Goodman be upset with me if I leave my counter to you?"

Miss Wheeler waved that aside. "This gentleman evidently wants you to assist him in Men's Furnishings, so that's what I imagine Mrs. Goodman would want you to do." She walked to stand beside Beatrix behind the glove counter. "I've not had but three customers today since it's not raining. I'll be fine looking after your counter."

"Then it's settled," Norman said before Beatrix could summon up another protest. "Shall we?"

"I can't leave until the cash boy comes back with Miss Robinson's change, and I also need to finish packaging up her purchases because she wants to take the gloves with her instead of having them delivered."

Pulling out another piece of brown paper, Beatrix started wrapping the gloves, annoyance running freely when Norman began drumming his fingers on the counter.

"Stop that," she muttered.

"Stop what?" he asked.

"Making so much noise."

"I'm doing no such thing."

"Norman often fidgets when he's made to wait," Theodosia supplied, earning herself a grimace from Norman, although he did discontinue drumming his fingers against the counter.

Robert returned with Theodosia's change right as Beatrix finished tying a string around the package she'd assembled. After she handed it to Norman, who took it even though he was still throwing exasperated glances Theodosia's way, he jerked his head toward the aisle.

"*Now* are you ready to go?" he asked.

"You're very impatient," Beatrix said before she stepped out from behind the counter and nodded to Miss Wheeler. "I'll be right back."

"Take your time," Miss Wheeler said as Beatrix began making her way toward Men's Furnishings, Norman falling into step beside her while Theodosia trailed behind.

Even though Miss Wheeler had encouraged her to take her time, Beatrix knew taking her time with Norman could prove to be disastrous. The man was notorious for irritating her, which could very well provoke an argument between them, something that would certainly see her dismissed from her position. That meant her only course of action was to find the items Norman needed as quickly as possible and then send him on his way.

CHAPTER 13

"How many collars do you need?" Beatrix asked as she sailed down the aisle past a gleaming counter filled with buttons.

"No idea. How many collars do men normally purchase?"

"Depends on how many you still have at home and how many you go through in a given day."

Norman slowed his pace. "I don't normally go through many collars a day because I don't wear them when I'm working."

"But you're running low on them?" Beatrix pressed.

"Hard to say."

She stopped walking. "How can you not know how many collars you have?"

"Norman lives with his parents," Theodosia said, stopping by Norman's side. "He doesn't normally bother himself with trivial matters such as collars."

"Then why are you doing so today?" Beatrix asked.

Norman didn't bother to answer her. Instead, he frowned at Theodosia. "I don't live with my parents. I live in the carriage house behind their main house."

"You might as well live at the main house because that's where you take all your meals. Your mother also sends a maid to clean your apartment every day and has that maid collect your laundry,

which is then returned to your wardrobe after its been laundered."
Theodosia turned to Beatrix. "Norman's mother has always been
rather insistent about looking after him."

"Because he almost died after his horse accident?" Beatrix
asked.

Theodosia shot a look to Norman. "You told her about that?"

"Of course I did, what with how she was badgering me about
not properly riding the horse I was using to get away from the
train robbers."

Theodosia returned her attention to Beatrix. "You were badgering him?"

"*Badgering* isn't the word I would use to describe what I was
doing."

"Interrogating," Norman said with a nod. "That might be a
better word."

Beatrix resisted a smile. "Perhaps, but weren't we speaking about
your mother?"

Theodosia nodded before Norman could respond. "Indeed,
and I should probably clarify that she doesn't only dote on Norman because of his accident. She also dotes on him because she
believes his unusual mind is a gift from God, so she wants Norman
to make the most of that gift instead of concerning himself with
the more mundane realities of life."

Beatrix glanced to Norman. "And what do you think of your
mother's belief?"

He shrugged. "I had to get my unusual mind from somewhere,
didn't I?"

"But you're a man of science."

Norman smiled. "Ah, I see where you're going with this. You
wonder if I put much stock in matters of faith. And while there
are many men of science who don't believe in God, I don't happen
to be one of those."

He took Beatrix's arm, seemed to realize that wasn't the thing
to do since she was an employee and he was a customer, so he
released it and began heading across the store again, with her

walking beside him. "I've always thought it arrogant for anyone, especially men of science, to claim there is no God, for how can one explain the intricacies of life without God?"

"How *do* you explain the intricacies of life?"

"No idea. I'm of the belief that our minds are limited in that they can't grasp the full measure of God or how He created all the splendors of our world or how those splendors work. That's where faith comes in, something I struggle with at times since I enjoy being able to explain everything through mathematic equations or scientific experiments."

"I don't imagine there's a mathematical equation to prove the existence of God."

"Yet," he said with a smile, stopping directly in front of the Men's Furnishings department. He nodded to the two salesmen, who were both assisting fashionably dressed matrons, neither salesman giving him more than a cursory look.

"See, I told you I wasn't receiving good service here," Norman said.

"And while I could point out that your less-than-fashionable long hair might be partially to blame for their careless disregard, the Marshall Field's employee handbook explains on page five how employees are to treat every customer the same, no matter if that customer appears to be wealthy or not." With that, Beatrix surged into motion, locating the collar section with ease. Dismissing the paper collars with a wave of her hand when Norman lingered over one, telling him he deserved better, she moved to the linen collars, quickly selecting three different styles—the stand up, the wing-tipped, and the perry. Pulling twelve of each out of the drawers situated beneath the counter, she stacked them in a pile before gesturing for Norman to follow her to the belt section.

"How many belts do you need?"

The blank look on Norman's face was answer enough. Eyeing his waistline, she moved to the drawers where the stock was kept, pulled out three different styles in what she estimated to be Norman's size, then added those to the pile of collars.

"What else?" she asked.

Norman consulted his notepad. "I thought perhaps I should get a few pairs of half hose, as well as some, er . . ."

"Garters?" Beatrix finished for him, earning a nod from Norman in return.

"There's really nothing to be embarrassed about over purchasing garters, Norman—ah, I mean, Mr. Nesbit. It's not as if men's garters are thought of in the same way as ladies' garters."

"I could use some new garters," Theodosia said, causing Beatrix to jump because she'd not realized Theodosia was standing right behind her.

"Those will be found on the fifth floor," Beatrix told her.

Theodosia frowned. "Why wouldn't they be found here? Aren't they along the same lines as Men's Furnishings?"

"They're unmentionables, so they need to be treated as such," Beatrix said, earning another frown from Theodosia.

"I'll just purchase some in this department," she said a moment later, giving an airy wave of her hand.

Beatrix shook her head. "Men's garters and ladies' garters aren't interchangeable. Men's garters are secured below the knee, whereas ladies' garters are, ah, secured a bit higher up on the—"

"Thigh, yes, I know," Theodosia said. "But I rarely wear ladies' stockings. I prefer wearing men's half hose." She smiled. "Half hose is far more comfortable than stockings, and it's not as if anyone can see what I'm wearing since my skirts cover my legs."

"I did not need to know that about you," Norman muttered.

"It's not as if I've just disclosed something scandalous," Theodosia said before she nodded to Beatrix. "I could also use some new half hose too, so you might as well show me the selections you were going to show Norman."

Realizing it was hardly her place to tell Theodosia that words such as *leg* and *thigh* were to be avoided at all costs in mixed company, Beatrix surged into motion again, choosing garters for Norman and Theodosia, as well as a nice selection of half hosiery for both of them.

Dusting her hands together after she'd organized their purchases on a counter, she pulled out her sales pad.

"What's that for?" Norman asked.

"I need to tally up all of your purchases before you can move on to looking for jackets."

"Aren't you going to help me with those?"

"I can't go to that department with you. The upper floors are only for seasoned salesmen and saleswomen, a rank I've yet to achieve. Just tell them you're interested in Prince Albert jackets and they'll take it from there." Beatrix looked over the items and began tallying them.

"You don't need to do that," Norman said. "I've already totaled my purchases for you."

"I've totaled mine as well," Theodosia added.

Norman shook his head. "I totaled your half hose and garters in with my total."

"I don't want you to buy my garters for me. That could cause all sorts of talk."

"No one will know they're for you since they're men's garters," Norman argued before he nodded to Beatrix. "I'm paying for all of it, and the total is—"

"Perhaps you should write it down," Beatrix said before he could finish. "That way I can know if you're right after I total everything up as well."

Even though Norman looked as if he'd like to argue with that, he scribbled down a figure on his notepad, then began drumming his fingers on the counter as she went about the daunting task of adding a very long list of numbers on her notepad, lifting her head and glaring at him when she lost track of a column after he started humming under his breath.

"Stop it. You're distracting me."

He sent her an amused look. "You don't need to add up the purchases. I assure you, the total I came to is not wrong."

Refusing a sigh, she returned to her task, finishing up a full minute later. After she slid her bill of sale across the counter, Norman glanced over it, his only response being sliding the number he'd written down back to her.

Annoyance was swift when she realized his total did not match hers, being off by twenty-two cents, and unfortunately she had the sneaking suspicion she was the one in error.

Pulling the bill of sale away from him, she scratched out the total she'd written down, replaced it with his, then forced a smile. "And there we have it. Would you care to charge this to your account, or would you like to pay cash?"

"I don't know if I have credit here."

"Of course you do," Theodosia answered. "Your mother arranged it for you years ago after you came into your majority and gained access to the trust fund your grandfather set up for you."

"You have a trust fund?" Beatrix asked.

"I do, and I apparently have access to credit at Marshall Field's as well, but I'll pay cash today." He smiled. "Are you certain you don't want to tally up the total again?"

"And have you distract me from getting the proper number by humming again? I think not."

"I've never heard you hum before," Theodosia said, lifting her head and abandoning a half hose she'd been inspecting. "Are you feeling well?"

"I'm fine," Norman said firmly. "I'm a little fatigued, though, from all this shopping, so I believe I'll forego looking for jackets today."

"Then all that's left to do is tell me whether you'd like to take all this with you or have it delivered to your house, and if that's the case, you'll need to provide me with your address."

Norman got a rather odd look in his eyes. "Are you asking for my address because you're curious where I live?"

"Don't be ridiculous." She turned to Theodosia and smiled. "It's been a pleasure meeting you, Miss Robinson, and I do hope you'll have fun at that ball. I'm sure Mr. Harvey Cabot is a delightful gentleman, no matter that Mr. Nesbit believes otherwise."

Norman let out a grunt. "*Delightful* is not a word anyone would use to describe Harvey. He's been known to bore people to tears, and you mark my words, once Theo remembers that, she'll change her mind about going to the ball with me."

"Considering you almost had Pinkerton men drifting off to sleep when you waxed on and on about your electrical research, you're quite the pot calling the kettle black," Beatrix countered.

"Theo enjoys discussing electrical research with me, and that right there is why I know she'll enjoy attending the ball with me over Harvey." Norman nodded to Theo. "You know I'm right about that."

Theodosia shrugged. "You're right about me enjoying our electrical discussions, but I won't be changing my mind about the ball. I've made a promise to Mr. Cabot, and I intend to honor it."

"But if you don't go with me," Norman began, "I'll be subjected to the company of either Miss Paulina Dinneen or Miss Caroline Ashburn."

"Those ladies aren't your only options," Theodosia argued.

"They are according to my mother, and—ouch. Have a care, Theo. You just stepped on my foot."

"I did it on purpose."

"Why would you do that?"

"Because the answer to your problem is right in front of you, but you're being annoyingly obtuse, something that's quite unlike you and does suggest you're soon to come down with some dreadful illness."

"I'm not becoming ill, nor is the answer to my dilemma right in front of me," Norman argued, which had Theodosia rolling her eyes before she actually pointed to Beatrix.

"She's right there. In front of you. Miss Waterbury."

"Oh dear," Beatrix muttered as Norman's mouth opened, then closed, then opened again, as if he couldn't decide what reply he should voice regarding Theodosia's unexpected declaration.

Taking pity on the poor man, Beatrix summoned up another

smile. "There's no need to worry I'm going to take what Miss Robinson just blurted out as an invitation, Mr. Nesbit. And with that settled, I think it's time for you to pull out your billfold, pay for your new items, and then get on with your day."

Norman narrowed his eyes at Theodosia before he pulled out his billfold, counted out the exact amount he owed for his purchases, then pushed the money over the counter.

"I'll leave it to Theo to arrange for the delivery of my items." With that, he sent Beatrix a curt nod and stalked out of the department without another word.

"What have you done to him?" Theodosia demanded after Norman disappeared from sight.

"I'm not the one who did something to him," Beatrix countered. "That, Miss Robinson, falls directly on you." She pulled out sheets of brown paper and began wrapping up Norman's purchases, ringing for a delivery and cash boy when she was finished. She then wrote down Norman's address that Theodosia rattled off to her as she waited for the delivery boy to arrive.

"You might as well send my items to Norman's house," Theodosia said. "I'll just retrieve them later."

"Which will give you the perfect opportunity to apologize to him," Beatrix said, handing the address she'd just written down to the young boy who'd shown up by her side, an address she might have already memorized for some peculiar reason.

When the cash boy arrived next, Beatrix handed over the money Norman had given her to pay for his purchases and pretended not to notice the irritated looks one of the salesmen was sending her as she nodded to Theodosia.

"I think that does it for today," Beatrix said.

Instead of taking her leave, Theodosia frowned. "Why do you think I should apologize to Norman?"

"Because he's your friend and you just embarrassed him."

"We're not friends."

"You are."

"The term *friend* has always seemed frivolous to me."

"Being friends with a person is not frivolous. In fact, friendship is essential to living a happy life, but now is not the time to discuss this further. I need to return to my department, and you need to go after Norman."

"I don't know where he went."

Beatrix refused a sigh. "I'm going to assume you and Mr. Nesbit came to the store together, which means he's probably waiting for you outside the front door, unless he decided to abandon you and take a train home, but that doesn't really seem to me like something he'd do. He's an annoying man, no question about that, but he's a gentleman, and a gentleman wouldn't abandon a lady, no matter the embarrassment that lady caused him."

"I don't know how I could have embarrassed him."

"You'll have to ask him about that, then."

"It would be simpler all around if you'd just explain it to me."

Beatrix chanced a glance to the salesman who'd now moved up beside her, hardly encouraged when he sent her a scowl. Glancing back to Theodosia, Beatrix forced another smile. "I'm afraid I really do need to get back to my department, Miss Robinson. I've prevailed on Miss Wheeler's kind offer to watch over my counter for long enough. I will offer you a small bit of advice, though, since you seem at a loss for how to proceed with Mr. Nesbit. Ask him to explain why he's upset with you, but do know that it has been my experience with gentlemen that when they're embarrassed, it's best to get right down to begging their pardon. That should go far in soothing his offended sensibilities."

"Norman's never struck me as a gentleman possessed of sensibilities."

Beatrix opened her mouth, but before she could say a single word to that, a loud clearing of a throat drew her attention. Turning, she discovered Mrs. Goodman standing a few feet away from her, a look of outrage on her face.

Beatrix rapidly bid Theodosia a good day, which left Theodosia looking somewhat confused, probably because of the abrupt end to their interaction, and then she forced her feet to move in Mrs. Goodman's direction, knowing the conversation she was about to have with the woman was going to be anything other than pleasant.

CHAPTER 14

"Explain yourself," Mrs. Goodman demanded as she stormed down the aisle, Beatrix having no choice but to trot along beside the woman since, clearly, she was in trouble again.

"What would you like to know?" Beatrix asked as they turned a corner that led not to her glove counter but toward the elevator.

"I'd like to know what possessed you to leave your department and go traipsing off to Men's Furnishings with Mr. Nesbit. This isn't a marriage mart, Miss Waterbury, and we here at Marshall Field & Company expect our associates to know that."

Beatrix stopped walking, but since Mrs. Goodman didn't bother to slow her pace, she charged after the woman, who was now standing in front of the elevator.

"Mr. Nesbit wasn't here because he's interested in marrying me," Beatrix began, ignoring the sniff Mrs. Goodman gave to that explanation. "He was here to find collars but—"

The elevator door opened, Mrs. Goodman gestured her inside, then after telling the elevator operator to take them to the sixth floor, she nodded to Beatrix. "We're on our way to Mr. Selfridge's office."

"Wonderful," Beatrix muttered, earning another sniff from Mrs. Goodman, which she pretended she didn't hear.

As the elevator whooshed upward, Beatrix couldn't help but conclude that her experience as a working woman was quickly turning into a disaster. She never would have thought in a million years that maintaining a position as a salesgirl would be such a daunting feat.

She'd been trying her hardest to do an acceptable job, but at every turn she kept finding herself being taken to task for matters she didn't believe warranted such chastisement in the first place.

It was a rude awakening to see how working women were treated, and knowing that she was powerless to do anything about that situation because she was determined to keep her job, well, it was downright maddening.

"Sixth floor," the elevator operator intoned, bringing the elevator to a stop with a pull of a lever before he swung the grate open and gestured them out.

"This way, Miss Waterbury," Mrs. Goodman said, heading down a narrow hallway that had framed paintings of different renditions of Marshall Field buildings hanging on the walls. Beatrix paused in front of a painting of a building with flames shooting out the windows.

"That depicts the fire of 1871."

Turning, Beatrix discovered Mr. Selfridge standing a few feet away from her, smiling pleasantly, although his good humor was sure to fade the moment Mrs. Goodman informed him of Beatrix's latest transgressions.

Wanting to delay that nasty business for as long as possible, Beatrix nodded to the painting. "Marshall Field & Company burned down?"

"It did, and twice at that," Mr. Selfridge said. "The first time was during the Great Chicago Fire of 1871. Marshall Field & Company was known then as Field, Leiter, & Company, and it wasn't spared."

Mr. Selfridge gestured to another painting. "After the '71 fire, State Street was almost completely destroyed, which is why Mr. Field and Mr. Leiter moved into a temporary building well away from the destroyed parts of the city, but they eventually moved back to State Street in a new building that sat on land Mr. Potter Palmer sold to the Singer Sewing Machine Company. Singer paid Mr. Palmer three hundred and fifty thousand dollars for the land, then spent an additional seven hundred and fifty thousand dollars to build a five-story structure that possessed a giant glass dome in the center of its mansard roof." He nodded to the painting again. "That's it right there."

"Impressive."

"I'm sure it was, given that Singer was charging Mr. Field and Mr. Leiter seventy-five thousand dollars a year in rent." He gestured to another painting. "That one depicts the building that was used next after fire destroyed the second State Street store in 1877."

"I had no idea Marshall Field's suffered so many disasters."

Mr. Selfridge nodded. "I find it important for our employees to understand the store's history, as well as to understand the history between Mr. Field and Mr. Leiter. They were partners for years, but tensions eventually built up between them. Mr. Field finally convinced Mr. Leiter to sell out his shares in the business after they moved to the building we're currently in, and that's when Marshall Field & Company was born."

Beatrix frowned. "Did Mr. Leiter want to sell his shares?"

"Doubtful, but retail is a cutthroat business, Miss Waterbury. Only the strongest survive. But enough of the history lesson," Mr. Selfridge said. "You must have a reason for being on this floor. Dare I hope you've come to tell me you've made another spectacular sale today?"

"That's not why I've brought her to speak with you."

Mr. Selfridge turned. "Mrs. Goodman. I didn't see you standing there."

"I didn't want to interrupt you while you were instructing Miss Waterbury on the history of Marshall Field & Company."

Mr. Selfridge settled a knowing eye on Beatrix. "Have you been disclosing too much information about our products again, Miss Waterbury?"

"She abandoned her post to escort Mr. Norman Nesbit and his companion to Men's Furnishings," Mrs. Goodman said before Beatrix could respond. "Poor Miss Wheeler, a young woman who never causes me any trouble, was left with the difficult task of watching not only her counter, but Miss Waterbury's counter as well."

"Perhaps we should take this into my office," Mr. Selfridge said, any sign of the recently cheerful gentleman having disappeared a mere second after Mrs. Goodman's disclosure.

Having no choice but to follow Mr. Selfridge and Mrs. Goodman down the hall, Beatrix soon found herself in a well-appointed office with a deep mahogany desk that sat in front of two long windows. After gesturing to the chairs in front of the desk, Mr. Selfridge moved behind the desk and took a seat. Leaning back, he nodded to Mrs. Goodman. "I'm listening." That was all it took for Mrs. Goodman to launch into a long list of Beatrix's supposed transgressions, ending with, "And while Miss Wheeler was reluctant to disclose where Miss Waterbury was, she finally told me that Miss Waterbury had gone off with Mr. Nesbit to Men's Furnishings. Miss Wheeler did tell me that she'd encouraged Miss Waterbury to assist Mr. Nesbit, but I'm convinced Miss Wheeler was being gracious and trying to cover for—" She jerked her head Beatrix's way.

"Would you like to dispute anything Mrs. Goodman has told me so far?" Mr. Selfridge asked, settling his attention on Beatrix.

"I believe Mrs. Goodman has been accurate in her assessment of the situation, although I wasn't attempting to thumb my nose at protocol. I just wasn't familiar with what a salesgirl was expected to do in that particular—"

A knock on the door interrupted her right as Mr. Selfridge's secretary poked her head in. "Mr. Blair, supervisor of Men's Furnishings, needs to have a word with you, Mr. Selfridge."

"Tell him I'm in a meeting," Mr. Selfridge returned.

"He's here about Miss Waterbury."

Mr. Selfridge shot a look of disbelief to Beatrix. "You may

leave, Mrs. Goodman," he said. "And please send in Mr. Blair." He then settled back in his chair and stared at Beatrix as if he'd never encountered a salesgirl quite like her before.

After Mr. Blair took Mrs. Goodman's vacated seat beside Beatrix, not bothering to even acknowledge her, he launched into an account of everything Beatrix had done wrong, with the most grievous offense, at least according to Mr. Blair, being the fact that she'd taken away an impressive sale from one of his salesmen.

Having held her tongue throughout Mr. Blair's entire tirade, Beatrix finally had enough. Sitting forward, she caught Mr. Blair's eye. "The only reason Mr. Nesbit requested my assistance was because he'd been all but ignored by your salesmen when he went over to select some items while I assisted his companion with choosing gloves."

"Neither Mr. Foster nor Mr. Rice would ever ignore a customer," Mr. Blair said with a sniff.

"Come now, Mr. Blair. From what I was told, your salesmen were assisting matrons known to be of the society set. You know that even with Marshall Field & Company expecting their associates to cater to every customer, some do get neglected when there's more than one known wealthy customer in a department."

"That never happens."

"It does. You just don't want to admit that in front of Mr. Selfridge."

Mr. Blair began quivering with indignation. "You're impertinence is not helping your situation, Miss Waterbury."

"I'm sure you're right, but since you've leveled unfair charges against me, I believe I have no choice but to defend myself, although I wouldn't say I'm being impertinent, more along the lines of brutally honest."

Mr. Selfridge sat forward. "You may go, Mr. Blair."

Even though Mr. Blair looked as if he wanted to argue some more, he rose to his feet, nodded to Mr. Selfridge, then strode from the room without a second glance at Beatrix.

An uncomfortable silence filled the air until Mr. Selfridge blew out a breath. "Why do you believe Mr. Norman Nesbit, a gentleman who belongs to one of the wealthiest families in Chicago, was being ignored by the salesmen?"

"In my humble opinion, that might have been caused by Mr. Nesbit's appearance. His hair is much too long at the moment, something I explained to him when he asked me that same question, and I believe his slightly derelict appearance had the salesmen believing he wasn't a gentleman with deep pockets."

Mr. Selfridge blinked. "You told one of our customers his hair was too long?"

"He asked."

"How did he respond to your answer?"

"He wasn't upset, if that's your concern, because he seemed genuinely curious about why he'd been ignored."

"Were you able to assist him with purchasing everything he wanted in Men's Furnishings?"

"I was, and I'm sure you'll be interested to learn that it was another impressive sale."

Mr. Selfridge narrowed his eyes. "But it was a sale that was taken away from a salesman."

"Who was ignoring Mr. Nesbit."

"If you would have given the sale to one of the salesmen in that department, that would have defused any resentment they now feel toward you."

Beatrix's brows drew together. "Why would I have done that?"

"Because it would have allowed one of them to add an impressive sale to his books for the day."

"It allowed *me* to add an impressive sale to my book, but . . ." She stopped talking, took a second to organize thoughts that were scattering every which way, then nodded. "You put more importance on the sales the men make than the sales the women make, don't you?"

"That's not a secret, Miss Waterbury. The men who work at Marshall Field are more competitive because they're here to advance their careers. Women, on the other hand, usually take up employment so that they may contribute to household expenses. They often don't advance because we don't have many high-ranking positions that are suitable for women."

"Well, perhaps I'm determined to become a saleswoman instead of a measly salesgirl."

Mr. Selfridge's brows shot up to his hairline. "Did you just call your position *measly*?"

"Slip of the tongue."

"You should watch that tongue of yours, Miss Waterbury. It's bound to get you into trouble."

"Excellent advice."

Mr. Selfridge settled back into his chair. "I suppose all that's left to do now is figure out what to do with you."

"Something needs to be done with me?"

"You abandoned your post, Miss Waterbury, and then you took away a sale from a salesman. Yes, something needs to be done with you."

Beatrix sat forward. "In the store handbook, it says that Mr. Field demands that we employees *give the lady what she wants*."

"And your point would be?"

"Well, even though Mr. Nesbit is not a lady, I was giving him, a cherished customer, what he wanted—that being my assistance."

"True, this is true," Mr. Selfridge said slowly.

"And while I did leave my glove counter, I did so at the request of a customer. I then proceeded to give that customer exactly what he wanted, and I also sold him large quantities of those items." She nodded. "That customer wouldn't have purchased a single item if I'd not complied with his request, which means I see no reason for you to discipline me because I was, after all, only doing my job."

"You have to be disciplined. Two supervisors have taken time out of their busy day to complain to me about you."

"Then they should have spent their time reviewing the situation more thoroughly, because I was not being derelict in my duties."

Mr. Selfridge blew out a breath. "While you've presented a most compelling argument, I still have no choice but to take disciplinary action against you because if I don't, it'll cause all sorts of difficulties on the sales floor." He turned and stared out the window, turning back to Beatrix a moment later. "Here's what I'm going to do. I'm taking you out of the glove department and reassigning you to the coat check. In all honesty, I believe you'll enjoy the coat check because you only need to take whatever coat, jacket, shawl, hat, or item a customer may hand you, then give them a retrieval ticket in return."

"That doesn't seem like too harsh of a disciplinary action," Beatrix said slowly.

"It's not, although it will be a fifty-cent reduction in your weekly pay."

Heat traveled up her neck. "You're reducing my weekly pay? If you're unaware, I only make seven dollars a week as it is."

"You'll still be making six dollars and fifty cents a week, but if you don't accept the demotion, you'll be making nothing."

Beatrix had never felt so helpless in her life.

That she believed a demotion was uncalled for was not in question, but what was in question was what she was going to do next.

She was clearly at a crossroads.

Unlike the other employees, she didn't need the position. But if she balked at accepting the demotion, she was going to be dismissed, and that would mean she'd never learn where her current path might have led her, and she'd be failing at the first real challenge she'd ever been presented with in her privileged life.

She didn't want to be a failure, which meant she was going to have to accept the demotion and reduction in pay, even though doing so left her teeth on edge.

Managing a nod as she rose to her feet, she summoned up the smile Marshall Field & Company expected of their employees. "I'm sure I'll *adore* working in the coat check."

"See that you do," Mr. Selfridge said curtly. "Because if you're sent to my office again, I will dismiss you, make no mistake about that."

CHAPTER 15

Norman could no longer deny that his life had turned downright peculiar.

Gone were the days spent working on his inventions and scientific experiments without distractions, and unfortunately, he was beginning to believe returning to those distraction-free days was not something that was going to happen in the foreseeable future.

He'd been certain that once he parted ways with Beatrix after their ill-fated adventure, his life would return to normal. However, he'd not seemed capable of resisting seeking Beatrix out, even when he had to resort to convincing Theo to go with him to Marshall Field & Company.

It was a decision he was now regretting, what with how Theo had all but invited Beatrix to the ball for him. Not that the thought hadn't crossed his mind to invite Beatrix to attend the Potter Palmer affair with him, but what gentleman wanted someone else to speak for him?

"What in the world are the two of you doing?"

Blinking, Norman turned and discovered Beatrix bearing down on him as he stood beside Theo on the wooden sidewalk outside Marshall Field & Company. She was now wearing a fashionable hat that had blue and green feathers attached to it, those feathers waving back and forth as she marched toward him.

For some reason, her eyes were flashing with temper, and given that the jacket she was wearing wasn't properly buttoned, leaving it bunched up on one side, he got the distinct impression she'd been in a hurry to leave the store.

He pulled out his pocket watch and consulted it. "I thought the store didn't close until six."

She waved that aside. "Mr. Field allows his female employees to leave earlier than the men so that we, being of the fragile set, won't be making our way home in the dark."

"Generous of him."

Additional temper flashed through her eyes. "Hardly not when he also evidently believes women don't need to be paid as much as men, nor, apparently, does anyone at that store believe women deserve to be promoted to higher positions. That right there is why I was just taken to task because I did not turn the sale I made through your purchases over to one of the men in the furnishings department."

"The salesmen didn't assist me with my purchases."

"Well, indeed, but they certainly were quick to complain to their supervisor about me stealing sales from them."

Theo raised a hand to her throat. "You weren't fired because you helped Norman, were you?"

Beatrix shook her head. "I wasn't fired, although I was demoted to the coat check room, which results in a reduction in my weekly pay. And Mr. Selfridge informed me that if I'm sent to his office again, I'll be dismissed on the spot."

"I need to have a word with Mr. Selfridge," Norman said, striding into motion only to be pulled to a stop by Beatrix before he'd made it very far.

"I don't want you to have a word with Mr. Selfridge, although I thank you for the gesture."

"But you were demoted because of me."

"It was my decision to assist you even though I had the sneaking suspicion that leaving my counter wasn't going to be considered acceptable by management."

Norman frowned. "Didn't Mr. Selfridge speak with that saleswoman who offered to watch over your counter, the one who encouraged you to go with me to select collars?"

"Mrs. Goodman spoke with her, but even after Miss Wheeler rose to my defense, Mrs. Goodman chose to lay all the blame directly at my feet, probably because she seems to believe I'm trouble." She glanced at Theo, frowned, then looked back to him. "But enough about my problems. Why were the two of you just standing in the middle of the sidewalk, staring at each other?"

Norman shrugged. "I was waiting for Theo to say something first after she caught up with me."

Beatrix arched a brow at Theo. "May I dare hope that you've only recently caught up with Norman?"

"I found him about five minutes after I parted ways with you," Theo mumbled.

Beatrix flipped up the face of a dainty watch that was attached to a bracelet around her wrist. "You do realize that was over forty minutes ago, don't you?"

"Theo and I haven't been standing out here for forty minutes."

"We have," Theo countered. "But I thought you were staying silent so I'd know how annoyed you were with me over the business about Miss Waterbury going to the Palmer ball with you."

A dull throbbing took root in the back of Norman's head. It was becoming abundantly clear that his life wasn't simply peculiar of late; it was rapidly moving toward the chaotic. He didn't enjoy chaos, tried to avoid it whenever possible, but it seemed to be closing in on him, causing him to act in a very un-Norman-like way . . . ever since he'd met Beatrix.

Theo turned a scowl on Beatrix. "You *have* done something to him, haven't you?" she demanded, thrusting Norman directly back into the chaos.

Beatrix rolled her eyes. "Why do you keep asking me that? I already told you I've not done anything to Norman. If you'll recall, I mentioned that you were to blame for him abruptly leaving the store, while also telling you how to rectify that situation, something you've evidently not attempted to do yet."

"I couldn't seem to find the right words."

"Would you care to have me assist you with that?" Beatrix shot back.

Theo began dragging the toe of her shoe in the dirt on the sidewalk, the action causing a weight to settle in the pit of Norman's stomach.

He'd been acquainted with Theo for years, spent hours every week in her company, and . . . he knew her. Any experiment he was working on, she was by his side, handing him whatever tool he needed or lending him her advice when an experiment failed.

She was incredibly intelligent and more awkward than he was in social situations, but she always tried to be helpful.

Realization hit him square in the face.

Theo had not deliberately set out to embarrass him with Beatrix. She'd only been trying to spare him the unpleasantness of having to attend the ball with Miss Dinneen or Miss Ashburn. He'd done her a disservice by storming off in a huff as well as by refusing to speak to her once she'd rejoined him.

Grabbing Theo by the hand and all but dragging her closer to Norman, Beatrix then gave Norman a bit of a push as well until no more than a few inches separated him from Theo.

"You two are probably the most intelligent people I know," Beatrix surprised him by saying.

"Thank you," he said in unison with Theo.

"I wasn't finished."

"Of course you weren't," he muttered.

"Intelligence aside," she continued as if she hadn't heard him, "you're both incredibly dense when it comes to what most people consider common everyday occurrences, such as the situation you now find yourselves in."

"Did she just insult us again?" Theo asked.

"I think she did."

Theo's nose wrinkled. "I might be a touch deficient with social expectations as pertains to interactions with others, Miss Waterbury—"

"Beatrix," she corrected.

"Beatrix then, but—"

"And shall I call you Theodosia?" Beatrix interrupted.

Theo's mouth dropped open for a good few seconds before she smiled. "That would be lovely."

Beatrix returned the smile. "Wonderful, and you were saying?"

It took a full minute before Theo spoke again, one she evidently used to gather her thoughts, a very unusual occurrence for Theo if there ever was one.

"Ah yes, as I was about to say," Theo continued, her cheeks a little pink, "I may be deficient when it comes to interacting with others, but I was going to take your advice in regard to Norman. I just hadn't sufficiently composed what I wanted to say to him before you happened upon us."

Beatrix nodded. "Perfectly understandable, but may I dare hope that you're ready now?"

Theo gave a jerk of her head and turned to him. "I'm sorry if I embarrassed you before with Beatrix. That was not my intention. I was merely trying to . . . ah . . ."

"Make it possible for me to attend the ball without Miss Dinneen or Miss Ashburn as my guest?" Norman finished for her when Theo faltered.

"Exactly."

"I just recently came to that conclusion as well, but allow me to extend an apology to you. It was not well done of me to storm off like that."

"I'd embarrassed you."

"You did, but I'm afraid I overreacted."

Theo inclined her head as the comfortable silence he was accustomed to whenever he was in her company settled around them, until Beatrix opened her mouth.

"Don't the two of you feel so much better?" she said cheerfully.

"And see, that wasn't very difficult at all, and now the two of you will be better prepared the next time you suffer a spat, something that friends occasionally suffer."

Norman frowned. "As has been mentioned before, by both of us, Theo and I aren't friends."

Beatrix released a snort. "Of course you are. One doesn't normally ask an acquaintance to participate in a shopping expedition, but here both of you are, standing outside Marshall Field & Company after spending time in each other's company while *shopping*. Furthermore—"

"There's a furthermore?" Theo interrupted.

"There's always a furthermore," Beatrix said.

"And while I'm sure you'd love to launch into what that furthermore entails," Norman hurried to say before Beatrix could continue, "I'd like to return the conversation to something I believe is more important, that being the reduction in pay you mentioned earlier. You never said how much of a reduction you're going to take."

"That's hardly more important than what I was going to say, but if you must know, fifty cents a week."

"I suppose that's not too extreme," Norman said slowly.

"It is when you were only making seven dollars a week to begin with."

Norman blinked. "Forgive me, but did you say seven dollars . . . a week?"

"I did."

"I feel a distinct urge to run down Mr. Marshall Field and have a nice chat with him. And before you argue with me about that, you should know that I live near Mr. Field on Prairie Avenue. Given the extravagance of his home, he's certainly capable of paying his employees more."

"I'm sure he is capable of paying more, but I don't want you to seek him out. Besides, he's not at the store today. I heard he's spending his time over at the dry goods warehouse on Madison and Market."

"Then that's where I'm heading," Norman said before he took off, pretending he didn't hear Beatrix's protests.

Striding around a group of ladies wearing enormous hats, he headed down the sidewalk, intent on getting to Madison and Market as quickly as possible.

A hand on his arm had him slowing his pace right as he got to the corner of the Marshall Field & Company building.

"You really can't run down Mr. Field to have a chat with him," Beatrix argued, her hand tightening on his sleeve. "He won't appreciate your interference in what is really only a small matter of one of his employees being disciplined for leaving her department."

He ignored that as he looked to the left and then to the right, coming to a complete stop when the traffic rumbling past him on State Street made it all but impossible to cross the street. "But Mr. Field is, without question, paying you too little."

"He pays all his female employees too little, but that's an accepted practice, at least from what I've been told, because working women enjoy the reputation that comes with being an employee at Marshall Field & Company."

"But you're being required to accept a decrease in what is already an unacceptable wage to begin with. Aren't you concerned that the decrease is going to leave you in an uncomfortable financial situation?"

"A loss of fifty cents a week will not ruin me financially."

Norman frowned. "But you're making very little as it is, and—"

The rest of what Norman wanted to say was interrupted when a man stumbled into him, which had him stumbling into Beatrix, which sent her careening into the street, right in front of a large delivery wagon.

CHAPTER 16

Norman felt someone grab him around the waist, but unfortunately that action did not break his fall. Instead, it got him to the ground more rapidly, which lost him the opportunity of getting to Beatrix.

Thankfully, Theo rushed past him and hauled Beatrix out of the path of the delivery wagon just in the nick of time.

Getting to his feet, he strode to Beatrix, looking her over with a sharp eye.

"Were you injured?"

She shook her head, her attention directed over his shoulder. "Where'd he go?"

"Where'd who go?"

"The man who pushed you."

Norman frowned. "No one pushed me."

Theo jerked her head toward a man who'd all but flown past them, his bowler hat bobbing through the crowd of people. "I think your Pinkerton man believes otherwise."

"I thought after the chat I had with Agent Cochran earlier that the Pinkerton men would let me know when they were trailing after me, but apparently I was wrong about that," Norman said slowly, squinting after the man who was, indeed, one of the Pinkerton men his mother had hired.

"And here I thought you were simply pretending not to notice him," Theo said, eyeing him suspiciously. "It's concerning, your behavior, but now is not the time to discuss it." She turned to Beatrix. "Are you certain you weren't injured? I was rather rough when I grabbed you."

"And thank goodness you did," Beatrix said, dusting off her skirt. "I would have been trampled for certain without your intervention. But let's get out of this crowd. I can't think with all these people swarming around us."

"I have a better idea," Norman said. "I'm of the belief that a nice cup of tea, paired with an even nicer meal, does wonders for clearing a person's head." He offered an arm to Beatrix, then offered his other to Theo. "Shall we repair to Kinsley's? It's only a few blocks away."

"Oh, I adore Kinsley's," Theo exclaimed, tugging him into motion as she nodded to Beatrix. "They serve the most delicious oysters there, and I must admit that I'm ravenous because Norman and I neglected to eat any lunch today." With that, she increased her pace, practically dragging him and Beatrix down the sidewalk.

It took all of ten minutes to get to Kinsley's, a well-established restaurant that offered different amenities on different floors. A guest could dine in the lunchroom or adjacent restaurant on the first floor, enjoy a meal at one of the two cafés located on the second floor, although one of those cafés was strictly for men, or reserve a private dining room on the upper levels.

"It's charming," Beatrix said, stopping to admire the striped awnings that covered the entrance door.

"Wait until you taste the food," Norman returned, heading after Theo, who'd already walked into the restaurant and was speaking with the maître d'. He gestured for them to follow him as he took them to the lunchroom and gave them a table by the window.

After holding Beatrix's chair for her, Norman went to do the same with Theo, but she was already seated. "I was going to help you."

"You usually don't bother to assist me into my chair."

"I've held your chair for you at numerous society events," he said, taking his seat.

"Which is expected because those are society events." Theo gestured around the room. "This is just enjoying a quick bite to eat, and you've never held my chair for me when we take time out of our day to eat."

Norman frowned. "Why have you never pointed that out to me before?"

"Because that would have reminded you that I'm not a gentleman."

"I'm well aware you're not a gentleman, Theo."

Theo shrugged. "Perhaps, but because you seem to hold women in less-than-high regard, at least as it pertains to their intellectual abilities, I didn't want to take the chance that you'd dwell overly much on my being a lady. That might have eventually led to me being deprived of the scientific research I enjoy."

"I hold your intellectual abilities in very high regard and value your input too much to ever want to discontinue our association."

Theo began blinking rapidly, but before he could ask her if she'd gotten something in her eye, a server appeared directly beside her, handing her a menu that she promptly disappeared behind.

Beatrix received a menu next, but she set it aside and nodded to Norman. "You may order for me."

"I don't know you well enough to know what foods you enjoy."

"But that's what will make this more of an adventure. I may be pleasantly surprised by a dish I've never tried before."

"Or you could be rendered nauseous if Norman chooses poorly," Theo said, peering over the top of her menu.

"Which will only add to the sense of adventure," Beatrix returned with a grin.

The sight of her grin had Norman's thoughts turning somewhat muddled, but thankfully Theo launched into telling the server what she was going to order, that being oysters and fresh bread. By the time the server turned to him, his thoughts had returned to relatively fine form, which allowed him to order exactly what Theo had ordered, but choosing chicken stew and salad for Beatrix, deciding it was the safest choice and shouldn't render her ill, even if it wasn't the most adventurous of meals.

Once they'd been served tea and coffee, Beatrix took a sip, then set aside her cup.

"Now that I can think clearly again, I'd like to return to the near disaster we almost suffered. I've been wondering if we might have been the intended victims of a pickpocket."

"I did feel someone grab me around the waist," Norman said slowly. "I just assumed that someone was trying to halt my descent to the ground."

"Pickpockets are normally more stealthy than that, having practiced their trade to where their victim doesn't feel a thing," Beatrix said.

"How would you know that?"

"I often travel to Five Points in New York, where many a pickpocket has tried to relieve me of my valuables."

Norman frowned. "What do you do in Five Points?"

"This and that," she said, which was hardly helpful, but before Norman could voice a complaint about her less-than-informative response, she continued. "If you weren't the intended victim of a pickpocket, though, I have to wonder if our accident was another attempt to part you from your research."

Norman took a sip of tea. "As I've said more than once, there's little likelihood the culprit now in possession of the faulty yet remarkably complex research has realized my duplicity."

Beatrix opened her mouth, but before she could voice what was undoubtedly going to be an argument on her part, the server returned. That server then went about placing small plates and slices of bread in front of everyone before he bowed and walked away.

Beatrix buttered a piece of her bread, took a bite, and sighed.

"Ah, delicious," she said before she smiled at Theo. "Because Norman is obviously reluctant to entertain the idea that someone could still be after his papers, allow me to change the subject so we won't spend our meal bickering. Tell me about the research you enjoy."

Theo immediately looked delighted, probably because no one usually bothered to ask her many questions. While Theo launched into a discussion about chemicals and chemistry, her science of choice, Norman watched as she became more and more animated, that animation increasing with every question Beatrix asked her.

Five minutes later, Theo abruptly stopped talking and frowned. "I once overheard a society lady state that a person should never monopolize the conversation, something I'm certainly doing. So enough about me. Tell me more about Marshall Field & Company. What time do you arrive for work in the morning?"

"We're expected to be at work a half hour before the store opens, which means I get there at seven thirty, and then leave between four and five."

"That's a lot of hours of work to only get paid what amounts to pennies more than a dollar a day," Theo pointed out.

Norman set aside his cup and nodded to Beatrix. "You're definitely earning a less-than-acceptable wage."

"I'm in full agreement with that, but there are relatively few positions available to women in respectable establishments, which allows those establishments to pay their workers so poorly."

"You can always come work for me," Norman said, refusing to wince when he realized he'd just made a most impulsive offer, one that was quite unlike him to make.

Theo immediately choked on the sip of coffee she'd taken while Beatrix stared back at him, her mouth slightly agape.

Taking a second to butter his bread, as well as to think through the implications of what he'd just said, Norman felt an unusual surge of anticipation flow through him.

That he'd not had any intention of offering Beatrix a job was not in question, but oddly enough, now that he considered the matter, it held a great deal of appeal.

He'd been worried about her for days, but if she worked for him, he'd be able to keep an eye on her, which would then allow him to return to his work without the distraction his worrying had caused.

"What type of work could Beatrix do for you?" Theo asked, drawing his attention.

Norman shrugged. "I could use an assistant."

Beatrix blotted her lips with her napkin, then sent him a smile that was filled with genuine warmth, one that left him feeling somewhat addled, which was not a feeling he was accustomed to in the least.

"You're a far more complicated gentleman than I gave you credit for at first," Beatrix began, "and while your offer of employment may be one of the nicest offers I've ever received, I'm afraid I can't accept it."

"Why not?"

"Because I don't know the least little thing about inventions or scientific studies. I also have this propensity for landing myself in the most unusual circumstances, which could prove detrimental to your research." She smiled. "You and Theodosia are seasoned scientists, and yet you still managed to blow something up that caused Theodosia to lose a good bit of her hair. The last thing you need is an assistant with no understanding of science, because, I assure you, I'd be more of a hindrance than a help. With that said, though, let me repeat that I do appreciate the offer even though I can't take you up on it." With that, Beatrix sent him another smile right as the server returned with their meals.

As they ate, their conversation turned to sights Beatrix wanted to see around Chicago, which was a surprisingly pleasant way to spend a meal, and before Norman knew it, dessert was being brought to the table—chocolate cake for him and Beatrix and apple pie for Theo.

"Would you look at all those women walking past the window,"

Theo said, setting down her fork. "They're wearing turbans on their heads, all of them in different colors."

Beatrix swiveled around in her chair. "Oh dear. That's Aunt Gladys and some of the women who live at her house. I completely forgot I was supposed to meet her after work because I'm attending a meeting with her this evening. I'll be right back." With that, Beatrix dashed away, still clutching her napkin in her hand.

"Have you ever met Miss Gladys Huttleston before?" Norman asked.

Theo took another bite of pie and shook her head. "Haven't had the pleasure, but . . ." She lowered her fork. "I think that's about to change, because if I'm not mistaken, Beatrix seems to be bringing her aunt to join us."

CHAPTER 17

Norman rose to his feet as Gladys Huttleston bustled into the restaurant. She immediately took charge of the situation by telling the server the women with her would sit at the table adjacent to where Norman was sitting, while she would be joining her niece at Norman's table.

Giving her turban a pat, Gladys settled her gaze on him and smiled. "Ah, Norman, fancy *running* into you again, and in the company of my niece."

Clearly Edgar had not been the only one to witness his sprints past the Huttleston house.

Taking the hand Gladys thrust at him, he placed a kiss on it, then helped her into a chair. After she was settled, he moved to the table where five other turban-wearing women were standing, helping each of them into their respective chairs, which earned him smiles all around, and a batting of eyelashes from Mamie, the woman who'd flirted outrageously with him when he'd delivered Beatrix to Gladys's house what seemed like a lifetime ago.

He didn't hesitate to return to his seat beside Gladys, who barely waited until he sat down before she began peppering him with questions.

"How is it, Mr. Nesbit, that you're currently enjoying a meal with my niece? Did you just *happen* upon her as she left Marshall Field & Company?"

Norman wasn't certain, but he thought Gladys might have sent him the merest hint of a wink.

He resisted a groan, but before he could answer her question, Theo sat forward, setting aside her fork.

"Norman and I were shopping at Marshall Field & Company because I needed new gloves," Theo surprised him by saying, although she might have immediately regretted speaking up when Miss Huttleston raised a monocle that was dangling on a chain around her neck, taking a moment to look Theo up and down before she nodded.

"Miss Theodosia Robinson, I don't believe we've ever been properly introduced." Gladys sent him a pointed look.

"Quite right," he hurried to say. "Miss Huttleston, this is an associate—"

"Friend," Beatrix corrected under her breath.

"Quite right again," he muttered. "As I was saying, this is my friend Miss Theo—or rather, Theodosia Robinson." He turned to Theo. "Theodosia, this is Miss Gladys Huttleston, Beatrix's aunt."

"You must call me Gladys, my dear," Gladys all but boomed, leaning over Norman to thrust a hand at Theo, who took it somewhat warily, giving it a bit of a shake, which seemed to satisfy Gladys because she withdrew her hand and set her gaze on him. "You must call me Gladys as well, Norman. No sense keeping it formal, what with how you seem to be friends—or at least I hope so—with my niece." She smiled fondly at Beatrix. "Poor Beatrix needs some friends here in the city, and I'd be much obliged if you'd step into that role." She nodded to Theo. "You too, Theodosia, but tell me, dear, what happened to your hair?"

Theo raised a hand to the hair in question. "I'm afraid an experiment Norman and I were trying went horribly wrong, as in it blew up and singed off half my hair in the process."

To Norman's confusion, Gladys's eyes began to sparkle right before she turned and waved to one of the women sitting nearby.

"Did you hear that, Blanche? Theodosia has burned off part of her hair. That will make her an excellent candidate for your new product."

Blanche, a woman wearing a turquoise turban, jumped out of her chair and hurried toward them, a distinct bounce in her step. She stopped directly in front of Theo, reached out a hand without a by-your-leave, and began inspecting Theo's chopped-off hair, smiling in satisfaction a moment later.

"I've never seen hair in this state before." Blanche bit her lip. "It'll be tricky, but I believe I can fix it. Might have to shape it up a touch to get rid of the worst of the brittle parts, but I shouldn't have to take more than an inch off."

Theo blinked. "I don't know if I'm willing to cut off any more of my hair, not with how much I've already parted with, and—"

"Best leave this to an expert," Gladys interrupted before she turned and nodded to a woman wearing a purple turban. "Della, do we have any available time this week to work Theodosia into our schedule?"

"Oh, I don't believe there's any need for that," Theo said weakly, a protest Gladys ignored as she kept her attention on Della, who was now rummaging around in a large bag she'd set by her feet, pulling out sheets of paper. She riffled through them and frowned.

"Tonight's out, as we're on our way to attend a lecture held by the Cook County Suffrage Association." She moved to another page. "Tomorrow's out as well because you have a Chicago Woman's Club meeting, followed by dinner at Mrs. Doggett's home." She considered the pages for a moment. "Saturday night you're scheduled to go to McVicker's Theater, and then Sunday isn't feasible either because we have church, and then we're taking a picnic lunch over to Mrs. Hanford in the hopes of raising her spirits after that nasty business of her daughter running off with that bounder who—" She stopped talking and shot a guilty look to Gladys. "Sorry about that. I included that tidbit in the notes I typed up, but that was for my personal benefit so I wouldn't forget to be solicitous of Mrs. Hanford's tender sensibilities."

Gladys inclined her head. "A prudent decision because Mrs. Hanford is still overwrought, but returning to the schedule?"

"Right," Della said, returning to the pages. A full minute passed before she lifted her head. "The Saturday after next is free. The only event scheduled is a seven-course dinner at home where Roberta and Susan are going to try to impress us with their culinary skills."

"Ah, marvelous," Gladys said, nodding to Theo. "Dare I hope you have no plans for Saturday after next?"

Theo shook her head rather reluctantly. "I don't believe so."

"No engagements with a young gentleman scheduled?" Gladys pressed.

"I don't normally have engagements with gentlemen," Theo mumbled. "Nor do I have a need of a schedule to keep track of those, due to the limited number of invitations I receive over a Season."

Norman frowned. "That's not true. You often accompany me to social events, and you do have a scheduled engagement in a few weeks with a young gentleman since you're attending the Palmer ball with Harvey Cabot."

"Harvey Cabot?" Gladys exclaimed before Theo could respond, the loudness of her voice drawing the attention of several diners. "Surely not, Theodosia. Why, he's not suitable for you in the least. You'd be much better off going with Norman since the two of you seem quite comfortable in each other's company."

"I'm not going with Norman," Theo said firmly. "I've already promised Mr. Cabot I'll go with him, and he's really not an unsuitable gentleman for me to attend a ball with. Why, when he came to ask me to go to the ball with him, he was ever so charming and even brought me a bouquet of flowers."

Norman's brow furrowed. "You never mentioned anything about flowers."

Theo lifted her chin. "Now I have." She turned back to Gladys. "But Mr. Cabot aside, I do not have plans on the Saturday after next, but—"

"Then it's settled," Gladys said before Theo could finish what was clearly going to be a protest on her part. "We'll expect you at the house at . . . shall we say six? That'll allow you to enjoy what I know will be a most exciting meal before Blanche attacks your hair."

A tinge of pink began to stain Theo's cheeks. "The meals at your home can be considered exciting?"

"The last time Roberta and Susan fixed a dinner," Blanche said, "they tried to light a sauce on fire, but it caused an explosion and food went everywhere."

The trepidation residing in Theo's eyes disappeared, replaced with curiosity. "Did they include too much alcohol in the sauce, or was extreme heat to blame for the explosion?"

"You'll be able to ask Roberta and Susan those very questions when you join us for dinner," Gladys said with a nod, which sent her turban listing to the left. Pushing it back into place, she settled a smile on Theo, who was now staring at the turban, blatant curiosity in her eyes. "Is something amiss, dear?"

"I was merely wondering why all of you are wearing turbans."

Gladys gave her turban a pat. "Oh, well, that's easily explained, and is all due to—"

Blanche suddenly interrupted her by clearing her throat in a very dramatic fashion.

Gladys frowned. "Whatever is the matter with you, Blanche?"

Blanche jerked her head in Theo's direction. "Do you believe it wise to go into the turban business, what with how I'm soon to get an opportunity to test out my new product on Theodosia?"

"Ah yes, quite right" was all Gladys said to that before she turned to Norman. "Because you're apparently not going with Theodosia to the Palmer ball, may I be so forward as to inquire who you'll be taking instead?"

Norman shifted in his chair. "Weren't we just talking about turbans?"

Gladys gave an airy wave of her hand, sending her many bracelets jangling. "Not much else to say about those except that we feel they're very fashionable and are hopeful this particular trend will catch on soon." Her gaze sharpened. "Returning once again to the ball, who are you escorting?"

"Ah . . ." Norman began.

"His mother believes he should take Miss Pauline Dinneen or Miss Caroline Ashburn," Theo said, finishing for him when he continued to sputter.

"That will never do," Gladys declared. "Those two ladies, while charming and the perfect pictures of decorum, will bore you to tears." She nodded. "You'll take Beatrix."

Beatrix sent her aunt a scowl. "You can't order Norman to escort me to the ball. Besides, what if he doesn't want to take me?"

Gladys quirked a brow in his direction, which had him swallowing and turning his attention Beatrix's way.

"I wouldn't, ah, mind taking you to the ball."

Gladys laughed even as she patted his arm. "How marvelous, Norman, although I do believe I'll need to fit you into my schedule as well because you could certainly use a bit of help regarding how best to secure a lady's agreement to attend an event with you."

"I never said I'd go to the ball with him," Beatrix said, which, oddly enough, caused his stomach to lurch.

"Of course you will," Gladys contradicted. "Ladies enjoy having an opportunity to dance, and I know you're no exception to that." She smiled. "Now, mind your manners and tell Norman you'd be delighted to attend the ball with him."

Beatrix threw up her hands. "Fine, I'll go to the ball with you, Norman." She shot a look to her aunt. "Happy now?"

"Ecstatic."

Unexpected relief slid through Norman until a troubling thought struck. "Will I be escorting you to the Palmers' ball as well, Gladys?"

"Don't be ridiculous," Gladys said. "Edgar will be accompanying me."

"Your butler?" Norman asked.

"Indeed. And now, with all of that settled, I'm in desperate need of some tea and cake."

The next thirty minutes were some of the most unusual minutes

Norman had ever passed, probably because he'd never been in the company of such unusual women before.

The conversation swirling between the two tables was what one could only describe as rousing. Gladys and her band of turban-wearing women first launched into a discussion about politics, which he always thought was a subject one shouldn't discuss in company, given the animosity such a topic could bring out in people. They then began an earnest debate about the labor unions and how those unions were attempting to secure better hours and working conditions for the laborers. After that, Mamie broached the subject of bustles, which again, he'd thought was a subject that women never broached while in mixed company. However, because Theo sat forward and was listening intently to every word uttered about bustles, he sat back in his chair and didn't lodge a complaint, learning more than he ever thought he would about the subject.

After Gladys and the women polished off most of their tea, coffee, and cakes, Blanche abandoned her table and pulled up a chair right beside Theo, where she immediately started inspecting Theo's hair again.

Theo, after sending Blanche a startled look, began trying her best to ignore Blanche's attention, resetting her attention on the women sitting at the other table, who were now earnestly discussing the best theaters in Chicago to see a show, but at a reasonable price. Norman couldn't help noticing the clear longing in Theo's eyes as she watched the other women interact, although what she was longing for, Norman couldn't say.

"Good heavens, would you look at the time," Gladys exclaimed after she'd pulled out a gentleman's pocket watch. "We're going to be late." She returned the watch to her reticule, blotted her lips with her napkin, set the napkin aside, then clapped her hands, drawing everyone's attention. "Ladies, we must take our leave." She then gestured to one of the servers, who immediately stepped up to their table.

"The check, if you please," she told the man.

"My treat," Norman said, nodding to the server. "You may bring me the check."

Gladys nodded in approval as he helped her from her chair. "You are a surprisingly delightful man, and I certainly hope I'll see you running through Hyde Park again."

"You've been running in Hyde Park?" Beatrix asked, moving closer to him, so close in fact that a hint of her perfume drifted to him, a scent he found most compelling.

"Norman enjoys trying new places to run so that he doesn't become bored with his chosen method of keeping himself in fine form," Theo said for him, earning his eternal gratitude when he realized he'd allowed Beatrix's perfume to render him all but mute.

"Seems to be working for him since his form is very fine indeed," Mamie said, which earned her a roll of the eyes from Gladys, who then bid him a hasty good-bye before she hustled Mamie out of the restaurant. The rest of the women followed quickly behind.

"Do let me know if you hear anything of interest from the Pinkerton man," Beatrix said, a statement that left him wincing because he'd forgotten all about the near disaster they'd experienced.

"We'll be certain to do that," Theo said briskly as Beatrix nodded, bid them a good evening, then hurried to catch up with her aunt.

Retaking his seat because he'd yet to settle their bill, Norman ran a hand over his face. "This has been a very interesting afternoon."

Theo didn't hesitate to nod, her gaze settled on Gladys, who was now bustling past the restaurant window, her pink turban bobbing. "I have the uncanny feeling that I'm soon to find myself taken in hand by Gladys Huttleston."

Norman grinned. "I'm afraid you might be right about that, although if it makes you feel better, she seems to want to take me in hand as well."

Theo turned from the window. "Too right she does. She effectively maneuvered you into agreeing to take Beatrix to the ball with relatively little protest on either your or Beatrix's part."

Heat crept up his neck. "I couldn't very well have refused to take her, not with how you first extended her an invitation on my behalf earlier. Then, with Gladys all but insisting I escort Beatrix to the ball—"

"You're fond of her."

"Gladys is an acceptable sort."

"Not Gladys," Theo said. "Beatrix. You hold her in some type of affection, and now I understand why you insisted we visit Marshall Field & Company today. I am, however, still confused about how you knew Beatrix was working at the store, unless you've actually taken to running in Hyde Park as an attempt to encounter Beatrix by happenstance, or to learn her daily schedule."

Norman's first impulse was to deny everything, but he pushed that impulse aside because . . . he *was* fond of Beatrix. He found her fascinating, more fascinating than he found electrical circuits at the moment, a notion that should have been incredibly disturbing but wasn't for some unfathomable reason.

"I suppose I'm rather fond of her, at that," he finally admitted. "And while you're certainly going to find this surprising, I feel compelled to admit to you that I have been running around Hyde Park in the hopes of checking on her."

Theo's eyes crinkled at the corners. "Well, thank goodness you've decided to admit that to me. Here I've been growing more and more concerned about your odder-than-usual behavior, but now I understand the reason behind it." She considered him for a long moment before she gave a decisive nod of her head. "You're going to need some help."

"With what?"

"Wooing her."

"I didn't say anything about wanting to woo Beatrix, and do people even call it wooing anymore?"

"No idea. I'm not exactly up to date on matters like that." Theo's nose wrinkled. "But even if you're not intending on wooing her, you admitted you hold her in affection, so I have to imagine you'd like her to hold you in some type of affection as well."

"You don't believe Beatrix is fond of me?"

"Well, she might be, but it's difficult to say for certain, what with how annoyed she seems to be with you at times."

"I do have a tendency to annoy her."

Theo lapsed into silence as the server returned with the bill. After settling the bill, Norman tucked his billfold away right as Theo sat forward.

"We need to go to the bookshop, and if they don't have what we need, we'll need to go to the library."

"Why?"

"Because I believe the first order of business is to get Beatrix less annoyed with you. There must be books printed on that subject, and they may very well lend some insight into steps you can take to have Beatrix return your affection."

"I doubt there are any books that can give advice about that."

"Sure there are," Theo argued. "There's an entire section at the bookshop dedicated to etiquette books, after all, and I'm certain that mixed in there are suggestions about how to win the affections of a lady." She smiled. "We simply need to look at this like any other experiment we've done. We'll try out different theories until we land on one that has Beatrix becoming less annoyed and more charmed by you."

"Charmed might be wishful thinking on your part."

"I'm sure you have charm in you, although it must be buried somewhere deep down inside."

"I don't know, Theo . . . dosia." He winced. "There I go again, addressing you as Theo, which suggests I'm incapable of charm since you've made it clear you prefer Theodosia over Theo."

She smiled. "I don't actually mind it when *you* call me Theo, and I have to imagine it would be difficult for you to change now, what with how long we've known each other."

"Well, that right there shows that *you* are certainly capable of being charming as well as gracious, but I'm going to make a concerted effort to be more mindful about what you like and don't like in the future. I'm afraid I've been sadly remiss with that over the years, and for that, I do beg your pardon."

She began blinking rapidly, taking a second to dash her napkin over her eyes.

"Are you all right?" he asked slowly. "Got something in your eye?"

"I'm fine," she said, abandoning her napkin. "Do you realize that this is the first time in our long acquaintance that we've actually exchanged personal tidbits?"

Norman's lips curved. "So it is, but I could have done without learning that you prefer men's garters and half hose over more, ah, feminine articles of clothing."

Theo grinned. "The look on your face was priceless. I know I shouldn't have said that about the garters, but I just couldn't resist."

"You're very odd."

"As are you, which is why I imagine we really *are* friends, aren't we?"

"I imagine we are at that," Norman agreed, rising from his chair, then helping Theo out of hers. Taking her arm, he noticed that her eyes were suspiciously bright, and this time he knew without a doubt that it was not because she'd gotten something in them.

Giving her arm a pat, he walked with Theo out of the restaurant, feeling quite as if his world had changed yet again, but he found that this time it didn't bother him in the least.

CHAPTER 18

Beatrix opened her eyes and barely managed to swallow a shriek when the first thing her gaze encountered was a black creature staring down at her, its eyes glittering in the dimness of the room.

That creature, or rather the oddly stealthy cat by the name of Phantom, continued its perusal for another ten seconds, until it lifted a paw and began grooming itself. Shifting her attention past Phantom, Beatrix discovered an additional six cats sitting on the very end of her bed, all of them regarding her with unblinking eyes, a situation that, in all honesty, was incredibly unnerving.

She looked back at Phantom. "I'm going to have to insist you discontinue this habit you've adopted of waking me up by sitting on my chest. I assure you, I'm more than capable of waking up without your assistance." Beatrix pushed herself up on her elbows, which had the desired effect of Phantom moseying his way across her stomach, stepping a dainty paw to the black and gold coverlet Aunt Gladys had chosen to match the Egyptian style of the room, then leaping to the floor. He then crept silently across the room and out a door that was barely open.

Returning her attention to the six cats still on the end of her bed, she received what seemed to be condescending looks from all of them before they jumped silently to the floor and padded out of the room as well.

Throwing aside the covers, Beatrix swung her legs over the bed and shoved her feet into slippers before shrugging her way into a dressing gown. She gave a bit of a stretch, then switched on a gas lamp sitting on a small table. Light immediately flooded the papered walls covered with images of pyramids and camels, the furniture made out of unusual Egyptian artifacts, such as ancient spears making up the backs of chairs, and, Beatrix's favorite, the gigantic four-poster bed that had yards and yards of billowing fabric cascading over the posts.

At the moment, that fabric was tied to the bedposts with multi-colored cords because Beatrix had wanted to avoid the tempta-tion of lingering in a cozy cocoon of silk, her filled-to-the-brim schedule not allowing her that particular luxury at the moment.

"Good morning, dear," Aunt Gladys said, strolling through the door, the lime green turban on her head paired with a lime green dressing gown. "I saw the cats wandering from your room, and I'm just tickled to death they've taken to you."

"They haven't taken to me, Aunt Gladys. Frankly, I'm somewhat confused as to how they got into my room because I distinctly remember shutting my door last night after we returned from the Christian Woman's Temperance meeting. If you ask me, they're unusually crafty creatures, and I'm almost convinced they've some-how learned to open doors."

"They don't know how to open doors. I open your door just a crack when I wake up in the morning so that the cats will know it's time to wake you up for the day."

"As I told Phantom, I'm perfectly capable of waking up on my own. I've always been an early riser, even before I took up a posi-tion, and I am now going to beg you to discontinue opening my door in the morning because I have the strangest feeling your cats are in the process of plotting my demise."

"Has anyone ever told you that you're delightfully dramatic?"

"I'm not dramatic in the least. I'll have you know that yesterday when I woke up and discovered Phantom sitting on my chest, he licked his lips in a most telling fashion and then he went about the troubling business of stretching out a paw, probably so I would be certain to take note of his sharp little claws."

Aunt Gladys sat down in the nearest chair, readjusting her turban when it listed to the left. "How curious. I imagine Phantom and the rest of the cats are taking your measure and then will decide if you're worthy of their affections."

"Who said I want their affections?"

"Shh, they might hear you, and cats understand more than we think."

"A concerning idea," Beatrix said right as a quiet knock sounded on her door, and Edgar stuck his head into the room.

"I've brought you a breakfast tray, Miss Beatrix. Everyone decent?"

"Of course we're decent," Aunt Gladys returned with a warm smile. "And how thoughtful of you to make certain dear Beatrix eats a good breakfast before she goes off to join the workforce."

Edgar let out a grunt as he wheeled a tiered cart into the room that had a silver coffeepot on it, as well as a few different plates covered with silver domes. Stopping the cart beside a small table stamped with Egyptian figures, Edgar turned to Beatrix with a smile.

"Wasn't certain what you'd care to eat today, so I had Roberta make you an assortment of dishes." He lifted a dome from one of the plates, revealing fluffy eggs, potatoes, and toast, which he placed on the table before gesturing her forward. "Best get to it, Miss Beatrix. Starting a day with a good meal is imperative to keeping up your stamina, and yesterday you only made it through half your meal, stating you were running late and needed to get dressed."

Beatrix's stomach took that moment to rumble, which had Edgar sending her a pointed look, one that had her moving to the table and taking a seat. "While it is a lovely treat to be served in my room every morning," she began, placing a well-ironed linen napkin on her lap, "I'm relatively certain it's not an occurrence most working women enjoy."

"You are *not* most working women," Edgar countered, sending a disgruntled look to Aunt Gladys, who'd taken a seat opposite Beatrix and was already sipping the coffee Edgar had poured for her.

Edgar returned his attention to Beatrix. "Your aunt and I are currently in disagreement about your employment at Marshall Field & Company. She is still of the belief that having you work at the store will lend you an improved sense of empathy for working women. I, on the other hand, believe that after careful observation of how you've comported yourself since you joined us in Chicago, you already possess a great deal of empathy for women."

"Honestly, Edgar, you make it sound as if I'm unaware of just how exceptional my niece is, when that's not true in the least," Aunt Gladys grumbled before she nodded to Beatrix. "With that said, I still believe your stint at Marshall Field & Company will encourage you to throw yourself firmly into the suffrage movement, much more so than you already have. You've already had your eyes opened regarding the obstacles working women face on a day-to-day basis, what with your suffering a demotion before you'd been employed at the store for even a week. That experience alone has left you understanding the plight of the working poor far better than if you'd merely read about it in a newspaper."

Edgar inclined his head at Aunt Gladys. "While I agree that Miss Beatrix has gleaned some valuable experience through taking up a position, I'm not comfortable sending off an American heiress day after day to the mean environment Miss Beatrix now finds herself in."

Aunt Gladys narrowed her eyes on Edgar, picked up a piece of toast, and nibbled on it, apparently unwilling to continue a conversation Beatrix suspected she and Edgar had had often as of late.

"You've not mentioned much about Norman the past few days,"

Aunt Gladys said after she polished off her toast. "Has he come around to the store to see you?"

Edgar released a huff. "I thought we agreed you wouldn't delve into any matchmaking in regard to Miss Beatrix because you've been known to create disasters when you try your hand at that."

"I'm sure I have no idea what you're talking about."

Edgar turned to Beatrix. "Last year, your aunt decided that Miss Georgia Lancaster, a lovely young lady with no prospects, would be the perfect bride for Sir Julian Newcastle, an aristocrat from England who'd come to Chicago to find a bride."

"I would have thought he'd go to New York City to do that," Beatrix said.

"My thought as well," Edgar said. "But after Gladys convinced Sir Julian that Georgia was a lovely young lady, he proposed to her within two weeks of meeting her. Then it came out that Sir Julian was under the mistaken belief that Georgia was Gladys's ward and, as such, would be given a large dowry once she married." Edgar shook his head. "Sir Julian all but fled Chicago when he discovered the truth, and last I heard, he married a mining heiress from Nebraska and is now living high on the hog back in England."

"I was perfectly agreeable to settle a dowry on Georgia. Sir Julian just never gave me an opportunity to announce that," Aunt Gladys complained.

"Because the bounder ran off into the night, leaving poor Georgia embarrassed and dejected."

"True, but Georgia is now happily married to Mr. Marcus Thurman, so all's well that ends well."

"Whom she found without any interference from you."

As Aunt Gladys and Edgar continued to squabble, Beatrix began shoveling forkfuls of eggs into her mouth, wishing she were anywhere except in the middle of the squabbling. Washing the eggs down with a glass of juice, she pretended she didn't notice that Aunt Gladys was now glaring at Edgar, who was glaring right back at her aunt, an unusual action for a butler to take with his employer, which left Beatrix wondering if . . .

"I have matters to attend to, so if you'll excuse me," Edgar said, turning on his heel and stalking from the room.

"He's such a delightful man," Aunt Gladys exclaimed right as Phantom slipped back into the room and immediately sidled up to Beatrix, rubbing up against her leg quite as if he wanted to make certain she knew he was back.

She elected to ignore the cat, turning her attention to her aunt. "How long has Edgar worked for you?"

"Thirty years, give or take." She released a sigh. "I always thought I'd eventually marry the man, but as the years pass by and he doesn't broach the matter with me, I'm becoming resigned to the fact that I'll always be a spinster, surrounded by more and more cats."

"I thought you never wanted to marry."

"Oh, I didn't," Aunt Gladys returned. "But that started to change probably after Edgar had been with me for fifteen years or so. That's when I realized he'd become quite essential to my life, but he doesn't seem willing to move past the fact that he's the butler and I'm, well, me." She took a sip of coffee, set aside her cup, then smiled. "But my disappointment aside, let us return to the subject of another delightful man. You've not mentioned much about Norman since I joined you at Kinsley's, what was it, seven days ago now?"

"I haven't seen Norman since then."

"He's not been to the store to visit you?"

"Not since last week, which was, again, seven days ago."

Aunt Gladys sat back in her chair. "Ah, so you've been counting the days since you last saw him. Interesting."

"I haven't been counting the days. You just mentioned it was seven."

"And you're disappointed that he's not been by the store to see you?"

"Only because I told him to keep me abreast of any news the Pinkerton man may have discovered about that accident we suffered. I've been waiting on tenterhooks to learn if anything's been uncovered, but Norman has neglected to give me a report on the matter."

"He is known about town as an absent-minded sort."

"He's not absent-minded in the least," Beatrix argued. "Granted, he does occasionally become distracted with unusual mathematical equations, but if you ask me, Norman takes advantage of his unusual mind by using it as an excuse to keep people at a distance."

"Hmm . . ." was all Aunt Gladys said to that.

"Should I even ask what you meant by *hmm*?"

"I would think it's obvious."

"Not to me."

Aunt Gladys poured herself another cup of coffee, added cream and sugar, took a sip, then smiled. "You understand him, and you've done so in a remarkably short period of time. It's telling."

"It isn't."

"It is because I don't believe many people take the time to try to understand Norman Nesbit, but you've evidently done exactly that, which means you're interested in him."

"He's an interesting man."

"That's not what I said. You're fond of him."

"I never claimed differently."

"Perhaps I should have said you're overly fond of him."

"I'm not sure I appreciate the direction this conversation is traveling," Beatrix said, taking another bite of eggs. She swallowed and frowned. "And because of what happened with Miss Georgia, I'm now going to recommend you cease all thoughts of matchmaking because, as Edgar pointed out, you're apparently not very good at it."

"Do you recall what verse the sermon was centered around last Sunday?" Aunt Gladys asked.

"What does that have to do with anything?"

"Humor me."

"Well, it was a verse from Isaiah, and I mentioned to you at the time it seemed appropriate because it centered around looking to the right or to the left, and then hearing a voice in your ear, saying 'this is the way, walk in it.' If you'll recall, I thought it was timely because I'd just been pondering the path I was supposed to take when I was facing dismissal from the store and felt compelled to take the path that would keep me employed."

Aunt Gladys beamed at her. "Exactly. That then had me pondering the verse as well, and I came to the conclusion that the path you're meant to take may include something to do with Norman."

"An odd conclusion to be sure."

"It's not when you consider the unusual circumstances that brought Norman into your life." Aunt Gladys nodded. "He's already very protective of you, and didn't hesitate to try to whisk you away when he thought I was a madwoman. Why, I'd not be surprised to learn his action left you a bit weak in the knees."

Beatrix blinked. Truth be told, she had felt a tad unsteady after Norman had set her down, but in all likelihood, that was simply a result of having lost the feeling in her feet after having them dangle over his arm for such an extended period of time.

"He suits you," Aunt Gladys proclaimed.

"He does not suit me."

"He does because he's your exact opposite and you know what everyone says about opposites—they attract."

"Or try to kill each other."

"There is that, but I believe Norman needs you. He's always been rumored to live for his work, but a man can't live on work alone. You're a lady who embraces life to the fullest and enjoys living from one adventure to the next. And"—she held up a hand when Beatrix opened her mouth—"you need him because he's different, and he'll never bore you." Aunt Gladys leaned forward. "Your mother has lent me the impression that you have no interest in society men, having used a nonexistent relationship with a Mr. Thomas Hamersley as a way to dissuade society men from pursuing you. That suggests to me that you're not interested in gentlemen most ladies would be keen to become better acquainted with. Norman might be perfect for you because he's not your typical gentleman."

"He's the most annoying man I know."

"Which is exactly my point, dear. Can you recall any other gentleman who elicits that type of emotion from you?"

"Well, no, but with that said, Norman's given me no indication he's romantically interested in me."

"He went shopping at Marshall Field & Company. If that's not an indication that he's at least curious about you, well, I don't know what is."

"He was at Marshall Field & Company to purchase gloves for Theodosia."

"Or so he told you," Aunt Gladys said right as Phantom jumped straight up into Beatrix's lap, then took to watching her as she tried to finish up a piece of bacon.

"I'm not giving you any of this," she told the cat.

"He might stop planning your demise if you share with him. Phantom loves bacon."

"An excellent point," Beatrix said, breaking off a piece of the bacon and holding it out to Phantom, who immediately devoured it. A second later, she found herself surrounded by cats, all of them mewing up a storm, their meows turning to contented purrs after she dispensed the rest of her bacon.

Shooing Phantom from her lap, Beatrix rose to her feet. "While I certainly hate to end this most unusual conversation, I need to get ready for work, so . . ."

"Fine, I'll leave you in peace . . . for now," Aunt Gladys said as she got up from the table and sailed out of the room, the cats trailing after her.

Shaking her head, Beatrix headed for the bathing chamber. After finishing up in there, she hurried to her wardrobe, choosing another plain white blouse paired with a black skirt. As she buckled her shoes, thoughts of Norman drifted to mind, ones she couldn't seem to banish with any success.

He *was* the most annoying man she'd ever known, but there

was something about him that appealed to her. In all honesty, her knees had gone just a touch weak when Norman and Theodosia had shown up at the store the previous week, which could very well mean that her aunt was on to something and that she was, surprisingly enough, becoming more than fond of a man she'd originally thought she'd never hold in any affection.

CHAPTER 19

As the barber at the Palmer House Hotel went to fetch a sharper pair of scissors, Norman smiled at Gemma and Oscar, who were huddled together on a bench with their heads bent over a pad of paper, making a list of supplies needed to build a peddle-boat.

He'd not had any intention of bringing them along to the barber's this morning. However, Constance had shown up while he'd been enjoying breakfast, needing their mother to watch Gemma and Oscar while she attended a scheduled engagement because the children's tutor had fallen ill. Norman had offered to watch them instead, earning Gemma and Oscar's undying gratitude after his mother mentioned something about hosting a tea party complete with dolls for the two of them.

"How's it coming?" Norman asked.

Gemma lifted her head, eyes shining with excitement. "I think we have almost everything listed, but are you certain we can get all these parts? I don't have much pin money left this week because I spent mine on . . ." She stopped speaking, sent Norman a guilty look, then bent back over her notes.

Norman resisted a grin. "Might your pin money have gone to those roller-skis you and Oscar were determined to make?"

Oscar began nodding before Gemma elbowed him, which had

him stopping mid-nod as he sent Gemma a grimace, crossed his arms over his chest, and presented her with his back.

Gemma heaved a sigh. "Sorry, Oscar. I shouldn't have done that."

Oscar, clearly a boy who couldn't hold a grudge long, turned around. "Apology accepted, but you might as well tell your uncle Norman about the roller-skis. I bet he could help us make them work so that we wouldn't go crashing into things, like that vase you haven't told your mother you broke."

"Dare I hope it wasn't an expensive vase?" Norman asked.

Gemma shook her head. "Afraid not, and I won't have enough pin money for the next five years to pay for it. It was from France—a present to Mother from Aunt Alice." She scratched her nose. "Maybe I should send a telegram to Aunt Alice since she's in Paris right now and see if she could find another one of those vases."

Norman frowned. "Alice is in Paris?"

"She's been there for months. She's taking an extended tour of the continent with Uncle Wallis."

"Is she really?"

"How could you not know that your other sister is in Paris?"

It was a worthy question, and one that, regrettably, he knew the answer to far too well.

He'd not known his oldest sister was in Paris because he rarely bothered to take the time to know anything about his siblings.

His family had always treated him with the utmost care, as if because of his accident as a youth and then because of his unusual intellect, he needed to be sheltered from the nuances of everyday life.

Unfortunately, he'd taken their care for granted, had never even voiced an appreciation for that care, and over the years, he'd undoubtedly turned into a most self-centered gentleman.

It was an uncomfortable truth, but now that he'd become aware of it, he was going to have to remedy matters and with all due haste.

Family, he was beginning to realize, as well as friends such as

Theo, was far more important than any invention or scientific discovery. Friends and family made life enjoyable, a notion he'd only begun considering after becoming acquainted with Beatrix. *She* was a lady who enjoyed life to the fullest and embraced the experiences life offered.

"What do you think he's doing?" Norman heard Oscar ask. "He's gone all glassy-eyed."

"He does that all the time when he's figuring out a mathematical equation. No need for concern."

"I'm not figuring out a mathematical equation," Norman said right as the barber returned with a different pair of scissors in his hand.

"Then what were you thinking about?" Gemma pressed.

"I was thinking about Alice being in Paris and me not realizing that. However, speaking of my world-traveling sister, I believe she gave me an identical vase to the one you broke."

Gemma's little face lit up. "She did?"

"Indeed, and because my vase is collecting dust in my closet, I'd be happy to give it to you, but only after you tell Constance what happened to her vase."

In the blink of an eye, Gemma was by his side, surprising him when she threw her thin arms around him and gave him a hug, holding on for a good few seconds.

"Thank you, Uncle Norman. I won't forget this," Gemma said, stepping back.

"You're welcome, and with that settled, how about you rejoin Oscar so my barber can get on with seeing after my hair?"

"Looks to me as if your hair hasn't been seen after for months," the barber, Mr. Farley, said, snapping open a cape that he drew around Norman as Gemma scampered away. "What would you like me to do with this today?"

Norman dug into his pocket, pulling out a folded-up advertisement Theo had ripped out of a *Harper's Bazaar* fashion magazine. He handed it to Mr. Farley. "I've decided I'd like to look like this man."

The barber glanced at the page. "You're certain you want such a dramatic change? This gentleman's hair is cut remarkably short."

Norman nodded. "According to research I've been doing with a friend of mine, ladies are said to be partial to shorter hair on gentlemen these days."

"Ah, so you've got a certain young lady in your sights and want to impress her, do you?"

"At this point, I'm only hoping that she doesn't get annoyed with me so often."

"Tricky business there," Mr. Farley said as he began sprinkling a great deal of water over Norman's head.

It took Mr. Farley forty-five minutes to cut and shape Norman's hair, during which Gemma and Oscar kept wandering up to join him, both children voicing their opinions on the progress Mr. Farley was making. After taking a final snip of Norman's hair, Mr. Farley stepped back and nodded to the children.

"What do you think?"

Gemma's nose wrinkled as she considered Norman. "You don't look like my uncle Norman anymore."

"Who do I look like, then?"

"You look like a man of business," Oscar said when Gemma seemed to be at a loss for an answer.

"Do I really?" Norman asked as Mr. Farley handed him a mirror and then told him he'd be back directly to brush away all the stray bits of hair from Norman's neck as well as to shave him.

"I don't know what everyone is going to make of this new you," Gemma said slowly as Norman held up the mirror, blinking at his reflection.

Gone was the dark, untidy hair that was always hampering his view, replaced with a style that looked exactly like the advertisement he'd given to Mr. Farley. "He must really want to impress a girl," Oscar declared loudly, drawing the attention of every gentlemen getting a cut or a shave in the barber shop, all of whom then sent him knowing looks.

"Who is she?" Gemma asked, stepping closer to Norman.

Finding it more than peculiar that he was now being interrogated by an eight-year-old, Norman was spared a response when Mr. Farley returned, shooing the children back to the bench so he could attend to shaving Norman.

Two hours later, and after Norman treated Gemma and Oscar to an early lunch at one of the restaurants in the Palmer House Hotel, he stepped out of the hansom cab he'd rented and onto Prairie Avenue, turning to help Gemma to the ground while Oscar jumped out on his own.

"When are we going to get the parts for the peddle-boat?" Gemma asked, surprising him when she took hold of his hand as they walked toward his mother's house.

"I'll see to getting all the parts tomorrow because I'm meeting up with Theo today to do some shopping."

Gemma gave their entwined hands a swing. "I never knew you and Theo enjoyed shopping."

"It's a recent development, but I won't be shopping tomorrow, so if your tutor is still under the weather, you and Oscar may return here tomorrow afternoon after I've had an opportunity to get all the parts needed for your boat."

"We're going to help you build it?"

"It's your boat, Gemma, so yes, you should help build it."

"How much do you think those parts are going to cost me?"

"You're eight. That's hardly old enough to worry about paying for parts. I'm buying everything."

Gemma gave another swing of their hands. "You've never bought me anything before."

"I suppose I haven't, so I'd best put some effort into making up for that unacceptable lapse."

"Mother's been afraid there's something wrong with you, and I think she may be right. You're acting odder than usual."

"Would you feel better if I allowed you to pay for the parts?"

Gemma grinned. "Not at all because you see . . ." She glanced over her shoulder to look at Oscar, who'd stopped a few paces behind them to tie his shoe. Turning back to Norman, she lowered her voice. "Oscar's birthday is next month. I want to get him some chemicals to add to his chemistry set."

"That's a very thoughtful gesture, Gemma. He's lucky he has you for a friend."

Gemma shook her head. "I'm luckier, Uncle Norman. Oscar is always there for me, no matter what outlandish plan I might want to try out. Not everyone has such a good friend, so I want to give him something special for his birthday." She smiled. "He's like your Theo."

A sliver of guilt slid through Norman because he didn't know when Theo's birthday was, which meant he'd certainly never presented her with anything special on her birthday.

Clearly he had more restitutions to make with his friend and his family than he'd realized.

"I think she might be here," Gemma said, pointing to Theo's pony, Rosie, who was hitched to the hitching post. "Will she be at Grandmother's house, or will she be in your workshop?"

Because Theo had thrown herself into their current experiment, the one that would hopefully see Beatrix less annoyed with him, Norman knew she was not in his workshop, but in his apartment above his workshop. She'd undertaken the daunting task of sifting through all the clothing that he'd had no idea his mother had purchased for him over the years, that clothing having been stored in an enormous closet in her attic.

It had taken Norman and Theo an entire afternoon to lug everything from the attic to his apartment—conveniently on an afternoon when his mother had been out of the house—which had allowed Norman the luxury of moving his unexpected wardrobe without being barraged with questions.

"I imagine she's up in my apartment, trying to organize my clothes for me."

"Why would she want to do that?"

Thankfully, Norman was spared an explanation when Oscar ran up to join them.

"Can we take your electrical conveyance vehicle for a drive today?" Oscar asked.

Norman nodded. "Of course. I charged up the battery two days ago, but since I have yet to figure out how to keep it charged for any length of time, I doubt the two of you will get past that tree again."

After helping Gemma and Oscar get the vehicle started, Norman watched them drive slowly away before he strode through his workshop, his gaze glancing over the new electric engine he'd all but abandoned ever since he and Theo had taken up their latest and most highly unusual experiment.

That he felt not a single urge to step over to the engine should have been concerning, but he had more important matters to attend to, the most important of which was changing his clothing and getting on his way with Theo to pay a visit to Beatrix at Marshall Field & Company.

Taking the steps that led to his apartment on the second floor of the carriage house, Norman walked into the room that served as his sitting room, coming to an abrupt stop when the first thing that met his gaze was his sister Constance standing with her hands on her hips as she surveyed mounds and mounds of clothing strewn everywhere. Theo was on the other side of the room, flipping through a fashion magazine as she held a gentleman's jacket that he'd recently learned was a single-breasted, four-buttoned, sack suit, done up in a pattern called the corkscrew—information he never thought he'd need to know but now was never going to forget.

"Constance," he finally said. "What are you doing here?"

Constance turned, but instead of responding, she regarded him with wide eyes and then abruptly took a seat directly on top of a pile of men's trousers.

"What have you done to yourself? I can see your face."

Norman took a step into the room. "I paid a visit to a barber."

"He cut off all your hair."

"Well, not all of it, but, you see, that's what barbers are supposed to do—cut a gentleman's hair."

"But you look quite unlike your normal self."

"That's what Gemma and Oscar thought as well. They've decided I look like a businessman."

Constance glanced behind him, her eyes going from wide to narrowed in a split second. "Where are Gemma and Oscar? Don't tell me you forgot you had them with you and left them downtown."

"They're taking a spin in my electrical conveyance vehicle, and honestly, Constance, I was hardly going to forget I had them with me. But again, what are you doing here? I thought you were supposed to be at a meeting all afternoon."

Constance shrugged. "I decided to leave the meeting early because the discussion was turning heated, what with how the ladies can't seem to agree where the Chicago Public Library should be moved."

"Theo and I were just at the library, and it didn't seem as if it needed moving. The upper floor of City Hall provides a more-than-ample space."

"Chicago deserves a library that is only a library," Constance argued. "But tell me this, were you and Theo at the library searching for more electrical research papers . . . or were you there searching for articles related to fashion, a subject I never thought either of you would take an interest in?"

Norman shot a look to Theo, who sent him a look in return that clearly said she wasn't going to become involved in this particular conversation, leaving him to believe Constance had already taken it upon herself to question Theo endlessly about why there were fashion magazines strewn about, along with piles and piles of clothing.

"Uncle Norman!" Gemma exclaimed, bursting in the room, Oscar nowhere in sight. "The engine died again, and we didn't even make it to the tree this time."

Norman frowned. "Troubling to be sure and suggests I might have come to a standstill with my theory on double currents, but where's Oscar?"

"He's pushing the electrical conveyance vehicle back to the workshop."

Gemma looked around, frowning at the mess, before her gaze settled on Constance. She practically skipped to her mother's side, dodging shoes, hats, and walking sticks. "I didn't see you there for a second, Mother."

Constance smiled. "Did you have a nice time with Uncle Norman?"

"We did. We watched him get his hair shorn off and then he took us to lunch at one of the fancy restaurants in the Palmer House."

Constance turned to Norman. "I'm still confused why you got your hair cut in that particular style."

"It's because of a girl," Gemma said before Norman could answer.

Constance's eyes began to gleam. "I knew it. There is a girl. Who is she?"

Norman settled for a shrug, which had Constance turning to Gemma. "Who is she?"

Gemma frowned. "I'm eight, Mother. It's not as if Uncle Norman is going to confide all the details to me."

Constance shot a look to Norman before she nodded to Gemma. "I need to have a bit of a chat with Uncle Norman, dear. What say you go find Oscar and then the two of you can go up to Grandmother's house? She's setting out a lovely tea for you and Oscar to enjoy with another new doll she's purchased for you."

"I think Oscar and I would rather stay here," Gemma said, gesturing around. "Uncle Norman could use some help getting his room tidy, and Oscar and I wouldn't mind helping him, not when he's agreed to help us make a real peddle-boat."

Constance glanced to Norman again. "You've agreed to help them build a peddle-boat?"

"He's already drawn up the plans for it, Mother, and he let me and Oscar make a supply list for him while he was getting his haircut."

Constance narrowed her eyes on Norman even as she gave an

airy wave in Gemma's direction. "Grandmother's waiting, dear. You'd best get on your way."

Gemma immediately took to looking stubborn, clearly unwilling to head off to see her grandmother. She glanced to Norman, her lips curving just a little before she returned her attention to her mother. "I can't go yet because I promised Uncle Norman I'd fess up to something I've done."

Constance frowned. "You must really not want to have tea with Grandmother and a new doll if you're willingly confessing to something."

"Or maybe I'm wracked with guilt with what I've done and know I'll feel much better after I get it off my chest."

"Does Gemma always sound like she's thirty instead of eight?" Theo asked, looking up from her fashion magazine.

"Afraid so," Constance said before she nodded at Gemma. "Very well. Out with it. What have you done now?"

It took Gemma less than a minute to confess, ending with, "Me and Oscar tried to put the vase back together, but that didn't work very well. But it turns out Uncle Norman is willing to give you the same vase that Aunt Alice gave him, so I'm hopeful you won't be too cross with me."

Constance laid a hand on Gemma's shoulder. "I'm not cross with you, Gemma, because I know you didn't mean to break my vase. Although I will expect you to fess up sooner the next time one of your inventions goes awry."

"I will, I promise."

As Constance gave Gemma a hug, Norman strode as best he could through the sitting room and into his bedchamber. Darting into his closet, he retrieved the vase Alice had given him, dusted it off on his jacket, then returned to the sitting room, handing the vase to his sister, surprised when she sent him a frown.

"This is a very expensive vase, Norman, and one a future wife of yours may enjoy, or perhaps that girl Gemma mentioned earlier."

"Beatrix isn't a girl, she's a lady, and—" He stopped talking and winced as Constance immediately took to looking like the cat who'd spotted a nice dish of cream.

"Gemma," Constance said rather absently. "Time for you to see Grandmother."

"But it's just getting interesting."

"Gemma . . ."

Gemma's little shoulders sagged. "Oh, very well. But I do hope someone will see fit to fill me in on what Uncle Norman says. I'd like to know if I'm going to get a new aunt sometime soon." With that, she turned on a small heel and stomped out of the sitting room, her stomps continuing as she made her way down the steps.

The second the door to his workshop banged shut, Constance rounded on Norman. "Who is Beatrix?"

Norman pulled out his pocket watch. "While I would love nothing more than to divulge all the pesky details I'm sure you want to know about Beatrix, I'm running out of time. Theo and I have an engagement planned for this afternoon, one that is long overdue since it took us longer than expected to go through some very interesting research, and—"

"Sit," Constance interrupted, pointing a dainty finger at a chair that was overflowing with jackets.

"I don't think she's going to let you out of here until you tell her about Beatrix," Theo said, setting aside the fashion magazine she'd been clutching and stepping forward.

His eyes widened when he got his first good look at her.

Theo had never been one to concern herself with fashion, but apparently she'd been taking to heart some of the articles they'd been sharing of late because she was wearing what looked to be a walking dress, but it was one he'd never seen before and looked as if it might have been pulled out of an old trunk, given that the blue it had once been had almost faded to gray. More curious than the color, though, were the flowers she'd attached to the dress, ones that had apparently been fresh flowers when she'd attached them to the fabric but were now wilted.

"It would appear Norman's not keen to answer my question,

Theodosia," Constance said. "Which means I'm going to need you to tell me all about this Beatrix."

"I wouldn't want to deprive him of the pleasure of explaining Beatrix to you."

Norman pulled his attention away from what seemed to be a large dollop of glue running from one of the flowers and nodded to his sister. "Because I'm sure you're going to begin badgering Theo about the matter, and because I know she isn't comfortable with that kind of direct questioning, what do you want to know about Beatrix?"

"Since when have you begun being considerate of what Theo is or is not comfortable with?"

"Do you want to know about Beatrix or not?"

"Sorry. I'm listening."

Five minutes later, and after he'd explained how he'd come to know Beatrix, Norman ended with, "I've decided I'm rather fond of her, which is why Theo and I decided I needed to make some improvements in the hopes that Beatrix may decide at some point she's fond of me as well."

Constance tapped a finger against her chin. "Let me see if I'm understanding this correctly. You've become fond of a woman who works at Marshall Field & Company?"

Norman nodded.

"Interesting," Constance said. "Although I'm not overly surprised that you don't seem concerned about her lack of societal standing, because that's never been something you've worried about, even if the gossips are going to come out in droves if you begin courting her."

"Gossip has never bothered me."

"True, but again, there will be a lot of that, especially since Beatrix is the niece of Miss Gladys Huttleston, an eccentric lady about Chicago if there ever was one."

"Gladys is actually a rather nice woman," Norman felt compelled to say. "But speaking of Gladys, I'm certainly going to have a chat with Alice when she returns from Paris about those stories she told me about Beatrix's aunt. Here I've been under the misguided notion that Gladys was guilty of abducting orphans when that wasn't true at all."

Constance's lips twitched. "You were always remarkably gullible, and I'm afraid I also may have told you some exaggerated stories when we were younger."

"You told me stories too?"

"Indeed, but because I feel slightly guilty about that, how about if I make it up to you by assisting you with what you should wear today?" She nodded to the jacket Theo had been considering. "That's a bit too much for a shopping expedition, so let me see what else I can find."

Twenty minutes later, Norman was dressed in a blue tweed suit paired with a matching blue shirt and blue waistcoat. He was also wearing the wing-tipped collar Beatrix had chosen for him, his tie done up in what he'd learned was called the Avondale knot, which, thankfully, Constance had known how to tie.

Stepping up to the mirror, he looked himself over, pleased with the reflection he saw, then turned, faltering for a second when he caught sight of his mother, whom he'd not heard enter the room. "Hello, Mother. I thought you'd be having tea with Gemma and Oscar by now."

Mary narrowed her eyes at him. "I was having tea, but then felt compelled to seek you out after Gemma asked me if I knew a Beatrix." Mary arched a brow at Constance. "I well remember how you were at Gemma's age, my dear, always overhearing things not meant for your ears, so I thought it might be prudent for me to come out here and see if any of you can explain to me who Beatrix is."

When Constance didn't say a thing, his mother turned to him, and when he stayed silent on the matter, she turned to Theo.

She folded within a minute of being the recipient of Mary's rapid-fire questions.

"Beatrix Waterbury is a delightful lady who works at Marshall Field's in the coat check, and she's the lady Norman's taking to the Potter Palmer affair because he didn't want to go with Miss Dinneen or Miss Ashburn," Theo said in a rush.

Mary pinned Norman with a scandalized gaze. "You're taking a coat check girl to the Palmer ball?"

The conversation only went downhill from there.

CHAPTER 20

"Be careful with that, girl. It's ermine, and as such it deserves to be handled with the utmost care."

Keeping her smile firmly in place, Beatrix accepted the ermine wrap Mrs. George Blossom all but dumped into her arms. The less-than-careful handing over of her wrap suggested that Mrs. Blossom wasn't all that concerned over its treatment but had made her demand in order to make sure that the two ladies in her company knew the wrap was ermine, and thus, expensive.

"It certainly is a luxurious wrap, Mrs. Blossom. I'll take extra care with it while you shop," Beatrix said as she handed the lady a claim ticket.

"I would hope you treat every garment with extra care, whether it be ermine or not." With that, Mrs. Blossom spun on her heel and marched away, whispering furiously to the two ladies marching alongside her.

"Don't mind her," Miss Dixon, one of the other two coat check girls, whispered as Beatrix hurried down the long rack, searching for a space to hang Mrs. Blossom's coat. "She's always unpleasant."

Miss Jaycox, the other woman working in coat check, nodded as she bustled past Beatrix, carrying a gentleman's overcoat of charcoal gray, along with a black hat. "Indeed she is, but we've encountered worse."

Hoping that someone worse than Mrs. Blossom wasn't waiting next in line, Beatrix hurried back to the counter and took a blue jacket from a lady who had two adorable little girls holding on to her skirts. Beatrix smiled at the girls, her smile fading when the lady released a sniff and hurried the girls away.

Over the week since she'd been reassigned to the coat check, Beatrix had experienced more than her fair share of nastiness from people who apparently believed it was their right to deliver such slights because she was a coat check girl.

Frankly, their slights were only fueling her desire to become more involved with the suffrage movement, because if women *could* obtain the vote, they'd then hopefully begin to see their circumstances improving through better work opportunities and greater chances for advancement.

As it stood now, what with how men ruled over work environments and had final say in the positions women were permitted to accept, working women were resigned to taking on positions such as the one Beatrix currently held, positions that hardly improved their circumstances.

Striding down the rack of coats again, Beatrix hung up the lady's jacket before heading back toward the counter, where the line was getting longer. Her pace slowed, though, when she caught sight of Miss Dixon and Miss Jaycox simply standing by the counter, both of them giggling as they chatted with a well-dressed gentleman.

That giggling was frowned upon was not in question, which had Beatrix squaring her shoulders, knowing an intervention was in order before Mrs. Goodman arrived on the scene.

Edging around Miss Dixon, who was actually fluttering her lashes at the gentleman standing on the other side of the counter, Beatrix summoned up a smile, her smile dimming when she got her first good look at the man.

He was dressed to the nines, sporting a well-tailored jacket that showed off his broad shoulders and was tapered to perfection, accenting the trimness of his waist. A gray-and-blue-striped tie knotted in the Avondale style sat against a brilliant white wing-tipped collar.

Lifting her head when she realized she was giving the gentleman a more-than-cursory glance, Beatrix sucked in a sharp breath when she got her first good look at the man's face, releasing that breath when the gentleman sent her a grin.

"Hello, Miss Waterbury."

The floor beneath her feet seemed to tilt when she realized that standing in front of her was none other than Norman Nesbit, but he'd changed, drastically so.

Gone was the long brown hair she'd become accustomed to, replaced with a style that was brushed carefully away from his face. The absence of hair straggling into that face allowed her to realize that while she'd always thought Norman was attractive in an absent-minded scientist sort of way, he was actually a devastatingly handsome man.

Peculiar as it seemed, she found herself missing the disheveled Norman, because that Norman she'd been getting to know, but this new Norman, well, she had no idea what to make of him.

"What in the *world* have you done to yourself?" she finally managed to get out, wincing when she realized her voice sounded a bit squeaky.

His grin widened. "Visited a new barber, one over at the Palmer House." He leaned closer. "He took forever to shape up my hair, time I worried was wasted, but because you seem to have immediately noticed the difference, I'm now of the belief it was time well spent."

"You've done more than simply cut your hair."

Norman nodded. "Indeed." He brushed the sleeve of his jacket. "Went through my entire wardrobe with Theo and my sister Constance and found numerous items I didn't even remember I had." He presented her with a bow. "What do you think?"

"Ah . . ."

Someone coughed behind Norman, which had Beatrix's scattered thoughts snapping back into place. However, before she could do more than nod at the lady standing behind Norman, impatience oozing from her every pore, Norman turned and smiled at the lady, who immediately returned his smile, all of the impatience she'd been directing at Beatrix disappearing in a flash.

"Forgive me," Norman began, taking the hand the lady didn't even seem to realize she'd held out for him. "I'm holding up the line, an inexcusable offense." He placed a kiss on the hand. "Mr. Norman Nesbit at your service."

The lady's eyes widened as her cheeks turned pink. "Good heavens, Mr. Nesbit. I didn't recognize you. I'm Mrs. Samuel Allerton, a friend of your sister Alice."

Norman inclined his head. "But of course you are, and do forgive me for not recognizing you immediately. I fear it's been far too long since I've had an opportunity to greet you."

As Mrs. Allerton launched into when she thought she'd last encountered Norman, which seemed as if it might have been a few years prior, Beatrix took another moment to look him over, the floor seeming to tilt under her feet again when she realized the brilliant white collar he'd chosen to wear was one she'd picked out for him.

Why that small detail would have the ground feeling unstable was somewhat befuddling, but before she could dwell on that, Norman was assisting Mrs. Allerton with her wrap, smiling charmingly at the lady, the charm in that smile doing absolutely nothing for the state of Beatrix's balance.

". . . simply delightful to see you, Mr. Nesbit," Mrs. Allerton all but gushed as Norman continued smiling at her. "Do give your sister my best."

"I'll be certain to do that, Mrs. Allerton, once she returns from Paris, but we seem to be holding up the line, so perhaps we should bid each other *adieu*."

Mrs. Allerton glanced over her shoulder, frowned at the ten

ladies waiting behind her to check their wraps, then nodded to Norman, who then finished helping her out of her coat. She sent him a warm smile before she turned to Beatrix, the smile disappearing in a flash. "My claim ticket."

Beatrix summoned up another smile, passed a claim ticket not to Mrs. Allerton, but to Norman, who was holding out his hand, then watched as he gave the ticket to Mrs. Allerton, returning the smile that lady gave him before she turned and glided away.

"I'm going to need you to hand over Mrs. Allerton's wrap so I can hang it up," Beatrix said after Norman turned around to face her.

Norman's brows drew together. "I recently read that a gentleman is never to hand over items that need to be hung to a lady who is not his wife, which is leaving me in a bit of a quandary."

"Where did you read that?"

"*Harper's Bazaar*, so maybe I should nip back there and hang up Mrs. Allerton's wrap so that I'm not committing what the author of that article said was a grave offense in regard to proper decorum."

"You can't come behind the counter, Norm—er, rather, Mr. Nesbit. That'll get me dismissed for certain, so . . ." She held out her arms, which had Norman placing the wrap somewhat reluctantly into them.

Hurrying to hang it up, she stepped beside Miss Jaycox, who was hanging up a shawl she'd taken from the woman who'd been standing behind Mrs. Allerton.

"You *know* that fine-looking gentleman?" Miss Jaycox whispered. "The one Mrs. Allerton called Mr. Nesbit?"

"I do."

Miss Dixon sidled up next to her, grabbing a hanger that she threw a black cape over. "But how do you know him? On my word, he's absolutely delicious as well as charming."

"I suppose he does come across that way, but frankly, I'm beginning to wonder if he's recently blown something up. Surely that would be responsible for the extremely different gentleman who has shown up at Marshall Field & Company today compared to the gentleman I've come to know."

Leaving Miss Dixon and Miss Jaycox looking somewhat confused, Beatrix all but sprinted back to the counter, coming to an abrupt halt at the scene unfolding before her eyes.

Norman was assisting another lady with her jacket, smiling and chatting about the weather, of all things, as he assisted her. Turning, he inclined his head to Beatrix before he nodded to a line of additional wraps placed in a row across the counter. He then proceeded to rattle off a list of names that the wraps belonged to, beaming a smile at Beatrix as he informed her that those ladies were waiting to be given claim tickets.

By the time Beatrix, with the aid of Miss Dixon and Miss Jaycox, managed to hand out tickets and then hang all the wraps Norman had apparently assisted all the ladies out of, her forehead was beaded with perspiration, and annoyance was flowing freely through her veins.

Depositing a lovely silk wrap that belonged to Mrs. Hallberg, she marched back to a counter that was, thankfully, devoid of additional wraps as well as ladies. Norman stood there all alone, humming a cheerful tune under his breath.

"What is the matter with you?" she demanded, which had his humming coming to a rapid end.

"What do you mean?"

"You're acting beyond peculiar, which is peculiar in and of itself since peculiar seems to be a common state for you."

Norman frowned. "I'm not acting peculiar in the least."

"You've been engaging in idle chitchat with ladies I'm convinced you barely know."

"You're the one who went on and on about how idle chitchat was an activity that everyone should embrace."

Beatrix yanked a handkerchief from the sleeve of her blouse, blotting her still-perspiring forehead. "Perhaps I did, but I certainly wasn't expecting you to try your hand at chitchat while assisting ladies with their wraps at the coat check." She took another dab at her forehead. "If you've neglected to notice, Mrs. Goodman has made three passes by here, and, given the scowling she's been doing, I'm certain I'm going to be in for a rough time of it once you get on your way to wherever it is you're going next."

"I'm off to Men's Clothing next because I'd like to purchase a few of those Prince Albert jackets you recommended."

Her pesky knees took that moment to go decidedly weak.

"Dare I hope everything is going according to plan?"

Beatrix glanced past Norman and found Theodosia standing to his right, but any greeting she might have extended to Theodosia died on the tip of her tongue when she got a good look at the woman.

Wearing a dress that gave shabby a new meaning, Theodosia had apparently decided to try to brighten up her ensemble by attaching random bits of wilting flowers to the fabric. On Theodosia's head was a brown hat with additional flowers glued to it, along with what appeared to be some type of stuffed bird, although the species was unrecognizable because it looked as if the bird had suffered a severe squishing at some point in time.

"I'm not certain we can claim success with our research just yet," Norman said, pulling Beatrix's gaze from Theodosia to settle on him. "She's clearly annoyed with me."

"Of course I'm annoyed with you," Beatrix shot back. "You've disrupted the coat check, and I'll be fortunate not to find myself dismissed." She turned to Theodosia. "May I dare hope that the two of you have recently blown up Norman's workshop again?"

Theodosia's brows drew together. "Why would you hope we've done that?"

"Because that's the only explanation I can come up with to explain Norman's odder-than-usual behavior today."

Theodosia's eyes widened before she turned to Norman. "You're right. I don't believe we *can* call this a success because she's more annoyed with you than ever."

Norman nodded. "Agreed. It's most perplexing because I adhered

186

to the research we gathered, and none of that research suggested that chivalrous behavior would evoke annoyance."

Before Beatrix could ask a single question about that puzzling statement, Mrs. Goodman came into view, bristling with animosity.

"Is there a problem here, Miss Waterbury?" she demanded.

"Of course there's not," Norman said before Beatrix could speak. "Miss Waterbury is performing her job as a coat check girl admirably, as are the other two women." He leveled a cool eye on Mrs. Goodman. "Why would you believe there's a problem?"

Mrs. Goodman took a step closer. "Miss Waterbury seems flustered."

"Of course she's flustered," Norman returned. "She's been running back and forth for almost twenty minutes, hanging up wraps and dispensing claim tickets. You'd be flustered as well if you were required to work so strenuously instead of waltzing around the first floor, dispensing gloom."

Miss Dixon and Miss Jaycox, who'd been standing next to Beatrix, waiting for additional customers, turned as one and bolted away, both claiming they needed to fetch more hangers from the stock room.

"There's the Norman I know," Beatrix said as Mrs. Goodman stormed away. "But before you truly do get me dismissed, perhaps you should go see about those jackets you want to purchase."

Norman brushed a piece of lint from his sleeve. "I have no idea why you believe my behavior could possibly get you dismissed. I've simply been trying to be helpful."

"Which is curious in and of itself, but again, you need to go away."

"We're going to have to do more research," Theodosia muttered as Norman nodded in agreement.

"Research for what?"

"Never you mind about that," Norman returned. "But obviously the research Theo and I have done over the past week has not been sufficient to aid us in our experiment."

"You've been doing research all week?"

Norman nodded. "Of course we have. Why else do you think we never got around to stopping in to see you to tell you that the Pinkerton man didn't come up with much about the accident?"

"Well, other than that he discovered that the man who ran into Norman had a horse saddled and waiting for him, suggesting he wanted to be prepared for a quick getaway," Theodosia added.

Beatrix opened her mouth to ask more questions but closed it a second later when a lady strolled up to the coat check. Sending Norman a pointed look, she breathed a sigh of relief when he strolled away with Theodosia on his arm, leaving her to get back to her job.

The next fifteen minutes passed with no unexpected surprises, until she returned to the counter after retrieving Mrs. Blossom's ermine wrap and watched that lady sail off without a word of thanks. That's when she discovered Norman wandering ever so casually back and forth a few feet in front of the coat check, sporting a Prince Albert jacket done up in a fine gray wool.

"What do you think?" he mouthed, striking a pose before he began wandering again.

"Nice," she mouthed back, earning a smile from him before he wandered out of sight.

He was back twenty minutes later, wearing a green jacket, and then twenty minutes after that wearing a plaid one.

"Definitely not," she said, earning a scandalized look from Mrs. Randolph, to whom she'd just given a claim ticket. "I beg your pardon, Mrs. Randolph. I was not speaking to you, but to . . ."

The rest of her apology died straightaway because Mrs. Randolph was already stomping away, aggravation evident in her every stomp.

"That lady should avail herself of an etiquette book. She was exhibiting very rude behavior," Theodosia said, popping up beside the counter so suddenly that Beatrix jumped.

"You just scared me half to death," Beatrix said, smoothing back a curl that was escaping its pins.

"Sorry about that," Theodosia said. "But speaking of being scared, thank goodness you dissuaded Norman from that plaid suit. It was dreadful, but he wasn't taking my word for it."

"There aren't many gentlemen who can wear that type of plaid," Beatrix said right as Norman strolled up to join them, still wearing the plaid in question.

"I don't know why the two of you don't care for this jacket," he began. "I find it to be smashingly fashionable."

"Plaid may occasionally be considered fashionable, but that's a really bold pattern and not one you should wear."

"I don't look dashing in it?"

"*Dashing* is not the word that springs to mind, although—"

"I would think Mr. Marshall Field is opposed to his coat check girls flirting with the customers, especially since your flirting is apparently the reason behind you neglecting to realize you have customers waiting to check their wraps."

Norman and Theodosia turned as one to the gentleman who'd just spoken.

"Mr. Cabot," Theodosia exclaimed as the man released the arm of a lady dressed in a lovely blue walking gown. "Fancy seeing you here."

Mr. Cabot, a rather handsome man, if one enjoyed the overly fastidious type, what with how his dark hair was expertly styled and his clothing looked as if it came straight out of a fashion magazine, stepped forward and presented Theodosia with a bow. "Miss Robinson, isn't this a delightful surprise? Your father didn't mention a word about you shopping at Marshall Field & Company when I stopped by to see him earlier today." He snagged hold of Theodosia's hand, raising it to his lips and placing a kiss on a glove Beatrix had only recently sold her.

"My father and I rarely exchange our plans for the day with each other," Theodosia said as she withdrew her hand and turned her attention to the lady accompanying Mr. Cabot. "Miss Burden" was all she said before she began to fiddle with one of the flowers, which started to shed its petals as soon as she touched it.

"Miss Robinson," Miss Burden returned with an inclination of her head. "On my word but you're looking rather interesting today. Are those fresh flowers attached to your . . . is that a walking dress?"

Theodosia looked down at her gown. "I imagine it might be a walking dress, although I'm not certain about that. I only found this dress the other day when I was searching through old trunks in my attic."

"And how delighted you must have been to find that frock," Miss Burden chirped, taking a step closer to Theodosia. "May I assume you'll be wearing something just as delightful to the Palmer ball?" She nodded to Mr. Cabot. "Mr. Cabot is quite pleased you agreed to attend the ball with him, and I do hope you'll be just as pleased to learn that the two of you will be joined by me and my escort for the evening, Mr. Clement Moore." She tilted her head. "Are you familiar with Mr. Moore?"

"Can't say that I am."

"He's most sought-after within Chicago society," Miss Burden continued. "I'm sure the two of you will become fast friends before the night is through."

Beatrix glanced at Norman, who was frowning as he looked to Mr. Cabot, then to Miss Burden, then to Theodosia, then back to Mr. Cabot. He was obviously trying to puzzle something out in that extraordinary brain of his, but his silence wasn't exactly helping Theodosia deal with a most unusual situation.

"May I take your wrap, Miss Burden, and your jacket, Mr. Cabot?" Beatrix asked pleasantly, drawing their attention.

Mr. Cabot nodded before he helped Miss Burden out of her wrap and tossed it at Beatrix before he shrugged out of his jacket and threw that at her as well, his hat following a second later.

Annoyance was swift and only increased when Miss Burden smoothed a hand down the front of her walking dress before she turned a smile on Theodosia.

"Do you like *my* dress, Miss Robinson?" Miss Burden all but purred. "I recently had it made for me after seeing a fashion plate in a magazine."

"I think I saw that plate," Theodosia said as she eyed Miss Burden's gown. "And I do like it. You look very charming." She turned to Beatrix. "Doesn't she look charming, Miss Waterbury?"

Before Beatrix could do more than nod, Miss Burden was drawing herself up, looking scandalized. "Miss Robinson, surely you must know that it's not quite the thing to draw a salesgirl into a conversation. I couldn't care less what—Miss Waterbury, did you call her?—thinks about my appearance."

"Where are my manners?" Norman said pleasantly, although a vein had begun throbbing on a forehead that was no longer covered with hair. "I've completely neglected to introduce all of you. Miss Waterbury, this is Miss Amelia Burden and Mr. Harvey Cabot. Miss Burden, Mr. Cabot, this is Miss Beatrix Waterbury, newly arrived from New York."

For a second, Beatrix was certain Miss Burden was going to ignore the introduction, but then she gave a short bob of her head toward Beatrix as Mr. Cabot did the same. She then held out her hand. "Our tickets if you please, Miss Waterbury."

Less than thirty seconds later, Miss Burden and Mr. Cabot were strolling away, tickets safely stowed in Mr. Cabot's pocket.

"Was it only me, or was that a most uncomfortable encounter?" Theodosia asked, her gaze lingering on Mr. Cabot and Miss Burden.

"I've always found Miss Burden to be an unpleasant lady," Norman said with a frown before he smiled at Theodosia. "Which is exactly why he wanted to escort you to the ball. You're a very pleasant sort, and Mr. Cabot has evidently realized that, which is why he certainly invited you to attend the Palmer affair instead of Miss Burden."

To say Norman's declaration took Beatrix by complete surprise was an understatement.

She'd realized almost straightaway that Mr. Cabot had not been expecting to see Theodosia at the store, given the expression on his face and the way he'd immediately released Miss Burden's arm. Norman had apparently noticed that as well, but had obviously been trying to reassure Theodosia about Mr. Cabot's interest in her, something that was so kind, and yet so unexpected, that Beatrix found herself feeling somewhat tingly all over.

"Mr. Cabot seemed twitchy," Theodosia said, looking to Beatrix. "Wouldn't you agree?"

Before Beatrix could respond, Mrs. Goodman appeared again, sending Beatrix a telling look, which had her encouraging Norman and Theodosia to return to Men's Clothing.

Thankfully, they didn't argue with her, leaving Beatrix free to get back to her job.

Glancing at a clock twenty minutes later, she breathed a sigh of relief when she realized she was almost done with her shift for the day. Relishing the idea of soon being able to kick off shoes that were pinching her toes, Beatrix moved to the counter right as a well-dressed lady stopped in front of it.

Before Beatrix could do more than nod, the lady flung her wrap Beatrix's way, the heavy brooch that was attached to the wrap smacking her in the head.

A sharp pain immediately followed, and after grabbing hold of the wrap, Beatrix held it away from her, not wanting the blood dribbling from her hairline to stain the garment.

"You might want to show greater care the next time you check your wrap, madam," she heard come out of her mouth before she could stop herself.

The lady drew herself up, not even flinching when her gaze settled on the blood. "What did you say to me?"

The condescension in the lady's tone had Beatrix drawing herself up as well. Laying aside the wrap, the heavy brooch making a thud against the counter, she pulled out her handkerchief and began dabbing at the blood. "I *said* you should have a care with how you fling your things at people because, if you've neglected to notice, your brooch cut me."

It really came as no surprise when, less than ten minutes later, Mrs. Goodman was standing in front of the coat check counter, informing her that, while Mr. Selfridge was away in New York, Mr. Bailer, the man who'd hired Beatrix, wanted to see her without delay.

CHAPTER 21

"Ah, Norman, there you are, darling. Had a nice run, did you?"

Norman used the tail of his shirt to blot his dripping face, turning to find his mother advancing toward the carriage house, determination in her every step, something that had him shuddering ever so slightly. Forcing a smile, he nodded. "It was a nice run, Mother, although it wasn't as peaceful as I would have liked, not with Agent Cochran wheezing so much as he ran beside me."

Mary drew to a stop beside Norman, looked around, then frowned. "Where *is* Agent Cochran?"

"I left him by the front fountain. He was in desperate need of a rest, so last I saw of him, he was sticking his bare feet in the water, looking quite as if he was about ready to toss up his accounts."

"I do hope he doesn't toss up those accounts directly into the fountain. That would be most unpleasant."

"Indeed, although he wouldn't be in that danger if he'd taken my suggestion of changing out of his clothes and making use of the running attire I offered to lend him after he insisted on accompanying me on my morning run. What I offered is much cooler than what he was wearing and more appropriate to run in."

"You're not wearing running attire, dear." Mary gestured to his clothing. "You're wearing what's known as bathing attire, complete with a striped sleeveless shirt, which one normally expects to see a gentleman wearing when he's at the beach, not running down Prairie Avenue."

"True, but bathing attire is far more comfortable than the trousers and tight shirts some gentlemen wear when they participate in strenuous activity. And even bathing attire isn't as comfortable as the short pants I tried out, something you insisted I abandon before I made it past the main house."

"Those short trousers showed entirely too much of you."

"So you said, and quite adamantly. That is exactly why I abandoned them, not wanting you to suffer a fit of the vapors every morning when you glimpsed me running—well, that and I didn't care to suffer through lectures from you over breakfast."

"I rarely lecture you."

"You do, as can be proven by how often you bring up the need for a Pinkerton man to dog my every step, even though I've stated time and time again that I don't need one. It's not as if the culprit behind the theft of my research papers has had enough time to figure out he's in possession of faulty information, nor do I expect him to come to that realization for months."

"You were accosted on the street only a few days ago."

"Perhaps, although I'm convinced I was simply the target of an inept pickpocket." He dashed a hand over a forehead that was still perspiring. "However, because I know you'll fret if I insist on getting rid of the Pinkerton men, I'll let them continue following me for now, even if I do feel it's a waste of their time and your money."

"That's surprisingly thoughtful of you dear."

Norman frowned. "Why is it surprising?"

Mary returned the frown. "Why would I not be surprised? You've never been one to concern yourself with how much I fret about you."

"Of course I have."

"No, you haven't, but your surprising thoughtfulness aside, I do have a reason for seeking you out."

Refusing a groan, Norman pulled out his pocket watch, took

note of the time, and tried not to smile. Returning the watch to his pocket, he nodded to his mother. "And while I would love nothing more than to engage in a discussion with you, Theo will be here within the next ten minutes to pick me up. We're going to the factory to fetch some steel to begin building that peddle-boat for Gemma and Oscar. Can't very well show up at one of our factories in bathing attire, can I?"

"We can hold our discussion while you're getting changed."

Realizing there was no sense arguing because his mother was clearly not going to be put off, Norman blew out a breath before he took his mother's arm, walking with her through his workshop, then up the steps to his apartment. Opening the door, he gestured her inside. Mary settled her attention on him the moment they reached his sitting room.

"I recently had a lovely chat with Mrs. Martin Tripp" was how she started their discussion.

"Who?"

"Mrs. Tripp, one of the ladies with whom I play whist every Thursday. She has a daughter who made her debut last year, a lovely young lady by the name of Blossom, and, as it turns out, Blossom is in need of an escort to the Palmer Ball."

"I'm already escorting someone to the ball, Mother, as you very well know."

Mary waved that aside. "A girl from Marshall Field & Company is not an appropriate guest."

"Beatrix is completely appropriate, and besides, it would hardly be acceptable for me to renege on my promise to escort her." He smiled. "You did insist I take all those decorum lessons in my youth, and I well remember the rule that states 'gentlemen shall not beg off a planned engagement unless a death has occurred.'"

"But Blossom is a most lovely girl."

"So is Beatrix."

Mary's gaze sharpened on Norman's face. "You believe this Beatrix is lovely?"

"I think it's time I get changed before Theo shows up."

"Fine" was all his mother said to that as she spun on her heel. "I'll just occupy myself by tidying up this place until you're done. I thought you said you'd already put your sitting room to rights after the disaster it was when you had all those clothes strewn about, but evidently I misheard you."

Norman cast a quick look around the room, the hair standing up on the back of his neck when his gaze settled on Theo's fashion magazines, ones he'd stacked on a table but were now scattered about, a few of them having fallen to the floor.

He didn't hesitate to take a firm grip of his mother's arm before he hustled her toward the door.

"What are you doing?" Mary demanded.

He didn't slow his pace. "Someone's been in here, Mother, because this room was perfectly tidy when I left for my run. That means there *is* some skullduggery afoot, and I may have use of those Pinkerton men after all."

Three hours after learning someone had snuck into his rooms—in broad daylight no less—tossed his belongings about, and then managed to escape undetected, Norman still couldn't seem to puzzle out the incident to satisfaction.

Yes, there were many men he'd met while in New York who'd been overtly interested in his research and had wanted to either work with him or buy his research outright, but not one of them had seemed to possess the intellect needed to have been able to realize so quickly that he'd altered the research he'd left behind after the train heist.

That whoever responsible was willing to resort to breaking into his home lent the whole affair a rather desperate air.

The only consolation he had was that Agent Cochran was convinced the person was no longer on his mother's property, having discovered horse tracks some distance away from Norman's workshop. Those tracks suggested the would-be thief had left a horse hidden behind some bushes and had used that horse to make a stealthy departure before Norman returned from his run.

Clearly, that person had been keeping a close eye on Norman, which meant Norman was going to have to make an effort to deviate from his normal schedule in the hopes of thwarting any new plans the potential thieves had in mind.

Using a wrench to twist a bolt into place, he crawled out from underneath a generator at the Nesbit Steel Factory, realizing his attempt at distracting himself from the troubling situation at hand had not been as successful as he'd hoped, not with how furious he still was.

His mother could have happened upon the criminal, or criminals, at any time, or . . . Gemma and Oscar could have happened upon them while scavenging about in his workshop, a thought that had his fury level rising exponentially.

Because whoever had tried to locate that research had been unsuccessful that morning, as his papers were still safely stowed away in a safe he'd created to look like an abandoned washing machine, that meant there would certainly be additional attempts to locate his papers. His mother had grasped that point immediately, which was why she'd already hired more Pinkerton men to guard not only him, but also to guard her property.

Those Pinkerton agents had arrived promptly after receiving the note Agent Cochran sent them, and their presence was the only reason Norman had felt comfortable leaving his home—that, and his mother had plans for the afternoon and wouldn't be at home anyway.

After rising to his feet, Norman accepted a towel from Mr. Daniel Batchelor, an engineer at Nesbit Steel Factory, and began wiping the grease from his hands. Attempting to push his disturbing thoughts aside, knowing they'd come barreling back to torment him soon enough, he nodded to Daniel. "I rerouted some circuits and found a few breaks in the cables. I took care of those, and as soon as Miss Robinson returns with that magnetized ring I told you about, I'll install that and the generator should work more efficiently."

"Sure do appreciate it," Daniel said. "This particular generator fails about three times a week, forcing us to shut down some areas of production while we get it up and running again."

Norman frowned. "Do you frequently encounter difficulties with the machines?"

"Every single one of them has their problems, but your father and brother have numerous engineers such as myself on the job, so we're always able to get operations up and running again." Daniel shrugged. "Just takes a lot of time throughout the week."

"What seems to be the problem now?" a voice called from behind Norman.

Turning, Norman found his older brother, Stanley, striding his way, coming to a stop directly in front of Daniel. Stanley shot a look to Norman, frowned for all of a second, then his mouth dropped open. "Norman, I didn't recognize you at first. Where's your hair?"

A touch of the anger still lingering in Norman's veins faded as he stepped forward and shook his brother's hand. "I left a great deal of it behind at the barber shop."

"It's about time. What are you doing here?"

"I dropped by the factory to pick up some steel to use for a peddle-boat that Gemma, Oscar, Theo, and I are in the process of making." Norman glanced to Daniel. "But then I came across Daniel, and he told me about the generator. Because I welcomed the distraction, I figured I might as well have a look."

"Distraction from what?"

"Long story." Norman nodded to the generator in question. "I recalibrated a few things, which should see it performing better, and after Theo brings me a certain part, I'll get that installed and that'll have the generator up and—"

"Theodosia's here?" Stanley interrupted, glancing around as he raised a hand and took to smoothing down his hair.

"Not presently. She's gone off to get a part, but she'll be back directly."

"Ah, so she drove you here?"

"No, I came with Mort, but Theo drove her wagon beside us."

Stanley blinked. "Who's Mort?"

Norman shrugged. "That's a long story as well, but what are you doing on the factory floor? I thought you usually spent the afternoons in your office, going over orders."

Stanley blew out a breath. "Seems to me as if you and I have quite a few things to catch up on. Let's go to my office so we can exchange stories in a quieter setting."

Finding that to be an excellent suggestion, Norman nodded before he turned to Daniel. "Would you send Miss Robinson up to Stanley's office when she returns?"

"Certainly," Daniel said, returning the nod. He then nodded to Stanley before he walked away.

Falling into step beside his brother, Norman moved across the factory floor and up a flight of stairs. Walking into Stanley's office, he took a seat on a chair that had seen better days as Stanley closed the door.

After taking a seat behind a desk brimming with paperwork, Stanley considered Norman for a long moment before he shook his head. "Mother's been saying for a few weeks now that there's something the matter with you, and I have to say, given that you just took it upon yourself to fix a generator, she might be right."

"Nothing's the matter with me, and I'm sure I've fixed a machine here or there for you."

"No, you haven't."

Norman frowned when not a single instance sprang to mind where he'd fixed anything at any of the factories his family owned. "I feel I must beg your forgiveness for that lapse because it's inexcusable that I've never offered to help before."

Concern flickered through Stanley's eyes. "You're dying, aren't you?"

"I'm not dying."

"Then you've lost all your money, and this is your way of buttering me up to extend you a loan."

"Don't be insulting. My wealth has increased tenfold this year through investments I made with the Standard Oil company."

Stanley frowned. "You make investments?"

"Of course I do. I take an hour every week to scan the stock market, then purchase stocks I believe are going to trend well."

"And you are successful with your investments?"

"I just told you I've increased my fortune tenfold this year alone."

Something that looked very much like disgruntlement flickered over Stanley's face. "Is that why you didn't want me to invest your money years ago, after you came into your trust from Grandfather Nesbit?"

"Yes, but I would have thought you knew that from the moment I declined your offer."

"How could I have possibly known that?"

Norman began drumming his fingers against the arm of the chair, until he remembered Beatrix telling him that particular habit was annoying to others. "Why do I get the impression that you've been annoyed with me for quite some time about this?"

"Because it *was* annoying, especially because you never bothered to explain to me why you were declining my offer. I thought you were being arrogant."

"Arrogant?"

Stanley nodded. "You've never been keen to accept advice or assistance from anyone, which I've always thought was driven by intellectual arrogance."

"Huh" was all Norman could think to respond to that as truth suddenly hit him from out of nowhere. "I do wish I could deny that, but I'm afraid you're right, which means I owe you an apology for being arrogant as well as for annoying you."

"Should I take that as an apology for *all* the times you've annoyed me?"

Norman blinked. "I've annoyed you often?"

"You're my younger brother, Norman. Of course you've annoyed me often."

"Would you find me less annoying if I offer to make some investments on your behalf? I seem to be more than adept at increasing fortunes."

"There really is something dreadfully wrong with you, isn't there?"

"Nothing is wrong with me."

Stanley ignored that. "Have you blown something up recently and suffered a concussed head?"

"I haven't blown up anything for a few months now, having set aside some of my more volatile experiments after Theo lost a great deal of her hair and part of an eyebrow when an experiment went rather wrong."

"What could you have possibly been doing that caused Theodosia to lose her hair and an eyebrow?"

"We were trying to improve upon Ludwig Boltzmann's theory about statistical derivations of physical and chemical concepts, especially entropy and the distribution of molecular velocities in the gas phase, which . . ." Norman trailed off when he noticed his brother looking a bit glassy-eyed. "But forgive me. I've recently been told I come across as a complete bore when I start pontificating on my experiments or research. Allow me to say that our experiment involved gas, but we misjudged the heat we were using, and it, well, blew up, taking Theo's hair with it."

Stanley sat forward. "Someone actually told you that you're a bore?"

"In great detail."

The corners of Stanley's lips twitched. "I don't imagine anyone has ever told you that before."

"It was a novel experience, but upon further reflection, I came to the realization that I *am* a bore at times. That point was further driven home when I was reading *The Gentlemen's Book of Etiquette and Manual of Politeness* by Cecil B. Hartley. He wrote, and I'm paraphrasing here, that a gentleman must never speak of his own business or profession, because to confine the conversation to the subject or pursuit of one's own specialty is considered vulgar."

"You've read a book on gentlemen's etiquette?"

"I've read several, all of which seem to agree that a gentleman should not flaunt his intelligence and instead adopt a more modest air, which will allow those around him to feel free to converse about any number of subjects without fearing their own intellects may be thrown into question."

Stanley regarded Norman for a long moment, an odd look in his eyes, before he picked up a pen and began twirling it around. "You reading etiquette books can only mean one thing. . . . You've finally decided to court Theodosia."

"What?"

"Theodosia. You've finally realized her worth and have decided to court her."

"Don't be ridiculous. Theo and I will never be anything other than friends."

Stanley blinked. "But I thought . . ."

"You thought what?" Norman pressed when Stanley stopped talking.

"I thought the two of you would eventually settle down together because she's the only woman you ever spend any time with."

"Theo and I are far too similar to ever want to settle down together." Norman caught his brother's eye. "But why are you asking about my relationship with Theo?"

Something odd once again flickered through Stanley's eyes before he smiled and shrugged. "Shouldn't I be interested in my brother's friends?"

"I find your interest rather curious."

Stanley waved that aside. "It's not curious at all, but speaking of curious, I'm curious as to whether or not you're taking Theodosia to the Palmer ball."

"She's going with Harvey Cabot."

"Harvey Cabot?" Stanley got up from his chair and started pacing around the room. "He's a bounder of the worst sort, flitting from one lady to another with little thought to the trail of broken hearts he leaves behind. Why would Theodosia want to go to the ball with him?"

"I believe because he asked her. Her father threw his full support behind the invitation."

"Harvey's a lazy, spoiled man who lacks ambition and—"
Stanley stopped walking and peered at Norman. "Do you think
Theodosia holds Harvey in high regard?"

"I think she may have been flattered that he was showing an
interest in her, until she witnessed him behaving rudely to Beatrix
at Marshall Field & Company the other day."

The moment he realized he'd spoken Beatrix's name out loud,
Norman knew he'd made a grave mistake because Stanley's gaze
sharpened on him and he immediately pulled a chair directly in
front of Norman and sat down. Fifteen minutes later, after one of
the most intense interrogations Norman could remember, Stanley
leaned back in his chair and crossed his arms over his chest.

"So let me see if I have this correct. You and Theo have taken it
upon yourselves to research how to impress a lady through fashion
magazines and etiquette books?"

"We have, and I have to say, I've been rather surprised with
how much information is out there about the matter. Some of it
is very insightful."

Stanley frowned. "And has that Mort you mentioned earlier
been helping you with this research project as well?"

"I haven't had an opportunity yet to see if Mort will be beneficial to the project or not."

"You're going to have to explain that more sufficiently."

Norman smiled. "I suppose that was rather vague. But you see,
Mort, I'm sure you'll be surprised to hear, isn't a gentleman. He's
more along the lines of a noble steed."

"You've purchased a horse?"

"Mort's a mule."

Stanley blinked. "I don't believe I've ever heard a mule being
called a noble steed."

Norman's lips began to curve. "I'm sure you haven't, but I
find that calling Mort a noble steed is amusing, especially since
it seems to aggravate Theo." He shook his head. "She's the one
who insisted I acquire a noble steed in the first place. Apparently,
she realized that every romance book she's taken to reading of

late—done so for pure scientific research, of course—has the hero riding a noble steed. That's what convinced her I needed to get one, and no amount of arguing on my part would change her mind."

"You could have refused."

"Don't think I didn't consider that. But what you might not know about Theo is this—she's relentless when she gets an idea in her head and wouldn't stop pestering me about acquiring a horse. She even tracked down a horse auction being held at the Washington Park Club and immediately began pestering me to attend. Since her pestering was making it very difficult to work on the design plans for Gemma's peddle-boat, I agreed to attend the auction—not that I agreed to purchase a horse there, mind you, but merely agreed in order to stop the incessant badgering."

"A horse auction would have been filled with horses—an animal you detest."

"I've recently read that a gentleman should be possessed of a brave and adventurous spirit, something Theo pointed out in the midst of her badgering."

"I . . . see."

"The skepticism in your tone suggests you don't see at all, and even though being surrounded by so many horses left me uneasy, that feeling disappeared straightaway the moment I laid eyes on Mort."

"The mule?"

Norman nodded. "He was standing some distance from all the horses, and he looked so out of place that I found myself drawn to him. One look into his sad, dejected eyes, and I knew he was the noble steed for me." Norman smiled. "Mort's a peculiar animal, and I found it rather fitting that I, a gentleman known to be peculiar as well, would acquire a peculiar mode of transportation."

"You've ridden this mule?"

Norman nodded. "Tossed up my accounts the first two times I took him around the block because he didn't have an even gait. That's since been resolved because Mort only needed to become adjusted to someone riding him, and now I'm quite convinced we make a fine sight as we amble along."

Stanley sat forward and shook his head. "I never thought you'd ride again, which means this Beatrix must be of great importance to you, especially since it's becoming abundantly clear you're going to extreme measures to try to impress her."

"I wouldn't say I'm going to *extreme* measures."

"You're riding a mule about town. I'd say that's fairly extreme." Stanley caught Norman's eye. "Are you, by chance, taking her to the Palmer affair?"

"I am."

"And does anyone know that?"

"Theo and Constance do. Mother too."

Stanley's eyes widened. "Bet that was an uncomfortable discussion for you since Mother was overwrought when you started bringing Theodosia to society events, but a salesgirl, well, I suspect she was downright apoplectic."

Norman winced. "She didn't reach the apoplectic stage, but she did take to lecturing me over the danger of becoming involved with a woman *not of our station*, concerned that Beatrix was only interested in me because of my money." He blew out a breath. "I thought that would be the end of it, but then Mother tracked me down earlier today to continue trying to discourage me in regard to Beatrix."

"I take it she wasn't successful with that?"

"She didn't have the opportunity to claim success, not after I realized someone had tried to burglar my rooms while Mother was still attempting to make me see matters her way."

Stanley sat forward in his chair. "Someone tried to burglar your rooms and you're only now getting around to telling me that?"

It took another ten minutes to explain that situation to his brother. "So now I have no choice but to accept that someone is still out to steal my papers," he finally finished. "Which has, unfortunately, brought danger to the front door of the family."

Stanley narrowed his eyes. "That does seem to be the case, but if there's such a threat, why in the world did you send Theodosia back to your workshop to fetch a part for one of the machines? She could even now be in real danger, which means—" Stanley got up and bolted for the door, disappearing a second later.

Before Norman could even get out of his chair, or contemplate to satisfaction why Stanley seemed to be bringing Theo into the conversation so often, he heard Theo's voice drift through the doorway, followed by a very un-Theo-like giggle, proving that she'd not encountered any danger. Although, given the giggle, he might be wrong about that.

CHAPTER 22

Before Norman could fully process the idea of a giggling Theo, Stanley was escorting Theo into the room, beaming a bright smile at her, one she was certainly returning.

"I see you've returned in one piece," Norman said, rising to his feet. "Stanley was concerned that I'd been careless with your welfare by asking you to go back to my workshop after the burglary."

Theo's cheeks turned pink. "How kind of you to worry, Stanley, but I had Agent Cochran with me the entire time. He's of the belief that since there are now so many agents guarding the house, it would be foolish for anyone to make another attempt to break into Norman's apartment." Theo nodded to Norman as she held up the magnetic ring for the generator. "This was exactly where you said it would be, and I left your suit, tie, and fresh shirt with Stanley's secretary, who promised to hang them up so they won't get wrinkled."

"You brought my brother another set of clothes?" Stanley asked as he offered Theo his arm, which had her face turning pinker than ever, before he escorted her to the nearest chair, making a big to-do about getting her settled. He then excused himself, telling Norman and Theo he'd be back directly after he spoke to his secretary about bringing coffee in for them.

Taking a moment to check in with Agent Cochran, who'd been lingering in the doorway, Norman felt relief flow over him when the Pinkerton man assured him there'd been no further trouble, and that his parents' entire property was now sufficiently guarded and would continue to be guarded until the culprits behind the burglary were apprehended.

After thanking Agent Cochran for the update, Norman returned to Stanley's office, finding Theo staring off into space before she evidently realized he'd returned, which had her turning to him.

"What's wrong with Stanley?" were the first words out of her mouth.

"What do you mean?"

"He took my arm to escort me all of five feet and has begun calling me Theodosia when he normally calls me Miss Robinson. Now he just went off to fetch us coffee. It's very unusual behavior for him." She tilted her head. "Do you suppose he's recently taken to studying etiquette books as well?"

"Why would he do that?"

"Perhaps he's sweet on a lady and has decided, as you have, that he needs to improve the way he interacts with ladies." Theo shrugged. "Maybe he's practicing his charm on me since I'm the only woman around."

"Why do you seem disappointed about that?"

"Who said I'm disappointed?"

"Your face says you're disappointed."

"I'm sure my face isn't saying any such thing."

"I'll be happy to fetch a mirror so you can see that disappointment for yourself."

"Theo doesn't need a mirror," Stanley said, reappearing through the door. "She looks lovely today, as she always does."

Norman's world shifted once again because, clearly, Stanley was not *practicing* being charming. He was, without a doubt, fond of Theo. And Theo, if Norman wasn't mistaken, was fond of Stanley, which explained why she'd looked so disappointed when she'd been considering that Stanley was sweet on someone else.

Sitting back in his chair, Norman looked at Theo for a few seconds, then switched his attention to Stanley, then back to Theo, then Stanley, then . . .

"Why's he doing that?" Stanley asked, taking a seat directly beside Theo, who smiled a smile that one could almost consider flirtatious—if it wasn't coming from Theo, that is.

"He's thinking, and apparently, very strenuously. He often stops talking when he thinks like that."

"Do you find it as disconcerting as I do?"

"You get used to it after a while," Theo said right as Stanley's secretary, Mr. George Lennox, entered the room, carrying a tray that held a battered coffeepot and mismatched cups. Placing the tray on top of some of the paperwork on Stanley's desk, he inclined his head and quit the room.

Theo moved to the coffeepot and poured out three cups. She added two cubes of sugar to the cup she handed to Stanley, one cube to the cup she handed to Norman, then took the last cup for herself, not adding a single cube because she always preferred her coffee black.

The notion that Theo knew how many cubes of sugar Stanley took in his coffee was telling in and of itself, and it suggested she'd been observing Stanley far more closely than Norman had realized over the years.

Retaking her seat, Theo took a sip of her coffee. "What were the two of you discussing before I arrived?"

Stanley smiled. "We were discussing Mort, an animal Norman told me you were responsible for badgering him into purchasing."

Theo released a snort. "I didn't badger him to buy Mort. *I* chose a magnificent black stallion that I thought warranted the name of noble steed. However, when I turned to point that stallion out to Norman, he wasn't there. I found him talking to Mort, and before I could formulate a suitable argument against the mule, Norman had already bought the creature."

Norman released a snort of his own. "I then bought *you* that stallion because you were so put out with me, so I'll thank you to discontinue making disparaging remarks about Mort, something I'm certain must hurt his tender mule feelings."

Theo nodded to Stanley. "I don't say disparaging things about Mort. Norman's exaggerating because he got annoyed with me earlier when I happened to mention that Mort seems to have only two speeds—slow and stop." She smiled. "But Sebastian, my new stallion, suits the term *noble steed* most admirably because he's fast and beautiful, although he does have a slightly questionable nature."

"There's nothing slightly questionable about Sebastian's nature," Norman argued. "He's a nasty beast that scares both Mort and me half to death. That's why I insisted you attach Rosie, your pony that is certainly feeling dejected by your acquiring of Sebastian, to your wagon today to spare Mort and me heart palpitations."

Theo narrowed her eyes. "I've yet to find a single instance in any of our research books, fashion magazines, or even novels where anyone has been impressed by the sight of a man riding a mule."

"Mules are a dependable mode of transportation."

"If you don't need to arrive at your destination in a timely fashion."

Ignoring that remark, Norman turned to Stanley. "Weren't you going to explain to me why you've taken to being out on the factory floor so much?"

Stanley grinned. "I think I'd rather continue listening to you and Theodosia discuss Mort."

"There's nothing more to discuss. Mort is a reliable mule, and that's all I have to say about him. But returning to the factory?"

Stanley's grin faded. "We're experiencing some labor issues at the moment, mostly because the men are clamoring for an eight- or, at the very least, ten-hour workday. There's been talk of a strike, which is why I'm now spending so much time on the factory floor."

Theo sat forward. "My father's been concerned about strikes at the Pullman company ever since the Haymarket Riot this past spring."

Stanley sat forward as well, the action leaving him inches from Theo, who was now turning rather pink in the face again. "The Haymarket incident was troubling. Even though the men responsible for throwing those bombs in the midst of the policemen who'd come to disperse the rally were apprehended, there's still an undercurrent of unrest brewing in the city."

Norman's brow furrowed. "The Haymarket Riot happened last May. This is October. I would think, given the time that's elapsed, that any lingering resentment caused by that unfortunate event has dissipated."

"The only way that resentment is going to dissipate is if all the owners and investors in our Chicago factories agree to abandon the twelve-hour workday."

"Wouldn't it be prudent to at least consider reducing the weekly hours required to avoid potential strikes and additional riots?" Norman asked.

Stanley shook his head. "Demand for steel and iron always fluctuates. When demand is high, we need our workers to work twelve-hour days in order to earn as much profit as we can so that when demand decreases, we can continue on without having to close any of our factories."

"I could help increase the efficiency of the factories by updating the machinery," Norman offered. "That might allow you some negotiation room when it comes to reducing hours."

"That would take you months, if not years, to complete."

Norman shrugged. "I am a Nesbit, Stanley. It's past time I begin acting like one and take an interest in the family business."

Stanley narrowed his eyes. "What about your inventions and your scientific research?"

"It'll be there for me when I have a spare moment."

Stanley's eyes narrowed another fraction. "But what about becoming the first scientist to perfect different ways of harnessing electricity?"

Norman waved that aside. "If we're actually able to improve the efficiency of our many factories, that would be considered an important achievement as well. It could benefit other factories throughout the country, thus improving people's lives much more than any electric vehicle I may eventually invent."

"I believe I'm going to like Miss Beatrix Waterbury," Stanley surprised him by saying. "She's obviously responsible for this new-and-improved you. Even without having met her, I know she'll be a woman I can appreciate."

"Beatrix does seem to have had a marked influence on him," Theo agreed, exchanging smiles with Stanley that almost seemed sappy. "Just imagine the influence she could have on him if they continue their association."

"He might become an entirely different person altogether."

"I *am* sitting right here," Norman muttered. "But if the two of you are done with whatever this is you're doing, which looks like a spot of flirtation if you ask me, I'd like to know, Stanley, if the offer I just made to take an interest in the family business is one you're going to accept."

"We weren't flirting," Theo and Stanley said in unison, before they smiled at each other, smiles that were sappier than ever.

Norman lifted his hand to rake it through his hair, until he remembered he didn't have much hair left on his head these days. "Fine, you weren't flirting. But returning to my offer?"

Stanley stared at Theo for another ten seconds before he finally pulled his gaze from her and nodded to Norman. "Of course I accept your offer, Norman, as well as greatly appreciate it. And if you are successful with improving our efficiency, Father and I will certainly be able to discuss decreasing the hourly workday, something that may very well help save our factories in the end." He shook his head. "You're going to have to broach this idea with Father, though."

"You don't think he will approve?"

"Oh, he'll approve. I just don't think he'll believe me if I tell him about your unexpected offer."

Even though Norman wanted to argue that point, he knew Stanley was right. He'd never shown an interest in the family business before, which meant their father would be skeptical about the offer unless it came directly from Norman.

Rising to his feet, Norman strode over to Stanley, extending his hand to his brother. As Stanley stood and took the hand, giving it an unexpected squeeze, Norman realized in that moment that he was finally, and after far too many years, taking the first step to truly becoming a part of his family. Curiously enough, he knew he had Beatrix to thank for that.

CHAPTER 23

"Any plans for this evening?"

Beatrix looked up from the box of table linens she'd been un-packing and smiled at Miss Joan Caton, a woman who worked beside her in the Bargain Basement, the department where Beatrix now found herself since she'd been relieved of her duties at the coat check.

"I'm having dinner with my aunt," she replied. "What about you?"

"I'm off to enjoy a show at the Columbia Theater with some other Marshall Field & Company girls. You're more than welcome to join us if you're not looking forward to spending the evening with your aunt."

"How kind of you to offer. And while an evening at the theater sounds lovely, I don't want to disappoint my aunt, and dinner with her, odd as this may seem, is always an adventure."

"Perhaps next time," Miss Caton said before she took a step closer to Beatrix and lowered her voice. "Everyone is appalled about you getting yanked out of the coat check and sent to the Bargain Basement. Why, if you ask me, you should have been pro-moted for having the gumption to reprimand Mrs. Sturgis. She's a nightmare every time she comes into the store, and it's unaccept-able that she injured you and then complained when you brought the injury to her attention. I suppose, though, that you must have been relieved to have been sent here instead of getting dismissed. It's most unusual for management to be so forgiving when an employee offends a customer, even if that customer is wrong."

Beatrix knew full well that the only reason she'd not been dismissed was because Mr. Selfridge had been in New York when she'd had her encounter with Mrs. Sturgis, which had left Mr. Bailer responsible for disciplining her.

After arriving in his office, Beatrix had found Mr. Bailer in a most agitated frame of mind, his agitation a direct result of the dilemma he found himself in. He was quick to inform her that her behavior was cause for immediate dismissal, but he wasn't going to dismiss her because Miss Gladys Huttleston had personally requested he consider hiring Beatrix in the first place. Aunt Gladys apparently terrified poor Mr. Bailer, although he hadn't seemed aware of the relationship Beatrix shared with her aunt.

Mr. Bailer had then proceeded to hem and haw about what should be done with Beatrix, finally settling on sending her to the Bargain Basement, stating that Mrs. Sturgis had demanded that she never see Beatrix again. Reassigning Beatrix to the Bargain Basement would evidently assure that never happened because apparently Mrs. Sturgis never stepped foot in the part of the store that offered customers goods at an inexpensive price.

Beatrix had been beyond put out over the notion she was being disciplined because an insufferable customer had all but accosted her. However, she'd been downright dumbfounded to learn she was going to suffer yet *another* reduction in pay.

In all honesty, she was beginning to think, what with how often she was suffering demotions, that there might come a day when she was paying the store for the privilege of working there.

Her dumbfounded state had only increased when, after Mr. Bailer had informed her of her reduced circumstances, he'd handed her another copy of the Marshall Field & Company handbook, insisting she read it cover to cover right there in his office. That demand had made it impossible to see Norman again because she didn't finish the book until the store had closed for the day. Norman, unfortunately, was nowhere to be found once she left the store and took to the street.

She'd actually considered taking the train to Prairie Avenue and seeking him out at his house—what with how she'd memorized his address—because she'd felt the strongest urge to tell him all about the grievances she'd suffered that day, until she'd realized it would hardly be acceptable for her to seek out a gentleman at his house, no matter the reason.

That she'd felt compelled to seek Norman out in the first place was telling in and of itself.

"After you finish unpacking that box, Miss Waterbury, you may leave for the day, as may you, Miss Caton."

Shaking aside her thoughts and sending Mrs. Hartford, the supervisor of the linen department, a smile, Beatrix quickly finished her task. She then walked through the Bargain Basement with Miss Caton and up the stairs to the employee room, where she'd left her coat. After bidding Miss Caton good-bye, she headed for the stairs.

"Miss Waterbury, wait up," Miss Dixon, her former co-worker from the coat check, called from behind Beatrix, catching up with her a moment later. "I've been hoping to run into you. How's the Bargain Basement? I've heard it's a madhouse down there at times."

"Oh it is, but the customers who shop in the basement are far more pleasant than the ones who shop on the main floors, so I'm not upset at all about my recent demotion."

"Mrs. Sturgis was in the store yesterday, probably to make sure you weren't still manning the coat check counter." Miss Dixon shook her head. "She's a nasty piece of work, but that wasn't why I was hoping to run into you. It's about Mr. Norman Nesbit. He came looking for you three days ago after you'd been called to Mr. Bailer's office. He then came to the store yesterday as well and seemed most concerned when I told him you no longer worked in the coat check but had been reassigned."

"Norman was at the store yesterday?"

Miss Dixon smiled. "Looking for you." Her smile dimmed. "I'm afraid I was unable to fully explain what had happened to you because Mrs. Goodman came skulking about. But"—she leaned closer to Beatrix—"I heard him tell Miss Robinson, the lady who was accompanying him again, that he wouldn't be able to track you down after work yesterday because he had a commitment with his niece. I wanted to tell you all that so you would know he's been asking about you. In my humble opinion, I believe that suggests that Mr. Nesbit is sweet on you."

Beatrix tripped over the bottom step. Regaining her balance, she headed for the employee exit. "He's not sweet on me."

Miss Dixon stepped with Beatrix through the door and began walking down the sidewalk beside her, pulling Beatrix to a stop a few seconds later as she grinned and nodded to something across the street.

"You're wrong about that because Mr. Nesbit's right over there. . . . But is he sitting on a donkey?"

Beatrix spun around and peered across the street, blinking when she spotted Norman, who was, indeed, sitting on top of an animal. She turned back to Miss Dixon. "I think that may be a mule."

"An odd choice to be sure, but he's waving at you."

Turning again, Beatrix discovered that Miss Dixon was right, and that Norman was waving at her, although Theodosia, who was standing beside a pony attached to a wagon, was, curiously enough, leafing through a book.

"I should see what Norman wants," she said, which earned her another grin from Miss Dixon.

"I believe I've already stated what he wants—and that would be you."

Returning the grin even though she was fairly certain Miss Dixon was wrong in her conclusions, Beatrix told her to enjoy her Sunday off, then headed for the street.

Waiting for an open buggy to pass, Beatrix began making her way through traffic, coming to an abrupt stop right before she reached the sidewalk when she saw three men on horses charging directly for Norman.

That they were all wearing kerchiefs over their faces was not an encouraging sight.

"Norman, watch out!" she yelled, charging forward.

Before she could reach him, though, the mule he was sitting on surged into motion, carrying Norman down the street at a most rapid rate of speed, the hat on his head being left behind as he struggled to get control of his mule.

"Whoa, Mort, whoa!" she heard him yell, apparently still unaware that he was coming under attack, two of the riders now in hot pursuit. The third rider, however, had run afoul of Theodosia, who'd taken a swing at him with the book she'd been leafing through, knocking that man off his horse.

Thankfully, another man galloped into view, throwing himself off his horse and at the man Theodosia was now whacking with the book.

Relieved that Theodosia was getting assistance from a man who was evidently one of the Pinkertons responsible for keeping Norman safe, Beatrix spun around and headed after Norman. Racing down the street, she dodged carriages and wagons, until she spotted Norman a moment later.

He was no longer on the mule but lying in the street, one of the handkerchief-wearing men trying to wrestle a satchel away from him.

She stopped in her tracks when she saw the other man, one who was still on his horse, pull out a pistol and aim it directly at Norman. Fumbling with her reticule, she withdrew her pistol purse and took aim.

"Lower your weapon or I'll shoot!" she yelled.

When the man didn't lower his weapon, but instead turned it on her, she flipped out the trigger on the bottom of the purse right as a gunshot rang out.

After she lurched to the right, her relief was swift when she didn't feel a bullet tear through her, but then the man took aim at her again, and she didn't hesitate to pull the trigger, thankful in that moment that her father had had the foresight to make certain she knew how to aim and operate a gun.

Satisfaction was immediate when the man dropped from his horse and landed on the ground, reaching for his shoulder, where a small stain of blood was already forming. That satisfaction, however, was short-lived when the man jumped from the ground and began advancing her way, menace in his every step.

Raising her purse again, she pulled the trigger, horrified when nothing happened and the man kept advancing.

"Beatrix, run!" she heard Norman yell right as the man stopped directly in front of her.

"You!" he roared. "I should have known."

Sweat beaded her forehead and began running down her face the moment she recognized the distinct scar running up from where the kerchief covered the lower half of the man's face.

It was the man who'd tried to rob her on the train, the same man who'd threatened to shoot her then, and given the rage she now detected in his voice and the horrifying sight of him raising his hand and training his pistol on her again, she was all but certain that this time he *would* shoot her.

Norman broke free of the man who'd been trying to wrestle his satchel away from him and flew at the man threatening her, tackling him to the ground.

Norman and the man rolled over and over again, and then Theodosia was rolling with them, having jumped on the back of the man after he'd rolled Norman beneath him.

"Good heavens, is that Miss Robinson?"

Turning, Beatrix found Mr. Harvey Cabot standing beside her, his mouth slightly agape as he stared at the sight of Theodosia thrashing around on the ground. A second later he apparently came to his senses and leapt forward, pulling Theodosia from the melee before throwing himself into it.

Grappling with the man who was all but smothering Norman, Harvey planted a fist in the man's face as Norman lumbered to his feet and dashed a hand over a nose that was now bleeding. He immediately turned to the man who'd been trying to steal his satchel, who was now bolting down the street, the mule Norman had been riding chasing after him.

"Give me your pistol purse," Norman yelled to Beatrix.

Rushing to his side, she thrust the purse at him. "It misfired just a minute ago so it might not be of much help."

Norman nodded, tossed his satchel to her, then was off, racing down the street after his mule and the assailant.

"He's getting away."

Turning, Beatrix discovered Harvey Cabot lying on the ground, blood smeared on his face, his jacket torn, and his trousers covered in the filth that littered the street. The man with the scar was already leaping up into the saddle of his horse, kneeing his horse into motion.

Temper flashed anew when she realized there was little chance she could capture the man since she was on foot, nor would the Pinkerton man be of any assistance because he was in the process of securing the man Theodosia had first subdued. Her temper soon turned to trepidation, though, when the scarred man turned his horse in her direction. Realizing that the man was after Norman's satchel and would probably resort to deadly means to get it, Beatrix turned and bolted across the street toward Marshall Field & Company, hoping to find safety and concealment amongst the well-heeled customers.

Before she could make it to the front door, though, police whistles rent the air. When she turned around, she saw the scarred man racing away, apparently unwilling to face arrest, even if that meant leaving Norman's satchel behind.

Ignoring the curious looks of the ladies who were whispering behind gloved hands outside of Marshall Field & Company, Beatrix hurried back across the street and found Theodosia helping Harvey Cabot to his feet.

"Ah, Beatrix, thank goodness you're all right," Theodosia said, releasing Harvey's arm and apparently not noticing that he immediately began to wobble about. "I was so afraid that man was going to run you over with his horse before the police arrived."

"The two of you all right?" the Pinkerton agent asked, appearing by Beatrix's side with one of the assailants in tow, a man who now had his hands firmly secured behind his back.

"We're fine, Agent Cochran, but Norman went after one of the men," Theodosia said.

"Which way?" Agent Cochran demanded.

Beatrix nodded down the street.

Agent Cochran pushed the man he'd apprehended toward Harvey Cabot and nodded. "This is James McCaleb. He's a habitual criminal and is known to be crafty, but I need you to see after him so I can go after Mr. Nesbit. Do not allow him to get away."

Before Harvey could do more than blink, Agent Cochran was in motion, racing down the street.

"How am I supposed to see after this criminal when I don't even have a pistol to—"

Whatever else Harvey had been about to say got lost when James McCaleb suddenly headbutted Harvey, which had him dropping like a stone to the ground. McCaleb then bolted away, moving remarkably fast for a man without the use of his hands.

Beatrix, with Theodosia by her side, took a step forward, preparing to run after the man. But she was pulled to an abrupt stop a few seconds later by Harvey, who had gotten rather unsteadily to his feet.

"You two have no business chasing after a criminal. You're ladies, and as such, you need to leave this nastiness to the discretion of men," Harvey rasped, keeping a firm grip on Beatrix's arm when she tried to tug it away from him.

"Release me," Beatrix said between gritted teeth.

"I think not," Harvey returned before he frowned at Theodosia. "Your father would never forgive me if I let something happen to you. Why, it's bad enough you threw yourself into a brawl, but I'll not tell your father the details of that if you behave yourself from this point forward."

Theodosia shoved back a hat that had slipped almost over her eyes. "You overstep yourself, Harvey. You have no authority over me, and I'll thank you to remember that."

"Your father and I have an understanding in regards to you," Harvey said, continuing to hold Theodosia's arm although he did release Beatrix's.

"I don't know you nearly well enough for you to have any type of understanding with my father." Theodosia shrugged her way out of his hold. "Do know, however, that I intend to have a chat with Father at my earliest convenience since he's suffering from some type of misunderstanding about the two of us."

"I would think his expectations should already be clear to you," Harvey argued. "Surely you've realized how amiable he's been to the idea of me escorting you around town."

"You're taking me to a ball," Theodosia said impatiently, looking around. "That's not escorting me around town." She nodded to something over Harvey's shoulder. "Seems like half the city's police are descending on the scene. We should give them our account of what happened, which will hopefully assist them with apprehending the criminals."

Beatrix nodded, tightened her grip on the satchel, then fell into step with Theodosia as Harvey trailed after them. They were quickly approached by three officers, who immediately began taking notes as they recounted their stories.

As she talked to the policemen, Beatrix saw numerous customers from Marshall Field & Company pass by, as well as numerous employees. But whereas the employees sent her looks of concern, the customers regarded her with suspicion, as if she'd done something wrong and was now being interrogated by the police about it.

She couldn't help but wonder—and not for the first time—how those ladies would have reacted if they knew her as Miss Beatrix Waterbury, grand American heiress, instead of a salesgirl from a store they frequented.

"There's Norman," Theodosia said. "He must have lost the

man he was chasing as well, but . . . oh dear, he seems to be experiencing some difficulty with Mort."

Excusing herself from Officer Stewart, the policeman who'd just finished questioning her, Beatrix turned her attention to a most curious scene unfolding half a block away.

Norman was standing in the middle of the street, gesturing to a mule that appeared to have turned stubborn since the animal was not moving a single inch, blocking traffic in the process.

"Should I assume that's Mort?" Beatrix asked.

Theodosia nodded. "Indeed. Norman only recently purchased him, even though I told him mules have a tendency to be tricky, but he wouldn't listen." She shook her head as Norman tugged on Mort's reins to no avail. "Bet he wishes he'd listened to me now."

"While I'm more than intrigued about why Norman would have purchased a mule, I believe he needs some assistance."

After handing Norman's satchel to Theodosia, Beatrix slipped through the congested traffic, stopping a few feet from Norman.

He was looking the worse for wear, his clothing dirty and his face smeared with blood, while a distinct trace of annoyance radiated from him as he tried to pull Mort into motion.

"You're trying my patience," Beatrix heard him say. "And while you're obviously feeling very disappointed that you were unable to catch that criminal, we have important matters to attend to now, such as ascertaining that Beatrix and Theo haven't been harmed. That means you need to stop being muleheaded and come with me."

"Theodosia and I are fine," Beatrix said, which had Norman lifting his head, relief replacing the annoyance as he looked her over. "As for your mule, may I suggest you simply release the reins and walk away from him? Mules are complicated creatures, and Mort may be testing you at the moment to see how much he can get away with. I would advise you to not allow him to do that because you'll never be able to manage him properly after that."

Norman frowned. "You think I should let go of the reins?"

"I do. That will show him you're the boss, and he should eventually follow you." She glanced at Mort and frowned. "Although mules are unpredictable, so my advice might be way off the mark."

"Since I don't have any other thoughts about how to get him to move, I'm willing to give it a go," Norman said, dropping the reins and striding Beatrix's way, taking her arm once he reached her side. "Shall we?" he asked, tugging her forward without so much as a single look back at Mort.

Beatrix tried to sneak a peek but stopped when Norman shook his head. "Aren't you even curious as to whether or not he's following us?" she asked.

"'Course I am, but at the risk of allowing him to believe he's got the upper hand, I'm going to ignore my curiosity for the moment." With that, Norman increased his pace, not slowing down until they were a few feet away from Theodosia and Harvey.

"Harvey's looking rough," Norman said, nodding to Harvey. He was standing beside Theodosia, who'd retrieved her book from the ground and was, peculiarly enough, reading it again.

"The poor man got headbutted by James McCaleb, the one and only criminal we captured, who then made a rather spectacular escape."

"He got away?"

"He did. Theodosia and I tried to go after him, but Harvey, unfortunately, intervened. He apparently thought that we, as women, had no business pursuing a member of the criminal persuasion."

Norman's hold tightened on her arm before he nodded. "Odd as this may seem, for once I find myself in full agreement with Harvey."

Chapter 24

For some unfathomable reason, the second after those words left his mouth, Beatrix's nose shot into the air. She then sent him a glare, shrugged her arm free, and stomped away. Mort, to Norman's surprise, trotted past him a second later, not bothering to spare Norman a single glance.

Finding himself more than a bit bewildered, Norman strode after Beatrix, catching up with her in no time. "Forgive me, but I get the distinct impression that I've somehow annoyed you again."

She stopped in her tracks and plunked her hands on her hips. "Of course you annoyed me. Here I was beginning to believe you were coming around in regard to how you view women, but apparently, I was wrong about that."

"What do my views on women have to do with any of this?"

"You just said you agree with Harvey, after I told you that he took Theodosia and me to task for wading into the fray."

Norman blinked. "I agree with Harvey because the two of you could have been grievously injured, and that would have distressed me more than I can say."

Beatrix blinked back at him. "Oh."

"Yes, oh, but I do apologize if what I said came out wrong." He smiled, and then winced when the action reminded him he'd recently taken a blow to the face. "The only excuse I have, though, is that I fear I'm not myself at the moment, not after what just happened, and what happened earlier today."

"What happened earlier today?"

"Someone broke into my home, but—" Norman looked up and gestured to the officers still milling around—"perhaps now isn't the moment to get into all that."

"I'll expect you to tell me everything at some point," Beatrix said, moving into motion again until she reached Theo's side, Mort stopping directly beside her, where he proceeded to nuzzle Beatrix with his nose.

"That's an interesting animal you've got there," Harvey said to Beatrix, dabbing at a small trickle of blood running down his cheek with a handkerchief.

"He's Norman's."

Harvey sent a nod Norman's way. "Ah well, I suppose you have your reasons for owning a donkey, Norman, and I must say it does fit your reputation as an eccentric about town."

"Mort's a mule," Norman pointed out. "I purchased him at an auction because he's rather odd, quite like myself, and he was being overlooked because all the horses at the auction were prime specimens."

Harvey frowned. "You bought him because he's odd?"

"That, and I overheard a man say Mort was destined for the glue factory if he wasn't sold that day, which made it impossible for me not to buy him."

Beatrix moved closer to him and placed her hand on his arm. "You saved him from the glue factory?"

The touch of Beatrix's hand on his arm sent a jolt racing through him, one that left him feeling as if his brain had been scrambled as well.

"He did," Theo said, looking up from where she'd been riffling through an etiquette book and pulling Norman from a state of what could certainly be considered shock. "I think it speaks to Norman's sensitive nature."

Not certain he was comfortable with Theo delving into his sensitive nature, because from what he'd read, sensitive natures in gentlemen left ladies with the impression they were not manly men, Norman opened his mouth, but swallowed the argument he was about to make when Beatrix sent him a smile.

It was a lovely smile, filled with genuine warmth, which made him think that perhaps he'd been wrong about the whole sensitive nature business.

"Oh, lovely, you still have my pistol purse," Beatrix said, interrupting his thoughts as she nodded to the small pistol he was clutching in his hand. "Were you able to get it to fire again?"

Before Norman could answer, Harvey stepped forward. "What do you mean, fire it again?" He nodded to Norman. "Did you shoot at those criminals?"

"I didn't. Beatrix did. Hit one of them in the shoulder."

Harvey's eyes went wide as he considered Beatrix. "You shot a man? How did I miss that?"

"You were preoccupied," Theo returned. "And before you start lecturing Beatrix about the inadvisability of her shooting a man, she had no choice in the matter. If she'd not pulled out her pistol and taken action, Norman could very well be dead right now."

Harvey turned to Norman. "Why would anyone want to shoot you?"

Having no reason to avoid the question, Norman shrugged. "Someone's been trying to steal my research pertaining to double electrical currents. The danger has apparently escalated, what with how my home was burgled this morning and how I was just set upon by some of the same men who tried to divest me of my research when they held up a train I was recently on."

Harvey blinked. "Who would possibly want to steal your research? Seems a curious thing to want to steal, and most scientists, myself included, take pride in making new discoveries on our own."

"I've narrowed down my list of suspects considerably of late, although given recent events and the unexpected intelligence of the person evidently behind the attempts to steal my research, I'm going to have to rethink that list."

Harvey tilted his head. "Who do you believe *is* trying to steal your research?"

"I originally thought it could be any of the men who attended that meeting about electricity in New York with me, yourself included at first."

Harvey seemed to swell on the spot. "I'm insulted you'd even consider me a suspect."

Norman frowned. "I said you were a suspect *at first*. I've since changed my mind."

"As I would expect you to, but . . ." Harvey returned Norman's frown. "What made you change your mind?"

"Because I'm aware of your limitations as a scientist, and . . ." Norman's voice trailed off when Beatrix cleared her throat in a rather telling fashion.

"What?" he asked.

"You obviously suffered a blow to your head, quite like Mr. Cabot did, which is the only explanation I can think of to explain why you were just about to insult Mr. Cabot's abilities as a scientist."

"I'm sure Harvey's well aware of his limitations and should be relieved that those limitations are exactly why he's no longer on my list of suspects."

The look Beatrix shot him next was filled with exasperation, but before she could voice that exasperation, Theo lifted her head from her book.

"I just read the most excellent advice."

Beatrix frowned. "What is it?"

"It says that good humor is the only shield to protect oneself from the barbs of satirists, and that you're supposed to be the first to laugh at a jest made against you because then others will laugh with you instead of at you."

"What does that have to do with anything?" Norman asked.

Theo shrugged. "Well, nothing, but it's interesting, isn't it? And it might come in handy at some point."

"As riveting as that is, Theodosia," Harvey began, "if we could return to the topic of Norman's research, I feel compelled to state loud and clear that I am *not* responsible for the attempted theft of his work." He handed Norman his satchel, something Norman hadn't even realized Harvey had been holding. "As further proof, I'm now returning Norman's satchel to him that Theodosia thrust at me when she decided she needed to look something up in one of her books. If I *had* been the culprit, I certainly wouldn't be doing that, now, would I?"

"Unless you just decided that it would benefit your claim of innocence by not running off with the satchel, which would certainly muddy the waters and throw suspicion in another direction," Theo argued as she looked up from her book again.

Harvey's brows drew together. "I'm doing nothing of the sort, but dare I hope you just blurted out that bit of nonsense because of another passage in that ridiculous book?"

"There's nothing ridiculous about Cecile B. Hartley's book. And I was just reading that a gentleman must never stop another gentleman in the street during business hours because there's a chance that will delay said gentleman from important matters of business."

Harvey stared at Theo for a few seconds before he nodded. "I believe this is where I offer to escort you home because you're evidently overwrought, which is the only explanation I can come to, given that I don't believe this is quite the time to be leafing through a book on what seems to be general manners."

Theo wrinkled her nose. "While I thank you for the offer, I'm not returning home after this. I've been invited to attend a dinner with Miss Gladys Huttleston, and if I return home, I'll be late. And that engagement, I'll have you know, is why I've been leafing through this book at what you must see as a most unusual time, but I'm about to be served a seven-course meal and I have no idea what to expect in regard to proper cutlery."

Harvey opened his mouth, but before he could say anything, Miss Amelia Burden suddenly burst on the scene, stumbling to a stop when she reached his side.

"Mr. Cabot, what's happened to you? I was just at Marshall Field & Company and learned that a shooting had taken place on the street, and—" She stopped talking and drew in a deep breath. "I came to see if the rumors were true, but you've not been shot, have you?"

Harvey took hold of Miss Burden's arm and gave it a pat. "I'm fine, although I'm sure I must look a sight." He nodded to Norman. "I happened upon Norman right as he was being accosted by a group of criminals I've recently learned are determined to steal his research. I, as a gentleman, had no choice but to throw myself into the madness, especially after I realized Miss Robinson had apparently thrown herself on top of a man who was trying to tear Norman's satchel straight out of his grasp."

Miss Burden turned to Theo. "Surely Mr. Cabot is mistaken and you weren't tussling with a member of the criminal set, were you?"

Theo had returned to her book and didn't bother to so much as look up. "I couldn't very well ignore that Norman was being assaulted."

Miss Burden nodded to Harvey. "You should escort Miss Robinson home immediately. She's clearly suffering the effects of her recent misadventure."

"I already offered," Harvey said. "She declined because she's made arrangements to attend a dinner engagement with Miss Gladys Huttleston and doesn't care to be late."

"Why would anyone willingly attend a dinner with Miss Huttleston?" Miss Burden asked. "She's an unpleasant woman, odd most would say, and—"

"I suggest you have a care before you say any additional disparaging comments about Miss Huttleston," Beatrix snapped.

Miss Burden raised a hand to her throat. "On my word, you're that coat check girl from Marshall Field & Company. And while

I have no idea what you're doing involved in all this, *you* should have a care in how you speak to me, unless you'd like to find yourself dismissed from your position for behaving so rudely toward a valued customer."

"We're not currently in the store, Miss Burden," Beatrix said shortly. "Which means I don't need to have a care in watching what I say to a woman making disparaging remarks about Miss Gladys Huttleston."

"Why would you care what I say about Miss Huttleston?"

"She's my aunt."

Miss Burden blinked. "But you're a coat check girl."

"I've recently been demoted."

Miss Burden blinked again. "But your aunt is rumored to be one of the wealthiest women in the city."

"Indeed" was all Beatrix said to that right as Agent Cochran strode into view and made his way directly for Norman.

"He got away," Agent Cochran said, shaking his head. "But at least we have James McCaleb. He might, under a bit of pressure, divulge the names of the other two men."

"James McCaleb escaped," Beatrix said, nodding to Harvey. "He overpowered Mr. Cabot and ran off."

Agent Cochran ran a hand through his hair, his hat nowhere in sight. "I should have known James would try something like that, but I didn't want to leave Norman out there unprotected with so many men of the criminal persuasion running loose." He blew out a breath. "On a positive note, though, at least we have one name of someone who most certainly can shed some light on the earlier events of the day. I don't imagine it will take long to track James down, not with how many Pinkerton men are now working on this case."

"Pinkerton agents are involved with all this?" Miss Burden asked.

Beatrix frowned at Miss Burden before she nodded to Harvey. "Perhaps it would be for the best, Mr. Cabot, if you were to escort Miss Burden home. She seems flustered by what's happened, and the last thing any of us need is for her to suffer a fit of the vapors. Theodosia will be fine because I'll ride with her to my aunt's house, so there's no need to fret about leaving her unprotected."

"I *would* like to go home," Miss Burden proclaimed, holding out her hand to Harvey. "I would also appreciate you escorting me there because I drove my pony cart to the store earlier, but I certainly don't feel safe right now."

Harvey looked at Theodosia, who was once again reading, then back to Miss Burden, then returned his attention to Theodosia and cleared his throat. "If you've no objections, Miss Robinson, I'm going to escort Miss Burden home. I will, however, call on you tomorrow."

Theo waved that aside. "There's no need for that, Harvey. I'll see you on the evening of the Palmer ball. I'm sure you've already told my father what time you'll be by to pick me up for that ball, so that's soon enough to see you again."

Miss Burden looked Theo up and down, her brow wrinkling. "I'm sure you're much relieved, Miss Robinson, that the Palmer ball is still some time away. You'll have plenty of time to scrub that dirt from your person and get yourself presentable, although I'm not certain much can be done with that hair of yours."

Irritation began trickling through Norman's veins. "I'm certain Theo will look lovely at the ball, Miss Burden, dressed in the first state of fashion, if I'm not mistaken."

His irritation increased when Miss Burden looked Theo over again and pursed her lips. "If you say so, Mr. Nesbit, but looking lovely might be a somewhat insurmountable goal for Miss Robinson." With that, she grabbed hold of Harvey's arm and together the two of them hurried away, Miss Burden whispering furiously into Harvey's ear.

"Are you certain you won't change your mind about attending the ball with that man?" Norman asked, which had Theodosia abandoning her book and looking up.

"According to numerous etiquette books, a lady never reneges on a promise, and I did, unfortunately, promise Harvey Cabot

I'd attend the ball with him." She snapped her book shut and tucked it under her arm. "I have no idea, though, why you said I'd be dressed in the latest fashions when you know I'm wearing my one and only gown."

"Couldn't seem to help myself."

"Yes, well, now I'm in a bit of a pickle because I know that awful Miss Burden will enjoy nothing more than mocking me when she sees me dressed in my slightly shabby ball gown."

Norman frowned, considered that for a moment, then nodded. "I'll take care of it."

Theodosia blinked. "Take care of what?"

"Never you mind," Norman said before he turned to Beatrix and handed her his satchel. "This is for you."

"You're giving me your research papers?"

He shook his head. "My research papers aren't in there, although I should have realized someone might mistakenly believe that and chosen a different type of bag to carry what *is* in there. That might have spared us our recent drama."

Beatrix opened the latch and frowned as she pulled out the object nestled inside. "Is this some type of club meant to be used as a weapon?"

"It's not a club. It's a prosthetic limb I made for Hubert. I finished it late last night and wanted you to take it to him today. I'm hopeful he'll find it more comfortable than that peg leg he's currently wearing." He helped her unwrap the fabric he'd wrapped around the limb. "I made it out of steel, and it has a suction socket to keep it firmly attached as well as a polycentric knee, which I won't bore you with what that means, and an articulated foot."

For the longest moment, Beatrix didn't say a thing, but then she lifted her head, her eyes sparkling quite as Theo's had done when they'd decided they were friends.

"Thank you, Norman," she said quietly. "Hubert will love this, and it was very kind of you to take the time to make him something that will certainly improve his quality of life."

234

The most curious feeling took that moment to settle in the very pit of his stomach, a feeling that then spread throughout his body and left him rather warm. He took a step toward Beatrix, powerless to do anything else, and then he reached out and drew her toward him, right before he lowered his head and kissed her.

CHAPTER 25

The moment Norman's lips touched hers, Beatrix felt a shock run through her, one that was obviously responsible for her foot lifting of its own accord, something she'd read about in the romance novels she enjoyed but certainly had never experienced before.

A second later, she felt something jab into her stomach, realizing it was the prosthetic limb. A second after that, she realized they were standing in the middle of a busy sidewalk, and . . . it was not exactly the right setting or moment for her to be enjoying a kiss with Norman.

Tearing her lips from his, Beatrix took a step back, faltering because her foot had yet to return to the ground. Flailing about, she grabbed hold of Norman's arm, concern immediately replacing the shock she'd been feeling when she glanced at his face and found him staring at her, quite as if he was experiencing some manner of shock as well but hadn't snapped out of it just yet.

Glancing past Norman, Beatrix found Theodosia leafing through her book like mad, shaking her head and muttering until she finally stopped on a page, lifting her head a moment later.

"While this is certainly an unexpected development between the two of you, not to fret," Theodosia said, catching Beatrix's eye. "According to this book, as long as Norman immediately asks for your hand in marriage, there will be no unfortunate repercussions for the kiss the two of you just shared in front of an entire crowd, if you neglected to realize that."

Beatrix felt the most unusual urge to laugh, until Norman blinked and began looking as if someone had knocked him over the head with something heavy.

"We have to get married?" he asked, the note of disbelief in his voice going far to banish any urge Beatrix felt to laugh, replaced with an urge to kick the man.

"Of course not."

"But Theo just said it's expected after we, ah . . . kissed—a kiss I'm going to assume was noticed by more than a few people."

Beatrix gestured around at the crowded sidewalk, where not a single person was seemingly paying them the least little mind. She looked back at Norman. "No one noticed anything, probably because everyone's preoccupied with getting home in time for dinner."

Norman's brows drew together. "I'm sure someone must have witnessed our kiss."

"I did," Theodosia said, holding up her hand.

"Yes, well, you don't count, Theodosia," Beatrix returned. "And besides, you must realize that Norman's unexpected kiss was simply a result of him suffering some adverse effects from the madness we just experienced. I believe that sensitive nature you mentioned earlier might have been to blame."

Norman narrowed his eyes on her. "I'm not having an adverse effect to any madness, and I'm not all that sensitive."

Beatrix arched a brow. "Does that mean it's a frequent occurrence for you to kiss an unsuspecting lady on the street?"

"Can't say that I've ever done this before."

"Then for goodness' sake, put that unusual mind of yours to work, which will then allow you to conclude that your recent behavior was some manner of anomaly."

"My mind is in fine working order. It's working so well, in fact, that I have to consider what Theo suggested."

Beatrix waved that aside. "Honestly, Norman, even though we did enjoy a rather pleasant kiss, there's no need for talk of marriage."

His eyes narrowed another fraction. "You found our kiss to be merely pleasant?"

"Indeed."

"Perhaps I should give it another go. I'm sure I'm capable of delivering a more-than-pleasant kiss."

"Absolutely not, and with that settled, we're going to put this matter behind us for good." She nodded to Theodosia, who missed the nod because she was once again thumbing through her book. "We should get on our way, Theodosia. If you've forgotten, my aunt has plans for you this evening, ones I'm going to assume she's anxious to begin."

Theodosia lifted her head. "I thought Gladys was only going to serve me dinner and then have one of her friends try to fix my hair."

"That's some optimistic thinking on your part," Beatrix said, pretending not to notice that Theodosia's eyes had gone wide and that she'd begun muttering under her breath about "terrifying situations," followed by her hair not being that bad after all.

Returning the prosthetic limb to the satchel she'd dropped to the ground at some point, probably the second Norman's lips had touched hers, Beatrix nodded to Norman, who was watching her far too intently and looking remarkably disgruntled.

"I'm off to make certain Agent Cochran has no further questions for me, and then I'm going home," Beatrix said.

"Just like that? With no further discussion about what transpired between the two of us?"

"Yes." Turning on her heel, she marched her way over to Agent Cochran, who greeted her rather warily, lending the impression he'd witnessed the kiss but was too polite to mention it. Thankful for that small favor, she was quickly told that there was nothing further he needed from her, since he'd already informed the police about what little he knew of their attackers. He then nodded to Officer Stewart, the policeman who'd taken down her account of events, and told her that Officer Stewart was going to be accompanying her home since dangerous criminals were still afoot.

Not having a reason to argue with that because she certainly didn't want to suffer another ambush, Beatrix thanked Agent Cochran before she moved to rejoin Norman and Theodosia.

That those two were whispering to each other was somewhat concerning, especially when their whispers came to a rapid end the second they caught sight of her.

"Am I interrupting?" she asked, earning a nod from Norman and a shake of the head from Theodosia.

"Shall we get on our way?" Theodosia all but chirped, an unusual state of affairs because Beatrix had never heard the woman sound quite so chipper. "My pony and wagon are just over there, next to Mort."

Norman's eyes widened. "I forgot all about Mort."

"Which you might not want to do again since you are now responsible for that animal's welfare," Beatrix said.

"I would have remembered him at some point, but . . ." Norman looked over to where Mort was standing by Theodosia's wagon, his eyes closed and body completely still. "Do you think there's something wrong with him?"

Beatrix glanced to Mort. "I believe he's sleeping, which might put him in a more amiable frame of mind, making him keener to cooperate with you—after he wakes up, that is."

Norman tilted his head. "Perhaps you should be the one to wake him up since he does seem to like you more than me."

"I'm not waking him up, and the only reason he gravitated to me earlier was because I've always enjoyed animals and they can sense that." She caught Norman's eye. "If you want Mort to like you, you might begin showing him more affection. You could also go off and find a carrot at one of the local groceries and give it to him when you do wake him up."

Norman's brows drew together. "I hardly believe Mort will hold me in any great affection if I abandon him to the sidewalk while I go off to find him a carrot."

Beatrix glanced around, then nodded to a young boy who was waiting to shine shoes. "I bet he'd watch over Mort if you offer to pay him. But only give him half up front and then promise him the other half when you return so you don't find yourself missing a mule."

"Sensible to be sure."

"I'm nothing if not sensible."

"And stubborn as well, what with you being—"

Theodosia cleared her throat in a very telling manner, which had Norman stopping midsentence and sending his friend a quirk of a brow, which she returned, before he blew out a breath and shrugged. "Fine, I've nothing else to say on that matter." He nodded to Theodosia. "I'll be by the Huttleston house later to see you safely home. Don't even think about leaving there until I come to fetch you." He pulled out his pocket watch and frowned. "However, since I've just realized I'm running short on time, I'm off to . . ."

"Buy Mort a carrot?" Beatrix finished for him when Norman simply stopped talking.

Norman shot a look to Theodosia before he returned his attention to Beatrix. "Indeed." With that, he strode over and had a quick word with Agent Cochran. He then set his sights on the shoe-shine boy, who grinned in delight over whatever Norman said to him before moving to stand beside the still-sleeping Mort as Norman strode away.

"Why do I get the feeling he's not off to purchase a carrot?" Theodosia asked.

"What else would he be off to purchase?"

Theodosia winced. "I'd rather not dwell on that because there are endless possibilities at this point, what with the gauntlet you threw down at Norman's feet."

Before Beatrix could ask a single question about that, Theodosia was moving toward her wagon, barely waiting for Beatrix to take her seat beside her on the bench before she got Rosie, her pony, ambling down State Street.

"I don't know where your aunt lives," Theodosia said.

"Hyde Park," Beatrix said before she rattled off the address.

Theodosia nodded as she urged Rosie into a trot, steering their way through the crowded street with a practiced hand.

"What gauntlet did I throw down?" Beatrix asked after they'd left the worst of the traffic behind.

"You told Norman you found his kiss merely pleasant."

"I wasn't complaining about it."

Theodosia blew out a breath. "I didn't say you were, but I have to imagine Norman was hoping for higher praise, such as you found his kiss to be invigorating or perhaps exhilarating." She tilted her head. "Did you truly not find it to be either of those things?"

Beatrix released a sigh as she considered the question.

The truth of the matter was—of course she had.

His kiss had been responsible for her foot kicking up, an action she'd never thought to experience. That she'd even had such a reaction to his kiss left her reeling.

She was a lady who'd decided that she might never marry. But ever since she'd met Norman, she'd been feeling all sorts of peculiar. She'd begun to wonder if her aunt was right and that the unexpected path she now found herself on actually did include not only a chance to understand the plight of the working woman, but also had something to do with Norman.

Beatrix blinked as another terrifying thought sprang to mind.

For the briefest of moments, after Theodosia had announced Beatrix and Norman needed to get married, she had realized that she wasn't exactly opposed to that idea and might have been just a touch disappointed when Norman seemed so shocked with the notion.

"You do know that Norman will put a concerted effort into proving to you he's capable of delivering a more-than-pleasant kiss, don't you?" Theodosia asked, drawing Beatrix from her thoughts.

"Surely not" was all Beatrix could think to say to that, the very idea of Norman attempting to kiss her again leaving her feeling rather tingly all over.

"I'm afraid so, although because it didn't seem to me that you weren't enjoying his kiss—not that I intended to gawk at you while the two of you were kissing. I don't imagine you're too concerned about him kissing you again, are you?"

"How do you know I was enjoying his kiss?"

"Your leg shot up." Theodosia nodded. "I recently read about that in an article in *Harper's Bazaar*. A rising leg often accompanies an exceptional kiss, especially if a lady is overly fond of the gentleman kissing her."

"I never claimed to be overly fond of Norman."

Theodosia didn't seem to hear that as her eyes went rather distant. "I imagine my leg might very well kick up if the gentleman I hold in affection ever kissed me."

Relieved to have a reason to avoid further talk of her kiss with Norman, Beatrix placed a hand on Theodosia's arm. "I didn't realize you held a certain gentleman in affection."

Theodosia's cheeks turned pink. "I must admit that I do, but this particular gentleman is beyond my reach. He's far too handsome to be interested in someone like me, and besides, he has ladies fawning over him at all the society events. That he's yet to settle on a specific lady, even though he's in his thirties, suggests he's a man with very discerning tastes, which means he'll never return my affection because . . . well . . . look at me."

Beatrix squared her shoulders. "I am looking at you, Theodosia, and what I see is an accomplished woman possessed of an unusual intellect as well as a woman who has proven herself to be a fast friend to a man many must find difficult. Any gentleman would be fortunate to be the recipient of your affection." She tilted her head. "Does this gentleman have any idea you hold him in high esteem?"

Theodosia's eyes widened. "I should say not, nor am I planning on allowing that to ever happen. It would certainly make time in his presence uncomfortable, and I'd have to take to planning out my visits with Norman to make certain this gentleman wasn't—"

"He's friends with Norman?" Beatrix asked when Theodosia went silent.

"I've said too much," Theodosia muttered before she turned Rosie down a different street, smiling brightly at Beatrix a second later. "Weren't we discussing Norman and that gauntlet you've thrown?"

"I find myself not nearly as curious about that right now."

Theodosia ignored her. "What you need to understand about Norman is this—he's very focused when he comes up against a challenge, and he'll definitely see your remark about a pleasant kiss as a challenge. Although . . ." Theodosia bit her lip. "Since he and I have been taking great pains to have him avoid annoying you, it will be interesting to see how he goes about it."

Taking a second to direct Theodosia to turn Rosie down another street, Beatrix glanced over her shoulder to make certain Officer Stewart was still following them, then wrinkled her nose. "What do you mean, you and Norman have been taking great pains to learn how to avoid annoying me?"

"Aren't we almost to your aunt's house yet?"

"No, we still have a good ten minutes to go, so out with it."

For a second, Beatrix didn't think Theodosia was going to cooperate, but then she released a sigh right before she launched into an explanation regarding what she and Norman had been doing over the past week, finishing by saying, "But even though Norman's been attempting to adhere to the rules of the general manners and etiquette articles we've researched, you still seem to get annoyed with him often, which is forcing us to rethink our theories."

"Am I to understand that I'm some sort of experiment to the two of you?"

"When you put it that way, it sounds slightly insulting."

"It is insulting, although I'm still incredibly bewildered regarding why Norman felt it necessary to go to such extremes in the first place."

For a moment, Theodosia didn't respond, but then she blew out a breath. "Because he's fond of you and wanted you to return that fondness."

Beatrix felt a distinct flutter in her stomach. "Just because he frequently annoys me doesn't mean I'm not fond of the man."

Theodosia settled a stern eye on Beatrix. "You just recently told me you never said you were overly fond of Norman."

"I did say that, didn't I?" Beatrix asked weakly, even as she realized there was no good way to extract herself from what was turning into a very interesting, yet revealing conversation. "I suppose what you need to know about me is this—most gentlemen of my acquaintance are careful to never annoy me, which is why I find Norman somewhat refreshing."

Theodosia steered her wagon around a large hole, turning to Beatrix after she got Rosie back on the right side of the lane. "Refreshing is encouraging, and I hope you'll also find it refreshing and not annoying when Norman puts a concerted effort into changing your mind about his kissing abilities."

"How exactly would he go about doing that?" Beatrix asked slowly.

"By finding other opportunities to kiss you, of course."

CHAPTER 26

"You've not said much in response to my declaration about Norman's plans regarding kissing," Theodosia said to Beatrix in a low voice an hour later as they sat around a large table, waiting for Aunt Gladys to signal for their first course to be brought in.

"There's really nothing else to say about the matter," Beatrix returned, placing a stiff linen napkin on her lap and then nodding at Theodosia to do the same.

"I'm sure there's much to say, and frankly, there are many questions I find I now have about kissing, questions you may be able to answer since, clearly, you've been kissed, whereas I, well, I've not had the pleasure of that experience," Theodosia whispered before she placed her napkin in her lap, the seven other women at the table following suit. The only woman who lived under Aunt Gladys's roof who was not in attendance was Miss Colette Balley, who'd gone off to help her sister with a sick child.

"Nicely done, ladies," Aunt Gladys boomed, drawing Beatrix's attention while earning a sigh from Theodosia, who'd obviously been hoping to continue their kissing discussion.

It wasn't that Beatrix was opposed to discussing kissing. However, given that Theodosia would undoubtedly divulge whatever was said about the matter to Norman, what with how she didn't seem to grasp that women expected each other not to divulge secrets that may be rather embarrassing, it would be for the best to delay the discussion until Beatrix had ample time to consider the matter.

"I hope all of you are famished," Aunt Gladys said, reaching for a small bell resting beside her and giving it a ring. "It's time for the first course, and our esteemed chefs this evening, Roberta and Susan, have chosen quail eggs in aspic with caviar."

"What's caviar?" Mamie asked.

"I don't think you should start asking questions again, Mamie," Blanche said. "The last time we were served a fancy meal, you asked what terrapin was and then spent the remainder of the meal going on and on about a turtle named Franklin."

"Even thinking about eating poor Franklin should have made everyone queasy," Mamie shot back.

"Caviar is fish eggs," Aunt Gladys said firmly. "It's a delicacy, and since I'm sure none of you have ever had pet fish eggs, no one should get queasy."

Mamie frowned. "I'm not so sure about that. Fish eggs sound revolting, unless they're scrambled and cooked up."

"They're eaten raw," Aunt Gladys said, looking over her shoulder to the door and frowning. She picked up the bell again and gave it a vigorous ring, watching the door for a good few seconds before she blew out a breath. "Edgar is apparently put out with me again."

"He did seem annoyed after Miss Beatrix told everyone about the attack outside Marshall Field & Company," Della said, looking up from where she'd been scribbling something onto a notepad. "I've just been writing down an account of everything Beatrix and Theodosia told us so that nothing will be forgotten. I'll type up my notes later on this evening."

"An excellent idea," Aunt Gladys proclaimed. "Once the culprits are apprehended, they'll be taken to trial, and your notes may be able to aid a prosecutor with winning a case against these men, especially if Beatrix and Theodosia remember something they share here that they forgot to tell the authorities." She looked to the door again, picked up the bell, and gave it another ring, this time more vigorously than the last. When Edgar did not appear in the doorway, Aunt Gladys rose from her chair and marched out of the room.

A mere thirty seconds later, she breezed back in again. "Good news, ladies," she exclaimed. "Edgar, I'm pleased to report, is not put out with me. He's been helping Hubert with that new leg Norman made for him. They're having a few difficulties getting it attached."

Theodosia removed her napkin from her lap and rose to her feet. "I may not have much proficiency with maneuvering my way around a table set with all this cutlery," she began, nodding to the cutlery in question, "but I'm more than proficient with matters involving prosthetics. If you'll excuse me, I'll be back directly."

Aunt Gladys beamed at Theodosia as she quit the room, then sat back down and turned her smile on Beatrix. "She's such a delightful lady and has so much potential. I have to imagine she'll take Chicago society by storm after we get done with her."

"I'm not sure Theodosia will be comfortable with that," Beatrix said slowly.

"Being comfortable is overrated," Aunt Gladys returned as Edgar strode into the room, Hubert right behind him, with Theodosia bringing up the rear.

"Ah, I see Theodosia got your leg on properly, Hubert, and in no time at all," Aunt Gladys said.

Hubert grinned. "She knows what she's about with this leg," he said before he proceeded to walk up and down the dining room, his gait still slightly stiff, but he was moving much better than Beatrix had ever seen him move. "The foot part works almost like a real foot, and the leg is incredibly comfortable, something I never expected."

"What a lovely happenstance it's turning out to be, having Norman drop into our lives as he did," Aunt Gladys proclaimed before she sent a pointed look Beatrix's way. "Why, one could claim without hesitation that Norman's arrival in our lives has presented us with unforeseen opportunities that may very well enrich our lives, something I'm certain Hubert agrees with, given the freedom his new leg is sure to bring him."

"Indeed it will," Hubert said, still walking back and forth across the dining room. "I'll never be able to thank Mr. Nesbit enough for his unexpected kindness."

Beatrix's heart missed a few beats.

Norman *had* shown an incredible kindness by creating a new leg for Hubert, a kindness that had certainly taken her by surprise, but a kindness that spoke to who Norman really was.

He was not just a man possessed of an unusual mind, but a man who truly could make a difference in the world, although she wasn't certain he understood that quite yet.

"Can we please get on with this meal?" Roberta demanded from the doorway. "Creating a seven-course meal and then serving it so that it may be fully enjoyed is all about the timing, and our timing is soon to suffer if we don't start serving everyone their food."

Aunt Gladys nodded. "An excellent point, Roberta, but I must mention that it's rare for a professional chef to speak so crossly to her customers."

Roberta rolled her eyes. "I don't know of any professional women chefs, Gladys. We're always considered lowly cooks." With that, she disappeared from view, Hubert and Edgar trailing after her.

Less than five minutes later, the first course was served, followed by six more courses. The menu Roberta and Susan had chosen was an ambitious one. Potage Saint-Germain followed the caviar, then came *Homard Thermidor*, which Beatrix had to explain to Mamie was lobster with potatoes. Mamie didn't balk over eating that course, but she did balk at *tournedos aux morilles*, tender beef with wild mushrooms.

Mamie apparently didn't trust mushrooms so refused to eat that course, earning a lecture from Roberta, who'd stepped into the room to see how the dinner was progressing.

Aunt Gladys had been forced to intervene, sending Roberta

back to the kitchen after reminding her that *really* great chefs, of which Roberta should consider herself to be, never wasted their time berating a guest since they found that type of behavior beneath them.

The rest of the courses were spent enjoying the different dishes, which consisted of *cailles aux cerises*, which were quails with cherries, *consommé Olga*, and then the final course, chocolate-painted éclairs with crème. Aunt Gladys spent the meal dispensing instructions regarding proper table etiquette, even though she didn't bother to reprimand some of the ladies when they all but devoured the éclairs, although she did send Mamie a quirk of a brow when Mamie picked up her plate and licked the last bit of crème from it.

Sitting back in her chair as Edgar and Hubert cleared the last of the plates, Beatrix set aside her napkin and smiled at Roberta and Susan, who'd just walked into the room, anxious to discover what everyone had thought of the meal they'd prepared.

"That was excellent," Beatrix said, Theodosia nodding in agreement before she gave her stomach a pat.

"I'm stuffed to the gills," Theodosia added.

"Which I'm sure Roberta and Susan adore hearing," Aunt Gladys said, "but if you were in polite company, that is a remark that should be avoided."

"Duly noted," Theodosia said with a smile right as a loud gong sounded and everyone jumped.

"Wonder who that could be?" Aunt Gladys asked while Edgar strode from the room to answer the door.

"Perhaps it's Norman," Theodosia said. "He told me he'd be by to escort me home, but he's going to be in for a long wait since we've yet to get to my hair."

Beatrix smoothed a hand over her own hair, earning a telling look from her aunt in the process, which she ignored. Butterflies immediately began churning in her stomach, but those butterflies lost flight when Edgar walked back into the room holding a large package wrapped in brown paper, no Norman in sight.

Theodosia nodded to the package. "What do you want to bet that's from Norman, and is the first step he's taking to try to make you more amiable to accepting more kisses from him?"

The entire room went silent as Aunt Gladys leaned forward, her eyes gleaming in a most concerning way. "You never mentioned a word about Norman and kissing."

Beatrix forced a smile. "Must have slipped my mind."

Aunt Gladys arched a brow. "I highly doubt that. So what happened?"

"He kissed her," Theodosia said when Beatrix faltered.

The gleam in Aunt Gladys's eyes intensified. "Did he really?"

Theodosia nodded. "Right in the middle of the street, in front of everyone, and—"

She stopped talking when Beatrix kicked her under the table and frowned. "I never took you for a clumsy sort, Beatrix, but you've just lost control of your foot and kicked me."

"It wasn't clumsiness on my part." Beatrix turned to Aunt Gladys. "And to settle this matter once and for all, Norman only kissed me because he was swept up in the moment after the attack we suffered in the street."

"She then annoyed Norman," Theodosia interjected, "by telling him she found his kiss merely pleasant, and—"

Beatrix placed her foot directly over Theodosia's and pressed down in a rather determined fashion.

Theodosia stopped talking as her brows drew together. "Since you recently claimed you weren't being clumsy when you kicked me, may I now presume you're all but smashing my foot into the floor because you don't want me to expand on the kissing business?"

"We're going to have to have a long discussion on what friends are expected to keep to themselves," Beatrix returned.

"We're friends?"

"Of course we are."

Theodosia's eyes turned suspiciously bright. "I've never had a woman friend before."

"And now you have an entire room filled with them," Aunt Gladys proclaimed, which had all the women nodding their heads in agreement as well as Edgar and Hubert. "With that settled, and because it seems as if Beatrix is not going to divulge all when it comes to Norman, perhaps you should give Beatrix that package you're holding, Edgar."

Edgar shook his head. "It's not for Miss Beatrix. It's for Miss Theodosia."

"For me?" Theodosia asked slowly. "Why would someone send me something here instead of having it delivered to my house? And who would send me something anyways?"

Edgar walked over to Theodosia, setting the package directly in front of her after Hubert made space. "You'll have to open it up to discover all that."

Biting her lip, Theodosia ripped away the brown paper, then opened the large box, staring at the contents for a long moment, apparently rendered speechless.

Scooting her chair closer, Beatrix looked into the box and discovered a beautiful ivory gown with hundreds of glass beads attached to the fabric, glittering in the light cast from the chandelier.

"I don't understand," Theodosia whispered.

"There's a note." Beatrix plucked the note card from where it had been lying on top of the gown and handed it to Theodosia.

She opened it with hands that were now trembling, her eyes turning bright with unshed tears as she read it. She drew in a breath and lifted her head. "It's from Norman. He bought it at Marshall Field & Company, and he wants me to wear it to the Palmer ball, writing that he's been told it's a gown worthy of the phrase *in the first state of fashion*." She dashed a hand over her eyes before she grinned a somewhat wobbly grin. "He also included that I'm not to take a knife to the hem if it's too long but to ask if anyone here is proficient with alterations."

Half the women now gathered around Theodosia lifted their hands.

"Norman certainly knew what he was about, sending that gown

here," Aunt Gladys said. "What a dear friend you have in him, Theodosia, one who clearly cares about you and wants to ascertain you'll face no unkind scrutiny at the ball." She clapped her hands and nodded all around. "Ladies, it's time to take Theodosia under our wings, which means . . . to action."

Before Beatrix knew it, she and Theodosia, along with the rest of the women, had abandoned their outfits for loose-fitting trousers and blouses. They then moved to the parlor, where Edgar had placed linen sheets on the floor and hardback chairs on top of those sheets.

"I thought I was simply going to have my hair trimmed," Theodosia said warily as Blanche stopped mixing something in a large bowl and frowned.

"Your hair needs more than a trim." She nodded to the bowl. "I'm going to start by putting this on your head and allowing it to sit. Hopefully my concoction will diminish the brittleness, which will then allow me to know how to proceed with cutting and styling it."

Even though Theodosia had been remarkably silent throughout the meal, spending her time observing the antics of the women surrounding her, the mention of a concoction had a sparkle settling into her eyes. She strode to Blanche's side and immediately began throwing questions Blanche's way regarding what ingredients she was using and what the purported benefits would be, and then went on to throw out suggestions of her own that might improve Blanche's concoction, such as the addition of olive oil.

The enthusiasm Theodosia was showing suggested she might have found a new avenue to put her unusual mind to work—one that might someday see her becoming involved with the beauty industry that was only now beginning to advance in the country.

"I'm ashamed to admit I never realized how desperately Theodosia needed female companionship," Aunt Gladys said quietly, stepping up beside Beatrix. "I should have known, what with how she's been raised by a father who is known to be consumed with his work, but I didn't."

"You know now, and I have a feeling you're going to make certain Theodosia doesn't suffer from a lack of female companions ever again."

"Too right I won't." Aunt Gladys smiled and nodded to Theodosia, who was now sitting in a chair, having an oily mixture spread over her face. She then nodded to Hubert, who was helping Edgar rearrange a few chairs for some of the women, his limp having all but disappeared. "I've been thinking that there have been so many unexpected blessings of late, what with Theodosia finding friends and Hubert gaining a new leg. God certainly knew what He was about when He sent you into our lives, and by sending Norman through you as well. If you ask me, there's a plan afoot, and I'm looking forward to seeing how it continues to unfold."

Beatrix ignored the pointed look Aunt Gladys sent her next, but she couldn't ignore her aunt's words. Her friendship with Norman had clearly brought about benefits to those around her, his unexpected generosity leaving her with the distinct notion that he was a man with a great deal of potential. She couldn't deny that there was something appealing about the idea of her being around when he reached that potential.

"I'm looking for my next victim," Blanche called as she nodded to Beatrix. "Ready to have your face revitalized?"

Pushing all thoughts of Norman aside, Beatrix took a seat in the chair Blanche was pointing to. "What are you going to be doing to my face?"

"I'm going to put a mixture of lemons and cucumbers on you to see if it'll lighten up a few of your freckles."

Hoping those were all the ingredients Blanche was going to be slathering over her face, Beatrix forced what she hoped was an enthusiastic smile, which was all the incentive Blanche needed to get to work.

Fifteen minutes later, and after every woman had their faces covered with a variety of mixtures—from special herbs, fruits, vegetables, and even flour—Blanche announced that to enjoy the greatest benefits from her mixtures, they needed to completely relax, which meant all the lights needed to be turned off and silence maintained for a full thirty minutes.

After Edgar and Hubert turned off all the lights in the parlor, they left to turn off the lights throughout the house after Blanche insisted it would help with the relaxation business.

Beatrix swallowed a bubble of amusement as she sat in a pitch-black room, the smells of lemon, lime, and a variety of other scents mingling in the air.

"Sure is dark in here," someone remarked, which earned her a shush from Mamie, who was sitting on the other side of Aunt Gladys.

Grinning, Beatrix closed her eyes, finding it impossible to relax because thoughts of Norman immediately sprang to mind.

There was no denying that he was becoming important to her, and while she didn't regret her declaration that there was no need for them to marry because of a kiss, she couldn't help but wonder what marriage to a gentleman like Norman would be like.

She'd told Theodosia that she'd found his frequently annoying ways refreshing, and that was certainly nothing less than the truth. For years, gentlemen had gone out of their way to accommodate her, even with her having allowed society to believe she shared an understanding with her very good friend Thomas Hamersley. But even with them knowing she was supposedly spoken for, they'd still treated her with kid gloves because of her status as a grand American heiress.

Norman had never treated her with kid gloves, had proceeded to annoy her every other second, and had even attempted a most outlandish experiment with her as the subject, not realizing how she relished the annoying banter they frequently shared between them.

It was a—

A loud crash sounded from above them, causing everyone to jump. Aunt Gladys actually fell out of her chair and landed on the floor with a thud right as the angry screeches of cats rang out.

"We need some light," Beatrix yelled, which had Mamie striking a match she pulled from a pocket, the light from that match help-ing Blanche find the switch that turned on the electrical lights her aunt had recently installed throughout most of the house. As soon as light flooded the room, Beatrix raced for the door, Theodosia and the rest of the women close behind her.

Skidding to a stop when she reached the foot of the staircase, Beatrix glanced up, finding a man running down the steps, being chased by a herd of cats.

The scar on his face had the blood running through her veins turning to ice, but instead of trying to attack her, the man she'd shot only that afternoon raced past her and for the door, wrench-ing the door open and disappearing through it a second later, the cats in hot pursuit.

CHAPTER 27

That Norman *wasn't* dumbstruck by the sight of a man scrambling over the fortress-like fence that surrounded Gladys's house with a pack of cats leaping over that fence after him spoke volumes about the state of his life of late.

Kneeing Mort and giving a tug on the reins to set the mule after the rapidly fleeing man, Norman released a grunt when Mort refused to move. Thankfully, Agent Spencer, the Pinkerton who'd relieved Agent Cochran for the evening, was already chasing after the man, his horse apparently far better trained than Mort was.

The gate guarding the entrance to the Huttleston house creaked open, but before it was open more than a foot, another man came dashing though it, pounding down the lane as two additional cats raced through the gate, yowling up a storm.

The moment Mort caught sight of these particular cats, he bolted into motion—not after the fleeing man, but in the opposite direction. As he tried to get control of a mule that was now moving faster than Norman had thought possible, he caught a glimpse of women dressed in flowing trousers and billowing shirts racing through the gate and giving chase to the man, their faces completely covered in one of Blanche's latest beauty concoctions, if Norman wasn't mistaken.

It was a good five minutes before Mort decided to stop, and he didn't stop gradually. One minute he was galloping along, and the next he wasn't, the abrupt halt of forward motion sending Norman sailing through the air and landing with a thud on the ground.

"I'm going to have to get back to my electrical conveyance vehicle unless you start behaving like a proper mule," he told Mort, lumbering to his feet and rubbing an elbow that had taken the brunt of his fall.

Mort moseyed over to a grassy spot, sent Norman an injured look out of his big brown eyes, then proceeded to close those eyes, apparently in need of a nap.

"This is hardly the time for that nonsense," Norman told him, but when Mort didn't so much as move a single eyelash, Norman threw up his hands, turned on his heel, and began striding back down the lane, hoping Mort would eventually decide to join him at the Huttleston house.

By the time he reached the house, women were streaming back through the gate, a row of cats slinking behind them. His gaze immediately settled on Beatrix, knowing it was her even with her face covered in something questionable and her hair hidden beneath a turban.

That he could identify her so easily was not a surprise.

Beatrix had somehow become permanently etched into his very soul, and he knew he'd always be able to pick her out of a crowd. She had also become important to him, important in a way no one had ever been before.

"Norman," Beatrix exclaimed, breaking away from the crowd to rush his way. "What happened to you?"

"Got thrown from Mort."

Beatrix blinked, the action causing the paste on her face to shift, a paste that gave off the distinct smell of lemons. "Where's Mort now?"

"Taking a nap back that way," he said, gesturing up the lane that was dimly lit by a few gas lamps. "I think Mort might have an underlying fear of cats, so I'm not certain he'll rejoin us. Although I'm not quite sure about that fear, what with how he didn't bolt when the first cats leapt over the fence . . . but perhaps he didn't see those cats." He shook thoughts of Mort aside. "Any luck with the men I saw fleeing from the house?"

Beatrix released a sigh. "Afraid not. The man we were chasing had a horse waiting for him, and since we were all on foot, he got away. But Phantom, he's the black cat, jumped on the man as he was in the saddle and went after the man's face with his sharp little claws."

"That must have taken the man by surprise."

"Oh, it did, but then he gave Phantom a backhand, which sent the poor cat flying, and off the man went. I doubt Phantom will be keen to jump on a horse again."

"Mort will appreciate that." Norman pulled out a handkerchief and took a swipe at a clump of something that was about to dribble off her chin. "What is this?"

"Lemon paste mixed with mashed cucumbers and some type of oil." She grinned. "Blanche is trying to create a formula that will lighten a lady's skin. She believes I'm the perfect candidate because of my freckles."

"You want to get rid of your freckles?"

"Not particularly, but in the interest of assisting Blanche with what she hopes will turn into a lucrative beauty business someday, I'm willing to lose a few freckles or perhaps lighten them up."

"I like your freckles. They make you, well, you."

Beatrix beamed a bright smile at him. "No one's ever said that about my freckles before."

"Well, now someone has," he returned with a smile right as Gladys and Edgar strode up to join them.

"I cannot believe someone had the audacity to break into my house," Gladys exclaimed.

"There were two of them," Edgar pointed out before he glanced past Norman and frowned. "And given that the man walking up the street—a Pinkerton, if I'm not mistaken—is holding two cats and doesn't appear to have a man in custody, I believe it's safe to say that both men escaped."

That was soon confirmed when Agent Spencer reached them.

"He got away," the agent said, disgust evident in his voice. "It was James McCaleb, which leads me to believe the men came here to steal what they weren't able to steal this afternoon. He had a horse stashed up the lane, and even though the man suffered a cat attack, he still managed to jump on his horse and evade capture."

A sense of guilt was immediate.

Norman took a step closer to Beatrix. "This is my fault because they were clearly after that satchel I gave you earlier, evidently not knowing that it didn't contain my research papers."

"You can't blame yourself for this, Norman," Beatrix said. "We couldn't have known that one of those men evidently saw me take the satchel from you."

"I should have considered that," Norman argued. "It's quite unlike me to neglect such an important consideration, but now that I'm getting a better grasp of how desperate someone is to secure my research, you may be assured that I'll not be so careless again." He caught Beatrix's eye. "In fact, in order to keep you safe, I'll not be letting you out of my sight for the foreseeable future."

To his relief, Beatrix put up not a single argument to that, until he told her he wanted her to give up her job at Marshall Field & Company.

CHAPTER 28

"I've noticed there always seems to be a certain someone, as in Mr. Norman Nesbit, waiting to pick you up every evening over the past week and a half."

Swallowing the bite of sandwich she'd taken, Beatrix looked up and found Miss Dixon standing beside the table in the employee lunch room, smiling back at her.

Beatrix motioned Miss Dixon closer and lowered her voice. "Norman has turned remarkably stubborn about escorting me home ever since we were set upon by criminals right outside the store last week. Those very same criminals then broke into my aunt's home, which is why I haven't protested Norman's insistence on picking me up from work every evening."

Miss Dixon's eyes widened. "I heard rumors that you ran afoul of some criminals over a week ago but was hopeful that was just idle gossip with no basis in fact."

"Afraid not, which is why Pinkerton men have been roaming around the Bargain Basement this week. They check on me twice an hour, even though I tried to convince Norman there's little threat to me while I'm in the store."

Miss Dixon released a sigh. "How romantic."

"Or annoying." Beatrix shook her head. "I'm sure management

will be most displeased if they realize Pinkertons are in the store because of me, but—"

"Is there a Miss Waterbury in here?" someone called from the doorway.

Beatrix raised her hand. "I'm over here."

The man in the doorway sent her a curt nod. "Mr. Bailer wants to see you in his office."

Finishing the last bite of her sandwich as she rose to her feet, Beatrix headed out of the room, sending Miss Dixon a reassuring smile when that woman sent her a look filled with alarm. Taking the stairs to Mr. Bailer's floor, she hurried down the hallway and arrived at Mr. Bailer's office, his secretary hustling her straight inside a moment later. As soon as she slid into the chair that sat directly across from Mr. Bailer's desk, Beatrix soon found herself pinned under Mr. Bailer's gaze—and a nervous gaze at that.

"Miss Waterbury," he began, tugging on his collar, "I'm sure you know why you've been summoned."

"Someone's mentioned the Pinkerton men who keep coming to check on me?"

Mr. Bailer gave another tug of his collar. "Pinkerton men are keeping tabs on you here at the store?"

"No, they're checking on my welfare, which is not the same as keeping tabs on me. That would imply that I've done something wrong."

"Word has reached my ears that you have done something wrong because you apparently shot a man."

"Purely in self-defense, and in the defense of a friend of mine."

Mr. Bailer abandoned his collar and took to drumming his fingers on the desk. "We've had complaints about that very incident."

"From whom?"

"From a customer who witnessed whatever chaos you managed to become involved in last week. This customer came to see me just this morning, her visit delayed because of a nasty cold she's been suffering, but she personally witnessed you being questioned by the police last week. She recognized you as being a woman she'd seen working in the coat check, so she felt compelled to report your unacceptable behavior to me once she felt well enough to leave her house." He caught Beatrix's eye. "You must understand that we at Marshall Field & Company cannot retain an employee who has allowed herself to become involved in something so, well, tawdry."

Beatrix stiffened. "I wasn't involved in anything tawdry. I was the victim of a crime."

"You should have left the thieves to the discretion of men. Men, my dear, are equipped to handle such unpleasantness, while women, on the other hand, are not."

"I'm not certain how you expect me to respond to that."

"There's no response for you to make. With that out of the way, I must now inform you that I have no choice but to terminate your employment with Marshall Field & Company, effective immediately."

Temper began crawling through her veins. "Aren't you concerned that Miss Huttleston will be very upset with you for terminating me?"

"I do find that notion concerning, but since I'm fairly certain *I'll* be dismissed if I don't dismiss you, I'm willing to brave Miss Huttleston's wrath even if I'm not looking forward to that."

"But I wasn't even working when I had my interlude with criminals."

"You obviously neglected to memorize that handbook I gave you because there's a full page in it regarding how an employee can be terminated if they damage their reputation, and thus the reputation of this fine establishment. I assure you, shooting a man certainly damages your reputation as well as ours." He gestured to the door. "I believe that'll be all, Miss Waterbury. Good day."

Beatrix felt heat climb up her neck and settle on her face as she rose to her feet. "That's it? You're not going to allow me an opportunity to explain the circumstances behind the shooting?"

"I've heard all I need to hear about the matter, and with that said, good day again, Miss Waterbury." Mr. Bailer pushed a button on his desk, which had his secretary walking through the door a blink of an eye later. She moved to Beatrix's side, took her by the arm, and the next thing Beatrix knew, she was standing on the street outside Marshall Field & Company, jobless.

Knowing there was nothing left to do but return to her aunt's house, she stomped down the street, trying her best to get her temper in check but not having much success with that.

Her dismissal was outrageous, and the very idea she had no available recourse set her teeth on edge.

Stomping all the way to the train station, she headed for the ticket counter, stopping in her tracks when Blanche and Mamie, both wearing turbans of vivid pink, rushed past her. Mamie spun around a second later, calling out to Blanche, who stopped and turned as well.

"Beatrix," Mamie exclaimed. "Thank goodness. We were just on our way back to the house, but time is short and perhaps you can help us."

Beatrix frowned. "Help you with what?"

Blanche swiped a hand over a forehead that was drenched in perspiration. "Colette's been arrested."

Of all the women who lived under Aunt Gladys's roof, Colette Balley, a shy and retiring woman who'd come to live with Gladys after experiencing a troubling incident with a manager at the slaughterhouse where she'd been working, was the last woman Beatrix would have expected to get arrested.

"What happened?" she demanded.

Mamie shook her head. "Colette, if you'll recall, missed our dinner last week, having gone to assist her sister with a sick child. She's not returned since, which is why Blanche and I decided to check on her today. When we arrived at Colette's sister's house, we were informed by Colette's brother-in-law, an unpleasant man who drinks too much, that Colette and his wife had been arrested, and they're still in jail because he refused to pay their bail."

Beatrix frowned. "But why were they arrested, and why, pray tell, wouldn't Colette's brother-in-law post bail?"

Blanche blew out a breath. "Colette's brother-in-law was stingy with details, but from what I could gather, their arrest was apparently a result of a protest at the slaughterhouse where Colette used to work and where her sister still does. As for why he wouldn't post bail, I have to imagine he's one of those men who doesn't support women protesting anything and has decided his wife can rot in jail for all he cares."

"Do you know what jail Colette's in?"

"She's been taken to the House of Correction located on the far southwest side of the city."

Beatrix nodded to Blanche. "I'll go there immediately, but you should go and fetch Aunt Gladys because I might need help." She nodded to Mamie. "You'll come with me?"

Mamie returned the nod. "Don't know what we'll be able to do, unless you have money for bail."

"I have money" was all Beatrix said to that, and after watching Blanche head off for the train, she and Mamie hurried to a line of hansom cabs for rent, climbing into the first one she reached and telling the driver to take them to the House of Correction.

The ride through the streets of Chicago was done mostly in silence, Beatrix taking the time to gather her thoughts and brace herself for dealing with men of authority, who were often quick to dismiss any concerns voiced by women, something she'd experienced during the two times she'd been arrested.

Luckily for her, though, she had a father who hadn't hesitated to bail her out of jail, but she could only imagine how helpless the women currently behind bars were feeling, what with their lack of access to funds that would secure their freedom and marriage to men who didn't approve of their actions and were refusing to pay the bondsman what Beatrix knew, from prior experience, were minimal fines.

Climbing from the cab once they reached the House of Correction, Beatrix wasn't surprised when the driver refused to wait until she was finished inside, even though she'd offered him a substantial amount if he'd agree to wait.

"What's wrong with men these days?" Mamie muttered, shaking her head as the hansom cab trundled away. "First we learn that Colette's brother-in-law didn't bother to get his wife and Colette out of jail, then that driver leaves the two of us here in a most dangerous part of town, and that was after I fluttered my lashes at him and . . ." Mamie stopped talking, her eyes widened, and then she was smiling broadly and batting her lashes like mad right as Agent Cochran, the Pinkerton man Norman felt was best suited to watch over Beatrix, jumped out of a hansom cab and began striding their way.

"Care to explain what you're doing here, Miss Waterbury? Or why you didn't bother to wait for me or another Pinkerton to accompany you here? Or better yet, why you left Marshall Field & Company early?" Agent Cochran demanded. "I'm fortunate I caught sight of you leaving the store, although I have no understanding why you abruptly left the train station and came here, a circumstance that had me scrambling to catch up with you."

Beatrix winced. "Would you believe I completely forgot I was supposed to apprise you of any changes to my schedule, that forgetfulness brought on, no doubt, by my unexpected dismissal from my position earlier?"

Agent Cochran blinked. "You were dismissed?"

"It appears Marshall Field & Company has a policy regarding their employees shooting anyone."

Agent Cochran narrowed his eyes. "That's ridiculous. You only shot that man because he was threatening you." He cracked his knuckles. "Want me to have a talk with whoever dismissed you?"

As Beatrix shook her head, Mamie batted her lashes at a furious rate. "What a delightful man you are, Agent Cochran, and here I was just complaining about men and their lack of chivalrous behavior, but then you show up and . . . well . . ." Mamie smiled and took hold of Agent Cochran's arm, earning a rather surprised look from him in return, although he didn't shrug from Mamie's hold. "I hope you'll accompany us into the jail because we may very well need your assistance getting Colette released." She shook her head. "Poor Colette is a most anxious type, preferring to spend her time knitting and talking to Gladys's cats. I can't imagine the terror she must be feeling over finding herself locked away in jail."

Agent Cochran tilted his head. "How did a knitting cat lover manage to get arrested in the first place?"

Beatrix shrugged. "There was limited information available as to how it happened, but I'm hoping we'll be better informed soon."

Moving into a large waiting area, Beatrix paused as she looked around, setting her sights on an officer who was stationed behind a desk that had a long line in front of it. After they waited for over thirty minutes, it was finally their turn.

"We're here to secure the release of Miss Colette Balley," she told the officer, who had a nameplate stating he was Officer Greenwood. Beatrix felt irritation flowing freely when Officer Greenwood barely glanced at her before he settled his attention on Agent Cochran.

"What's Colette Balley in for?" he asked Agent Cochran.

"I have no idea," Agent Cochran said, withdrawing his Pinkerton badge from his pocket and handing it to the officer, who sat up a little straighter in his chair after he caught sight of it.

"She was obviously arrested for no good reason," Mamie said, immediately bristling when the officer let out a grunt and sent her a roll of his eyes.

"Not like I haven't heard that before," he muttered as he began running his finger down a very long column of names. He stopped halfway down the page. "Here she is." He lifted his head. "She was arrested for causing a disturbance at the Owen Slaughterhouse last week. Her bail has been set at ten dollars."

"Ten dollars?" Mamie all but shrieked. "How's a poor, single woman supposed to post a bail like that?"

"She should have thought about that before she caused a disturbance."

Beatrix lifted her chin. "I'll pay it as well as the bail for her sister."

"And the sister's name would be?" Officer Greenwood asked.

"No idea." Beatrix turned to Mamie. "Do you know?"

Mamie frowned. "I think Blanche called that man Mr. Brightman, or maybe it was Bingham, or . . . well, it could've been any name starting with a B."

Beatrix returned her attention to Officer Greenwood. "It appears I'll need to get the name from Colette, so if you'll kindly have someone escort me to her cell, I'll get that information and then you can make arrangements to have Colette and her sister set free."

Officer Greenwood frowned. "If this sister was arrested for the same disturbance, her bail will also be ten dollars. You have that much money on you?"

Beatrix gave a jerk of her head right as Agent Cochran stepped closer to her and lowered his voice.

"Need I remind you, Miss Waterbury, that you just lost your position? Twenty dollars is a lot of money, and I'm not certain it's wise for you to spend your funds on bail when you're currently jobless."

Beatrix waved that aside. "While I thank you for your concern, Agent Cochran, there's no need for you to worry about me." She nodded to Officer Greenwood. "I'm capable of paying the bail, so you may call for someone to take me to Colette so we can get her and her sister out of here with all due haste."

For a moment, she thought Officer Greenwood was going to refuse. But then he slid a glance to Agent Cochran, who in all honesty was a rather intimidating man, being at least six feet tall and sporting wide shoulders, and gestured for another officer to join him. That man, an Officer Kelly, after getting instructions from Officer Greenwood, motioned for Beatrix to follow him. With Agent Cochran on one side of her and Mamie on the other, Beatrix moved through the main room and down a long hallway, forced to stop when Officer Kelly drew out a set of keys to open the first of many locked doors that led to where the women were held.

Having been arrested and secured behind bars before, and twice at that, Beatrix knew what to expect—despair, weeping, taunts from inmates behind bars, and an atmosphere that seemed to suck the soul right out of a person.

Passing by three cells filled with gaunt-looking women, Beatrix soon found herself standing in front of a cell that had two women huddled up together on a cot, one of those women being Colette.

Mamie rushed past Beatrix and stuck her hand through the bars, ignoring a protesting Officer Kelly in the process.

"We're here to get you out, Colette," Mamie said, which had Colette lifting her head, blinking a few times, then jumping to her feet and dashing to the bars, taking hold of Mamie's hand and looking quite as if she was never going to let go.

"Thank goodness you're here," Colette said, her voice trembling and tears in her eyes. "I asked to have a note sent around to Gladys a few days ago but was told that since my brother-in-law had been informed of my arrest, then my note wasn't going to be delivered."

Beatrix rounded on Officer Kelly. "That sounds like a clear violation of Colette's rights."

"We don't cater to criminals here, but we would have gotten around to sending her note out at some point, if she was still here in a month."

"That's . . . outrageous," Beatrix sputtered, taking a step toward Officer Kelly but stopping when Agent Cochran took hold of her arm.

"You won't do Colette any good if you get yourself arrested," he said quietly. "Perhaps you should allow me to take it from here?"

Knowing Agent Cochran was right, and knowing she'd be of no use to anyone if she let her temper get the best of her, Beatrix gave a slight nod.

Agent Cochran stepped closer to Colette, securing the name of her sister, Ada Bingley, which he immediately gave to Officer Kelly. He then nodded to Beatrix. "I think we need that bail money now."

Colette peered at Beatrix through the bars. "You're getting me and my sister out?"

"Of course," Beatrix said, distracted a second later by the sight of four officers moving into a nearby cell, one of them pushing a cart that held large brown jugs on it and some manner of tubing that was hanging off the side.

"Why do I get the feeling something horrible is about to happen?" she asked to no one in particular.

"They're here to try to force Ada's co-workers from the slaughterhouse to eat," Colette whispered, her hands tightening around the bars, her sister joining her at the bars a second later. "They stopped taking meals after their husbands refused to post their bail. They wanted me and Ada to stop eating as well, but Ada's got children who depend on her, so she wouldn't risk her health. We got placed in another cell after we decided to eat, but the warden has been threatening to make the women eat, and he must have decided today's the day."

Beatrix squared her shoulders. "That's barbaric." With that, she strode forward, slipping past Agent Cochran when he tried to snag hold of her arm. "I'll be fine," she said, which earned her a scowl from Agent Cochran as he fell into step beside her.

"Mr. Nesbit's not going to be pleased with either of us if we get arrested," Agent Cochran muttered right as Beatrix stepped in front of the four men, blocking their way.

"Officers," she began, "a moment of your time, if you please."

All four of the officers scowled at her, impatience oozing from their every pore.

"Step aside, ma'am," one of the officers said. "You're interrupting official business."

Beatrix lifted her chin. "Too right I am, although if what I've learned is true, and that you're about to force women to break their hunger strike, I'm interrupting a torture session, not official business."

One of the officers scratched his nose and shrugged. "We don't have any other choice in the matter. Can't very well let those women die. Wouldn't look good on the department, would it?"

"There is another choice," Beatrix returned. "You could release them."

"They can't post bail," another officer said. "Their husbands are refusing to do that, and if we were to let them loose without paying, it would send a bad message to other women looking to break the law."

"We didn't break any laws," a woman said, moving to the front of a cell and peering through the bars. "We were only protesting the conditions at the slaughterhouse after one of our co-workers got fired because she got sliced up by a machine that broke."

The officer behind the cart released a grunt. "All of you were blocking the entrance to the slaughterhouse, encouraging other workers to join you. It was disrupting production and the owners demanded we act, which we did." He nodded to Beatrix. "If you don't want to join them in this cell, I suggest you move aside and let us get on with this."

Right there, in the middle of her mean surroundings, understanding struck.

She'd been placed on an unexpected path that had started with her banishment from New York, which had then given her the unexpected opportunity of taking up a position where she'd gotten a taste of what it was like to be a working woman.

The thought had struck her more than once that her unexpected path had been God's way of opening her eyes to the daily injustices working women faced, and now, what with how she'd ended up in this dismal place at exactly this specific time, after experiencing a surprising dismissal from her job, it was clear she was facing a new fork in the road, one where she might very well find that purpose Aunt Gladys had been talking about.

Unlike the women who were currently behind bars, she was not as helpless as she'd thought.

She was an American heiress—a grand heiress, at that—and it was past time she put that status to work for something other than securing the latest fashions or traveling the world on her family yacht.

Squaring her shoulders, she regarded the four officers in front of her and then sent them a nod. "There'll be no need for your barbaric action today, officers. You've stated that these women are still here because they can't make bail, but I'm here to tell you I'll pay their bail. That means you can set them free—immediately."

To her surprise, one of the officers shook his head. "It's too late for that. We have orders to see this through. The warden wants to make an example of these women to discourage disorderly conduct from any women who consider protesting their employment conditions."

Beatrix crossed her arms over her chest. "You can't ignore my offer to pay their bail. That's against the law. But speaking of the law, now that I think about it, were these women not offered an opportunity to seek an attorney's counsel?"

"They couldn't pay their bail, so they wouldn't have been able to afford any counsel."

"But were they given the opportunity to even seek out counsel? Surely there must be resources in this fine city of yours that offer representation for the poor."

When none of the officers answered, Beatrix turned her attention to the woman standing directly behind the bars of her cell. "You weren't offered any counsel?"

The woman shook her head. "They let us send notes to our husbands, but that was all we were offered." She shook her head again. "Me and the other women have been thinking that Mr. Tripp, he's the main owner of the slaughterhouse, paid off people to make sure all of us suffer as much as possible. He wants to make sure no other workers give him any trouble."

Beatrix rounded on the officers, all of whom were now shifting around on their feet.

"Is this true?" she demanded, her demand ignored as one of the men began jangling his keys before he fit one into the lock.

Beatrix moved to block the door. "I'm afraid I can't allow you to proceed with your plans because, you see, I'm determined to pay the bail for all of these women, and you are then going to release them." She glanced at the gaunt-looking women, all of whom were now pressed against the bars of the three cells they were held in, taking a moment to do a quick count.

"There are ten women from the slaughterhouse, plus Colette and her sister?" she asked.

"That seems right," Agent Cochran answered when none of the officers did.

She reached into an inside pocket sewn into her skirt, pulling out a roll of bills. She then counted out the bills, finding she was twenty dollars short. She lifted her head. "I only have one hundred dollars on me, but I have additional funds at home. I just need to send for it."

"We don't have time to wait for that," the officer behind the cart said.

Beatrix narrowed her eyes. "If you think I'm going to step aside and allow you to proceed, you're gravely mistaken." One by one, she looked each officer directly in the eye. "All of you should be ashamed of yourselves. You must know this is wrong, and yet you're using your orders to go through with it as if you don't have a choice in the matter." She gestured to the women behind bars. "These are mothers you're so anxious to abuse, and daughters, and may very well be your neighbors. How, pray tell, has it happened that you've allowed yourselves to forget that?"

"It's not as if we're going to take enjoyment in following our orders," one of the officers finally said. "And again, since you're only short twenty dollars, most of the women will be spared."

"All the women will be spared."

Turning, Beatrix discovered Aunt Gladys marching their way, Blanche on one side of her, a gentleman in an expensive suit on her other side. That gentleman immediately introduced himself as an attorney, right before he announced that all bail had been paid and all the women were to be released immediately.

Given the fury residing in Aunt Gladys's eyes, Beatrix knew that her aunt would be more determined than ever to advance the cause of women. And given the real-life lesson Beatrix had just experienced, she knew without a doubt that she'd finally found a worthy purpose in life, one she'd never be able to ignore.

CHAPTER 29

"Where's Theodosia? I thought she'd be here for the big launch of Gemma and Oscar's peddle-boat."

Looking up, Norman found Stanley moving to join him where he was standing at the back of a wagon Mort was hitched to. Mort had apparently decided he no longer wanted Norman to ride him after the cat debacle, but had graciously condescended to pull the wagon holding the recently completed peddle-boat, but only after Norman had bribed him with more than a few carrots.

"I've not seen Theo much this past week," Norman replied. "She's been spending most of her time with Blanche at the Huttleston house."

Stanley frowned. "Who's Blanche?"

"She's a woman who wants to take the beauty industry by storm. Theo's been using her extensive background in chemistry to help Blanche reformulate recipes, which will hopefully curb some of the unfortunate effects Blanche's creations have caused— such as hair falling out and hives."

"I doubt any lady would want to buy a beauty product that has her breaking out in hives."

Norman smiled. "Indeed. However, Theo's been joining me every afternoon as I wait for Beatrix to get done for the day at

Marshall Field & Company, so I imagine she'll show up here at some point, then go with me to fetch Beatrix."

"You fetch Beatrix from work every day?"

"Didn't really have a choice in the matter, not after realizing Beatrix's life has been placed in jeopardy because of me." Norman raked a hand through his hair. "It would have been far easier to keep an eye on her if she would have agreed to abandon her position. But because she adamantly refused to do that, Edgar, Gladys Huttleston's butler, and I came up with a plan. He escorts Beatrix to the store every morning, and I meet her every afternoon when she gets off work. I've then arranged for Pinkerton men to check on her while she's at work, just to make certain she's safe."

"If you're escorting Beatrix home every afternoon, and you're coming to the factory every morning and staying until lunch with me and Father, when are you finding time to work on your electrical research?"

"I've not done a bit of research in weeks," Norman said, using a rag to rub a smear of grease off the peddle-boat. "After I'm done at the factory, I've been helping Gemma and Oscar with their peddle-boat as well as giving them science and mathematics lessons because their tutor is still under the weather."

"How's that going?"

"Surprisingly well. Gemma is far more advanced intellectually than I realized, which makes instructing her incredibly satisfying. And while Oscar isn't as accomplished as Gemma is, he's still remarkably bright and eager to learn." Norman set aside the rag and caught Stanley's eye. "I've been considering taking up teaching, perhaps at the college level. I've been hounded to teach at different colleges for years, and now might be the perfect time to explore that option."

Stanley frowned. "Why now?"

Norman shrugged. "Because one of the stipulations I'll make before accepting a position will be to include women in my classes. That might eventually benefit Gemma once she reaches college age because perhaps it'll prove that women deserve a chance in the world of scientific study."

"Are you *sure* you're not dying?"

Norman grinned. "As I told Father the other day after he asked me the same thing, no, I'm not dying."

"You're acting quite unlike your normal self, although I have to say I'm enjoying this new, un-normal you, even if it is somewhat unsettling."

Norman inclined his head. "Thank you, I think, but I have to mention that you've not been acting normal of late either, what with how often you bring Theo into our conversations."

"I don't bring her up all that often."

"You do, and you also still seem incredibly put out that she's attending the Palmer ball with Harvey Cabot instead of you."

Color creeped up Stanley's neck. "I never said I wanted to take Theodosia to the ball."

"You didn't have to. Your constant scowling whenever the topic of the ball comes up speaks for itself."

Stanley tugged on his collar. "Theodosia hasn't mentioned anything to you about what she thinks of me, has she?"

"No, and even if she had, I wouldn't divulge that information to you, because according to numerous etiquette books I've recently read, a gentleman does not disclose personal information about a lady to anyone unless he has express permission to do so."

"But I'm your brother."

"And Theo's my best friend, and as such, I'm compelled by that friendship to keep any secrets she may disclose to me. And before you start arguing with that, what say you give me a hand getting this boat into the water?"

Even though Stanley tossed Norman a look that had annoyance stamped all over it, he didn't hesitate to help, pulling the boat from the wagon bed and then carrying it with Norman to the lakeshore. Gemma and Oscar immediately joined them, their eyes bright with excitement.

"Think the paddles will work the way we want them to?" Oscar asked as he dropped to the ground and peered at the paddles they'd attached to the back of the boat.

"I have no doubt the boat will operate exactly as I told you it will," Norman returned, smiling when Gemma plopped down on her stomach beside Oscar, peering at the paddles as well.

"Aren't you afraid the chain will rust?" she asked.

"Not unless you intend on pedaling for days, something I wouldn't advise since the weather, with it being almost the end of October, is turning questionable."

Gemma was on her feet a second later. "Then Oscar and I should immediately launch the boat, before that questionable weather turns up."

"You can't take the boat out on the water until your mother shows up, which should be in"—Norman consulted his pocket watch—"fifteen minutes."

"That's forever from now," Gemma complained.

"It's not, but to pass the time, I suggest you and Oscar go back to the wagon, give Mort a few pats to keep him in an amiable frame of mind, then get yourselves into those flotation devices I made for you."

Gemma frowned. "Why do we have to wear those? Are you afraid the boat might sink?"

"No, but I am afraid that one of you may get distracted by an unusual fish, or a gust of wind may whip up some waves, sending you into the lake."

"Oscar and I know how to swim."

"You're wearing the flotation devices and that's that." Norman nodded to Stanley. "Your uncle Stanley was forced to go into the water the last time the two of you went boating. I have recently read, though, that swimming is a most acceptable exercise for a gentleman to participate in, running being nowhere to be found in that book, which is a shame since it is my exercise of choice . . ."

He stopped talking when Gemma and Oscar scampered away without a single word, heading toward the wagon.

He turned to Stanley and quirked a brow.

Stanley grinned. "Children, if you're unaware, aren't really keen to suffer through dissertations, especially ones that have something to do with appropriate exercises for gentlemen."

"I would think Oscar would find that fascinating, being that he'll one day be a gentleman and will need to decide what manly exercise he should pursue."

"He's eight, and at the moment, the only thing he and Gemma are interested in is getting their new boat on the water. That also explains why they're now trying to wrestle themselves into those flotation devices you made them." Stanley nodded to where the children were doing exactly that, grinned again, then returned his attention to Norman. "I hope you don't take this the wrong way, but you're surprisingly good with the children, and that you're so concerned for their safety has left me questioning if I know you at all."

"You're surprised I'm concerned about the safety of my niece and her friend?"

"I've insulted you, haven't I?"

For the briefest of moments, Norman wanted to agree that he was insulted, until he remembered that he'd never shown any attention to any of his nieces or nephews before, let alone their friends, and thus had never shown any concern about their safety.

It was an unfortunate state of affairs, but since he'd decided he was going to do his utmost best to make amends for the neglect he'd shown his family, he caught Stanley's eye and shook his head. "You have every reason to be surprised about my newfound interest in our family, so no, I'm not insulted. I've been self-centered for most of my life, consumed with my own affairs, thinking that I was justified with that unfortunate behavior because of my unusual intellect. I've recently realized that perhaps I've been wrong in the path that I, as well as Mother, believed God had set out for me, because that path wasn't leading me to a place where I could put my intellect to use helping people. To my chagrin, I've realized I've been pursuing science as a way to benefit myself, hoping to earn accolades from fellow scientists, and even hoping to create a viable electrical vehicle so that I'd no longer be burdened with the inconvenience of traveling around without the benefit of a horse."

"You still don't have a horse," Stanley said, sending a pointed look to where Mort seemed to have fallen asleep again on his feet.

"But I now have the means to travel freely about the city without waiting for trains or rented cabs, even if Mort doesn't always want to deliver me to my intended destination. But speaking of horses . . ." He nodded to where two riders were galloping their way.

As they drew closer, he recognized Beatrix, the mere sight of her sitting so competently on her horse leaving him smiling. He'd not seen her ride since their train adventure, but she made a most impressive sight, moving at ease with her horse, while her companion seemed a touch unsteady in the saddle, although he wasn't certain who she was riding with.

"Is that Theodosia?" Stanley asked, shielding his eyes with one hand as he peered at the other woman riding alongside Beatrix.

Norman's gaze flicked over that woman again, then flicked over the black stallion, one that turned out to be Sebastian, Theo's new horse. "I believe it is."

"What's she done to herself?"

"I think Gladys Huttleston and her friends have taken her in hand."

Stanley began moving toward the ladies, looking over his shoulder. "Theodosia didn't need to be taken in hand. She's always been perfect just the way she is."

Before that incredibly telling remark could settle, Norman suddenly realized that Beatrix, who'd already dismounted from her horse, shouldn't have been at the lake in the first place because she was supposed to be working.

Striding forward, he reached her side in a blink of an eye. Taking hold of her hand, he brought it to his lips. "What's wrong?"

Beatrix's nose wrinkled. "Why would you assume something's wrong?"

"You're supposed to be at work."

She blew out a breath. "Oh, yes, quite right. I'm not at work because I've been dismissed from my position."

"What?"

"I know, it was a shock to me as well, but I haven't had much time to dwell on the matter because after I was dismissed, I then found myself traveling to a jail to secure the release of Colette Balley."

Norman took hold of her arm right as Agent Cochran rode up to join them, looking remarkably windblown.

"Dare I hope Agent Cochran was with you when you went to this jail?" Norman asked.

"He was, but since you've clearly got a million questions, allow me to explain."

By the time Beatrix was done explaining, Norman had more questions than answers—one of those being how Beatrix had acquired the funds needed to post bail in the first place because she hadn't been employed long enough to amass fifty dollars, let alone one hundred dollars.

Before he could voice a single question, though, a carriage arrived on the scene, his mother, father, and Constance stepping out, Constance holding the hand of her youngest son and his nephew, Christopher.

Christopher immediately tugged his hand free and dashed for Gemma and Oscar, who were now waddling their way into the lake, the flotation devices he'd made for them impeding their progress.

"Is that your mother?" Beatrix asked.

"It is, and also my father. Would you care to meet them?"

"It would be rather rude if I didn't."

Norman frowned. "I suppose you're right, but after the day you've already had, I'm not sure you're up for meeting my mother. She can be somewhat difficult at times."

"I've dealt with more than my share of difficult ladies" was all Beatrix said to that.

Knowing it would be futile to argue with her, even though Norman was relatively sure Beatrix had never encountered anyone like his mother before, he turned his gaze on his parents, finding them speaking to Theo, who was looking quite unlike herself.

Gone was the drab gray walking dress she often wore, replaced with a green walking dress in exactly the same style that Theo had recently shown him in a fashion magazine. On her head was a jaunty hat with a single feather attached to it, the hat angled in a way that drew attention to short curls that no longer looked singed, but vibrant.

Stanley, Norman couldn't neglect to notice, was beaming at Theo, suggesting that even though he'd stated the old Theo was perfect, he wasn't finding much to object to about her new appearance.

"Can we finally get this boat into the water?" Gemma bellowed, drawing everyone's attention.

"Let me get Gemma and Oscar settled, then I'll introduce you," Norman said when he realized Gemma and Oscar were in the process of pulling their peddle-boat into the water. Gemma slipped and tumbled into the water, her flotation device causing her to immediately bob to the surface.

"It's far too chilly, Gemma, for you to be taking a swim," Constance called, catching up with Norman as he hurried to the lake. She caught his eye and grinned. "Is that your Beatrix back there?"

"She's not my Beatrix, not exactly, but yes," Norman returned, frowning when he realized Gemma was beginning to bob her way out into the lake, which had him running for the water. After helping Gemma out of the water and on to the seat of the peddle-boat while Oscar scrambled in of his own accord, Norman turned and found little Christopher looking forlorn.

"I'll take you out next, Christopher," he said, earning a grin from his nephew. Giving the boat a push, he reminded Gemma and Oscar that they were to keep to the shoreline, then stepped back as they drifted away.

A second later, they were giggling in delight, pedaling like mad, their giggles increasing when the boat began chugging away, clearly working.

"I think we might have a situation over there," Constance suddenly said, waving a hand to where he'd left Beatrix.

Trepidation settled over him when he turned and discovered his mother advancing on Beatrix, determination in her every step.

"That is, indeed, a situation," Norman said right before he broke into a run, hoping he'd be able to intercept his mother before she did something unfortunate, such as convince Beatrix it would be in her best interest to maintain her distance from him.

CHAPTER 30

"I see you've decided to wear one of your gowns from Worth to the ball tonight."

Beatrix swiveled around on the stool, immediately regretting it when Mamie, who'd volunteered to style Beatrix's hair because Blanche and a few of the other women had gone off to Theodosia's house to get her ready for the ball, pulled her hair. Beatrix smiled at the sight of Aunt Gladys gliding into the room. Her aunt was looking resplendent in a gown of palest ivory, the diamond choker encircling her neck matching the diamond bracelets on her wrist.

"You're looking very well turned out tonight, Aunt Gladys, but you're not wearing a turban," Beatrix said.

Aunt Gladys gave a pat to hair that was a beautiful shade of strawberry blond, done up in a sophisticated chignon, a sparkling tiara adding a touch of sophistication.

"I've only been wearing turbans so often because Blanche made a bit of a miscalculation with her ingredients when she attempted to return my hair to its natural color." Aunt Gladys nodded to Beatrix's hair. "I once had hair exactly your shade, but over time it faded. Blanche was certain she could recreate the color, but disaster ensued, and I ended up with bright orange instead of red."

"I thought you and the rest of the women were wearing turbans as some sort of fashion statement," Beatrix said.

Aunt Gladys grinned. "I'm sure the turbans were some sort of statement, although fashionable isn't what I'd consider them." She turned her grin on Mamie. "It was delightful, though, how all of you started wearing turbans as well, Mamie, as a way to support me and make Blanche feel better until she rectified her mistake."

As Mamie returned the grin, Beatrix frowned. "Why did Blanche stop you from answering me when I questioned you about the turbans a few weeks back?"

"She didn't think Theodosia would be keen to allow her near that disaster Theodosia was sporting on her head if she learned Blanche was notorious for creating disasters of her own."

"I suppose that does make sense," Beatrix said, turning front and center again, which had Mamie releasing a huff. "Sorry, Mamie. I moved again."

"Lucky I wasn't wielding the hot tong just yet," Mamie muttered. "But I expect you to sit perfectly still from this point forward because while I'm capable of styling hair, I've never styled hair for anyone going to a fancy ball before. If you don't want to look like one of the performers at the dance hall where I used to work, I suggest you cooperate."

"Honestly, Mamie," Aunt Gladys began, "by the snippiness in your tone, I'm getting the distinct impression you're still put out over not attending the ball tonight."

Mamie picked up the hot tong, which Beatrix wasn't certain she should be doing if she *was* in a put-out frame of mind, and all but attacked Beatrix's hair with it. "How could I not be put out?" Mamie demanded, before she began counting under her breath, stopping at fifteen to uncurl the piece of hair she'd been working on before moving to another. "I'm sure I would adore attending this ball, and yet, instead of preparing myself for an evening of frivolity, I've been recruited to get Beatrix looking shipshape—not that I mind helping you, Beatrix. You've been more than delightful to me ever since you arrived at your aunt's house."

Beatrix suddenly smelled something burning. "I think it's been over fifteen seconds."

"Oh yes," Mamie said with a wince before she uncurled the piece of hair wrapped around the tong. She winced again as she gave the curl a bit of a fluff. "Don't think I scorched it too much."

Beatrix's eyes widened. "Most people don't want to hear the word *scorched* when it comes to their hair."

"No one will be able to tell. I'll just tuck the scorched part underneath another curl."

"That's hardly reassuring."

Mamie ignored her and turned to Aunt Gladys. "You could have taken me as your guest this evening instead of Edgar. He attends balls with you often, and I'm sure he wouldn't have minded sitting this one out so that I was given a chance to attend. He's considerate that way."

"And clearly you feel I'm not considerate."

"That has crossed my mind a time or two," Mamie muttered as Aunt Gladys settled herself into a chair, shaking her head.

"It's because I *am* considerate that I didn't invite you to join me," Aunt Gladys argued. "You've only recently abandoned a life that had you working in a dance hall. We've barely scratched the service of the etiquette rules that are required for anyone attending a formal affair, which means you're nowhere near ready to don a ball gown and mingle with society. You've much to learn, patience being at the top of that list."

Mamie set aside the tong. "That's your advice? To be patient?"

"Patience is a virtue."

"So says the woman who's been waiting years for Edgar to figure out there's nothing wrong with marrying his employer." Mamie began gathering Beatrix's curls on the top of her head. "If you ask me, your patience with him might not amount to anything if he never comes around to admitting he holds you in a great deal of affection."

Aunt Gladys leaned forward. "You believe Edgar holds me in affection?"

"The man has worked for you for over thirty years," Mamie shot back. "And in case you've neglected to realize, you're not always that pleasant to be around. You're very set in your ways, you're bossy, and, well, I could go on and on, but I don't want to annoy you overly much since I do appreciate you giving me a home to live in, which does speak well of your generous nature."

"My generous yet unpleasant and bossy nature," Aunt Gladys muttered, earning a grin from Mamie.

"Exactly, but my point was that, because you're rather flawed, Edgar obviously must hold you in great affection. Otherwise, why would he have stayed with you all these years?"

"I pay him a more-than-generous salary."

"Which could be one reason he stayed," Mamie admitted, "but I imagine it's because he cares for you."

"An encouraging thought to be sure, but enough about Edgar and me." Aunt Gladys nodded to the gown Beatrix was going to wear that night. "May I assume you've chosen Worth to wear for a reason other than it's a spectacular gown and you're certain to look enchanting in it? Perhaps as a form of armor against all the tongues that will certainly be wagging about you this evening?"

Beatrix smiled. "All the gowns I brought with me are from Worth. They'd only recently arrived from Paris before Mother sent me packing. I wasn't certain what to expect with you in Chicago, but thought I might as well bring a few of my new gowns just in case I had need of them."

"Bet you never considered that I'd send you out to work once you got here."

"Never entered my head, but I don't believe I've thanked you nearly enough for suggesting I take on a position. I certainly have a new appreciation for the working woman and the daily trials she faces. I'm also certain that appreciation will assist me greatly as I go forward with my work with the suffrage movement."

Aunt Gladys nodded. "There's much work to be done, and I think that if the two of us combine efforts, we'll be able to help women get the resources they need, such as attorneys and the like."

"I'm hopeful my parents will be as encouraging when I tell them I've decided to put some of my fortune to good use to fund that endeavor."

"I'm sure Annie will be delighted about your future plans, especially since providing resources to women in need is less likely to see you arrested as often as you would be if you merely continued attending rallies like you did in New York."

"I bet Beatrix's mother would be more delighted to learn her daughter has attracted the notice of Mr. Norman Nesbit," Mamie interjected before she released a dramatic sigh. "I have to think Norman made a most splendid figure as he raced to your rescue at the lake the other day, after his mother began interrogating you about why you were interested in her son."

"His intervention was certainly a chivalrous gesture," Beatrix agreed before frowning. "Although I don't believe he helped the situation with his mother when, after he realized she was accusing me of using my feminine wiles on him because I was interested in his fortune, he told her to have a care with how she spoke to me because I was going to become part of the family someday."

"A declaration of his future intentions if there ever was one," Aunt Gladys said with a nod. "Why, if you ask me, that was almost a proposal of marriage."

"It did come across that way, although Norman and I have yet to discuss the matter in detail. In actuality, he's not said another thing about it since his mother stormed off that day."

"That was over a week ago," Aunt Gladys pointed out.

"True, but Norman has yet to broach the subject, and since he is the one who made that declaration, I believe he should be the one to clarify what he meant."

"I'll have a word with him," Aunt Gladys said briskly. "Norman probably doesn't grasp the importance of clarifying what he meant."

Beatrix's eyes widened. "Oh, there's no need for you to—"

"There's every need," Aunt Gladys interrupted. "And I'll be happy to intervene."

"I believe it's time to get me dressed," Beatrix said firmly, rising from the stool to move to where she'd laid out her unmentionables. Picking up a silk stocking, she drew it up her leg and secured it with a garter. After doing the same with her other leg, she handed Mamie her corset, which Mamie pulled around Beatrix's light chemise, pulling far too rigorously on the laces.

"I can't breathe," Beatrix muttered.

"But your waist looks amazing," Mamie countered.

"But no one will be able to appreciate how amazing it looks if I'm unable to attend the ball due to fainting dead away here in about a second."

Even though Mamie immediately took to grumbling, she loosened Beatrix's laces, then helped her with her petticoats, and finally settled a small padded bustle over the petticoats. Beatrix lifted her arms, and Mamie drew the gown carefully over Beatrix's hair, tugging it into place before she set about using a buttonhook on the two hundred seed pearl buttons that marched down the back of the gown.

Beatrix slipped into her shoes, turned, then smiled at Aunt Gladys, who was looking her over with a sharp eye. "What do you think?"

"You look enchanting."

"Do I look like a lady capable of using my feminine wiles to capture the attention of a particular gentleman because I'm interested in that gentleman's fortune?"

Aunt Gladys's eyes sparkled. "You're far more annoyed with Norman's mother than you've let on, aren't you?"

"Perhaps I am, because her conclusions about me were incredibly insulting. Insults aside, though, I am going to disclose to Norman and his mother that I'm not a fortune hunter, what with me being an heiress and all. I was actually going to disclose my heiress status to Norman last week, but then we got distracted with the peddle-boat after his mother left, and I haven't seemed to find the appropriate time to tell him the full truth about me since." She smoothed down the skirt of her gown. "Frankly, what with how astute Norman is, I've been wondering if he's already figured out I come from money. He knows that I did, after all, have the funds needed to bail out those women from jail."

Before Aunt Gladys could respond to that, a knock sounded on the door, interrupting their conversation as Edgar called through the door that Norman had arrived.

"I shouldn't keep him waiting."

"No, you shouldn't, nor should you assume he knows about your wealth," Aunt Gladys said before she handed Beatrix her reticule. "You should tell him tonight about your fortune, although perhaps you should wait until after dinner is served. Men tend to react better to unexpected news when they're not suffering from hunger pangs." She gave Beatrix's cheek a pat. "Off you go, then, dear. I'll be down directly. I just need to fetch my wrap from my room."

Beatrix nodded, thanked Mamie for her assistance, then headed out the door of her bedchamber.

Edgar was waiting for her in the hallway, looking very dashing in a formal black evening suit, paired with a white shirt, white waistcoat, and white tie.

"You look lovely, Miss Beatrix," Edgar began, offering her his arm. "Dare I hope you're looking forward to this evening?"

Beatrix tilted her head, considering the question for a moment.

In all truthfulness, she *was* looking forward to the evening, no matter that she knew she'd be scrutinized by Chicago's finest.

It had been months since she'd had an opportunity to dance, and even though she'd made the claim often that she did not enjoy all the frivolities that society offered, in hindsight, that wasn't the full truth.

She missed the hum of a dinner party and the dancing at a ball as well as taking in the theater and riding through Central Park in the afternoon, which allowed her to chat with many of her friends.

Being presented with the unusual opportunity of taking up a position had allowed her to fully appreciate the life she'd been given, while also causing her to realize the realities of people who'd not been born into a life of luxury. Life for people with limited funds consisted of hardships Beatrix had never considered, such as feet that ached from standing on them for hours and worries about getting dismissed from positions that kept roofs over heads and food on the table. Those realities left an impression on Beatrix that she knew she'd never forget.

"Difficult question, was it?"

She shook aside her thoughts and grinned. "Apparently so, but yes, I am looking forward to the evening ahead."

Edgar leaned closer to her. "I'll be watching out for you, Miss Beatrix. You're sure to encounter ladies who saw you working at Marshall Field & Company, and I would hazard to guess that those very ladies, once they see you on the arm of one of Chicago's wealthy bachelors, will not want to make the evening pleasant for you."

"Thank you, Edgar. It's no wonder my aunt is so fond of you."

"And I'm fond of her as—" Edgar abruptly stopped talking, cleared his throat, then gestured her forward. "Norman is waiting."

Knowing Edgar had revealed more than he'd intended, Beatrix smiled and walked down the hallway. Moving down the stairs, she made her way to the receiving room, where Norman was waiting.

The sight of him left her grinning.

Even though he was looking dashing in his formal evening attire, he'd wound a scarf around his face, obscuring half of it. His eyes, however, could clearly be seen, and those eyes were directed at cats that had formed a semi-circle around him, all except for Phantom, who was winding his way around Norman's legs, purring up a storm.

"Ah, Beatrix," he began, lifting his head. "I could use some . . ." His words trailed to nothing as eyes that were watering rather profusely widened.

"Assistance?" she finished for him, striding forward and bending over to snag Phantom, her attempt failing when Phantom released a hiss and batted a paw at her.

"You're a menace," she told the cat before Edgar stepped in, scooped Phantom up, and strode from the room, the other cats following a second later.

She shook her head and returned her attention to Norman, who'd yet to say another word and was still staring at her with wide eyes.

"I forgot you're sensitive to the cats," she said, which didn't earn her so much as a blink from Norman in return.

"I should have had Edgar close them off in a room before you arrived," she tried again, earning a single blink from Norman, who continued to remain mute.

She took a step closer to him. "Are you all right?"

He lowered the scarf and frowned. "Hard to say."

"Are you having a reaction to the cats?"

He shook his head, then shook it again, quite as if he thought the shaking might resolve the issue. "It's not the cats," he finally said. "I'm having a reaction to you."

"What type of reaction?"

"One that has me feeling as if I've been struck by one of the electrical currents I've been trying to perfect, all due to your incredibly unexpected appearance."

Her lips curved. "My appearance has left you feeling as if you've been struck by electricity?"

"Quite. An unusual sensation to be certain."

Warmth began spreading through her. "I do believe you've just given me the oddest yet nicest compliment I've ever received."

Norman tilted his head. "That would suggest you're feeling somewhat agreeable toward me, which means this might finally be an appropriate time to delve into what I said last week about you joining the family."

Beatrix's pulse kicked up just a notch until she thought about what he'd actually said. "Have you purposefully neglected to broach that topic with me?"

"Of course I have. You've proven yourself to be a lady with a, forgive me, slightly questionable temperament, and I knew right after I told my mother you'd be joining the family that you were annoyed by my proclamation. Because of that, I also knew I'd need to approach the topic with you as delicately as possible, while also wanting to do so when you weren't annoyed with me."

"I haven't been annoyed with you all week."

"Your tone right now suggests differently."

Beatrix blew out a breath. "I suppose it does at that."

Norman took hold of her hand, brought it to his lips, and placed an unexpected kiss on it. "Which means now is hardly the moment to continue on with this particular conversation." He smiled. "Your aunt mentioned that you enjoy dancing, so perhaps, after I've had the opportunity to waltz you around the dance floor a few times, you'll be in a less annoyed frame of mind and more amiable to the idea of me broaching the matter again."

The thought of Norman waltzing her around caused her pulse to pick up again and also had any annoyance she'd been feeling toward him disappearing in a flash.

CHAPTER 31

It was a night that could certainly see his life changing, especially if he could somehow convince Beatrix that she wanted nothing more than to marry him.

Granted, he'd not offered her an acceptable proposal of marriage yet, nor had he been expecting to all but declare his intentions to his mother the week before, but ever since he'd done that, he'd been contemplating the idea of marriage . . . frequently. That contemplation had convinced him he truly wanted to marry Beatrix, which meant all that was left to do now was formally ask her for her hand.

He'd been hoping to do that before they left for the ball, but since he'd apparently made an unexpected muddle of matters, he was going to have to try his hardest to avoid annoying Beatrix again. He didn't really try to annoy her often, though, it simply seemed to happen whenever he was least expecting it.

Stepping from the carriage after it came to a stop, Norman held out his hand and helped Beatrix to the ground, another jolt of what certainly felt like electricity traveling through him when she took his arm and gave it a bit of a squeeze.

"The Palmer House is lovely," she exclaimed, nodding to the building in front of them. "I'm certainly looking forward to seeing the interior as well as seeing how Chicago society turns itself out for a ball. I imagine Chicago society events are not that different from the ones in New York."

Something curious began to stir in the furthest recesses of his mind, but before he could contemplate what that something was, another carriage pulled up, and Stanley stepped out, followed by Constance and her husband, William Michelson.

Thankfully, his mother was nowhere to be seen.

"Norman," Constance called out, taking William's arm and hurrying up to meet them. "Don't you look dashing." She moved closer to Beatrix and grinned. "Beatrix, how lovely you look, and I'm sure you'll be relieved to learn that my mother has been delayed, something to do with a Pinkerton report that was just delivered to her, which means you'll be able to enjoy yourself, at least until she arrives."

Beatrix returned the grin. "I don't get the impression your mother is one who'd enjoy a public spectacle, so I've not been all that concerned she and I will find ourselves engaged in another spat this evening." She nodded to William. "And with that out of the way, may I assume this is your husband?"

"Good heavens, I'm completely neglecting my manners." Constance turned to her husband. "Beatrix, this is my husband, Mr. William Michelson. William, this is Miss Beatrix Waterbury."

After exchanging pleasantries with William, Beatrix turned to Stanley, who immediately took her hand, complimented her, then launched into what seemed to be an interrogation about when Theo was going to be arriving and if Beatrix felt Theo was looking forward to the night ahead with Harvey Cabot.

Beatrix, who had spoken with Stanley a bit at the lake after his mother stormed off, had very quickly realized Stanley was interested in Theo, and not in a strictly friends sort of way. She nodded to something over Stanley's shoulder. "Theodosia's just over there, and yes, she's with Harvey."

"But how does she *feel* about coming with Harvey?"

"I can't disclose what I may know about that to you. Theodosia and I are friends, and friends do not disclose confidences in such a willy-nilly fashion."

"Not even a hint?" Stanley pressed.

"No."

Stanley nodded to Norman. "She appears to be very loyal to her friends, a trait I'll make certain to point out to Mother when she finally arrives."

"I appreciate that, Stanley," Norman returned before he frowned. "Constance mentioned that Mother's been delayed because of a Pinkerton report. Should I be concerned about that?"

"I wouldn't imagine there's anything to be concerned about, given that Mother has demanded the Pinkertons deliver her reports often," Stanley said, turning his head ever so discreetly in Theo's direction before he sucked in a sharp breath. "On my word, she looks like an angel."

Norman settled his gaze on Theo. And while he wasn't certain she resembled an angel, she was looking quite unlike herself.

Dressed in the gown he'd selected for her with the help of five saleswomen at Marshall Field & Company, Theo was looking very well turned out indeed.

The ivory silk shimmered under the gas lamps, a direct result of the beads that one of the saleswomen insisted would have Theo standing out from many of the other ladies who would be in attendance at the ball. That the gown seemed to fit her to perfection suggested Theo had taken his advice and allowed Gladys and her many friends to alter the fit instead of Theo taking a knife to it.

Her hair, while still short, was arranged in a very feminine, very un-Theo-like style with curls all over her head and a tiara nestled amidst them.

"Harvey seems to be paying Theodosia far too much attention," Stanley said, and even though Beatrix tried to snag his arm, she missed, allowing Stanley to stride away, Theo in his sights.

"We should join them," Beatrix said firmly, taking Norman's arm and tugging him after his brother.

By the time they reached Theo, Stanley had a hold of Theo's

gloved hand, raising it to his lips as her face turned pink. Norman shot a look to Harvey and found him looking rather disgruntled. But Miss Amelia Burden, who was on the arm of Mr. Clement Moore, was not paying Mr. Moore, Theo, or Harvey the least little mind because her attention was firmly settled on Beatrix.

"Miss Waterbury," Miss Burden exclaimed, releasing Mr. Moore's arm as she stepped forward, her gaze running over Beatrix's gown. "What a delightful frock you're wearing. Did you purchase that at Marshall Field & Company, using the discount I've heard employees are given?"

Beatrix smiled even as a storm brewed in her eyes, something that should have terrified Miss Burden if she'd actually seen it, but her attention was still on Beatrix's gown. "While I certainly would have used my discount if I'd been in need of a gown, I didn't purchase it there."

Miss Burden's head snapped up. "Wherever did you purchase it, then?"

Beatrix ignored her and turned her attention to Theo, who was still standing remarkably close to Stanley. "Theodosia, you look stunning this evening." She nodded to Harvey. "Good evening, Mr. Cabot."

Harvey inclined his head. "Miss Waterbury."

Beatrix then sent a pointed look to Mr. Clement Moore, which Harvey missed because he was now frowning at Stanley, who was still holding Theo's hand.

Stepping forward, Norman performed the introductions, relieved when Gladys and Edgar joined them. Edgar's appearance earned a quirk of a brow from Harvey before he all but pulled Theo away from Stanley, telling her it was past time they made their way through the receiving line.

"This is going to be such a delightful evening," Gladys proclaimed as everyone began making their way into the Palmer House. Miss Burden all but left Mr. Moore behind as she fell into step beside Beatrix, her less-than-subtle attempts to discover where Beatrix had gotten her dress, or more important, how Beatrix had been able to afford such a lovely dress, causing the tempest in Beatrix's eyes to increase.

As soon as they joined the receiving line, Norman couldn't help but notice the whispers behind gloved hands, all of which were directed at Beatrix, who didn't seem concerned she was the object of speculation. She merely began inclining her head at all the whisperers, earning scandalized looks in return, which left her grinning.

"Aunt Gladys was right," she said, turning her grin on him. "This is going to be a delightful evening."

Moving through the grand hall and rotunda, Beatrix peppered him with questions about the hotel, which he tried to answer to the best of his abilities, but other than knowing that the hotel they were in was the second Palmer House, the first having burned to the ground during the great Chicago Fire of '71, Norman didn't have much more to tell her.

"One would think that since you grew up in Chicago, you'd know more about this place," Beatrix complained after he admitted he had no idea how many people claimed Palmer House as their permanent residence, something Beatrix had apparently read about in a newspaper.

"Oh, look," she exclaimed, nodding up ahead as they joined the throng of guests in the receiving line. "There's the ballroom, although it's officially called the dining hall, something I'm sure you didn't know."

He smiled. "But I've now committed that tidbit to memory and will never forget again."

She returned the smile. "You can pull it out if you're ever in need of a topic for idle chitchat, although . . ." Her smile dimmed. "You seem to be becoming most adept at idle chitchat, even with you claiming when you first met me that you don't care for that particular activity."

He gave her arm a squeeze. "I've had a change of heart about that. I've discovered that chatting is not the trial I imagined it to be and actually find it to be most enjoyable."

Beatrix blinked. "Do you really?"

"Indeed," Norman said before he pulled her forward to greet Mr. Potter Palmer and his wife, Bertha.

Bertha Palmer considered Beatrix very closely as Norman performed the introductions, and then surprised him when she leaned closer to Beatrix and whispered into her ear.

To his relief, Beatrix exchanged smiles with Bertha before she began tugging him toward the ballroom.

"What did Mrs. Palmer say to you?" he asked.

"She wanted to know if we'd met before, and I told her we had, and then told her where."

Norman slowed to a stop. "Where could you have possibly met Mrs. Palmer?"

"New York, during a performance at the Metropolitan Opera House." Beatrix pulled him back into motion again, not slowing her pace until she swept through the door leading to the ballroom. Coming to a stop, she glanced around. "I had no idea it would be so lavishly decorated." She nodded to a nearby table draped in fine linen and set with china. "That's Mrs. Palmer's prized French Haviland bone china, which she acquired on one of her European trips."

"How do you know that?"

"Because all the large plates are engraved with a gilded *P* in the center. I read about the plates in a series the *Chicago Tribune* has been running about the Palmers."

"Interesting, but if we could return to you, Mrs. Palmer, and the opera, under what circumstances were you presented to each other, and—"

Whatever else Norman wanted to ask got lost when a lady suddenly began waving enthusiastically to Beatrix from halfway across the ballroom.

"Izzie!" Beatrix exclaimed before she surged into motion, leaving Norman behind.

A moment later, Beatrix was being hugged by the lady she'd called Izzie before a large gentleman took Izzie's place, scooping Beatrix into a hug and earning a laugh from her in return.

"Beatrix knows Ian and Isadora MacKenzie?" Stanley asked, stepping directly beside Norman.

"Who?" Norman asked.

"Ian and Isadora MacKenzie," Stanley repeated. "Ian MacKenzie is an attorney who practices in Pittsburgh, but he's recently come to Chicago at the request of the union men to help with negotiations that may see the union men abandoning their determination to strike."

"Ian MacKenzie is a lawyer for union men?"

Stanley nodded. "Father and I are actually meeting with him on Monday, and you're more than welcome to join us. He used to be an attorney for the steel owners and investors, but he had a change of heart months ago and now only represents the interests of the laborers who work in the Pittsburgh factories. He's acquiring the reputation of being a man capable of successfully negotiated terms between the two sides. After I learned he was coming to town to speak with the union men, I reached out and invited him to a meeting." Stanley shook his head. "I'm curious, though, how Beatrix knows them. Ian MacKenzie, from all accounts, is a self-made man, which is why more than a few eyebrows were raised when he married Isadora. She's an American heiress and a member of the New York Four Hundred. Given that she's holding Beatrix's hand, I have to assume they're some manner of friends." Stanley frowned. "How do you imagine it came to be that Beatrix is friends with a member of the New York Four Hundred?"

Norman returned the frown. "I have no idea, although—"

"What in the world are *you* doing here, girl?" a voice boomed through the crowd as a path opened amidst the guests, revealing a society matron, her face mottled with outrage as she, unfortunately, advanced on Beatrix.

Any thought of the New York Four Hundred or why Beatrix seemed to be friends with one of its members disappeared in a flash as Norman strode into motion, determined to intervene on Beatrix's behalf, no matter if he was going to end up insulting a Chicago matron in the process.

CHAPTER 32

Beatrix noticed a distinct increase in the number of people whispering around her, but she didn't pay them any mind, not when she'd been given the unexpected delight of being reunited with her very best friend, the former Miss Isadora Delafield, now Mrs. Ian MacKenzie.

"What are you doing here?" she asked. "And where are the children, and how did I not know you'd be coming to Chicago?"

Isadora grinned. "It was a spur-of-the-moment decision." She turned to Ian, her grin replaced with a fond smile. "Ian's reputation as an advocate for laborers and unions has increased significantly over the past few months. That's why, when he received a letter from a Chicago union, asking if he'd be willing to travel here to help them resolve some issues that might spare this city a strike of significant proportions, he didn't hesitate to accept."

Beatrix smiled at Ian. "Seems to me as if you've certainly found your proper calling in life, Ian. May I assume you're enjoying representing the workers over representing the interests of the owners and investors of the steel mills and iron foundries?"

Ian returned the smile. "Indeed you may, and Isadora's been enjoying her work with the new orphanage we built in Canonsburg." He shook his head. "She was somewhat reluctant to set aside that work to travel with me to Chicago, until I reminded her that you were visiting your aunt here."

"I couldn't very well ignore an opportunity to see my best friend," Isadora said, turning to Beatrix. "Before I forget, the children wanted me to tell you that they're awfully sad they couldn't come to Chicago with us to see you. They're also awfully put out with Ian and me because we didn't believe it would be responsible to let them miss school, which is why they're back in Pittsburgh under the watchful eye of Aunt Birdie, the indulgent eye of Uncle Amos, and the soon-to-be-leaving eye of their governess, Miss Olive." Isadora blew out a breath. "I'm sure you'll be delighted to hear that she is soon to marry Ian's man of affairs, Mr. Jonathon Downing."

"How delightful," Beatrix said. "But I'm sure you won't have any difficulty finding another governess for the children. Prim, Henry, Violet, and Daisy are adorable, and any governess would be lucky to have them as her charges."

"We also need to find a nanny as well," Ian said, a pronouncement that left Isadora rolling her eyes and Beatrix speechless for all of a second.

Pulling Isadora into a hug, Beatrix gave her a squeeze. "You should have written me a letter about that significant circumstance. How lovely to learn you're expecting."

"I thought it would be best to deliver the news in person," Isadora said before she stepped back and smiled. "Do know that if we hadn't decided to come to Chicago, I was going to come visit you in New York for the holidays. I assume your mother, even with her being somewhat annoyed with you, will want you home for Christmas."

Beatrix winced. "I'm not sure about that. What with all the shenanigans I got up to in New York, and—"

"On my word, but this is beyond the pale," she heard a lady shriek behind her. "I'm speaking to you, girl, and your blatant rudeness in not even bothering to turn around to acknowledge me certainly proves to everyone in attendance that you, a disgraced employee from Marshall Field & Company, do not belong at this ball."

"Is that lady talking to you?" Isadora asked as Beatrix turned around and found none other than Mrs. Sturgis, the woman responsible for one of her demotions, standing a few feet away.

That Mrs. Sturgis was furious was not in question.

Her face was an unusual shade of purple, and her jowls, all three of them, were quivering in clear indignation.

Beatrix glanced around and found the guests surrounding Mrs. Sturgis directing their attention her way, their gazes ripe with anticipation.

"Did she say something about you working at Marshall Field & Company?" Ian asked, his brow furrowed.

"She did. I was a salesgirl, until I got demoted to the coat check, and then—"

"I got her dismissed from the coat check for being overly cheeky with me."

Isadora arched a brow at Mrs. Sturgis before she returned her attention to Beatrix and grinned. "We obviously have much to catch up on, but why am I not surprised you took up a position at a store or that you were being overly cheeky with a customer?"

Beatrix returned the grin, ignoring that Mrs. Sturgis had begun sputtering in outrage. "It was Aunt Gladys's idea for me to take up a position, but as for me being cheeky, I wasn't at fault in the least. I merely pointed out to Mrs. Sturgis, after she threw her wrap at me and her brooch gouged my head in the process, that she should show more care in the future." She leveled an eye on Mrs. Sturgis as she pushed aside a curl that Mamie had carefully arranged over the small scab on her forehead. "And you *should* show more care in the future as well as resist running off to management to complain about what was *your* unacceptable behavior, not mine. You cost me fifty cents a week in my pay, and I received another demotion because I got sent to the Bargain Basement after you complained."

Mrs. Sturgis's eyes flashed. "I was under the impression you'd be dismissed on the spot."

"You'll need to take that particular grievance up with the store, but you'll be pleased to learn that I have been dismissed—just not because of you."

Mrs. Sturgis glanced around the crowd. "This girl's very presence here is an outrage, and I'm appalled she was somehow able to get through the front door in the first place."

"She came as my guest."

Beatrix glanced past Mrs. Sturgis and found Norman fighting his way through the crowd, seemingly unconcerned when he shoved aside a gentleman and sent him stumbling. Taking hold of her arm, he sent her a smile, then turned to Mrs. Sturgis.

"I believe you owe Miss Waterbury an apology," he said pleasantly, his tone at direct odds with the temper in his eyes.

"I think not," Mrs. Sturgis returned right as an older gentleman joined her, his face wreathed in a smile as he nodded to Ian.

"Ah, Mr. MacKenzie. I was hoping I'd get an opportunity to speak with you this evening after I learned how well your meeting went today with the union men who represent my meat-packing factory." He turned his smile on Mrs. Sturgis. "How wonderful, dear, that you've apparently already met the oh-so-lovely Mrs. Ian MacKenzie, the lady I spoke to you about earlier, the one who"—he lowered his voice—"is a member of the New York Four Hundred, and the one you wanted to be introduced to."

Some of the color leaked out of Mrs. Sturgis's face. "I . . . I've not had the pleasure of an introduction as of yet."

"Can't have that," the man said, taking hold of Mrs. Sturgis's arm and pulling her forward. "Mr. MacKenzie, allow me to present my wife, Mrs. Sturgis. Marilyn, this is Mr. Ian MacKenzie and his lovely wife, Mrs. MacKenzie."

After stumbling through the pleasantries, a now-pale Mrs. Sturgis looked at Beatrix, then Isadora, and then to Ian before she returned her attention to Beatrix. "I don't understand how a salesgirl is acquainted with a member of the New York Four Hundred."

Before Beatrix could answer, Isadora sent her a slightly bewildered look, one Beatrix responded to with a quirk of a brow and a shrug. Isadora's lips curved just the slightest bit before she nodded, squared her shoulders, and turned her attention back to Mrs. Sturgis. "Beatrix and I grew up together. And then we made our debuts together."

Mrs. Sturgis turned paler still. "Your . . . debuts?"

Isadora nodded. "Indeed, as in debuts to New York society, but . . . were you unaware that Beatrix is a member of the New York Four Hundred as well?"

Beatrix felt Norman stiffen beside her, but before she had a chance to explain, his mother, Mary, stepped around Mrs. Sturgis. Stopping directly in front of Beatrix, she narrowed her eyes. But then, instead of saying a single word to Beatrix, she glanced around at a crowd that was beginning to press closer, then nodded to Norman. "We should take this somewhere private."

"Indeed," Norman said, taking Beatrix's arm and tugging her along in the wake of his mother, who was already sailing her way through the crowd and toward an exit.

"Would you like me to come with you?" Isadora asked, Ian by her side as they fell into step beside Beatrix.

"I would, but I believe this is going to be uncomfortable enough as it is. I'll find you after I'm done speaking with Norman and his mother."

"Do not do anything to upset Beatrix," Isadora said to Norman, who slowed his pace but didn't stop.

"I'm fairly certain she's the one who is about to upset me," he returned right as Ian drew himself up and took on a rather menacing air. "Interesting friends you have," Norman muttered as they left Isadora and Ian behind, walking through the doorway of the ballroom and finding Mary waiting for them.

"I've been friends with Isadora since we were in short dresses, although I've only become friends with Ian over the past year, after Isadora ran off from New York to escape a most dastardly duke who was determined to marry her."

Norman came to an abrupt stop and arched a brow. "She ran away because of a dastardly duke?"

Before she could answer, Mary marched up to join them. "This is no time for chitchat. We have important, and need I add, disturbing matters to discuss. Follow me."

It took all of five minutes to wind their way through the hotel, retrieve their wraps, and then walk outside, Mary not stopping until she'd traveled well away from any lingering guests who might care to hear whatever it was she was about to say. Moving to stand by the corner of the Palmer House, she whipped around and crossed her arms over her chest.

"Did I hear correctly that you're a member of New York high society?" was the first question out of her mouth.

Seeing no reason to deny it, Beatrix nodded. "I am, although why that appears to upset you is rather confusing. One would think my being a member of high society would alleviate some of the concerns you've had about my involvement with your son, since clearly I'm not after his money."

"You have money?" Norman asked.

Beatrix nodded. "I do. My father, Mr. Arthur Waterbury, has been rather successful with increasing the family fortunes over the years, and he's set aside a portion of that fortune for my personal use."

Norman's brows drew together as he took to regarding her far too intently, while Mary looked absolutely furious.

"Your father is *Arthur* Waterbury?" she demanded.

Having no idea why Mary would be mad about the fact that her father was Arthur Waterbury, Beatrix nodded. "He is."

Mary narrowed her eyes and looked more furious than ever. "Then I *was* justified in believing you were up to no good as it pertains to my son."

"I have no idea what you could possibly mean by that," Beatrix said slowly.

Mary moved to Norman and took hold of his hand. "I'm sorry to have to be the bearer of what I'm sure you're going to find distressing news, my dear, but you see, I was only recently given a new Pinkerton report. The agents were able to track down the apartment for one of the men, a James something or other. And while that man was long gone, he left behind some incriminating evidence."

Mary sent Beatrix another scowl before she returned her attention to her son. "There was a letter written to James by none other than the mastermind behind the attempts to steal your research papers—a letter that was signed by one Mr. *Arthur* Waterbury. He stated in that letter that final payment would be made to this James person just as soon as the authentic research papers were delivered to him."

"What?" Beatrix demanded, taking a step toward Mary, which earned her a glare before she looked back to her son.

"So you see, I *was* right about Miss Waterbury after all, because while she apparently didn't set her sights on you because of your wealth, she did set her sights on you to secure your research papers for her father."

"That's . . . preposterous," Beatrix all but sputtered

Mary shook her head. "It's not preposterous in the least, especially when it's now becoming clear to me exactly who you are— you're a spy for your father, sent to Chicago to ingratiate yourself with Norman. I'm now quite convinced that if the men your father hired were unsuccessful, your next order of business would have been to take it upon yourself to use those feminine wiles of yours to secure Norman's research for your father once and for all."

CHAPTER 33

Different thoughts swirled through Norman's mind, each one more disturbing than the next, until he felt as if his head might explode right there in front of the Palmer House, leaving bits of his unusual mind scattered about the sidewalk.

It was almost too much to take in—this notion that Beatrix had purposefully sought him out in order to secure his research, but why else would she have neglected to disclose to him at some point who she really was, and why had she taken up a position as a salesgirl if she was an American heiress?

"Did you begin working at Marshall Field & Company in order to illicit sympathy from me?" he asked, drawing Beatrix's attention as well as her temper, given the way her eyes gleamed.

"Don't be an idiot. Of course I didn't. If you'll recall, you and I parted ways and had no intention of ever seeing each other again *before* I took on my position at Marshall Field & Company."

"Surely you're not going to believe her, are you, dear?" his mother asked him, earning a snort from Beatrix in return.

"If I were trying to pull the wool over Norman's eyes," Beatrix began, "I assure you, I wouldn't try to do so by crafting such an unusual tale. Nor would I have subjected myself to the ridicule and condescending behavior I experienced every day at the hands of far-too-many snobbish customers in order to garner Norman's sympathy so that he'd . . . what? . . . hand over his research papers to me?" She turned to him. "Surely you must see that this whole conversation is ludicrous, as is the idea that I'm some sort of spy."

Doubt began worming its way through him until a completely valid thought sprang to mind. "But why didn't you tell me you were an heiress?"

She heaved a sigh. "I should have told you at some point, but after you came and saw me at the store, I was just becoming acclimated to my new situation—or perhaps I should call it an experiment, since you're rather familiar with those. If word had gotten out that I was this grand heiress, I wouldn't have been treated as merely a salesgirl. Instead, I would have been viewed as an outsider, rendering my experience at the store useless."

The doubt wormed its way forward again. "But you've had ample time to tell me since you first started working at the store."

"True, and I don't really have a good reason for why I didn't tell you, although there might have been a part of me that was hoping you, what with that unusual mind of yours, were figuring out on your own that I was a woman of some means."

"How could I have figured that out?"

"You told me numerous times that you're very observant, so you must have noticed how I wasn't overly concerned about losing my position, which I would have been if I needed funds. Last week, I thought you might question how I had enough money to post bail for all those women. And then, of course, there's the dress I'm wearing." Beatrix gestured to her gown. "How else would I have been able to afford to wear a gown from Worth?"

"You're wearing Worth?" Mary asked, stepping all of an inch forward.

"I am," Beatrix said.

Norman tilted his head. "I didn't even consider at first how you came to possess that gown, probably because the sight of you rendered me all but speechless."

"And that is exactly why Miss Waterbury should be ashamed

of herself," Mary said firmly, advancing closer to Beatrix until only a foot separated them. "I've sheltered Norman from vixens like you his entire life, and that I was not there when you convinced him you were some type of damsel in distress leaves me quite furious."

Beatrix's lips, oddly enough, began to curve. "I know I should be gravely insulted about being called a vixen, but I find the thought of myself cast in that particular role rather amusing."

Norman was not encouraged when his mother drew herself up and opened her mouth, then closed it again, apparently uncertain how to respond to that. Knowing it was past time he took control of the situation before it deteriorated further, Norman nodded to his mother. "I need to speak with Beatrix alone."

"Absolutely not."

"I'm afraid I must insist on that." Taking Beatrix's arm, he told his mother he'd catch up with her later, then hustled Beatrix down the sidewalk, not stopping until they reached the line of parked carriages. Glancing over them, Norman spotted his carriage and headed for it, not really surprised when Beatrix tugged her arm away from his.

"Where are we going?" she asked.

"Away from here," he said as they reached the carriage and he told the driver to take them for a ride through the city.

After a groomsman hurried to open the door for them, Norman followed Beatrix into the carriage. Settling into the seat opposite her, he nodded as the carriage lurched into motion. "I believe I deserve some answers."

"I'm not a spy, if that's an answer you're looking for."

"Then why did you withhold your true identity from me?"

Her lips thinned. "Did I, or did I not, introduce myself as Beatrix Waterbury when we first met?"

"You did."

"Well, there you have it. I didn't withhold my identity from you. I simply didn't tell you that I am also an heiress."

"You've yet to sufficiently explain your reasons for that. All you've said is that you withheld it to aid your acceptance into the working world."

She frowned and tilted her head. "I suppose I withheld that information from you at first because I found you so annoying. You were quick to make assumptions about me—one of the most annoying being your assumption that I was a spinster because of my opinionated nature." She sent him a smile that was hardly amused. "I found it oddly satisfying to allow you to continue on with your less-than-accurate assumptions."

Norman winced. "I imagine I might have come across as rather condescending at the time."

"Indeed. But I found it amusing, that amusement lending me the forbearance I desperately needed to refrain from shooting you again."

He felt his lips give a surprising twitch. "I appreciate that, but why didn't you mention you're Arthur Waterbury's daughter when I brought his name up at the train station?"

"When did you bring my father's name up at the train station?"

"When I was giving those men a list of possible suspects. I listed your father among them because he attended that meeting I was at in New York."

Beatrix released a snort. "You gave those men over one hundred names, Norman. Even the men who were writing all those names down were having a hard time keeping up with you. And while I'm sure I must have heard a handful of the names you rattled off, I stopped listening for a while after someone brought me a much-needed cup of tea."

The doubt was back in a flash. "You did have tea."

"I did, but to be clear about my father, he often attends scientific meetings in New York. But he has no need to steal your research papers. He's known to be a generous man with funding research projects, so there are more than enough men willing to hand over their research papers in the hopes of securing funding. Father has no reason to resort to theft for any research idea that may appeal to him."

Norman frowned. "But if you *are* a spy for your father, it would explain why you decided to spend time with me, even though you just admitted you found me very annoying when we first met."

Beatrix settled back against the seat. "You must realize that's ridiculous."

Norman looked out the carriage window, wondering how his evening, as well as his life, had turned so dramatic.

He'd always been a man who maintained a life devoid of drama, and yet it seemed to have become his constant companion ever since he'd met Beatrix.

Turning from the scenery, he shrugged. "It's not ridiculous, although I have to wonder if you've been growing concerned about my, well, increased interest in you."

"You're going to have to explain that a little more sufficiently."

"Very well, and I'll start by saying this—if you've been, as my mother suggested, using your feminine wiles to get close to me, you must have neglected to realize that I might become intrigued by those feminine wiles."

She released a snort. "I'll have you know that in my many spinster years on this earth I've never been accused by anyone of using my feminine wiles, probably because when people think of Beatrix Waterbury, I'm sure they would never think, 'Well there's a lady who knows how to use her feminine wiles to advantage.'"

With that, Beatrix reached up and flipped open the small window that opened directly beside the driver, calling for him to take her back to Hyde Park. She then snapped the window shut and got resettled on the seat, staring out the window for the longest time until she turned to him again.

"You're a logical man, Norman, and logic should tell you that you're being absurd right now. Someone has obviously framed my father because, again, as one of *the* wealthiest men in the country, he has no need to steal your research." She held up her hand when he opened his mouth to reply. "If you consider all of the time we've spent together, you should know that I'm not after your research either. I could have easily taken your papers after I shot you, but did I? No, I did not," she finished before he could answer the question she apparently hadn't actually posed to him.

"I also highly doubt, if I wanted your research," she continued, "and if I were working on behalf of my father, that I would have intervened when those criminals attacked you outside Marshall Field & Company, or when they held up the train in the first place."

Everything she said *did* have a certain logic to it, but she *had* withheld important information from him, and that, as far as Norman was concerned, was telling.

"Perhaps you intervened because you realized those men were going to be unsuccessful, and by intervening, you garnered my appreciation." He nodded. "Perhaps those men were at your aunt's house later that night to pass along information to you, and before you argue with that, how would they have known where to find you if they weren't working with you?"

"My aunt's address was among the other contents of my reticule that I dumped into that bag on the train."

"Oh."

"Yes, oh."

The next twenty minutes were spent in uncomfortable silence after Beatrix turned to the window again and refused to say another word, the light from the inside carriage lamp flickering over a face that was flushed with temper. What she was thinking, he had no idea, but he felt a most curious urge to comfort her as well as beg her forgiveness, even with him still convinced that she could very well be the spy his mother had accused her of being.

As the carriage slowed, Norman felt a sense of urgency to do something, although what that something was eluded him at the moment.

"We're here," Beatrix said, pulling her attention from the window and reaching for the door.

"I'll see you to the front door," he said.

"I'm perfectly capable of seeing myself to the door, Norman. I've had quite enough of you tonight and don't want or need you to see me the last few feet home." She settled eyes that were suspiciously bright on him. "You've insulted me without cause, and because of that, I feel free to finally admit something to you."

"You *are* a spy?"

She sent him a look that spoke volumes before she opened the door and stepped to the ground. Turning back to him, she caught his eye. "What I wanted to admit was this—I'd grown very fond of you, Norman, some might say exceedingly so. But you've done me a grave disservice this evening, jumping to conclusions before you did your proper due diligence. I have to believe you didn't become the scientist you are today by being so neglectful, but that you'd be so remiss in your care of me, well, it speaks volumes. Any fondness I might have had for you is now long gone, although I do hope that the fondness you once held for me will have you at least extending me an apology—in the form of a written note, of course—after I clear my father's name. After that apology, I'll not want to have any further contact with you."

Trepidation was immediate. "You're going to attempt to clear your father's name?"

"Of course I am, and to do that, I'm going to have to return to New York as soon as possible." With that, Beatrix shut the door and glided away, not turning back to look at him a single time before she disappeared through her aunt's gate and straight out of his life.

CHAPTER 34

Beatrix stepped from the hansom cab and onto the sidewalk of Fifth Avenue. After paying the driver, she stood on the sidewalk, appreciating the sight of her family home, feeling as if she'd been away for years instead of months.

Four stories tall and built of limestone, the house was created in a style that combined Italianate touches with the formality of French neoclassicism, and was a lavish display of opulence mixed with a hefty dose of refinement.

The front door, flanked by tall windows, opened, and then Mr. Parsons, the Waterbury butler, was striding toward Beatrix, frowning as he stopped in front of her.

"Miss Beatrix," he exclaimed. "We've had no word you were returning home. What's happened?"

Before she could answer, Mr. Parsons took hold of her hand as his gaze ran over her, concern in his eyes before he pulled her into his arms and gave her a good squeeze. Releasing her a moment later, he stepped back. "You're a mess."

Beatrix grinned. "I've just been on a train for hours and hours, so of course I'm a mess. But do know that nothing too troublesome has happened to me."

"*Too* troublesome sounds like a story to me," Mr. Parsons said firmly. "But before I hear the details of what I'm certain is going to be a disconcerting tale, you should go and greet your parents while I ring to have some coffee and cakes brought to the library, which is where your parents are currently engaged in their latest . . . ah . . . diversion."

"Should I ask what that diversion is this time?"

"Best to see it with your own eyes."

Exchanging a grin with him, Beatrix walked with Mr. Parsons into the house, the fresh scent of lemons greeting her. Lemon was a scent her mother adored, which was why the maids always polished the furniture with lemon paste and also spritzed the air with lemon water a few times a day.

Mr. Parsons gestured her down the long hallway that led to the library, telling her he'd join her there directly after he fetched the coffee.

Striding down the hallway, Beatrix heard her mother's laughter, followed by a hearty laugh from her father in response, and braced herself for whatever diversion they were pursuing now.

Arthur and Annie Waterbury enjoyed the reputation of eccentric couple about town, that reputation a direct result of the disregard they showed at times for what society expected of members of the New York Four Hundred. That her father was one of the wealthiest men in the country allowed them to disregard the rules at will, especially considering he was from a Knickerbocker family, which meant his position within society was solidly secure, no matter the antics he and Beatrix's mother got up to.

Easing open the door to the library, Beatrix stepped inside, coming to a stop and shaking her head at the sight that met her eyes.

In her absence, the library had undergone a bit of a transformation.

The floor-to-ceiling bookcases were currently draped in linen, and all the furniture was missing in the room, save for a few battered chairs that Beatrix had never seen in her life and a large table that was in the middle of the room, holding a potter's wheel on it.

Her mother, Annie, was sitting in front of the potter's wheel, a mound of clay whirling about, and her father, Arthur, was standing behind her with his arms around her, both of them apparently trying to mold the same pot together. Given that the clay whirling around on the wheel resembled a blob instead of any discernable object, it was apparent that they'd yet to master the art they were currently pursuing.

"It's no wonder the two of you are often the talk of the town, what with your unusual habit of always touching each other," Beatrix said, moving farther into the room as her mother's head shot up, as did her father's, right as the blob on the wheel collapsed, bits of it flying into the air when the wheel kept spinning.

"You need to stop pumping the foot pedal, darling," Arthur said before he abandoned the clay and moved around the table. "Beatrix, this is a lovely, although unexpected, surprise."

Annie nodded as the wheel came to a slow stop and she rose to her feet. "Indeed, it is a lovely surprise, but why didn't you send us word you were returning home? And what are you doing home in the first place, and better yet, where's Gladys? You didn't get yourself arrested again and she's sent you back to us, did you?"

"I didn't send word because, frankly, it didn't cross my mind, what with the more important matters I've had to think about of late," Beatrix said, holding up a hand when it seemed as if her father was about to hug her, but given that his hands were covered in clay, she wasn't really keen to have him do that. "And no, I wasn't arrested again, nor have I done anything to annoy Aunt Gladys. She wanted to travel to New York with me, but Edgar came down with a horrible sore throat right as we were getting ready to go to the train station. That unfortunate situation had me encouraging Aunt Gladys to stay behind because she was obviously concerned about Edgar and wanted to personally see after him."

Annie tapped a clay-covered finger against her chin. "Dare I hope that Edgar might be finally turning his thoughts to marrying my sister? He clearly adores her, and I've made a point to say prayers for him every now and again, praying that he'll eventually set aside his pride and realize he and Gladys belong together—and not as employer and butler."

"You knew that Aunt Gladys is more than fond of her butler?" Beatrix asked.

"She's my sister. Of course I knew, even though she's never bothered to broach the subject with me."

Arthur picked up a rag and began wiping the clay from his hands, sending an affectionate glance to his wife. "And while Gladys is always an interesting topic of conversation, darling, what say we momentarily shelve this particular subject and move on to why Beatrix has returned." He caught Beatrix's eye. "I thought the plan was for you to stay at Gladys's until at least Christmas."

"It was, but there were extenuating circumstances that had me cutting my visit short."

"And explaining those extenuating circumstances certainly deserves to be told while having coffee and cake," Mr. Parsons said, wheeling in a cart that had her mother's silver service on it.

As Mr. Parsons went about pouring out the coffee, Arthur strode from the room, returning a short time later, dragging a small table behind him. Her mother quickly excused herself to wash the clay from her hands.

"Why have you all but dismantled the library?" Beatrix asked as her father began pulling battered chairs around the table he'd brought in.

"Your delightful friend Mr. Murray Middleton told us the lighting in here was more conducive to working with clay because the floor-to-ceiling windows bring in just the right amount of natural light," Annie said, walking back into the room.

"You've recently seen Murray?" Beatrix asked.

Annie nodded. "We frequently see him because he's begun offering instruction in art." She shook her head. "Your father and I attended a few of Murray's classes on abstract metal sculpting, but we experienced somewhat of a problem with that."

"Your mother almost burned Murray's studio down when she

316

got too close to the flame we were using to heat the metal in order to make it supple," Arthur said with a shake of his head. "Before anyone knew it, the mitts she was wearing to protect her hands caught on fire. Murray's wife, Maisie, was quick to rush to your mother's aid, dousing her with the water from a vase of flowers an earlier class had been using as their subject matter."

Annie released a sigh. "Your father and I weren't overly surprised when Murray offered us private lessons, but only if we'd agree to take those lessons here."

Beatrix grinned. "I imagine he was most insistent on that."

"Indeed he was," Arthur said. "Which explains why the library is currently in a state of disarray, although because your mother and I have decided we really enjoy pottery, we might add an artist studio to the back of the house."

"Have you actually finished any pieces of pottery?"

"We haven't," Annie said cheerfully before she tossed a rather flirty grin to Arthur. "But it's been marvelous trying."

"You do know you're embarrassing me, don't you?" Beatrix asked.

Annie's smile was anything but contrite. "We've been alone now for weeks. Clearly we're out of practice with how to comport ourselves when our children are underfoot."

"Which does leave me questioning whether having the house to yourselves, save for all your staff, might have been a great incentive to banish me to the wilds of Chicago."

Annie's smile dimmed as she nodded to Arthur. "You've still got clay on you, dear."

"Which I'm sure is your way of saying you'd like a few minutes alone with our daughter," Arthur replied with a nod of his own. "I'll be right back."

"Give me at least twenty minutes."

Arthur smiled and strode from the room, Mr. Parsons following him, saying over his shoulder that he was off to fetch additional treats from the kitchen before closing the door behind him.

Annie moved to Beatrix's side and engulfed her in a warm

embrace, the scent of lemons mixed with clay leaving Beatrix smiling.

"I've missed you, my darling girl," her mother said before she gestured to one of the battered chairs. "Shall we sit?"

Taking a seat, Beatrix soon found herself under the unwavering stare of her mother.

"You've not been sleeping," Annie proclaimed.

"It's difficult to sleep on a train, even with Aunt Gladys reserving a private Pullman car."

"A more pleasant way to travel than what you probably experienced getting to Chicago."

Beatrix smiled. "You must know I wasn't overly bothered by having to take a passenger car to Chicago. It gave me an opportunity to meet new people, and I did have quite the adventure on that ride to Chicago."

"And I'm sure you'll explain that more sufficiently in a moment, but returning to your lack of sleep. You've never had difficulties sleeping before, even when you're on a train, which means . . . you've met a man, and one who is giving you trouble if I'm not mistaken."

"How did you come to that conclusion?"

Annie shrugged. "You and I have always been very similar, Beatrix. And the only time I ever experienced difficulty sleeping was after your father and I first met." She blew out a breath. "Your grandmother, Mrs. Howard Waterbury, didn't approve of me at first as a suitable bride for your father. My father, as you know, made his fortune in mining and had no illustrious ancestors to impress New York society when he moved here. Because of that, and because the Waterburys are firmly of the Knickerbocker set, your grandmother did everything in her power to dissuade your father from courting me."

"But he obviously wasn't dissuaded."

"He did have reservations, though, after his mother, sister, aunts, and even a few friends began telling him how unsuitable I was. He stopped calling on me for a good month without any explanation, which caused me more than a few sleepless nights, trying to figure out where the charming gentleman with whom I'd fallen in love had gone."

"Clearly that charming gentleman returned at some point since you've been married to him all these years."

Annie smiled. "He did, but only after I took matters into my own hands. You see, one day I'd taken my horse to Central Park, and Arthur was there with a group of his friends. He had the audacity to ride past me without so much as a doff of a hat, and something inside me snapped. I chased after him and told him he was being an idiot. I then told him that while he apparently felt I was socially unsuitable, four other gentlemen, all of whom actually wanted to marry me and didn't care about my lack of grand social status, had already approached my father to ask for his blessing to court me." Annie's smile turned smug. "Arthur came to his senses in a remarkably short period of time after realizing he was about to lose me forever, and that, my dear, was the end of my sleepless nights."

"What did Grandmother Waterbury think of that?"

"Oh, she wasn't pleased at first, but I managed to grow on her, and we eventually enjoyed an amiable relationship." Annie sat forward. "Is the trouble you're experiencing with a man a direct result of his mother?"

Seeing no reason to deny that a man was the root of her sleep deprivation of late, Beatrix nodded. "To a certain extent, but Mrs. Nesbit isn't worried about my social status, although she was at one time, when no one was aware that I'm an heiress or a member of the New York Four Hundred."

"You didn't let anyone know who you are?"

"I wasn't hiding it, but after Aunt Gladys arranged for me to take on a position at Marshall Field & Company, I decided that I wouldn't benefit nearly as much from that position if everyone there came to the conclusion I was only working in a store as some type of lark."

Annie was out of her chair and moving for the door in the blink of an eye. Opening the door, she let out a small shriek when Arthur and Mr. Parsons stumbled into the room, sheepish smiles on their faces as they then went about acting as if they'd not been eavesdropping.

"I've brought additional treats," Mr. Parsons proclaimed, walking out of the room again and returning a moment later, pushing a second cart.

"I'll help pour more coffee," Arthur said, and after he did exactly that, and after Mr. Parsons handed out fine bone china plates with cake, cookies, and fruit on them, everyone took a seat and turned their attention to Beatrix.

"Start with the store," her father suggested.

"I think she should start with the adventure she mentioned she had on the train getting to Chicago," Mr. Parsons said, a remark that suggested he'd been eavesdropping from practically the moment he'd left the room.

"I think she should start with the gentleman responsible for her sleepless nights," Annie argued.

"A Mr. Nesbit," Mr. Parsons said with a nod.

"How about if I just start at the beginning?" Beatrix suggested.

"That works for me," Arthur said.

It took over an hour to get most of the story out, what with how everyone kept interrupting her and demanding she expand on a few of her adventures—such as the train heist, the demotions and then dismissal from the store, the many suffragist meetings she'd attended, the remaking of Theodosia, her visit to jail, the cats who wanted to plot her demise, the relationship between Aunt Gladys and Edgar, and then . . . question after question about Norman.

"I'm still a little unsure about why you and Norman suffered such a disagreement with each other," Annie said slowly when Beatrix paused to take a sip of coffee. "Although I am beyond thrilled that you've finally met a gentleman you care about, which is what I was hoping would happen when I sent you off to stay with Gladys."

"I thought you sent me off to stay with Aunt Gladys because I'd landed myself in jail."

"Twice, dear, you landed yourself in jail twice, and don't think I've forgotten about that other time when you almost landed in jail, when you were with the oh-so-charming Poppy Blackburn." Annie regarded Beatrix over the rim of her coffee cup. "And speaking of Poppy, before I forget, she and her lovely husband, Lord Reginald Blackburn, are currently not in town, having gone to Kentucky to visit her parents. I believe they'll be back soon, what with Poppy expecting a new addition to their family right around Christmas."

"Then I'll see her when she returns since I'm not intending on going back to Chicago."

"You mustn't be hasty about that," Annie countered. "Before I got distracted with thoughts of Poppy, I was about to tell you the true reason why I sent you away from New York, and no, it wasn't because you landed in jail."

"Was it because I misled you about my relationship with Thomas Hamersley?"

"No, although I was certainly annoyed with you for being less than truthful with me about that relationship over the years." Annie smiled. "However, I eventually realized *why* you'd perpetuated what was basically fraud on your part, and that, my dear, is the true reason for sending you off to stay with your aunt."

Beatrix frowned. "I'm afraid I'm not following."

Annie took a sip of her coffee. "You used Thomas for years to keep other gentlemen at a distance—and not only gentlemen who might have been too interested in the wealth that's attached to your name. By having society believe you and Thomas would marry at some point, you were free to go about your life without being pursued, well, until Thomas went off and got himself engaged to Helene Leggett. After word about his engagement got out, you then made the claim to me that you'd decided long ago to never marry, but I don't believe that's true."

Setting aside her cup, Annie sat forward. "I believe you've always wanted what your father and I share—an unusual partnership in the eyes of society, but one that's always been filled with laughter and love." She exchanged a smile with Arthur before returning her attention to Beatrix. "God has blessed your father and me with a true love story, but I'm sure our love, being so unusual, must seem like an anomaly to most people, including you. That's why I believe you used Thomas as an excuse to not become romantically interested in any gentleman, saving you disappointment in the end."

"Until she met Norman Nesbit," Arthur said with a nod. "Who apparently, from what I've been able to grasp, became incredibly put out after discovering Beatrix was not merely a salesgirl, but an heiress."

Beatrix blew out a breath. "That's not the main reason Norman became incredibly put out with me, but I've not gotten to that point of the story just yet, what with all your questions."

"We'll be silent as church mice," Mr. Parsons said, setting aside his cup and folding his hands in his lap.

Beatrix resisted a smile. "That'll last for about a minute, but allow me to use that minute to explain. You see, Norman wasn't all that upset about learning I'm an heiress. What he was most upset about was learning there could be a chance I was a spy, interested in stealing those research papers I told you about."

"That's absurd," Annie said with a huff. "Was his mother behind that unfounded accusation?"

"She was, but in her defense, she made that accusation after a letter was discovered at the home of one of the criminals I mentioned earlier." She nodded to her father. "That letter appeared to be from you and left little doubt that you were responsible for attempting to divest Norman of his research."

CHAPTER 35

"You do realize that it would have been much easier all around if you'd figured out that Beatrix is not capable of the skullduggery you accused her of before she left to return to New York, don't you?"

Norman stopped in the middle of Grand Central Depot, wiped his perspiring forehead with the back of his hand, and arched a brow at Theodosia. "What did you pack in this trunk? I can barely pull it."

"Essentials, such as a large bottle of olive oil so I can continue on with the treatment Blanche and I developed to keep my hair in fine form as well as numerous jars of different creams I've been trying out to see which one makes my face softer."

"Clearly your idea of essentials differs from mine, but the next time I offer to run down a porter to manage our trunks, I suggest you don't argue with me."

Theo gave an airy wave of a gloved hand. "I can pull my own trunk, Norman, if you'd like. I only thought to save us time."

Before Norman could respond to that nonsense, Gladys marched up beside him, took hold of the handle of Theo's trunk, then marched away without a single word. Edgar sent Norman a look that proved that man was still put out with Norman before striding after Gladys, easily pulling his trunk and hers behind him.

"What are the odds that we'd just happen to travel to New York on the same train as Gladys and Edgar?" Norman asked.

"Not great," Theo returned as she watched Edgar weave his way through the crowd. "And even though we rarely encountered them on the trip here, what with them having their own private Pullman car while we rode coach, one would think some of the annoyance they're holding for you would have dissipated since we're obviously in New York so that you can make amends with Beatrix."

"That annoyance will disappear in a thrice if you *are* able to make amends with Beatrix," Mamie said, huffing her way up to them as she lugged a large trunk behind her. Blanche nodded in agreement to that as she stopped directly beside Norman.

"And if you can convince Beatrix you're worthy of another chance with her," Blanche began, "I imagine you'll once again find yourself in Gladys's good graces, although it may take a while longer for Edgar to come around. He's been very disturbed by the unfounded accusations you leveled against Beatrix." With that, Blanche sent him another nod, smiled at Theodosia, and took off after Gladys, with Mamie by her side.

Norman trailed after Blanche, finding that far easier now that Gladys had relieved him of Theo's trunk and he only had his to pull. "In my defense, those accusations didn't appear to be unfounded at first, what with that letter the Pinkertons found."

"Mr. Waterbury was framed," Mamie shot back over her shoulder. "Although by whom, well, that is the question of the hour, isn't it?"

"Too right it is," Theo agreed, but instead of speculating on that particular matter, she hurried to join Blanche, immediately launching into a discussion about whether or not they should try adding grapefruit juice to a new tonic they were developing that was supposed to help decrease the oil on a lady's face.

"Is this really the moment?" Norman asked when the two ladies slowed their pace considerably when their discussion turned earnest.

"Says the man who's been known to block traffic when he's crossing the street and comes to a mathematical equation he's never considered before," Theo shot back, although she paired her statement with a grin and did jolt into motion again.

Reaching a line of carriages for rent, Norman took Theo's trunk from Gladys, who sent him a sniff before she climbed into the carriage she'd rented, leaning out of that carriage a second later to pin him with a stern look. "Do not be a disappointment, dear. I expect you to extend Beatrix a heartfelt apology as well as extend one to her father for even considering the idea he resorted to theft in order to get your research papers."

Norman arched a brow. "Do you truly believe I traveled all this way to do anything *but* deliver apologies to Beatrix and her father?"

Gladys considered him for a long moment before she inclined her head. "Perhaps there's hope for you yet." With that, she retreated into the carriage, with Edgar following her a second later, but only after he sent Norman a scowl.

"See, you're making progress already," Mamie said before she jumped into the carriage, Blanche doing the same as soon as Mamie found her seat.

"We'd better follow right behind them," Theo said, waving a man forward to help get her trunk onto the hired carriage they were taking. "Gladys didn't bother to give us Beatrix's direction, and while I assume she lives on Fifth Avenue, it might take up precious time if we're forced to knock on every door in search of her."

Norman gave Theo his hand and helped her into the carriage, right as the hair at the back of his neck stood to attention. Turning, he scanned the crowd bustling outside of the depot.

"What is it?" Theo asked.

"I have the most curious feeling we're being watched."

Theo stuck her head out of the carriage, peered around, then frowned. "Who would want to watch us here?"

"No idea, but . . ." Norman looked around again but didn't see a single soul watching them, or even anyone who looked vaguely familiar. He told the driver to follow Gladys's carriage before he climbed into the carriage and took a seat.

Theo pressed against the window as they trundled their way through the streets of New York, excitement in her eyes. "I've never been to New York before," she admitted, her breath fogging up the glass.

"We'll have to make certain to take in some sights—after I settle matters with Beatrix, of course."

Theo sat back in the seat. "Dare I hope you have a plan to settle those matters?"

"Not a single one."

"That's not like you at all. You always have a plan." She immediately began rummaging around in the large bag she was carrying, pulling out a fashion magazine, along with an etiquette book. "Perhaps these will give us some suggestions."

Norman shook his head. "The few times I tried to follow proper etiquette and expected behavior didn't seem to impress Beatrix in the least."

"What do you mean?"

"Well, when I tried to assist her in the coat check by taking all the coats from the ladies, she got annoyed with me. But then when I gave her that leg for Hubert, she sent me the nicest smile, even though I'm sure giving a lady a leg isn't exactly proper."

Theo stuffed the magazine and book back into her bag. "Perhaps that means she's fond of the real you and not the person you tried to become in order to impress her."

"Which suggests our experiments pertaining to proper manners were ill-conceived from the start."

"On the contrary," Theo argued. "Our experiment proved that expected behaviors won't always work when the subject is not a typical subject, which you must admit, Beatrix is not."

"An excellent observation," Norman said as the carriage began to slow, and then pulled to a stop directly behind the carriage Gladys, Edgar, Mamie, and Blanche were in.

Reaching for the door, Norman stepped to the sidewalk, helped Theo out, then squinted at the house in front of him.

That the house was impressive was not in question, but the sheer size and detail given to every aspect certainly confirmed what Beatrix had been trying to tell him—the man who owned this particular house, that being her father, had no reason to steal anyone's research.

He should have listened to Beatrix, but his pride had gotten in the way, that pride having been wounded over the notion that she'd used him, made a fool of him, and worse yet, had toyed with his affections.

He no longer cared if his pride suffered, because he intended to make matters right with Beatrix even if that entailed begging her on bended knee for forgiveness because . . . well, he was more than merely fond of her.

She'd changed his world in a way he'd never expected, and in so doing, she'd allowed him to see his many, many flaws, which had then motivated him to take steps to correct those flaws, thus improving his life significantly.

He'd begun to form actual attachments with his family and with Theo—attachments that would have been all but impossible when he'd still been so self-centered and consumed with his work.

Beatrix was responsible for that, and yet, when his mother had presented him with Beatrix's duplicity, he'd allowed his pride to get in his way.

He'd be fortunate if Beatrix even accepted his apology, and while he was hoping to convince her to accept more than that—to accept him and all his flaws and idiosyncrasies—he couldn't blame her if she didn't.

"Are you going to come in the house with us or not?" Gladys demanded, pulling him out of his thoughts and back to the situation at hand.

"Coming in the house," he said firmly, moving to join Gladys, who was now marching her way to a front door that was already opening.

"Gladys," a man in a black jacket exclaimed, stepping aside as he gestured her into the house. "How lovely to see you. Your sister will be thrilled you've come to visit, as will Beatrix." He held out his hand to Edgar, which Edgar immediately took. "Happy to see you've recovered."

Edgar nodded. "It was a horrible illness, Mr. Parsons, but didn't last long." He sent a fond look after Gladys, who was already disappearing down a hallway. "Gladys watched over me like a hawk and even insisted on staying with me while Miss Beatrix returned here."

"Which I would think must have convinced you it's past time you . . . well, I'll leave it to you to figure out what you should do from here," Mr. Parsons said before he turned and smiled at Mamie and Blanche, both of whom were looking more than a little apprehensive. "Who do we have here?"

Edgar performed the introductions, his lips twitching when Blanche and Mamie curtsied to Mr. Parsons, a man who was clearly the Waterbury butler, before they hurried into the house.

"This is Miss Theodosia Robinson, a dear friend of this gentleman here," Edgar said next.

Mr. Parsons arched a brow at Norman. "And who is this gentleman?"

"That's Norman Nesbit."

"You may wait out here" was how Mr. Parsons replied to that, sending Norman a glare before he gestured Theo and Edgar into the house and firmly shut the door behind them.

328

CHAPTER 36

"Can't tell you how glad I am you've returned to New York," Murray Middleton said, galloping easily beside Beatrix on his horse, Wilbur, a delightful creature that her friend Poppy Garrison Blackburn had saved from a neglectful and abusive deliveryman. "What with Poppy and Reginald out of town and Maisie constantly rearranging the furniture in our new house, I've found myself at loose ends of late."

Beatrix wrinkled her nose. "I would think Maisie would want you to help her rearrange the furniture, what with how you seem to have an eye for matters like that."

"And normally she does. However . . ." Murray grinned. "She's in a somewhat delicate frame of mind at the moment, bursting into tears at the drop of a hat. I tend to hover when she cries, and apparently when a lady is, well, *expecting*, they're prone to dislike hovering husbands. Something to do with us having gotten them in that condition in the first place."

"Information I did not need to—wait." She smiled. "You're going to be a *father*?"

"Indeed, but the idea of fatherhood scares me half to death." He frowned. "What if I'm a horrible father, or what if we have a daughter and she decides to run off with some bounder Maisie and I don't approve of, and—"

"You'll be an excellent father, Murray, and I imagine if your daughter ran off with a bounder, you'd go after her and take care of it once and for all."

"I have grown more proficient with a pistol."

"I would imagine you have. See? Nothing to worry about."

"Practical advice for sure, and I have certainly missed that from you while you've been away."

"Since I doubt I'll be leaving the city again anytime soon, you may avail yourself of my practicality anytime you feel you need it."

Murray smiled before he sobered. "I'm sorry about all that business with that Norman fellow. Seems to me as if you'd grown fond of the man."

"I *was* fond of him, but I don't care to discuss Norman any further. Once I clear my father's name, I'll be done with Norman for good, and that will be that."

"You said your father hired the Pinkerton Agency to look into the matter."

"He has, and I've told the agent who came to the house all I knew about the men who'd been trying to steal Norman's research. And while I'm sure the Pinkerton Agency is more than up for investigating the situation, I'm currently feeling at loose ends. That is why I've decided to help by finding all the men who attended that meeting with Norman a few months back and interrogating them."

"A frightening thought to be sure, but speaking of frightening, do you think your parents might be growing tired of exploring their artistic natures?"

"You haven't gotten accustomed to their . . . ?"

"Unexpected gestures of fondness they're constantly giving each other?" Murray finished for her.

Beatrix grinned. "That's an interesting way of phrasing it, but yes."

"While I readily admit that there's something delightful about seeing a couple who've been married as long as your parents have still so obviously in love, it does take me aback when I happen to walk in on them and find them kissing or staring into each other's eyes."

"Rest assured, they never linger long with any new diversion, so by spring at the latest, I imagine they'll give up art and take on something else." She grinned. "Mother's been talking about learning how to box, so unless you've begun giving boxing instructions, you'll be safe."

"Good to know," Murray returned before he glanced past Beatrix and blinked. "On my word, that poor man should not be riding such a beast, what with how he doesn't seem comfortable in the saddle, but he's heading this way and . . . I think he's in trouble."

Beatrix turned in the saddle, discovering as she did so a man galloping her way, holding on to his horse for dear life, his hat long gone.

"Norman!" she yelled right as he thundered past her.

"Can't talk now, Beatrix," she heard him reply. "Got a bit of a situation here."

"He's lost all control!" Theodosia exclaimed, galloping into view and dashing past her.

Beatrix kneed her horse into motion, bending as low as she could over the sidesaddle. She then urged her horse faster when she saw Norman's horse, one of her father's high-spirited stallions by the name of Lightning—a horse Norman had no business attempting to ride—head for a row of hedges that was at least five feet high.

Two feet away from the shrubbery, Lightning came to an abrupt stop, and then Norman went sailing through the air and disappeared over the hedges.

While her horse, Tory, was perfectly capable of leaping the hedge, Beatrix had no idea where Norman had landed, so she reined Tory in, jumped to the ground, then rushed to the hedges, trying to peer through the branches.

"Norman? Can you hear me?"

A moan was his only response. Turning, she nodded to Murray. "Help me over?"

Murray immediately got down on all fours. "Don't know if you'll have enough height, but give it a go."

Beatrix stepped up on Murray's back, finding herself a few inches short, but then Theodosia gave her backside a hard shove, which had Beatrix moving upward at a rapid rate. She promptly tumbled over the hedge, landing directly on top of Norman, who let out an "Oomph."

"I'm so sorry," she said, scrambling off him. "Can you tell me where you've been injured?"

"I think you knocked the wind out of me just now, but . . . I've got an odd ringing in my head."

Bending over him, Beatrix began probing his head, concern flowing freely when she felt him begin to shake, until she realized he was laughing. Sitting back, she gave him a swat. "Is your head even injured?"

"Well, no, it might just be my ear since I landed on one of them, but the last time I told you I injured my head, you leaned over me exactly as you just did, allowing me to enjoy the most delightful scent of your perfume."

"You really *have* injured your head, haven't you?"

Norman pushed himself up to his elbows. "I don't have an injured head, Beatrix, although I am most assuredly suffering from an injured heart, a condition brought about by my own stupidity." He sat up before reaching out and taking hold of her hand, the action and his recent words taking her by such surprise that she didn't even try to tug her hand from his.

"I *was* an idiot, but I'm here to try to make amends," he said. "I've already spoken to your father and extended him a most fervent apology for even entertaining the thought that he was behind the continued threats to my research, so now I'm here to do the same with you."

"How did my father react to your apology?"

"He was quick to accept it, although he did launch into a rather scathing lecture about how I'd mistreated you. He told me he'd be happy to take me to Grace Church so that I could seek out the advice of a man of the cloth. However, when I hesitated about that because I really wanted to seek you out without delay, he then launched into a bit about how men of science should not dismiss religion but should embrace it since God is *the* only explanation for life . . . or something to that effect." He winced. "I must admit I missed some of it because your mother began whispering things to your father to add, and then your aunt Gladys chimed in, and then Edgar a moment later."

"Did you come to New York with Aunt Gladys and Edgar?"

"No, it was one of those unexpected happenstances I've been experiencing ever since I met you."

"Were you able to make amends with my father?"

"I believe so, although I'm relatively certain Gladys is still put out with me, because after I told him I wanted to borrow his fastest horse, she's the one who convinced your father that Lightning would be a good choice for me."

"She knows you don't ride horses, Norman."

He glanced at the hedges. "Clearly, although I'm getting rather proficient at tumbling off them."

"You should have told my father that, because he would have never chosen Lightning for you."

"I didn't have time. As I said, I wanted to get to you quickly, but in all honesty, even if I had admitted to your father that I am less than proficient at riding a horse, there is a possibility he still would have given me Lightning, what with the way he was going on about how I mistreated his daughter."

"Is everyone alive over there?" Theodosia called.

"We're fine," Norman called back. "How's Lightning?"

"I think he's snickering."

"Of course he is." Norman turned back to Beatrix and blew out a breath. "I owe you a heartfelt apology."

"Did someone tell you to add that heartfelt business?"

"Gladys might have mentioned it."

Beatrix pressed her lips together to keep from smiling. "Of course she did, but since you did travel all this way to apologize, I believe it would be churlish of me to do anything but accept it."

Norman rubbed his head. "Perhaps I *have* suffered some type of head trauma, because I swear you just accepted my apology, and with absolutely no fuss."

"I'm not a fussy kind of lady. I'm practical. I told you I wanted you to apologize to my father, which you have done, and then you apologized to me, although I'm not sure how you came to the conclusion I wasn't guilty of the charges your mother laid against me."

"Well, I wrote out a summary of everything, and after studying it for a full day, I—"

"Decided there wasn't enough evidence against me?"

"No. I abandoned the summary because it didn't matter. What mattered was that I know you—know you better than I've ever known anyone, including Theo—even though I've not known you for that long, if that makes any sense."

Beatrix blinked to keep the unexpected tears that were threatening to blind her at bay.

What Norman had said did make sense because . . . she knew him too.

He was annoying, opinionated, and too intelligent for his own good, but he made her laugh, was incredibly kind when one least expected it, and she found him more interesting than any man she'd ever known, and . . . she was rather certain she loved him.

He'd been willing to carry her straight out of her aunt's house when he'd thought she was in danger, and then he'd come to visit her at Marshall Field & Company, parading past her in the most outlandish jacket she'd ever seen, the sight of him in that jacket leaving her laughing. He'd also abandoned his work on his electrical conveyance vehicle to help his little niece and her friend build a peddle-boat, and then there was Hubert.

Norman, without anyone asking, had created a new leg for a man he didn't know, an act of kindness that spoke to his true heart, and an act that might very well have been the moment when Beatrix's fondness for the man had turned into something more.

"It makes perfect sense," she finally whispered when she realized he was waiting for a response.

He smiled. "That's a relief. I really didn't know how I'd go about explaining it any differently." He leaned closer to her. "And now that that's out of the way, I feel compelled to set matters completely right between us, and even though I'd intended to do this differently, I simply can't wait."

If she'd been standing, Beatrix was fairly certain her knees would have turned just a touch weak.

"Or perhaps you'd like for me to wait," he said, his gaze locking with hers. "From everything Theo and I have read, this type of moment is usually expected to be done in certain settings, and this"—he gestured to the hedge they were sitting beside—"doesn't lend itself to, well, . . . an expected setting."

"You're not really a gentleman who does the expected."

"True, probably because I'm a rather unusual man."

"I've recently discovered I find unusual to be most appealing."

A mere second later, Norman was drawing her to him, pressing his lips against hers in a kiss that was so unexpected and yet so completely perfect that Beatrix felt a shock run through her, one she was quite convinced felt exactly like what Norman's electrical currents would feel like.

"While I hate to break up such a touching moment, we got a man that wants to talk to you, Mr. Nesbit. And to make sure you come quiet-like, do know that I ain't got no problem with shooting one of you—and that one would be the woman, if that's in question."

CHAPTER 37

Norman leaned against Beatrix as they rattled along in a fast-moving carriage, his broad shoulder providing her with support as she swayed back and forth, her hands tied firmly behind her back.

Their captors were the same men they'd encountered in Chicago, although Beatrix hadn't quite figured out how those men had been able to find them or who the man was who wanted to speak with Norman.

She certainly couldn't tell where they were heading, not since she, as well as Norman, had scratchy bags over their heads, those bags giving off the distinct smell of potatoes.

"It's a most peculiar predicament we're in," Norman said calmly, as if they were taking a leisurely carriage ride instead of a ride where the driver seemed to think that all haste was required, the carriage actually having tilted up on two wheels when he'd taken a sharp turn.

"An understatement to be sure," she said.

"Indeed, although I now find myself wondering if you still find the unusual to be delightful, because this situation is certainly unusual, but I'm not sure how delightful you're finding it."

She felt the oddest urge to laugh. Only Norman would ponder such a matter while in the midst of an abduction, but that pondering spoke to the curious nature of his mind. Frankly, she found it charming, found him charming as well, even though he had the ability to be able to charm her one minute and leave her wanting to strangle him the next.

"Speaking of unusual, though," Norman said, interrupting her thoughts. "I've yet to finish settling matters between us, what with all the loose ends we still need to tie up, the greatest one being that of where we're going to go from here with the affection we most certainly share for each other."

She resisted another urge to laugh. "Forgive me, Norman, but since we're currently facing what I have to imagine is going to be a most unpleasant meeting with some man who is now desperate to obtain your research papers, this probably is not the best time to continue with the conversation we were enjoying before we were abducted."

"Too right it isn't," a voice growled from the seat opposite them. "You two should be preparing yourself for the trouble that awaits you, not behaving as if you're in the midst of a garden party."

"I've never been to a garden party," Norman returned. "Are those normally held in gardens, or are they called garden parties to lend the occasion a certain atmosphere?"

Beatrix grinned. "You're going to get us killed with statements like that."

"Enough of the flirting," the man growled again. "It's enough to make me want to lose my lunch."

"There's nothing wrong with a bit of flirting," Beatrix shot back. "My parents are very flirtatious with each other, and they've been married for years. I imagine you're only being so surly because you don't have anyone to flirt with, but you have only yourself to blame for that. Ladies, I'll have you know, don't care for men who embrace criminal activity."

"And here you were worried *I* would get us killed," Norman muttered as the man across from them released a grunt. "I am curious, though, as to why we've been abducted."

"My man wants your research—the real research. He's losing

patience, so me and Martin were sent off to snatch you. It was sheer luck to find you with the woman because we can use her to force you into giving our man what he wants."

Beatrix frowned. "But why go through the bother of following Norman to New York? Wouldn't it have been easier to abscond with his papers back in Chicago?"

"We was plannin' on doing exactly that, but then he took off for New York."

"How do you know he even has the papers on him?" Beatrix pressed.

Beatrix felt Norman stiffen beside her. "I, ah, might have let word about that get out down at my gentleman's club. Didn't want to take the chance of anyone tossing my rooms again while I was off to New York, not when Gemma and Oscar are known to wander through my workshop when I'm out of town."

Her heart skipped a tiny beat. "That was very noble of you, even if it did result in you being abducted, something I'm sure you weren't expecting to happen."

"I must admit I wasn't expecting an attack, nor did I even consider having a Pinkerton travel with me, because my decision to come to New York was a spur-of-the-moment decision, and hence, I didn't believe anyone with skullduggery on their minds would have enough notice to successfully follow me here."

"But you were followed, which suggests whoever is behind all this is more determined than ever to relieve you of your research papers."

Norman shrugged. "I'm perfectly willing to hand over my papers, but only after you get set free."

"I'm not leaving you to the mercy of some diabolical thief."

"It's not up for debate, and with that settled, I believe we're slowing down."

The moment the door to the carriage opened, Beatrix realized they were at a train station. Whistles sounded in the background, trains rumbled, and people called out to one another. The presence of so many people gave her a sense of hope, until one of her captors pulled her out of the carriage and slung her over his shoulder. He then whisked her up two steps and into some type of building, dumping her onto a surprisingly cushy surface, Norman tumbling beside her a second later.

"You weren't supposed to bring Norman back *here*," a man thundered. "You were only supposed to take the research papers from him."

"You said nab 'em, so that's what we did."

"I said 'nab them,' meaning the papers, not Norman, you idiot, and why in the world would you bring that woman along?"

"Thought we could use Mr. Nesbit's fondness for her to make him cooperate."

"Which would have been a great thought except for the fact that I never wanted Norman brought to me, let alone—"

"She's that Miss Waterbury, sir. You know, the woman that threatened to shoot me on the train, and then did shoot me in the middle of State Street. I'm lucky she didn't kill me and lucky that tiny bullet went clean through my shoulder."

"You've succeeded in creating a complication I didn't count on or want."

Beatrix struggled to a sitting position, knowing she'd heard the voice of the man speaking before, but she couldn't quite place who he was, or . . .

"Hello, Harvey," Norman said pleasantly, sitting up as well and lending her the support of his shoulder again. "May I dare hope that this is all some grave misunderstanding and that you're not behind all the skullduggery Beatrix and I have experienced of late?"

"Oh dear," Beatrix muttered.

"What?" Norman asked.

"Haven't you ever read any of those gothic novels where the hero and heroine find themselves in a dire situation but get out of that situation by keeping their wits about them?"

"An interesting question for you to pose at this particular time," Norman returned. "But no, I've never read a gothic novel in my life, so you're going to have to expand on whatever it is you're trying to say."

"I'm sure Miss Waterbury is of the belief that you shouldn't have revealed to Harvey that you know who he is because now, well, you've left us in a bit of a pickle."

Beatrix stiffened right as the bag covering her face was pulled off. Lifting her chin and squinting against the light, she discovered none other than Miss Amelia Burden standing before her, fury in her eyes.

"You, Miss Waterbury, are a menace," Miss Burden spat before she yanked Norman's bag from his head, tossed the bags to the floor, then stomped across what Beatrix realized was a private Pullman car. She stopped directly beside Harvey, who was looking at Miss Burden as if she'd lost her mind.

"Darling, are you certain it was wise to remove their bags? Now they can see us," Harvey said, earning a roll of the eyes from Miss Burden in return.

"Since Norman recognized your voice, there was no need to have them sit there with bags over their heads. It was a troubling sight to be sure, and besides, it doesn't matter that they've seen us since Norman knows it was you behind the skullduggery."

"If you've forgotten, the skullduggery was your plan, Amelia," Harvey argued.

Miss Burden gave a nod, sending her curls bouncing. "True, but I wouldn't have been forced to develop such a plan if you hadn't annoyed your father by being incapable of inventing a workable invention, or, at the very least, making one little impressive scientific discovery, or, better yet, figuring out a way to prove you can earn a living, things I've come to realize are beyond you."

She turned to Norman. "It was never personal. You simply seemed to me to be the easiest mark, what with your reputation for living in your own world most of the time." She shot another glare to Beatrix. "Unfortunately, Miss Waterbury seems to have had a most curious effect on you, making it far harder than I was anticipating to abscond with your electrical research."

"Why would you need my research in the first place?" Norman asked.

Miss Burden arched a brow. "To prove to Harvey's father that he's capable of earning money."

Norman arched a brow of his own. "Because?"

Miss Burden flung herself into the nearest chair. "Harvey's father decided that he won't loosen the purse strings until Harvey proves he has worth. Since that's going to be next to impossible for him, what with his propensity for laziness and enjoyment of leisurely pursuits, I felt there was no choice but to develop a plan that would convince Harvey's father he has some potential. After Harvey returned from his New York trip, we decided that the easiest way for him to make money would be to sell the most sought-after research presented in New York to the highest bidder." She nodded to Norman. "Lucky for us, Harvey knew that your work showed great potential and also knew that there were numerous parties interested in your electric research, parties who wouldn't balk at paying him if he was able to get his hands on it."

"They'd be comfortable purchasing stolen research?" Beatrix asked.

Miss Burden gave a wave of a hand. "Scruples are rare when it comes to matters of electricity."

Beatrix frowned. "But how were you going to explain to Harvey's father how he came up with that money?"

Another wave of a hand was Miss Burden's response to that. "Harvey will simply say he sold research he's been working on to an interested party." She smiled. "His father is desperate for Harvey to prove his worth, so I doubt he'll question Harvey extensively about the matter."

"Or at least you hope he won't," Norman said before he turned to Harvey. "How did you realize so quickly, though, that I'd left misleading research for your hired thugs to find? I would have thought my calculations were beyond you."

Miss Burden released a titter. "Harvey didn't figure that out. You told him, although you didn't know that, of course." She shrugged. "We knew that anyone interested in buying your research would need certain assurances that you'd had real breakthroughs with double electrical currents. Harvey also knew that you were un- likely to discuss your research with him, which is why I suggested he become involved with Theodosia. We hoped that she would be suitably impressed that a man like Harvey would even notice her and would then disclose things you and she talked about regarding your work."

"I find it hard to believe that Theodosia would have told anyone about the misleading papers I left behind."

"Oh, she didn't," Miss Burden said. "She's proven herself far too loyal to you to do such a thing, but . . ." She sent Harvey a smile. "Harvey was visiting Mr. Robinson one day, hoping to get in that man's good graces so he'd have a champion in his corner as he tried to squire Theodosia around town. Harvey may be shiftless at times, but he's rather sly, and he eavesdropped on the conversa- tion you and Theodosia were having that day when you paid her a visit. That's how he learned the papers he'd acquired were all but worthless, and that's when we adjusted our plan."

"Having your men attack me in the middle of the street after they ransacked my rooms, and then having them break into Gladys Huttleston's home was quite a readjustment of plans," Norman said dryly.

Miss Burden shot a look to the man with the scar, who was now rubbing the spot where Beatrix had shot him. "I didn't tell Martin and James to break into Miss Huttleston's home. They took it upon themselves to do that, most likely as an attempt to get back at Miss Waterbury after she shot Martin." Miss Burden leveled malevolent eyes on Beatrix. "You really have no one to blame but yourself for your current situation, Miss Waterbury. If you'd not interfered on the train, you wouldn't have been pulled into this mess, but I suppose annoying, nosy women like yourself just can't resist interfering in other people's business."

"Is that why you forged that letter framing my father, and somehow arranged for it to be found by the Pinkerton Agency? Because you wanted to get back at me for being nosy and annoying?"

Miss Burden shrugged. "Frankly, I had no idea at the time we created that letter that you were Arthur Waterbury's daughter. I only pointed out to Harvey after I learned that the Pinkerton Agency had been hired to investigate the attempted thefts of Norman's research that we needed a scapegoat. I then remarked that it was unfortunate we couldn't make *you* that scapegoat, what with how you're always sticking your nose in our business." Her lips curved the slightest bit. "Harvey then pointed out that he'd had an unsuccessful meeting with a Mr. Arthur Waterbury, who'd refused to extend Harvey so much as a single dime for future research purposes, and then wondered if perhaps you were some distant relation."

Miss Burden tapped a finger to her chin. "That got me to thinking that it would be amusing if you were a distant relation, which is why I forged the letter and signed it from Arthur Waterbury." She caught Beatrix's eye. "I must admit that I was more than amused to learn you're Arthur's daughter and completely delighted that you were cast in the unusual role of villain and spy."

She turned to Norman. "If you'd only continued to think of Miss Waterbury as a spy, we would not now find ourselves in this unfortunate situation, because you would not currently be in New York, nor would we have been forced to take the dramatic step of following you here."

Norman tilted his head. "Why did you follow me? I have to believe it would have been easier all around if you'd just waited for me to return to Chicago."

"Harvey's father has been relentless of late about Harvey proving his worth, which forced us to come after you." Miss Burden nodded. "Lucky for us, Harvey's father is heavily invested in the Pullman company, which is how we were able to secure this private car, and on the very same train you traveled to New York on." Miss Burden shook her head. "Unfortunately for you, the situation has taken a concerning twist, leaving me and Harvey with few options."

"I bet that's exactly what the villain would say in one of those gothic novels, Beatrix," Norman said, drawing everyone's attention. "I have to imagine that villain would then go on to say that it's time to dispose of the witnesses, which, of course, means kill them." He nodded to Miss Burden. "Am I right about that?"

Miss Burden blinked. "Murder might be taking the matter too far." She shot a look to Harvey.

Harvey rubbed a hand over his face. "Well, I suppose we could take Norman's research, sell it to the highest bidder, then flee to some far-off country to avoid any unpleasant consequences of our actions."

Miss Burden frowned. "I don't want to live in some far-off country."

"But you'll be with me, the man you've claimed, and often at that, you long to marry."

Miss Burden's frown deepened. "But surely you must realize that the money you'll receive from the research papers won't keep us in style for long, don't you?"

Harvey's forehead furrowed. "It seems as if I'm missing something here. I thought you wanted to marry me because you love me, which is why you thought up this plan in the first place so that I could finally win the respect of a father who seems to despise me."

"I never mentioned a word about being in love with you," Miss Burden shot back. "Nor do I suffer from a delusion you love me. Frankly, I've assumed you only want to marry me because I'm beautiful and look good on your arm."

"Those are some of the reasons," Harvey countered, having taken to looking disgruntled the second after Miss Burden claimed she didn't love him. "But since we're apparently disclosing all, the main reason I wanted to marry you was because of your father's fortune. I thought if matters couldn't be resolved with my father, I'd be able to live well on your money."

Miss Burden narrowed her eyes. "I don't have a large dowry. Father believes his money should be given to his one and only son, so there's no fortune coming your way through me."

"How unfortunate," Harvey said.

"I believe everyone here is in full agreement with that," Norman said. "But to get matters moving along, if you would unbutton my jacket, Harvey, since I don't currently have use of my hands, and then reach underneath my vest, you'll find my research papers."

Harvey blinked, shot a look to Miss Burden, then did as Norman asked, pulling out a sheaf of papers from Norman's vest a second later. He glanced through them, shuddered just a touch, then lifted his head. "We will need you to explain the finer points of this."

"And I'll do just that, but only after you let Beatrix go."

"So she can run off and summon the authorities?" Miss Burden asked. "I think not, which means you need to start explaining your research to us before I have Martin and James do something unpleasant to Miss Waterbury to encourage you to cooperate."

Norman, instead of arguing, drew in a breath and nodded. "Very well, although I suppose I should begin by stating that I have realized my research is flawed, more specifically . . ." and with that he began doing what he did best, pontificating on and on about his research and where he felt it needed work.

Fifteen minutes later, and with Miss Burden and Harvey looking rather bewildered, Norman finished with, "Any questions?"

Harvey hid a yawn behind his hand, then winced when Miss Burden gave him a swat. "Surely you must have a few questions after all that, don't you?" she demanded.

Harvey's brows drew together. "Surely *you* must have realized by now that I'm slightly intellectually challenged when it comes to science. In all honesty, I didn't understand most of what he was saying, and—"

A loud thump against the door interrupted Harvey, and before Martin and James could do more than jump, the door to the Pullman car flew open, Murray rushing in, pistol drawn. Behind him came Theodosia, brandishing a large beaded reticule she immediately aimed at James, who'd pulled out a knife.

"I knew help would arrive at some point" was all Norman said before he struggled to his feet and launched himself at Martin, head-butting the man because his hands were still tied behind his back.

As Beatrix struggled to her feet, Aunt Gladys flew into the room, followed by Edgar, who was also gripping a pistol and used that pistol to knock James's knife out of his hand. A second later, Annie and Arthur dashed into the room, her father launching himself at Martin, who seemed to be in the process of trying to strangle Norman.

"Beatrix," her mother yelled, grabbing James's knife from the ground. "Give me your hands."

Relief was swift when Beatrix felt her bindings fall away, but that relief was quickly replaced with horror when she turned and discovered Miss Burden holding Aunt Gladys around the neck, a knife pressed against Aunt Gladys's throat.

"I'm afraid all of you have forced my hand," Miss Burden shrieked. "I'll use this knife if I have to, I swear I will, unless I'm allowed to leave this room with no threat of injury to my person."

Beatrix glanced around the room, finding her father and Norman lumbering to their feet, an unconscious Martin lying on the floor. Murray and Theodosia were sitting on top of James, who seemed to have been secured with Murray's tie. Edgar was in the midst of a brawl with Harvey, but the moment he realized Aunt Gladys was in peril, he flung him aside. Harvey crashed into the side of the Pullman car and slumped to the floor.

"You will release her . . . now," Edgar said, drawing himself to his full height and taking a step toward Miss Burden.

"Don't come any closer, or I *will* hurt her," Miss Burden screeched.

"Don't be ridiculous, Miss Burden," Aunt Gladys snapped. "You're in enough trouble as it is, but if you add murder to the charges that are soon to be leveled against you, you'll never see your way out of prison. I don't think you'd do well with a long prison sentence considering there are no frivolities offered."

"Gladys . . ." Edgar all but growled.

Aunt Gladys smiled. "I'm speaking the truth, Edgar. She's distraught and isn't thinking clearly, so I thought I should point out the obvious to her."

"She has a knife pressed to your throat."

Aunt Gladys nodded, then winced, probably because the knife was making nodding somewhat painful. "I know, dear. She's also ruining the hairstyle Blanche spent precious time on earlier, and—"

In the blink of an eye, Aunt Gladys jabbed Miss Burden with an elbow and then stomped on her foot. Miss Burden's knife clattered to the floor, skittering directly next to Harvey, who took that moment to release a groan. He opened an eye, then immediately shut it, as if the situation was too much for him to handle.

"Harvey!" Miss Burden screamed. "You can't leave me to deal with all this. Grab the knife that's right in front of you and help me for once."

Harvey didn't move a single muscle.

Beatrix couldn't help herself, she snorted. "In all frankness, Miss Burden, you must have realized at some point that marriage to Harvey will always leave you dealing with everything."

Miss Burden pressed her lips together, sent Beatrix a scowl, then presented Beatrix with her back right as a policeman rushed into the Pullman car. He glanced around, pulled out a whistle, and gave it a blow, which resulted in five more policemen entering the car in short order.

Within ten minutes, the police had taken Miss Burden, Martin, and James into custody, Miss Burden screaming all the while that she was innocent and that her father would be having something to say about the unacceptable treatment she was experiencing. The two policemen holding on to her arms didn't seem concerned about that as they dragged her away, her screams falling on deaf ears.

Harvey, who'd refused to open his eyes even though Beatrix was relatively certain he was conscious, was placed on a stretcher and taken out last. He stirred feebly and opened his eyes as he passed her, then quickly closed them again, as if he couldn't bear the sight of her.

"Are you all right?" Annie asked, coming to stand beside Beatrix, smoothing a strand of her hair away from her face.

"I'm fine, but how did all of you become involved with this latest drama?"

Annie smiled. "We're family, dear, which means we're nosy when it comes to family matters. After Norman and that delightful Theodosia showed up with Gladys and Edgar, we told Norman where he could find you. We gave him a ten-minute head start before we followed, wanting to find out how he was going to make amends to you."

"They ran across Murray and me as we were giving chase to the carriage you and Norman were thrown in," Theodosia added, coming up to join Beatrix as she nodded to Murray, who was dabbing blood from a nose that was already beginning to swell.

Beatrix's eyes widened as she took a step toward Murray, remembering full well the aversion Murray had to blood. He waved her off as he took a seat on the floor of the Pullman car.

"I'm fine, and no, I won't be fainting today. Just need a second to compose myself. Is Norman all right?"

Beatrix turned and settled her gaze on Norman, who was wiping blood from his face with the sleeve of his jacket.

He was looking the worse for wear, but she'd never found him more appealing.

He looked up and sent her a hint of a smile, and then he was moving toward her, his gaze turning more intense the closer he got. His progress was delayed, though, when Edgar cut in front of him on his way toward Aunt Gladys, who was speaking to Arthur. She abruptly stopped that conversation when Edgar stopped directly beside her, took hold of her arm, and pulled her toward him.

"You could have been killed" were the first words out of Edgar's mouth.

"But I wasn't," Aunt Gladys pointed out.

"But you could have been," Edgar argued before he shuddered.

"The sight of that woman with a knife pressed to your neck took a good twenty years off my life."

"Which means you're now, what . . . about eighty-five?"

Edgar's lips curved just a touch. "Indeed, and at that advanced age, I should know better than to behave like a stubborn old man, resisting the notion of marrying you simply because of my pride, but . . . no more."

Aunt Gladys blinked. "What does that mean?"

"It means I love you—have always loved you—and it's past time I did something about that." He dropped to one knee, winced, then took hold of Aunt Gladys's hand. "I don't currently have a ring, but I would be honored if you'd agree to marry me."

Aunt Gladys considered him for a moment. "You do realize that I'm still a very wealthy woman, don't you?"

"'Course I do, and while that was the main reason I resisted the idea of marriage to you, I've now realized that your wealth doesn't matter. It also doesn't matter that people are going to be talking about us for years, what with me being a butler and you being a wealthy woman. The only thing that matters to me is you."

"I could always terminate your employment."

Edgar grinned. "True, but then I'd have nothing to do with my days but bother you."

Aunt Gladys returned the grin. "What a delightful prospect."

"Does that mean you'll marry me?"

"Of course I'll marry you, Edgar."

A second later, Edgar was on his feet, and then he was kissing Aunt Gladys, clearly unconcerned that they had an audience.

"Well, that's just unfortunate," Norman muttered as he came to stand beside Beatrix.

"You aren't happy for my aunt and Edgar?" Beatrix asked.

"Oh no, that's not it at all, but Edgar, what with his charming proposal, just threw into doubt what I hoped would be a rather spectacular moment for us."

The entire Pullman car fell silent as everyone turned Norman and Beatrix's way.

"I don't believe this is how you should go about this, Norman," Theodosia said, marching her way up to Norman as she pulled a fashion magazine from her bag. "And even though we recently decided to abandon the research we did, every article I read stated most emphatically that a romantic setting is a must for what I know you're about to do." She gestured around. "This isn't what I'd call romantic."

"Seems fairly romantic to me," Aunt Gladys said, her eyes twinkling as she settled a smile on Edgar.

Norman turned to Beatrix. "Perhaps I should wait."

Beatrix tilted her head. "I've never been an overly patient sort. So . . ."

"You want me to get on with it?"

"Indeed."

Theodosia threw up her hands and marched away, joining Murray on the floor.

After she got settled, Norman took hold of Beatrix's hand. "I made you a new pistol purse. Theo has it."

Beatrix wrinkled her nose. "You made me a new pistol purse?"

"And it's a lot better than your old one," Theodosia called, holding up the purse in question, one that was covered in brightly colored beads. "Gemma and Oscar helped put on all the beads, although Norman did promise Gemma you'd teach her how to shoot the purse someday, if he can convince you to—"

Norman cleared his throat, loudly.

Theodosia stopped talking for all of a second before she nodded. "Right, you're in the midst of something important so I'll just be quiet, but I do have to mention that you're the one who brought up the purse in the first place."

"I was stalling as I tried to get my scattered wits about me," Norman said.

"Perfectly understandable," Theodosia said. "May we dare hope your wits are no longer scattered?"

"I believe they're returning to order."

"Then do get on with matters, Norman," Theodosia encouraged. "It's turning into a very dramatic moment, and I believe I speak for all of us when I say we've had enough drama for today."

Norman nodded. "Too right you are, so . . ." He turned back to Beatrix. "Would you be so kind as to clarify why you wouldn't leave me when I told Harvey I'd tell him everything he needed to know after he let you go?"

Since that wasn't exactly what she'd been expecting Norman to say, Beatrix frowned. "I don't think there's anything to clarify about that."

"Of course there is."

Knowing Norman, what with him being a rather focused gentleman when he set his mind on something, wouldn't continue until she gave an answer, Beatrix blew out a breath. "Not that this should come as a surprise to you, but I didn't leave you because I'm inordinately fond of you."

"Are you merely fond of me or might you be a bit more than fond?"

"Well . . ."

"Because I'm more than fond of you," Norman interrupted before Beatrix could finish. "In fact, I love you, but if you're only fond of me, I won't bother saying anything else because I don't want to put you in the uncomfortable position of having to decline my offer of marriage, which you'll no doubt do if you're merely fond of me."

Beatrix found herself devoid of words.

Norman loved her, he'd said that out loud, and even though he hadn't actually proposed to her, he'd done exactly that in a very Norman way.

"I love you too," she whispered, which had his eyes widening before he, oddly enough, frowned.

"I suppose this is the part where I should actually propose to you, because I've just realized I didn't do that yet." He leaned closer to her. "Theo and I have researched the matter most extensively, and I have a few of the better suggestions in regard to extending a lady a proper proposal stored to memory."

"I think you did propose to me and in a very charming way, at that."

His lips began to curve. "Oh, well, right then, but I don't believe you said whether or not you'll marry me."

"I would have thought my declaration of love for you would have been a sure sign that yes, I would love nothing more than to marry you."

"You would love to marry me?"

"More than anything."

Norman's lips began to curve even more before he pulled her into his arms, and then he was kissing her in a way that was definitely more than merely pleasant.

Epilogue

"Is the bride nervous?"

Beatrix looked up from where she'd been waiting in a room reserved for brides at Grace Chapel in New York City, finding Norman sticking his head through the door.

"You're not supposed to see the bride before she walks down the aisle," she said.

"From all those articles and books Theo made me read, I know for certain that only pertains to the groom, and I'm not the groom today. Edgar is." Norman slipped into the room and drew Beatrix to him, giving her a kiss before he stepped back and smiled.

"And while I did just inquire as to whether or not Gladys is nervous, how are you doing, Mrs. Nesbit?"

Beatrix returned the smile, knowing she would never get tired of hearing herself addressed as Mrs. Nesbit. "I'm fine, although it's been rather difficult to keep Aunt Gladys in this room until the ceremony actually starts, what with how anxious she is to marry Edgar."

Norman consulted his pocket watch. "She only has ten minutes to go."

"She's been waiting thirty years."

"True." He glanced to Aunt Gladys, who was having her hair fussed over by Blanche as Mamie flitted about, rearranging the small train that was attached to Aunt Gladys's gown. "I'm still surprised Gladys agreed to get married in New York, and with all the pomp and circumstance I wouldn't have thought she'd want."

"She was concerned my mother was harboring a bit of disappointment over not being able to plan an elaborate wedding for me, what with how you and I decided to hold a very small wedding at the beginning of November, something I believe your mother was disappointed about as well." Beatrix smiled. "However, what with how elaborate the wedding and reception we're about to attend are sure to be, I'm certain my mother is no longer suffering from disappointment, although she might be suffering from exhaustion, given how much effort she put into making sure her sister's big day would be truly remarkable."

"And my mother is surely not still disappointed either, not after you told her you want to hold a spectacular ball at the end of January, introducing us as a newly married couple to Chicago society."

"Your mother has no reason for any disappointment," Theodosia said, stepping up to join them, looking rather smug. "I've asked her to plan my entire wedding to Stanley, and I've given her carte blanche."

Beatrix grinned as she looked Theodosia over, taking in the stylish gown she was wearing as well as the vibrant curls that had grown longer, their vibrancy a direct result of a new formula Theodosia and Blanche had created, one they were hoping to bring out into the world after the beginning of the year.

That Theodosia had blossomed since Beatrix had first met her was not in doubt. She'd formed a fast friendship with Blanche, enjoyed spending time with all of Aunt Gladys's friends, but more important, when she'd returned to Chicago from New York, Stanley had surprised everyone, including Theodosia, when he'd announced that he'd been in love with Theodosia for years, and he wasn't going to hide that love another day or give her a reason to ever attend a ball with any gentleman other than himself.

Theodosia had then thrown herself into Stanley's arms, proclaimed herself in love with him as well, and that had been that.

Norman's mother, to Theodosia's surprise as well as to her delight, had taken her soon-to-be daughter-in-law under her wing, providing Theodosia with the mother figure she'd never known.

Mary had also been quick to apologize to Beatrix, which had allowed Beatrix to begin building a relationship with the woman who would be her mother-in-law forevermore. That relationship was certain to suffer disagreements at times, what with Mary still having a tendency to want to shelter Norman, while Beatrix found it best to keep pushing him further into the real world.

"I was right about Harvey," Theodosia suddenly said, pulling Beatrix from her thoughts.

"What does Harvey have to do with anything?" Norman asked. "He's currently serving a very short stint in jail, thanks to the deep pockets of his father, but it's an odd time to bring him into the conversation."

"I know," Theodosia said, "but a thought just sprang to mind and I thought I'd voice it."

"What thought?" Norman asked when Theodosia stopped talking as she glanced past Norman and got a sappy look on her face.

"My brother's standing behind me, isn't he?" Norman asked.

"He is," Beatrix said as Theodosia swept past them, whispered something to Stanley, then returned. "He's saved me a seat."

"Thoughtful of him."

"Wasn't it, though?" Theodosia asked before she nodded. "And the thought I had was this—I told Harvey he could have been using his proclamation of innocence as a distraction to keep us from learning he was behind all the shenanigans, and I was right. That's exactly what he was doing, although I do believe Miss Burden was the true mastermind, even with her plan being less than well-developed." She grimaced. "Hardly seems right that her father got her released without jail time, although I suppose since she's been sent off to Egypt to stay with some obscure relative who enjoys looking for Egyptian artifacts, that is punishment enough. Miss Burden probably won't like trudging through all that sand."

"If all of you are done chatting," Aunt Gladys said, gliding up to join them, Blanche and Mamie by her side, "I'd like to get married."

"We should take our seats," Beatrix said.

"Before you do that, dear, I'd like a private word with you, if you don't mind."

After they waited until everyone else quit the room, except for Annie because she was standing up with her sister, Beatrix soon found her hand in her aunt's.

"I wanted to thank you, my dear, for barreling into my life and adding so much joy to it. Edgar and I have grown to love you dearly, and I do hope we'll see much of you and Norman after we return from the trip Edgar's planned for me."

"Since Norman and I will most likely still be living in your house because it's doubtful the house we're building on Lake Shore will be done until summer, I don't believe you'll have to worry about that."

Aunt Gladys smiled. "How delightful, but do know that even after you move out of my house, I'll be visiting you often. I'm looking forward to helping you with that new committee you're forming to advance the rights of working women as well as advance the work still needed to obtain the right to vote for all women."

Beatrix returned the smile. "And I look forward to your help. By the time you return, we should have the building completed on State Street and numerous attorneys hired on to lend legal counsel to women in need. Word has already gotten out about the assistance I'm going to be offering to women who have no place to turn when they encounter problems at work or with their unreasonable husbands. I hope other women of means may eventually join forces with me, which will certainly advance the rights of women in the not-too-distant future." Her smile widened. "Constance has already insisted on helping me, and even Mary wants to be included, deciding much needs to be done in order to ascertain that Gemma will be able to pursue her interest in science someday."

"Norman still planning to become involved with teaching?" Aunt Gladys asked.

Beatrix nodded. "He's not been having much luck getting the local colleges to agree to his terms of including women, which is why he's decided to add a large building on the land we've purchased on Lake Shore. He wants to use that building for science lessons available to women and men. He also wants to offer up the building for suffrage lectures, since that will lessen the chance of me landing behind bars again."

"He has certainly come around in his way of thinking about the suffrage movement," Aunt Gladys said with a smile. "Perhaps I'll even take one of his classes—after I get back from my trip around the country, that is. "

"You're not supposed to know the details of the trip Edgar planned for you."

Aunt Gladys waved that aside. "Why do you think I agreed to have your mother plan my wedding for me and hold it in New York? I knew Edgar procured a private Pullman car and intends to whisk me around the country, making it from one coast to another, stopping whenever something strikes our fancy. That's why I thought holding the wedding on the East Coast would make it easier to execute Edgar's plan, while also allowing your mother an opportunity to plan that extravagant wedding she always assumed she'd plan for you."

"All excellent decisions on your part, but how did you find out about Edgar's plan?"

Aunt Gladys smiled. "Mamie prevailed upon the delightful Agent Cochran to uncover the details for her."

Beatrix grinned. "Agent Cochran seems to be dropping by your house often these days."

"Indeed he does, which isn't all that surprising, what with his obvious interest in Mamie. I do believe a Pinkerton man may be exactly what she needed to keep herself out of trouble, even though she and Agent Cochran do seem to have the tendency to slip away often, what with how they enjoy holding hands and gazing longingly into each other's eyes."

"Norman and Beatrix seem to have that tendency as well,"

Annie said, stepping up to Beatrix and giving her a squeeze. "I'm delighted you finally found a gentleman who loves you wholeheartedly, and one who doesn't seem opposed to holding your hand, kissing you whenever he pleases, and—"

"I think the music has begun," Beatrix said, interrupting her mother before Annie could list all the ways Norman showered Beatrix with affection, affection that certainly took New York and Chicago society matrons aback, not that Beatrix was bothered by that, since she'd never really put much stock in the many opinions of society.

"It *is* the music," Aunt Gladys said, her eyes sparkling. "Which means it's time."

"Let me go take my seat."

After giving Aunt Gladys a kiss on the cheek, Beatrix rushed out of the room and down the aisle, grinning at her two very best friends in the world, Isadora MacKenzie and Poppy Blackburn, who were sitting with their husbands, Ian and Reginald.

Slipping into a seat beside Norman as the "Wedding March" began, Beatrix turned as Annie walked down the aisle, met halfway by Arthur, who kissed his wife in front of everyone before he escorted her to the front of the church, Annie sending Edgar a wink, which he immediately returned.

Everyone stood as Aunt Gladys entered the room. She'd insisted on walking down the aisle by herself, knowing that God, who'd always been by her side, would be walking beside her, giving her His blessing as she married the man she'd loved for so long, her Edgar.

Tears blinded Beatrix more than once as Aunt Gladys and Edgar exchanged their vows. And then they were finally pronounced man and wife, drawing applause from everyone.

With both of them beaming after Edgar kissed Aunt Gladys, they turned and moved down the aisle, their happiness a palpable thing.

"Who would have ever thought all of us would experience so many weddings in, what, just over a year?" Isadora asked, walking over to join Beatrix. Poppy waddled beside her, looking radiant and due to give birth any day.

"It's been quite the year," Poppy agreed, giving her stomach a pat, smiling as the children Isadora and Ian had adopted, Prim, Henry, Violet, and Daisy, dashed past. "Reginald's been feeling rather smug about your marriage to Norman, Beatrix, because he told me this past summer, after you stated to us you were destined for spinsterhood, that you'd be married by Christmas, and here you are, married by Christmas, and to a most unusual, yet delightful, gentleman."

Glancing to where Norman was having an earnest conversation with Ian, Isadora's husband, and probably about labor issues at the factories he was now involved with, Beatrix smiled. "He is a most unusual man, and I'm now convinced he was certainly placed in my path by God, although that particular path was not one I'd ever dreamed for myself, what with it being such a lovely path to find myself on."

Taking Isadora's hand, and then Poppy's, Beatrix lifted her gaze to the cross that was at the very front of the church right as the Bible verse her aunt had mentioned a few months before sprang to mind.

And thine ears shall hear a word behind thee, saying, This is the way, walk ye in it, when ye turn to the right hand, and when ye turn to the left.

Closing her eyes, Beatrix took a moment to say a prayer of thanks to God for directing her to a most unexpected path, one that had allowed her to find the love she'd always hoped to find. With a quiet "Amen," she linked arms with Isadora and Poppy, walking with her friends to join the husbands none of them had seen coming, content with the idea that all of them were certain to discover new paths throughout the years, paths that would bring even more laughter, happiness, and love into their lives.

Named one of the funniest voices in inspirational romance by *Booklist*, **Jen Turano** is a *USA Today* bestselling author, known for penning quirky historical romances set in the Gilded Age. Her books have earned *Publishers Weekly* and *Booklist* starred reviews, top picks from *Romantic Times*, and praise from *Library Journal*. She's been a finalist twice for the RT Reviewers' Choice Awards and had two of her books listed in the top 100 romances of the past decade from *Booklist*. She and her family live outside of Denver, Colorado. Readers can find her on Facebook and Twitter, or online at jenturano.com.

Sign Up for Jen's Newsletter!

Keep up to date with Jen's news, book releases, and events by signing up for her e-mail list at jenturano.com.

More from Jen Turano!

To escape an unwanted marriage, heiress Isadora Delafield flees New York. Disguising herself as a housekeeper, she finds a position at Glory Manor—the childhood home of self-made man Ian MacKenzie. Ian is unexpectedly charmed by Isadora and her unconventional ways, but when Isadora's secret is revealed, will they still have a chance at happily-ever-after?

Flights of Fancy, AMERICAN HEIRESSES #1

You May Also Like . . .

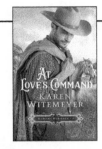

Ex-cavalry officer Matthew Hanger leads a band of mercenaries who defend the innocent, but when a rustler's bullet leaves one of them at death's door, they seek out help from Dr. Josephine Burkett. When Josephine's brother is abducted and she is caught in the crossfire, Matthew may have to sacrifice everything—even his team—to save her.

At Love's Command by Karen Witemeyer
HANGER'S HORSEMEN #1
karenwitemeyer.com

Growing up in Colorado, Josephine Nordegren has been fascinated by, but has shied away from, the outside world—one she's been raised to believe killed her parents. When rancher Dave Warden shows up at their secret home with his wounded father, will Josephine and her sisters risk stepping into the world to help, or remain separated but safe on Hope Mountain?

Aiming for Love by Mary Connealy
BRIDES OF HOPE MOUNTAIN #1
maryconnealy.com

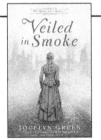

As Chicago's Great Fire destroys their bookshop, Meg and Sylvie Townsend make a harrowing escape from the flames with the help of reporter Nate Pierce. But the trouble doesn't end there—their father is committed to an asylum after being accused of murder, and they must prove his innocence before the asylum truly drives him mad.

Veiled in Smoke by Jocelyn Green
THE WINDY CITY SAGA #1
jocelyngreen.com

BETHANYHOUSE